Min Min

A Queensland Cadet Adventure

C.R. Cummings

Also By
CHRISTOPHER CUMMINGS

<table>
<tr><td>Kylie & Skip</td><td>Sugar & Spice</td></tr>
<tr><td>The Boy and the Battleship</td><td>Coast of Cape York</td></tr>
<tr><td>The Green Idol of Kanaka Creek</td><td>Kylie and the Kelly Gang</td></tr>
<tr><td>Train to Kuranda</td><td>Beyond the Barrier Reef</td></tr>
<tr><td>Endeavour Island</td><td>Behind Mt. Baldy</td></tr>
<tr><td>Kit in the Serpent's Lair</td><td>The Cadet Sergeant Major</td></tr>
<tr><td>The Mudskipper Cup</td><td>Cooktown Christmas</td></tr>
<tr><td>Davey Jones's Locker</td><td>Secret in the Clouds</td></tr>
<tr><td>Fourteen</td><td>Mischief at Mingela</td></tr>
<tr><td>Air Cadet</td><td>The Word of God</td></tr>
<tr><td>Spinifex</td><td>The Cadet Under-Officer</td></tr>
<tr><td>Below Bartle Frere</td><td>Through the Devil's Eye</td></tr>
<tr><td>Bowling Green Bay</td><td>Barbara in the Bush</td></tr>
<tr><td>Airship Over Atherton</td><td>The Smiley People</td></tr>
<tr><td>Cockatoo</td><td>Barbara at her Best</td></tr>
<tr><td>The Cadet Corporal</td><td>Barbara's Bivouac</td></tr>
<tr><td>Stannary Hills</td><td>*Min Min</td></tr>
</table>

Min Min

A Queensland Cadet Adventure

C.R. Cummings

DoctorZed
Publishing
www.doctorzed.com

Copyright © 2025 by Christopher Cummings

All rights reserved. No part of this book may be used or reproduced by any means, graphic, electronic, or mechanical, including photocopying, recording, taping or by any information storage retrieval system without the written permission of the publisher except in the case of brief quotations embodied in critical articles and reviews.

This 1st Edition published 2025 by DoctorZed Publishing

DoctorZed Publishing books may be ordered through booksellers or by contacting:

DoctorZed Publishing
10 Vista Ave
Skye, south Australia 5072
www.doctorzed.com

ISBN: 978-1-7636975-0-8 (sc)
ISBN: 978-1-7642181-9-1 (ebk)

A Cataloguing-in-Publication entry can be found at the National Library of Australia
www.nla.gov.au

This is a work of fiction. Names, characters, places, events, and dialogues are creations of the author or are used fictitiously. Any resemblance to any individuals, alive or dead, is purely coincidental. The views expressed in this work are solely those of the author and do not necessarily reflect the views of the publisher, and the publisher hereby disclaims any responsibility for them.

Cover design © Scott Zarcinas

Printed in Australia, UK & USA

DoctorZed Publishing rev. date: 24/07/2025

Dedication

TThis story is dedicated, with thanks
to

Cheryl Cummings

Partner, wife, co-driver, travel companion

and

Inspiration.

Also
To acknowledge, with respect,
those First Nations people
who inhabited this harsh environment
for 40,000 years.

And with admiration
for those European explorers and settlers,
especially the Scots,
who in the 19th Century tackled a place so different from
their own cool and green lands.

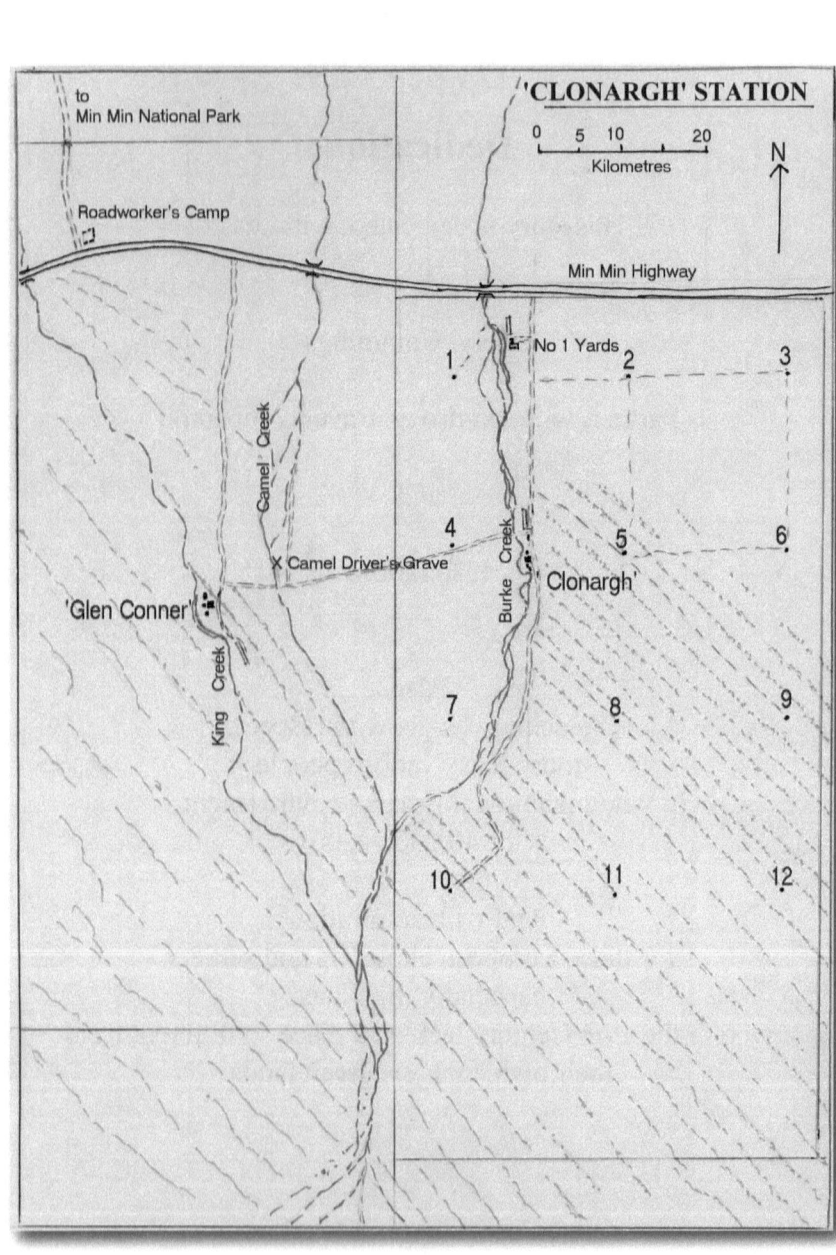

'CLONARGH' STATION

0 5 10 20
Kilometres

N

to
Min Min National Park

Roadworker's Camp

Min Min Highway

No 1 Yards

1 2 3

Camel Creek

4 Burke Creek 5 6

X Camel Driver's Grave 'Clonargh'

'Glen Conner'

King Creek

7 8 9

10 11 12

Chapter 1

DONNY

Min Min Shire in far Western Queensland.
10:00hrs. Second week of the September school holidays.
Air temperature: 36 degrees Celcius.

Donny MacAndrew, nine years old, slim and wiry and a real 'bush' kid and dressed like a stockman, stood next to his older cousin, Vaughan, and wondered why he had been idolising him all these years. They were both standing to one side at a new cattle trough and lick that Donny's father, Martin MacAndrew, was explaining to his two brothers. Uncle David, who was the eldest of the three, and Uncle James, who was the middle. The steel drinking trough was located in the centre of a vast, open stretch of almost bare country as this was on the edge of the Simpson Desert and the carrying capacity per square kilometre was low. Min Min Shire was the size of a European country like Hungary, but there were only 12 properties, cattle stations to the locals, and a population of a few hundred people. The climate was a challenge for people not used to it, and already Donny could see that the heat shimmer was giving the 'watery' effect off the land, forming minor mirages in the distance.

What was special about this drinking trough was not that it was brand new but that it was the only one on the property under a steel shade structure. At one end were two 'licks', one for salt and one for molasses. At the other end was a large plastic water tank and drinking trough with associated pipes and pumps, all controlled by a solar power array and linked to a radio and camera system. That meant the trough could be observed from the homestead and the water flow controlled from there by computer and any potential problems monitored. Donny was very proud of his dad for being so up-to-date and for installing the system.

Martin was explaining it to his brothers, Donny's two uncles. "I will progressively extend the system to all the bores and troughs on the property, as quickly as our available funds allow," he said.

7

This began a discussion on finance, which was why the three brothers had driven there that morning.

As his father talked, Donny glanced at Vaughan, who was 15 and a good head taller, and felt vaguely guilty because he was no longer impressed by the older boy. He had not seen Vaughan for three years and his memories over that time were of a big boy who was good at everything and who was friendly and helpful. During the last visit, Donny had come to hero-worship the older boy and the comments by his parents and grandfather had added to that aura. They had frequently made comments on how good Vaughan was and how well he was doing at almost everything. One consequence was that Donny had accepted this and felt quite inferior.

Now Vaughan was here on the family property, Clonargh Station, for a holiday visit and Donny was starting to form his own opinion. Vaughan and his parents lived in Sydney and were obviously not enjoying the desert environment. On being introduced, Vaughan had just nodded and then ignored Donny. Then he had seemed to go out of his way to make comments about how much better their house in Sydney was and their lifestyle. Donny had been particularly hurt by several put downs and cutting comments by Vaughan, who had implied that Donny and his family were just country hicks of no account.

This had even rankled Donny's father who had commented to his mother, "He doesn't appreciate that it is the property that gave his family their chance to move to the city."

Just the previous evening Vaughan had made a hurtful jibe about Donny's lack of education. That had really hurt because Donny believed he was getting a very good education. He was in Year 3 and mostly did Distance Education, by computer and the internet, and he tried very hard to do the work as well as he could. His mother kept him at it, helping and encouraging but not doing the work for him. Every term he spent a week on an 'In-reach' at Golden Dawn, the nearest town a hundred kilometres to the west, and twice a year he travelled to Longreach or Brisbane for another full-time class gathering. He really enjoyed these opportunities to meet his peers and the new experiences. But that was only part of his education because he also learned practical lessons every day when he helped his father doing real work out on the run: mending fences or machinery, caring for cattle or helping in the kitchen and workshop.

hand. His mind rapidly pulled up images of the country ahead of them. *More sand soon and then a dune. The dip between it and the next dune has a few trees and bushes but not many but after the second dune there is quite a bit of scrub. Maybe there?*

What he had in mind was using the dust, and he cudgelled his racing mind to try to visualise that bit of track.

A glance at the rear vision mirror showed him the white vehicle was even closer. It had slowed and pulled back in the thick dust, but they were now back on sand. Ahead the sand dune seemed to grow rapidly in size. It was not a high dune but stretched seemingly from horizon to horizon. Donny knew that many of the dunes were tens of kilometres long, some of them hundreds, and mostly running parallel to each other. They were anchored by a thin cover of vegetation so that they were about half open, bare sand of a salmon pink colour and a covering of plants. At that, time of year they had many small bushes whose white flowers made it appear as if parts of the dune had a sprinkling of snow. The flowers were interspersed with tufts of spinifex and other grass and clumps of saltbush and a few small, scrubby bushes. Having seen them all his life the scene was quite normal to Donny.

And he knew this dune. It was only a few metres high where the track crossed it so didn't suit his purpose. He was so busy scanning it, as much for cover and ideas, that he did not notice another patch of clay and hit more potholes in the bulldust. The Land Rover bounced and shuddered. Objects flew up and rained down. Donny cried out in alarm but kept control. He was driving much faster than he had ever driven before but did not dare slow down. Beside him, Vaughan was clinging to the dashboard wide-eyed and mouth open.

"Slow down! You'll crash and kill us," Vaughan cried.

"No!" Donny shouted back.

He pressed his lips together, still determined to try to get away. Dust billowed in, making them both cough and he was dimly aware that his teeth felt gritty and that he was blinking fast as sweat trickled down into his eyes. Grimly he clung on and concentrated.

Just in time he spotted what he thought was another bulldust filled hole and pulled the wheel to swerve around it. But he miscalculated and nearly lost control. The wheels bounced over a few big tufts of grass beside the track before he had them back on course. The dune seemed to rush toward them. The dust ended and he just had time to note that the pursuing vehicle had slowed and fallen back a bit to escape the dust.

At about 80kph they went up the side of the dune and Donny could only hope no-one was coming the other way on that narrow track. The Land Rover went over the top so fast that it was momentarily airborne and he felt his stomach go up and down.

Like hitting turbulence in a little plane, he thought.

The wheels landed with a crash, and they bounced but then settled and raced on. Donny noted that the next dune was at least a kilometre ahead and that the track to it was dead straight.

Can we make that? he wondered.

Already they had come further than he had thought he might. Once again, his thoughts focused on the types of vegetation ahead. He knew there were a series of widely spaced parallel dunes. In fact, he could clearly see the next one, and that between each was what his teacher had called a 'swale', which his father had commented was an oddly English word for such a geographical feature.

And the vegetation between each dune is often very different from the ones on either side, he thought.

His dad had pointed that out, suggesting that it was the local conditions of soil and moisture, etc that caused this. But for Danny the swale they were now crossing was no good. There were areas of knee-high grass and small clumps of trees, ironbarks and so on, but no real cover. And there were also bare, open stretches of 'gibber' desert, areas covered with small pebbles and rocks that were cemented together by salt and polished over hundreds of years by wind-blown sand.

And this bit of track was mostly sand with very little dust being flung up behind. A glance confirmed Donny's worst fears; the white vehicle was now close behind, and even as he looked he saw the barrel of a rifle come out of the passenger's window, followed by an elbow and a head.

Bloody hell! He is going to shoot! Donny thought.

With his attention now torn between steering to stay on the track and focusing to watch the man with the gun behind, Donny knew he was scared. But he was also familiar with guns and seeing the barrel of the gun tilt slightly down he thought he knew what the man was intending.

He's going to try to shoot our tyres, he reasoned.

A chill of impending failure gripped him and he felt ill.

Chapter 3

DANGEROUS DRIVING

How can I stop this? Donny thought.

He realised his palms were now slippery from perspiration and his eyes were stinging from the salty sweat trickling down his forehead. Gasping and coughing, he wiped one hand at a time as his brain went into overdrive. He knew he had to take fearful risks and the idea scared him.

Another glance showed the man he had nicknamed 'The Thug' lean out and start aiming the rifle, his aim complicated by the bumps and small swirls of dust. A glance ahead showed no areas of dusty track, just sand. By now Donny was almost hyperventilating with anxiety (He did not want to admit to being frightened!).

In a frantic attempt to spoil the Thug's aim, Donny noted a large area of flat, shiny, gibber desert ahead on the left. Reefing the wheel suddenly, he swerved the Land Rover off the track and onto it. He was just in time as he saw a puff of smoke and then heard a muffled bang.

Missed! I think! he told himself.

Emboldened by that little success, Donny swung the wheel the other way and the Land Rover swerved dramatically, the tyres crunching through the thin crust of gibbers and varnish and throwing up both dust and pebbles. More by good luck than good driving, a rollover was just avoided.

Vaughan again cried out in fright and grabbed at him. "Stop! Stop! You will kill us! He will shoot us!" he screamed.

"He's trying to blow our tyres," Donny snarled between gritted teeth, still grimly determined.

He swerved again, steering a slalom course on the gibbers and getting glimpses of the pursuing vehicle as he did. As nothing else had, the firing of shots convinced him of how serious the situation really was.

But I don't think the crooks will shoot us, he reasoned. He decided to keep going.

Vaughan looked back and blanched. "Stop! Stop please!"

"No!"

"You are a lunatic! You'll get us both killed!" Vaughan shouted.

But Donny just ignored him and swung the Land Rover right and then left in frightening skids, this time so fast he felt the outside wheels lift as centrifugal force took temporary control. He knew what to call it, both his dad and his teacher had warned him of its existence and the dangers.

There was another bang behind them and this time Donny heard a sharp, metallic noise, a whang!

That was a bullet hitting some steel part of the Land Rover rather than the rubber of the tyres, he reasoned.

They were now only a few hundred metres from the next dune and Donny knew they must go over it on the track.

If I try to drive up that sand dune this fast, we will just bog, he thought, having seen many vehicles stuck in soft sand and knowing he did not have time to stop and engage the transfer case for 4WD and 'low range'.

And the flat area of gibbers was coming to an end. Large clumps of spinifex and saltbush extended from the end of the gibbers to the base of the dune. With no other choice, he steered the Land Rover back over to the vehicle track, still avoiding steering straight for more than a few moments. Weaving and sometimes skidding, he made it back onto the track, bouncing hard over a small ridge of soil a grader had thrown up at some time in the past.

The Land Rover raced up a gravel incline put there by the station to ease the crossing of the next dune, which was steeper and several metres higher than the previous one. Once again there was a worrying few seconds of anxiety in case there was a vehicle coming the other way and nothing to see but sky.

The Land Rover flew over the crest and landed with a shudder and slipping of madly spinning wheels. But it was on the down slope. Donny gasped with a mixture of thrill and satisfaction and peered ahead.

I was right, lots of cover, he noted, seeing large areas of bushes and small trees ahead, mostly on the right of the road. *But how to reach them?*

It was plainly obvious they did not have time to stop and get out without the men catching them. The other vehicle was close behind.

With his mind still grappling with how to get away and hide, Donny kept going. They raced down the other side of the dune and out onto another long straight stretch of track. Another sand dune was just visible through the trees and looked to be several kilometres away.

And thankfully there was some more dust. But not enough, and Donny saw Thug again leaning out and aiming his gun. A spurt of fear helped Donny to accelerate, and then he steered a small weaving course. As he did, he heard the bang of the gun and flinched. There was another sharp noise from below and behind him, a *thunk*!

That bullet hit us low down, he thought.

Now he was sure they were trying to puncture a tyre. Beside him, Vaughan screamed and whimpered. Donny gritted his teeth and kept driving, ignoring Vaughan's pleas to stop.

And then they were on a patch of dust that shielded them for a few seconds. But ahead was a shallow depression. It wasn't really a creek line, just a small dip with rocks in the bottom, but Donny knew the crossing was rough and was forced to slow down to cross it safely.

As he did, he saw movement in the rear vision mirror. Through the billowing dust and very close behind was the pursuing vehicle! The image of its bull snout and shiny brand badge seemed to fill his vision. It looked so close that Donny braced for a collision. In his rapidly blinking eyes it appeared to be getting closer. For a fleeting second, he wondered if the crooks meant to hit them from behind.

Like the cops do in America, a 'PIT Manoeuvre' to push us out of control, he thought, recalling one of his dad's favourite TV programs, *American Police Chases*. But then he shook his head. The other car had abruptly braked, widening the distance. *No, they just nearly ran into us coming through the dust.*

A desperate idea formed in his mind. As he changed gears and accelerated up out of the dip, he glanced again at the front of the pursuing vehicle and frowned.

That's not a normal 4WD, he thought.

Vehicles were so much a part of station life that Donny had a very good working knowledge of vehicles, but he wanted to be sure. Turning to Vaughan, he shouted, "Vaughan, has that vehicle got a bull bar?"

"What?"

"Has that vehicle behind us got a bull bar?"

Vaughan twisted around and looked, then gaped as the front of the pursuing vehicle was still close behind them. Then he shook his head.

"No, It's an SUV."

That clicked in Donny's mind. He remembered his father speaking disparagingly about all those rich people who had big 4WD vehicles yet lived in a city and never went offroad at any time.

"Not real Four-Wheel Drives for the bush," his dad had said.

And no bull bar, Danny thought.

Almost every vehicle owned by people in the bush or outback had a strong steel frame bolted or welded to the front bumper bar in case the vehicle accidentally collided with a big animal, like a kangaroo. But most SUVs didn't. A glance in the rear vision mirror confirmed it, this one didn't.

At that, the idea crystalised in Donny's brain. It was going to be very dangerous, he sensed that, but he was determined.

Good. Now we need some dust.

And he was sure there was some before the next dune, which was now only a few hundred metres ahead.

Having made his decision, Donny glanced at Vaughan and yelled, "When we stop, get out and go right."

He was now so anxious he was gulping great breaths of air and felt light headed. It seemed as though everything was moving in slow motion. But before he was mentally ready, he noted thick clouds of dust swirling up behind them.

Now or never! Now, do it now! he told himself.

Another glance behind, and yes, the white vehicle had vanished into the dust, but when he got his last glimpse it was still travelling very fast. After taking one more great gulp of air, he took his foot off the accelerator and stood on the brake.

"Hang on!" he shouted at Vaughan, who had turned his head to stare at him in alarm.

The Land Rover shuddered and skidded in the dust, ploughing up more as it bounced and slid through several potholes, the impact of the tyres hurling up more dust. Donny hung on to the wheel with all his strength, struggling to stop the Land Rover going into a side slide or skid and rolling over. It was all he could do to hold it straight. And then the following dust cloud engulfed them and completely blotted out the scene as it swirled in the open back to fill the cab.

Donny hung on, hunching and holding his foot on that brake. At every moment he expected to feel a crash, but none came. The Land Rover shuddered to a stop.

Damn it! I've failed! he thought, a sick feeling of despair swamping his whole being.

But he wasn't ready to give up. Even as the dust started him coughing, he reached down for the gear lever to change into reverse, intending to back into the other vehicle.

But he never got time to change gears. Out of the dust came the SUV going slower but much too fast. Donny got a glimpse of a shadow in the dust cloud and just had time to snatch at the wheel to hold on before the other vehicle slammed into the back of the Land Rover.

Ker...rash!

The impact was so sudden Donny was flung forward against the wheel. He was braced ready for that but not for the sudden violent jerk that flung him back down into the seat. It felt like his arms were being wrenched out of their sockets and he cried out in pain. He heard Vaughan scream and saw his arms and legs flailing about in the orange haze. Then Donny lost his grip on the steering wheel just as there was another shuddering crash. The impact flung him back against the seat back and then bounced him forward again so that his chest struck the bottom of the steering wheel, winding him. More dust swirled.

Half stunned, he grabbed at the wheel and hauled himself upright. Despite feeling bruised and scared he began groping for the gear lever. He was aware that he was alive but so numb and shocked that he was unsure if he had been injured or not. As he hauled himself upright, more dust billowed in; but through a brief gap in it he got a glimpse of the SUV. Its nose was jammed right up against the tailgate of the Land Rover. Frantic to know what was going on, Donny looked back to see what the two crooks were doing. He was astonished to see nothing but dust and white blobs inside their cab.

What? What the bloody hell? he wondered as his hand found the gear lever.

Then it came to him, the white blobs filling the inside of their windscreen were the airbags, something the old Land Rover had never been fitted with!

We might have a chance, he thought.

He slammed the lever back into first gear, pulling himself forward to get his boots back onto the clutch and accelerator. He had to look down to do that and he only managed it with difficulty.

His original idea had been to smash the front of the SUV to wreck its engine and then to drive away. Now he tried to act on it. Pressing hard on the accelerator he slowly let out the clutch. The engine roared and the wheels spun, grinding up another blinding shower of dust and grit. But the Land Rover did not move forward!

Donny swore and tried again but it was at once obvious that the two vehicles were locked together.

Oh bugger! Donny swore.

His mind quickly considered the situation. Part of his plan had been to ram the Land Rover's towing pintle through the radiator of the SUV. Now he thought that might be what had happened.

It might be stuck there, he thought.

He tried again, the engine screaming but the towing hook did not come loose. Not being a quitter by nature he tried a fourth time before giving up. The dust, he noted, was still thick and offered some cover.

We have to run for it, he decided.

"Get out! Get out!" he screamed, his whole being galvanised by the urgent need to escape.

Vaughan was already doing that. He had been scrabbling for the door handle for some time, his face a mask of fear, dust and trickling blood. Now he reefed the handle up and flung the door open.

Then he was out and running.

Chapter 4

RUN!

Donny shook his head to clear it, and blinked to clear his eyes of dust and grit. His hand found the door handle and he pulled. It only moved a tiny bit. Now frantic to get out he hammered the handle up and down, swearing as he did. Suddenly it clicked up and he shoved outwards. The door swung open so fast that it rebounded to hit him as he went to climb out. Ignoring the blow, he pushed the door aside and then went to step down, only to have his boot catch on his hat. He swore and kicked at it, sending it flying out onto the ground. Donny did not even remember his hat coming off but now he noted that the water bottle that had fallen earlier was also on the ground near his hat.

We might need water, he thought as he jumped out. *And my hat too!* Wearing a hat when outside was so much a part of the lifestyle that he bent down and snatched up the water bottle and then his hat. *You need a hat in the desert,* he told himself as he clapped it on his head.

He looked hastily around to check on what the men were doing. His first glance just showed swirling dust and the inflated air bags filling most of the cab of the SUV. Where were the men?

Cracked windscreen, Donny noted, but no sign of the men. *Are they already out?* he wondered, his heart rate leaping even higher with a sudden spurt of anxiety.

A hasty glance around showed no sign of them. Then a horrible thought came to Donny: were the men injured in the crash? Or even killed? The idea that his actions might have seriously harmed people made him feel nauseous. Anxiously he stared at the cab of the SUV, even stepping closer to look.

I can't just run. I've got to see if they are alright, he told himself.

The notion of just leaving badly injured people in a car wreck tore at his emotions. His survival instinct was just to run, but his conscience and reasoning were stronger than that and he hesitated and stared. What he was particularly worried about was the possibility of the vehicles catching on fire. He could smell hot oil and diesel and that thought horrified him.

So he took three steps towards the SUV driver's door. He even put out his hand preparatory to opening the door. Then he saw a hand groping at the air bag and this was suddenly pulled aside and a very angry, blood-stained face appeared: the Ringer's. The man immediately saw Donny and glared, then shouted and began thrashing at the enveloping air bag.

Oh hell! He's really mad, Donny thought. He turned and ran.

For a dozen paces Donny sprinted forward past the front of the Land Rover and then he remembered Vaughan.

Where is he? he wondered, his eyes flicking around.

Then he saw Vaughan sprinting away along the road, his boots sending out little spurts of dust at each stride. Already the bigger boy was nearly the length of a football field away and Donny was astonished.

Bloody hell! Look at him go! he thought, setting out after him with a spurt of annoyance that Vaughan had ignored his yell to go right.

Donny was sufficiently in command of his battered senses to look around as he sprinted. He had previously noted that there was much less cover on the left side of the road, which was why he had shouted at Vaughan to go right. But he had to admit that the road was much easier to run along and every few seconds got them further from the men.

But we do need to take to the scrub!

As he ran, Donny continually glanced back. And now, when he was only about 50 paces from the vehicles, he saw what he had been dreading. The driver's door of the SUV swung open and a leg appeared and then Ringer slid out and stood clinging to the door.

Is he hurt? Donny wondered, guilt at possibly being the cause niggling at him again. *And what about the Thug? Oh bugger! There he is!*

Thug had slid out of the passenger's side and stood shaking his head. The sight sent surges of anxious energy through Donny's muscles and he increased speed, rapidly catching up on Vaughan who was only about 50 metres ahead.

Another glance back. *Oh no! Thug is reaching in for his rifle!*

Thug slammed the door and ran forward to near the front of the Land Rover. "Stop you bloody kids! Stop or I will shoot!" he shouted angrily.

Real fear surged through Donny's being. He was now experiencing such a range of emotions and physical pains that his whole being felt like a quivering bundle of nervous worms. Only his mind seemed to be functioning, although his legs kept running.

Crack!

Donny heard the noise and experienced a stab of pure fear and the physical sensation of wanting to void his bowels. He knew what that sound was.

That was a bullet! his mind told him, adding to the squirming emotions. His dad had taught him that a person hears the bullet go by before they hear the thump of the gun going off. *Travelling faster than sound, Dad said. You don't hear the one that hits you!*

Donny could not believe it, even though his senses told him it was happening. His eyesight confirmed it when he saw a spurt of dust several hundred metres ahead up the road, the bullet strike.

That must have just missed Vaughan too, he decided. And Vaughan had stopped and was turning. *What's he doing? Why doesn't he keep running?*

"Vaughan, keep running!" Donny yelled, or tried to as he was now getting short of breath. To his dismay, he saw Vaughan shake his head and put his hands up. "Vaughan, keep running!" he shouted as he quickly closed the distance.

Now he was twisting his head around to look back at almost very step, still not really believing that the man would actually shoot them. *That was a warning shot,* he thought. He had often seen his dad shoot a running fox or dingo at 300 metres or more and he was less than a hundred from the man. *If he had wanted to hit us, he could have done it easily,* he reasoned. *We weren't even jinking.*

He reached Vaughan and grabbed at him. "Vaughan, what are you doing?" he cried, even though it was obvious the older boy was surrendering.

Vaughan looked terrified. He was red in the face and gabbling. "They will kill us! We have to give up!" he cried.

"Crap!" Donny snapped. "That was just to scare us. They need us alive as hostages. Come on, keep running!"

He tried to turn Vaughan, but the bigger boy was too strong and broke free.

Donny looked back at the men and saw that Ringer had joined Thug at the front of the Land Rover, and that Thug was raising the barrel of his rifle again. A doubt crept into his mind and he hesitated. But it really irked him.

"I'm going!" he snarled, still determined to save his dad.

He turned and started running again while Vaughan started walking back with his hands high.

An anxious look back caused Donny to falter in his run. Thug was aiming the rifle, and it looked to be straight at him.

Thug shouted, "Give up, you little bastard, or I will shoot you!"

Donny jinked sharp right and headed for the bushes. As he left the road he ducked and jinked again, glancing back as he did. He was just in time to see Ringer reach across and push the rifle barrel up and away. The gun went off but by then it was pointing up in the air. Donny skidded to a stop and watched as the two men began a furious argument.

"You bloody idiot!" Ringer shouted. "A dead kid is no use to us. Then the cops will really track us."

"I just wanted to scare them and let them know I could hit them if I wanted to," Thug retorted.

It took Donny a few moments to grasp the situation. Then he shook his head. *I was right, they won't shoot us,* he decided.

Ringer's angry words confirmed that. Then Donny saw that Vaughan had stopped in obvious indecision.

"Vaughan! Vaughan, come on! Run! They won't shoot us!" he yelled.

Vaughan turned to look at him, indecision and anxiety all over his face. His hands came half down. Donny shook his head and yelled again, "Come on! They will try to catch us. We can outrun them. Run!"

Or I can anyway, he mentally added.

Vaughan looked both ways several times. By then the two men were struggling over the gun and yelling at each other.

"Run!" Donny called.

To his enormous relief, Vaughan turned and began running towards him. Donny grinned, then turned and resumed running. Another backward glance showed that Vaughan was following but that the two men had stopped arguing and were also running after them.

Donny dashed into the bush, leaping over the smaller tufts of spinifex and long grass and dodging around the bigger clumps and bushes. His eyes scanned rapidly ahead, trying to pick out the best route and also where the best cover was. To his relief, Vaughan followed him. By then they were more than a hundred metres ahead of the men and Donny thought he could outrun them.

I won the 400 and 800 metres on Sports Day, he reminded himself.

Within a minute, Donny had run another hundred metres. He was angling away from the road but trying to keep as far away from the men, very conscious that if he went straight into the bush it shortened the distance the men had to run to catch him. He tore through several spiky bushes which scratched but the stings meant nothing in his emotional state. Dodging around some trees and bushes, he glanced back and was heartened to note that the men were out of sight much of the time, the view blocked by the vegetation.

We can do this, he thought. But a look back at Vaughan made him amend that to: *Well, I can.*

Vaughan had fallen 50 paces behind and was red in the face, obviously terrified and already gasping for breath. Then he tripped. Donny gasped in angst and then with relief as Vaughan scrambled to his feet and resumed running. Donny grinned and gave him a 'Thumbs Up' before also resuming his run.

While ducking under the branches of a small tree, Donny felt his hat get swept off. For a couple of paces he ran on, thinking it didn't matter. But then he shook his head and ran back to snatch it up.

"I need it," he told himself, noting that Vaughan did not have one.

It made him aware that he was still clutching the plastic bottle of water and he nodded, determined not to lose that either.

If they chase us out into the desert, we will need water.

By this time the men were out of sight much of the time. Even their shouts to stop and swearing had died away as they got short of breath.

They aren't very fit, Donny mused, allowing Vaughan to catch up.

Vaughan tripped again but immediately scrambled back to his feet, casting a fearful glance behind as he resumed running. By the time he caught up with Donny, he was really gasping for breath and looking distressed. He slowed to a panting stop and began gasping huge shuddering breaths.

Donny grabbed at him. "Keep running or they will catch us!" he croaked, feeling half out of breath himself. "Come on! They aren't as fit as us!"

"But I'm not fit!" Vaughan gasped his eyes rolling and sweat pouring down his face. "They will catch us and then they will bash us for sure, even if they don't kill us."

"Crap!" Donny snarled. "They want us as hostages and that means alive and well. Now run! They think we are just kids who need our mummy and daddy. Run!"

That last he added from exasperation and the notion that Vaughan probably did want his mummy and daddy! Unkind thoughts about Vaughan being fat and unfit flitted across his mind, making him feel guilty.

At that moment, Donny caught a clear view of the men as they crossed a patch of open scrub. They were still at least a hundred metres behind. But Vaughan was now bending over and taking huge breaths. To Donny he looked like he was going to puke. Donny pointed to the men.

"Look, they haven't caught up at all. Now make an effort and run!"

But Vaughan, while he looked, just shook his head and continued sucking in huge breaths. That annoyed Donny.

"Oh, make the effort!"

"But they will catch us!" wailed Vaughan, straightening up but still sucking in air.

"No, they won't! They aren't all that fit. Look, they are just standing there arguing. Keep going." Donny snapped, pointing to where the two men had stopped in the shade of one of the larger trees.

But the men were now only about 75 metres away and Donny knew he could not wait any longer, so he shrugged and decided to leave Vaughan. Turning, he resumed running, weaving to keep clumps of scrub and big bushes between them and the men. When he looked back he was pleased to see that Vaughan had started running again.

Good! he thought.

Then things started to get worse. Sunlight indicated more open country ahead. Donny looked in all directions, wondering if there was somewhere they could hide. But there wasn't. Every patch of scrub or clump of trees was too small with the men that close. And it was open country ahead. Donny groaned and swore.

A claypan! No cover at all! he thought.

Ahead of him stretched a football field sized area of flat, white claypan, almost blinding in the bright sunlight. He slowed until Vaughan caught up. Vaughan came to a stop.

"What do we do? Can we go around it?"

Donny shook his head. "No. Takes us at right angles to those men, and they will see us. We need to sprint." He looked around and saw movement through the trees not far behind. "Come on, run!"

Without waiting to see if Vaughan was running Donny dashed out onto the open claypan. He had hardly gone ten paces before he heard a shout from behind him.

They have seen us. They are catching up, he thought.

Another spurt of adrenaline got him sprinting as fast as he could go. Thudding footfalls close behind told him that Vaughan had followed.

But the thudding grew fainter and fainter and was replaced by the sound of gasping, wheezing breathing. A glance behind showed Vaughan falling behind, and only about 50 metres behind him were the men!

Now Donny was torn between the urge to get away and the niggling feeling that he could not abandon his cousin.

"Oh bugger!" he swore again and slowed until Vaughan was beside him.

Reaching across he grabbed his sleeve and ran with him. As he ran, he kept glancing back. And what he saw brought a sardonic smile to his lips. Ringer was no closer, and the Thug was falling behind, a good ten metres further back.

No, they aren't very fit, he thought.

Vaughan began sobbing and croaked to let him go, but Donny shook his head and kept a tight grip. The other side of the claypan was only 50 paces, 40 paces, 30 paces. He glanced back. Ringer had slowed to a gasping walk and so had the Thug. The Thug made a half-hearted effort to lift his rifle but then Donny and Vaughan were across and into another belt of trees and bushes. The two men came to a gasping standstill. Donny kept them running for another 50 paces before also slowing to a gasping walk.

"Stop!" Vaughan gasped. "I need a break."

"Sorry, keep walking," Donny croaked.

Vaughan groaned and slowed to a plod. Donny was not impressed but slowed to stay with him. Then he saw the men start after them, and looming only a hundred metres or so ahead was a large sand dune. It was a much bigger dune than the previous ones and had a lot of open sand. And it stretched across their route as far as the eye could see in both directions.

Oh! This will be a bit of a challenge! Donny thought.

Chapter 5

SAND DUNES

As they got closer to the huge dune, Donny saw Vaughan stare up at it with dismay on his face.

"Oh, bloody hell!" he croaked.

The two boys came to a sweating, gasping stop on the open sand at the base of the dune. Heat reflected off it and seemed to engulf them in a hot cloud. Donny took a couple of deep breaths and then grabbed at Vaughan's sleeve.

"Come on, let's get it over with."

A glance over his shoulder showed the men coming through the trees and that added incentive. Donny tried to run up the dune, but Vaughan wouldn't run and both came to a slogging plod. Vaughan kept gripping his right side.

"I've got a stitch," he wailed.

Donny knew what that meant but wasn't very sympathetic. As a keen runner he often got twinges.

"Just bend towards it a couple of times. It's just your gut catching on the inside," he gasped.

He kept on going, appalled at how soft the dune was and how the sand started to slide under his feet.

This is the two steps forward and one step back, he told himself, remembering a comment by his dad. Then he remembered another.

"Vaughan, walk sideways, use the sides of your boots. It gives a better grip," he croaked.

Something to do with pressure to weight ratios, Dad said.

They both made a dozen gasping steps upward, the sand sliding under their boots at every step, before Vaughan slipped and fell to his hands and knees. Donny dragged him up and continued hauling. He was breathing so hard his heart felt like it would burst, and his eyes began going in and out of focus. Black dots danced across his vision. There was sand sticking to the sweat on their hands and arms, but Donny barely noticed the irritation.

They made another 20 steps and Donny began to hope they might make it. He was so stirred up and frantic to get over that crest that he started to swear and croak. He used all his strength to keep dragging Vaughan, who at least kept his legs moving. The word panic was flitting through Donny's mind as he struggled up. The heat, the hot sand, the glare, the sheer effort all draining his muscles!

Then Vaughan slipped again and lay there scrabbling and gasping. Donny really became frantic as he saw the two men appear out of the trees only about 50 metres back.

"Get up Vaughan! Get up!" Donny gasped. He felt like his heart would break as well as burst.

"I can't!" Vaughan croaked. His legs stopped moving and he lay there gasping.

"You must!" Donny shrieked, hauling again at Vaughan's sleeve.

A ghastly sensation of failure began to grip him, as well as anger. Then he had to stop as a wave of dizziness swept through him.

Failed! he thought bitterly.

Great shuddering gasps wracked him, and he could hear Vaughan sobbing. Then Donny's vision cleared for a few seconds and his spirits got an instant lift. The two men had arrived separately at the base of the dune, scarcely 25 metres away in a straight line, but they had also come to gasping stops. Donny could see their chests heaving and their eyes rolling and blinking as they tried to clear the salty sweat from them. That was one of his problems too, and he wiped his face and then instantly regretted it as some of the grit off his sweaty hand got into his left eye. He swore again and stared angrily at the men as they stood there gasping and glaring angrily back. His left eye he blinked rapidly in an attempt to clear it.

Thug glared up at him and hefted his rifle. "Give up, you little shit, and come down here!"

His whole tone and manner aggravated a defiant streak in Donny. His dislike and his temper flared.

"No way! Go away!" he shouted back.

He was already getting his breath back and he was very determined.

Thug took several more deep breaths and wiped sweat off his face with one hand and then returned it to his rifle. The rifle was pointed up at Donny. A spasm of anxiety made Donny worry that he had gone too far, but somehow he didn't care. Thug gasped some more and beside him Ringer was wracked by a series of hacking coughs which made him bend over.

Thug pointed the rifle. "Come back down or I will shoot you," he snarled.

At that, Donny jeered. "No ya won't! You aren't that big an idiot. You don't want to spend the rest of your life in jail for murder, and I'm sure yer bushie mate doesn't. You'll have ter catch us!"

As he said this, he saw Ringer look up and scowl at him. Ringer coughed twice more as he spoke quietly to Thug, who also scowled and then made to aim the rifle.

"Not if I shoot you in the leg," he retorted angrily.

At that, Donny did laugh. "You aren't that good a shot buster! You couldn't hit a bull on the bum with a banjo!" he said, using an expression of his dad's.

"You cheeky little brat! You wait till I get my hands on you!" Thug threatened.

Donny knew he had annoyed the man, but he didn't care. "If you shoot one of us you will have a wounded person you will have to carry back to the vehicles and then what? How do you get them to a doctor before they bleed to death or whatever?"

That caused both the men to scowl again, and Donny knew he had scored a vital point. And that gave him confidence. He now thought they could get away.

"You aren't fit enough to catch us. You are just an ugly townie thug and old Ringer there smokes too much. Come on, Vaughan, let's go."

With that Donny started struggling up the dune again. To his relief, Vaughan followed, being towed up by his shirt. By then Donny's breath had slowed but he could hear Vaughan panting like an old steam engine.

At that, Thug swore crudely and again aimed the rifle, but a gasping Ringer again moved over and pushed the barrel aside. Thug tried to shake the rifle free.

"Let go, Ringer!" he snarled.

"The kid's right, Benny. We have to catch them. Come on."

With that he started forward onto the bottom of the dune. Thug swore again and followed him, already gasping and with his chest heaving rapidly.

Donny saw them start and that galvanised him to try harder. "Come one Vaughan, run!" he ordered, again grabbing the bigger boy's sleeve and hauling.

Vaughan tried but he was so unfit and gasping that all the pair of them could achieve was a slow, upward plod, slipping at almost every step but making painful upward progress. A backward glance showed Donny that Ringer was starting to catch up but that the Thug was struggling just as much as Vaughan. Donny tensed ready to run or fight, he wasn't sure which he would do.

Then Ringer slipped and sprawled on the hot sand. He swore and scrabbled furiously to get traction, but his efforts seemed to make it worse. Then it came to Donny.

He grabbed Vaughan's arm and hissed in his ear, "Walk on the bushes, walk on the bushes!"

Following his own advice Donny did so and found immediately that it was a bit easier. The hardest action was lifting his feet high enough to get it on the bush or its uphill side. Every couple of paces there was a clump of spinifex or a saltbush and stepping on them limited the slipping. They began to make rapid progress. Behind them the two crooks swore and croaked at them to stop, in between rasping gasps for air.

The crest of the dune got closer and closer with every straining step and Donny began to feel hopeful, except he thought he remembered what was beyond this dune, open country with very little cover. And he was right. As his head came above the level of the top, he got a glimpse and his hopes went crashing. The next swale was at least a kilometre wide and most of the flat land in it was a gibber plain!

He and Vaughan staggered to the crest and Vaughan stopped for a second. But Donny kept him moving, knowing that Ringer was only a dozen paces behind. Going down was easier and he let go of Vaughan, which was just as well as both tripped and went sprawling and rolling down the hot sandy slope.

Scrambling to his feet, Donny continued down to the bottom of the dune, jumping some bushes rather than detouring. At every step he expected Ringer to come crashing down and grab him, but when Donny arrived sweating and gasping on the flat he saw through sweat-filled eyes that Ringer had stopped at the top. Vaughan came staggering down to join Donny at the same moment Thug struggled gasping up to join Ringer.

Donny stood there for a few seconds, hot breath rasping in his dry throat and then he turned and stared at the absolute wasteland ahead of him. It was almost flat, a shiny expanse of black gibbers that reflected the sunlight to look as though they were wet. The heat was reflecting up off the gibbers in visible waves and in the distance was the 'water' effect and the beginnings of mirages. The glare was horrible. He had walked across such gibber plains many times, but usually in the cool of the day or for short distances, so he quailed at the ordeal of running across this one at midday.

Sucking in a couple of dry, warm breaths, he bit his already dry lips and muttered, "Come on Vaughan, run!"

"I... I can't!" Vaughan croaked, but he started a staggering trot at Donny's physical urging.

As they ran out onto the gibber plain, Donny looked back, half expecting the crooks to actually shoot but instead he saw them just standing silhouetted against the sky. Then they both swore and shouted at each other.

They are having an argument, Donny thought, and then the men turned and vanished from view.

Vaughan noticed this and slowed down to a plod. "They've given up," he gasped with relief.

But Donny shook his head and pushed him to keep moving. A dismaying thought had come to him, and he voiced it now.

"No, they haven't. I reckon they are going back to get a vehicle."

His eyes swept around that vast, flat plain and he felt cold with fear.

"But their vehicle is wrecked, isn't it?" Vaughan queried, his voice a gasping wail.

Donny could only look at him with astonishment. "Yes, but I don't think the Land Rover is damaged much. All they have to do is separate the two vehicles."

He was sure two adult males would achieve that in no time.

"But they will need keys, won't they?" Vaughan said.

Donny shook his head. "No. I left the key in it. We always leave the keys in vehicles on the station. You never know who needs it in a hurry."

"But don't people steal them?"

"Vaughan! This isn't a city. Usually nobody comes on to a station unless they are locals or working," Donny replied.

Then Vaughan astonished him again. "But they can't drive them off a road, can they? They can't come here."

"Vaughan, it is a 4WD designed to drive off roads. Dad and the stockmen often drive across gibber plains like this when doing a job."

In fact, he was sure they had driven along this swale, and this was confirmed a few minutes later when they came to distinct wheel marks.

Vaughan looked shocked and defeated but he kept plodding along. Donny wanted to run.

"Run Vaughan, run! We need to get off this gibber plain before we are fried like an egg," he cried in impatient exasperation.

We need to be off it before those men come back in a vehicle, he thought, his eyes scanning around looking for cover.

There was almost none. The next sand dune was at least three quarters of a kilometre away and was also so long it extended out of sight to right and left. On the flat there were a few areas of short grass and some small patches of bushes but not a single tree.

And the air was stifling. It was so hot that breathing it felt like sucking in gaseous heat. The air dried out the throat and airways and eyes and Donny knew it meant death from heat stroke if they didn't reach both water and shade quickly. Tiny fingers of fear tightened around his heart. He started to wonder if he had made a bad mistake in running.

First, we must avoid the bad guys and then we need water, Donny reasoned.

He visualised the map of the property in his mind and began working out the best route to take. He knew that the vehicle track did a left turn after crossing the dune behind them. It then ran northwards parallel to the dune for several kilometres before crossing over the dune in front. It took him very little effort to bring up images of the country between each set of dunes and the other features of the vast property.

The best cover is along Burke Creek and that leads direct to the homestead, he told himself. Burke Creek flowed almost North-South. *And there are a couple of permanent waterholes along the way.* It seemed like the best option but after a bit more thought Donny shook his head. *No. Too obvious.*

So he changed direction slightly to his right and kept walking as fast as he could persuade Vaughan to go. But just walking across the gibber plain was a challenge. Much of the time the small, rounded stones were cemented hard together, and the surface presented an unyielding mass that almost hurt to walk across and where their boots left no mark he could see (Though he believed that the old Aborigines, the world's best trackers, could follow a man across such country). In other places the varnished and wind-polished pebbles formed only a thin crust which cracked and left very distinct imprints. And Donny lacked the experience to distinguish between the two. But the heat and the glare reflecting off the highly polished stones were the worst. He had to squint to see. So they just hurried on, sweating and panting in a circle of shimmering mirage 'water'.

Ten minutes later they reached the next dune. Vaughan went to sit down but Donny stopped him.

"Not here. In the bushes on the other side." This dune was also dotted with many small bushes so he was sure there would be cover there. Then he had another idea. "You go first, and I will brush out our tracks."

Selecting a suitable small saltbush, Donny pulled it up by the roots and then backed his way up the dune, carefully smoothing the sand as he went. It wasn't a very good job and looked obvious to his eyes, but he hoped it would not look like two sets of boot prints to anyone. As he did, this his eyes kept flicking to where he knew the vehicle track came over the last dune, about a kilometre away to the north-west.

But no vehicle had come into sight before he reached the crest, so he thankfully brushed his way over to where he found Vaughan slumped on the sand.

"Get up, Vaughan, we need to keep going," he said.

To his annoyance, Vaughan shook his head. "I can't. I'm buggered."

"We must! We need to get as far away as we can so they don't know where to look. Then we can lie down in short grass and not be seen."

Vaughan shook his head and pointed to the water bottle Donny was still clutching in his other hand.

"Give me a drink. I need a drink."

Donny was very reluctant to allow that. He was also annoyed by the tone, and it was on the tip of his tongue to say, 'Say please!'. He resisted the impulse and then grudgingly held the bottle out.

"You have half."

Vaughan snatched the bottle, unscrewed the lid and began gulping the water down. Donny watched with dismay. It was only a 750ml bottle and it was vanishing down Vaughan's throat at a great rate! He reached out and grabbed at it. Vaughan let go and sat there taking rapid breaths and looking defiantly guilty.

Donny studied the bottle. At least two thirds were gone. "I said half," he said in an aggrieved tone.

"Yeah, well, I'm bigger than you so I need more," Vaughan snapped back.

Bigger, fatter and less fit! Donny thought, giving the bigger boy a glare of disapproval. Then he put the bottle to his lips and drank the remainder. It tasted wonderful but was all gone much too quickly. *We certainly need more water,* he thought, anxiety about heat and dehydration being killers in that desert environment having been part of his whole life.

While Donny screwed the lid back on the bottle, he studied the flat ground across to the next distant dune. This area had small patches of gibbers but also had some distinct clumps of trees and bushes and a thin covering of short grass or spinifex over most of it.

Much better! he thought.

Looking down at Vaughan he pointed. "Come on, get up. Go that way. You lead down off the dune and I will brush the track out again."

For a few moments he thought Vaughan was not going to move but he then reluctantly got up and stumbled his way down the other slope. Donny followed, walking backwards while carefully brushing out the tracks as he went.

Once they were down on the flat, Donny took the lead, keeping both the empty bottle and his bush. He immediately changed direction to what he estimated as being north-east.

Vaughan was following him and asked, "Where are we going?"

"Back to the homestead of course, where else?" Donny replied, quite unable to keep the astonishment out of his voice.

"How do you know which way to go?" Vaughan asked, staring anxiously in all directions.

Donny looked at him in amazement. "By the sun and the sand dunes," he replied.

"Sand dunes?"

Donny was even more amazed. "Yes. Don't you know that the general trend of all the sand dunes in this desert is from south-east to north-west?"

"No. Why is that?" Vaughan asked.

"Something to do with the prevailing winds I heard Grandad say," Donny replied.

"Can we use the sun?" Vaughan asked.

Donny shook his head. "The sun isn't much use at this time of day. Too high overhead so you can end up walking in circles. Come on, let's go. We need to get to Bore No. 8 as quickly as possible."

"Why?"

"Before those men can get there to check."

Vaughan looked doubting. "How would they get there?"

"By the Land Rover. Now walk!"

How could he not realise that? Donny thought.

Chapter 6

CLONARGH STATION

Donny started off at a fast walk and was relieved to note that Vaughan was following. Their route was across another barren gibber plain. The heat was fierce and caused the air to dance and shimmer in waves.

We need to cross this as quickly as we can, Donny thought, glancing back to see how Vaughan was coping.

He was there but already plodding and falling behind. "Keep moving fast Vaughan or we will fry out here on the gibbers," Donny called. "And don't follow me. Make your own tracks and weave around a bit."

"Why?" Vaughan croaked, his face a red mask of distress.

"So we don't leave really obvious tracks if they get an aircraft or a helicopter," Donny explained.

He vividly remembered being up in a mustering chopper and the pilot showing him cattle and other animal tracks in the desert country.

"They couldn't, could they?" Vaughan queried, a picture of worry.

Donny shook his head and slowed to allow Vaughan to catch up. "Not easily. Not unless they have one handy."

Vaughan was so unfit and moving so slowly that Donny began to worry that he had made a serious mistake in bringing him.

I could easily have gotten away from those blokes on my own, he thought.

Another 15 minutes of hard walking had them at the next sand dune. It was another big dune that stretched right across their front from horizon to horizon and, like all the others, was dotted with a variety of bushes and clumps of grass and spinifex. The sand was so hot that when he put his hand down to steady himself, Donny gasped and quickly withdrew it. Vaughan had the same reaction and cried out on pain. He stopped plodding up and looked around in obvious distress. He was gasping open-mouthed and his eyes looked bloodshot.

Donny stopped and shook his head. "Breathe through your nose, Vaughan. Don't breathe through your mouth. It dries you out too much," he cautioned.

Vaughan just looked back, his chest heaving and perspiration making him blink. His appearance sent Donny's anxiety level up another notch.

To distract him he, said, "You just keep walking slowly up and I will try to brush out our tracks again," he added.

Vaughan stood there for another couple of minutes, gasping in great sucking gulps of air. Then he slowly started up the slope, plodding diagonally to avoid the steepness and to limit the slippage.

"It's too hot!" he wailed.

"Can't be helped," Donny replied.

"The sand," Vaughan added. "I can feel the heat through my boots."

Donny could only agree as he was experiencing the same boiling-at-the-bottom sensations. He became aware that he had stopped sweating.

That's not good, he thought.

His dad had taught him all about heat stress, heat exhaustion and heat stroke, and he began to experience little spasms of niggling fear, more out of concern for Vaughan than himself.

The boys reached the top of the dune and came to a stop. Donny only saw what he had expected, another vast flat area with a few bushes and patches of gibbers and claypan. But Vaughan was obviously dismayed and gaped at the extent of the flat area. In the distance, a kilometre or so away, another long sand dune, half hidden in the mirage effect, stretched right across their front.

Donny pointed down and almost pushed Vaughan to get him started.

"Come on, Vaughan. Keep going. We don't want to stop up here on top of the ridge. We stand out like a couple of country dunnies," he said.

Vaughan slithered and staggered to the bottom and halted on the firm ground, then asked the way again.

Donny was astonished. *I've already told him,* he thought. "North-east," he replied, only just managing to keep his voice neutral.

"Which way is that?" Vaughan answered.

Donny stopped beside him and put both his arms out, aligned with the sand dune. "All the main sand dunes run on the same direction, from south-east to north-west. If we cross them at right angles, we are going north-east."

"You sure?" Vaughan queried, blinking in the harsh glare.

"Of course I'm sure!" Donny snapped.

He had studied the map in his dad's office so many times he knew the layout of the property off by heart. Vaughan still looked doubtful, so Donny reached out to nudge him.

"I know the way, just walk with me," he managed to say in a flat tone.

"Where are we going again?" Vaughan queried.

"Number Eight Bore," Donny replied.

"I thought you said we were going to the homestead," Vaughan said, his voice almost a petulant bleat.

"I did, and we are. But we need water first and Number Eight Bore is the closest," Donny replied, rapidly becoming annoyed with Vaughan!

"Is it like the one we were just at?"

Donny shook his head. "Similar, but it's older and has no shelter."

"Is there a camera that the crooks might see us with?" Vaughan asked.

"Nope. Dad has only put in two and it all costs money, especially the radio network. Now stop yakking and walk."

"Are you sure there will there be water there?"

Donny had bite back a sarcastic retort. *Bloody idiot!* he thought. *Why would I go somewhere where I didn't know there was water?*

"Yes. I was there only two days ago, watering some stock," he replied.

What particularly annoyed him was that Vaughan and his parents had been at the homestead for five days before that and Vaughan had shown no interest in any station work. Instead, when asked if he would like to come with Donny and his dad, he had said it just bored him and he had stayed in his bedroom playing computer games. Donny was now almost completely unimpressed with the older boy.

His opinion rapidly got lower when Vaughan said, "And you are sure you can find it?"

"Yes!" Donny snapped, partly because of the implied insult and partly out of anxiety.

If I get my navigation wrong, we will miss the bore and both die of thirst. I hope we are going the right way!

"How far is it?" Vaughan asked.

That caused Donny a bit of a mental pause. "Less than twenty kilometres," he replied.

Vaughan was dismayed. "I can't walk that far in this heat," he cried.

"It will be less," Donny replied, his mind rapidly grappling with the figures involved while he tried to remember the rule for calculating the hypotenuse of a triangle.

Bugger! Mr Ross only covered that a month ago. I should have paid more attention in class.

"How do you know?" Vaughan challenged, coming to a halt on an area of dry grass.

Donny also stopped. He could see he needed to convince Vaughan to encourage him. "Look Vaughan, Clonargh Station is 4,000 square kilometres. It is eighty north south and fifty east west, a rectangle. It was settled by our great, great, great or something grandad way back in 1884."

"I know that," Vaughan replied in a sulky tone.

Donny sensed that the older boy did not like being lectured to, so he altered his tone slightly. "Well, one of those great, great grandads worked out that the only way this country could be any use was by drilling bores to get the artesian water. So he had twelve of them sunk. They are fifteen kilometres apart in four rows of three. The first row are numbered one, two and three and are ten kilometres south of the northern boundary. Four, five and six are just south of the homestead. Seven, eight and nine are the next row. I am aiming for Number Eight."

"We came from Ten?"

"Yes. So it is about twenty kilometres from it to Number Eight."

"What about Eleven and Twelve? Are they any use?"

Donny shook his head. "No. Eleven and Twelve have been out of use for years," he said. "They are right out in the desert country, and we haven't been running any stock in that area for a while."

He was about to launch into an explanation that the northern half of the property was flatter and had more grass and water and that they kept most of the 4,000 or so cattle they ran in that area. He also refrained from giving an explanation that the desert area around Bores 11 and 12 were so hard to reach as to be virtually inaccessible.

Vaughan now looked very doubtful. "You said ten kilometres earlier and now you are saying it is twenty from Number Ten to Number Eight."

Again, Donny was surprised. "Yes, well we covered between five and ten or so k's in the Land Rover and we've walked four or five since. It could be only about ten or twelve at the most," he replied, trying not to sound annoyed.

Vaughan made a face and grunted. He looked around in all directions, appearing to glare into the shimmering heat.

"I don't know if I can walk that far," he commented.

That really got Donny worried. "You have to try. You can't stay here. By the time I get help you will have died of heat stroke," he said.

To his relief, Vaughan began walking with him. Satisfied with the direction, Donny launched into a detailed explanation of heat illnesses.

"We are just like an engine," he said. "We need water to keep us cool. All the time we are perspiring, how much depends on the temperature and the humidity. The perspiration evaporates and that helps cool us."

"I know that!" Vaughan said with a sneer. "What is heat stroke?"

"Well, it is the third stage of heat illness and the most serious. During the stage before, which is heat exhaustion, you are still sweating and your skin is clammy to feel but you start getting dizzy and have difficulty thinking straight and make poor decisions. That is probably us right now."

At that, Vaughan looked very anxious. "So what else can we do?"

"Not a lot. We need to stick to our plan and get to water," Donny said.

He was very aware that he was experiencing some of the symptoms as he was developing a headache and his vision was starting to go blurry.

"So what happens?" Vaughan asked, stumbling over a tuft of dry grass and then swearing as he did.

"You don't have enough liquid in you to do everything, so the body withdraws the remaining fluids to keep the vital organs going, the heart and the brain. If the brain overheats you can suffer a stroke. And your skin goes dry and hot, that is one of the things to watch for. But you will also have lost a lot of salt, and you need that to generate the electricity that makes the nerves work. If you sweat it all out you can get cramps. You can suffer a heart attack from that too."

"So we have to get to water?" Vaughan commented. He looked both scared and exhausted.

Bloody hell! We have only walked a few kilometres, Donny thought. He had been starting to train for a 5-kilometre cross-country run and could do that in 25 minutes. *At this rate it will take hours!*

They plodded on in silence for the next few minutes. Donny found he was starting to blink and his headache got noticeably worse. He began to surreptitiously feel his skin to see how dry it was. The air was so hot it almost hurt to breathe it and he could feel the sun's rays burning through the material of his shirt.

I'm glad I've got my hat, he thought, which got him casting another worried glance at Vaughan who was visibly blinking and squinting in the glare.

After another twenty minutes they reached the next dune and slogged their way up it. Donny remembered to brush out their tracks, but he found it a real effort and was tempted to ask Vaughan to take over. On the crest they again came to a halt. But this time Dony smiled with satisfaction. The swale was only about half a kilometre wide but was mostly covered in grass and waist-high bushes. There were even a few trees. It was what he had been expecting, and it heartened him.

We aren't lost. I know roughly where we are, he thought.

But Vaughan looked dismayed and shook his head. "This is crazy," he muttered. "We will die in this heat."

"So we need to get to water," Donny insisted, eyeing the older boy with anxiety.

To end the discussion, he started down the other side. Vaughan followed with obvious reluctance. But the grass and the few trees made a significant difference. There was less glare and heat shimmer, and Donny took a course to move through the few patches of shade cast by the straggly small trees. He began to feel more cheerful.

Vaughan suddenly cried out and jumped back. "Eeeiow! Bloody hell!" he gasped.

Donny got a fright too, but more at Vaughan's reaction than by what had caused it. Two red kangaroos had stood up in the long grass a few metres ahead. They had been resting in a patch of shade and after a quick glance both animals began bounding away.

Bloody hell! Donny thought. *They are only kangaroos.*

"Are they dangerous?" Vaughan asked, his whole being one of readiness for flight.

Donny knew that a big kangaroo could attack a human but also knew it was unlikely. "Maybe, but it is so rare I have never known it to happen," he replied

Vaughan shook his head. "I heard that they stand on their tails and try to rip your guts out with their hind claws," he said.

A comment of his father's came to Donny, and he made a wry face. "They like to box too, so just knock them on their arse," he replied.

Even though he had got a fright as well he masked this and resumed walking. After watching the roos bounding away, Vaughan followed.

Twenty minutes later they reached the next dune, quite a low one that was almost completely covered in bushes and spinifex clumps. On reaching the top Donny again smiled with satisfaction. The next swale was also only about a kilometre across and had even more grass and several very distinct clumps of trees and bushes. Better still there were dozens of cattle dotted along it.

"Good!" he commented.

"Why?" Vaughan croaked as he staggered up to join him.

"Cattle," Donny replied, pointing to the nearest beasts.

"So? This is a cattle station, isn't it?"

"It means there is water not far away," Donny answered. "Great Grandad set the bores up so that the cattle or sheep only had to walk a couple of kilometres to the areas of grass. Come on."

Vaughan grumbled but followed Donny down off the dune. The boys set off across the flat, weaving around the spinifex clumps as much as possible to avoid being prickled. After a few minutes, Vaughan began to lag behind and Donny halted in the shade of the first tree he came to and waited.

"Come on, Vaughan! Not far to go now and we need to get there before those men think of coming to check," Donny snapped, getting a little bit tired of the older boy's grumbles and weakness.

"I need a rest," Vaughan croaked, coming to a staggering halt in the tiny patch of shade.

He looked ready to drop to Donny, which was a real worry but he was being needled by worry about the men, so he pointed to a small clump of trees a few hundred metres further on.

"We will have a break in among those trees. The shade will be better and we will have more cover," he said.

Vaughan grumbled again but Donny ignored him and resumed walking. It should have taken only three or four minutes but actually took twice as long and to Donny it seemed that every step they took was dragging the energy out of them. The heat and the glare were intense, and he became aware that small bush flies were now starting to bother both of them. The flies particularly annoyed them by crawling around the corners of their eyes and one even went up his left nostril.

Vaughan swore and swatted at them, nearly losing his balance as he did. "Bloody flies!" he shouted.

51

"It is because there is more cow dung around for them to breed in," Donny explained.

He was also irritated by the insects but could not see any point in getting too upset. They were just a normal part of life to him. He reached the clump of trees and found a patch of bare earth in among them in the shade. Vaughan joined him and slumped down, but almost immediately stood up and hit at his ankles and trousers.

"Ants! There are ants!" he cried in an accusing tone.

Donny resented the implication that the ants were somehow his fault, and he scowled and snapped back, "Of course there are bloody ants! This is the bush, you know."

Vaughan glared at him and stood there, leaning on a tree trunk and blinking in the glare.

"How much further?" he croaked.

Donny could only shrug. With an effort of will he resisted the temptation to tease by answering like a small child, 'Are we nearly there!'

"Not far I hope," he said instead.

"I'll wait here," Vaughan said.

Donny shook his head. "No you won't! I may not be able to find you again and you will just die in the heat. Then the ants will really get you."

"Don't be horrible!" Vaughan answered, on the edge of tears.

Donny shook his head and started walking again. He walked twenty paces before glancing back and was worried to note that Vaughan had stayed leaning on the tree, or almost clinging to it. But then Vaughan shrugged and started to follow.

This time Donny did not stop until he reached the next dune. It was only a few hundred metres but by the time he got to it he was aware that he had a blinding headache and that was starting to stagger and stumble. Vaughan looked to be in even worse case and when he reached him Donny grabbed his shirt and began dragging him diagonally up the slope.

It took at least five minutes to climb up the 25 metres to the crest. Donny was too worn out to brush out their tracks and he knew should approach the crest with caution but was too hot and exhausted to make himself do that. Instead, he plodded and struggled up until he could see over the top of the sand ridge.

As soon as he could, he let out a little gasp of relief. Off to his left, about two kilometres away, was a windmill and water tank.

Chapter 7

BORE NO. 8

"Bore Number Eight!" he croaked.

But it was right out in the open. The bottom of this swale was just a carpet of short grass with a few bushes and small areas of gibbers. There was not a tree to be seen.

No cover! Donny thought.

Donny pushed Vaughan down behind a bush and crouched under cover to scan the area. That was hard to do as the afternoon glare and the salty sweat in his eyes and the heat shimmer all made it hard to see. But after a careful squint in all directions he was satisfied there was no-one around.

"There doesn't seem to be anyone here," he commented.

Vaughan raised himself, blinking and squinting and stared towards the bore, saying, "How can you tell?"

"Well, there's nothing to be seen and the only cattle nearby are looking in our direction, and that bloody crow over there is staring at us," Donny replied. He stood up and reached down to grab at Vaughan's collar. "Come on! Let's get some water into us and get out of here."

Vaughan gave him a resentful look but got up and struggled the last few steps to the top. Then he slid and stumbled down, going sprawling across a bush near the bottom. Donny made a face and then followed, using his branch to brush out the tracks. He was surprised to find he was still carrying the empty plastic water bottle but was glad as he could use that hand to balance himself without having to touch the hot sand with his bare skin.

At the bottom, Vaughan was standing brushing sand off and spitting it from his mouth. He swore and glared at Donny. To lighten the atmosphere, Donny held his leafy branch up and forced a grin.

"You should get one so these. You could carry your own shade with you then."

Vaughan was not amused. "Get stuffed!" he croaked, glaring red-eyed at Donny.

Donny just shrugged and stepped past him, brushing out his own tracks until he was out on the grassy flat. The grass was only ankle high and mostly a dry yellow to grey colour but with patches of green.

From that winter rain we had a few weeks back, Donny mused. He set out at a fast walk on the firm ground.

Vaughan followed after a while, obviously having difficulty and slowly falling behind. Donny shrugged and continued as fast as he could walk on the flat ground.

I will go and get some water and bring it back to him, he decided.

For twenty-five minutes he plodded along on a course parallel to the sand dune and about 50 metres out from it. His planned route was to curve out towards the bore when he was closer to it. By then Vaughan was visibly staggering and looking very unhappy.

Donny slowed to let him catch up, thinking to urge him on. He was definitely no longer impressed by him. When Vaughan joined him, he restarted and they walked slowly side by side. The bore was now only about half a kilometre away in a diagonal line, so Donny angled towards it, still scanning in all directions.

As they walked, Donny, by habit, looked at the cattle in their path. There were perhaps fifty beasts that were scattered around nibbling the sparse feed. As the boys got closer, the cattle raised their heads and stood looking at them.

Vaughan eyed them warily. "They won't attack us, will they?" he asked.

Donny was again astonished. "Normally they won't. Just shout at them and wave your hat," he said.

That reminded him that Vaughan did not have his hat. *He is looking very red and sunburnt,* he thought. Worry caused a crease in his brow until Vaughan spoke again.

"You sure," he said, eyeing the cattle nervously.

"Yes, they are scared of us," Donny said. "As Dad says, 'We eat them, they don't eat us!' They are grass eaters."

"What do you mean?"

Donny had to make an effort to gather his thoughts in the intense heat. Part of a remembered conversation came back to him. "Dad says that all animals are scared of people. We are a hunter, with our eyes in the front."

"Eyes in front?"

"Yeah. It allows stereoscopic vision so we can judge distance better. You wouldn't want to throw a spear at a wild pig and miss. Dad says the animals with their eyes on the side are the grass eaters who spend half their effort looking over their shoulder to try to see what is creeping up on them. Dad says that all animals are frightened of humans as we kill."

"What about lions?" Vaughan queried.

"There aren't any lions in Australia," Donny answered.

"I know that! I meant in places like Africa," Vaughan retorted.

Donny ignored his anger. He was no longer intimidated by the bigger boy. He chuckled and said, "I know a good joke about lions."

In reply Vaughan grunted, so Donny went on, "There were these two wildlife photographers walking across the grassland in Africa when suddenly a big lion poked its head up out of the grass not very far in front of them. They both stopped and stared at it and then one bloke slowly knelt down and put his camera on the ground and began retying the laces on his Adidas running shoes. The other bloke looked down and said, 'Why do that? You can't outrun a lion.'. 'I don't need to,' the first guy replied as he stood up. 'I only need to outrun you!'.

It took a few moments before Vaughan got the joke and then he curled his lip. "Oh, that's not funny!"

Donny thought it was and gave a real chuckle. "It will be if we meet a big bull," he replied.

That got Vaughan looking anxiously at the cattle. "Is there one?" he asked.

Donny glanced at him and noted that he was visibly staggering. He had not seen one, so he shook his head, and said, "Don't think so, or not here anyway."

They were passing through the widely scattered herd by then and Vaughan kept looking anxiously at them. The cattle, in return, lifted their heads to watch them and a few even took a few paces closer.

"Why are they coming closer?" Vaughan asked.

Again, Donny shook his head. *He should know more about cattle than that,* he thought.

He said, "Because they associate humans with good things like salt and molasses licks."

"Why don't they run away?"

"Because they don't understand what is going to happen in a year or so," Donny replied.

He was so used to cattle and unafraid that he just walked confidently towards the water trough next to the raised water tank. Several beasts lowered their heads but then backed away.

Donny explained that Bore No. 8 was a typical older bore. The actual artesian bore, a pipe that went down for about a thousand metres, came out of the ground half a kilometre away. It then led across the top of the grass to go up and over the top of a large, corrugated iron water tank. Here, water was dribbling from the end of the pipe and into the tank, a wisp of 'steam' rising from it as it did. The artesian bore water was usually so hot it would scald and had to be allowed to cool before use. One of the main jobs on the station was to open the tap to fill the long steel water trough each evening so the cattle could drink when the water was cool enough.

"This will probably be the next bore Dad upgrades to a radio system so one of the men doesn't have to drive here to work the taps," he said.

As he and Vaughan got closer to the bore, Donny noted that the last hundred paces or so was just bare sand, thickly dotted with cow poos. He stopped on the edge of the clear area and then sent Vaughan on ahead. He then followed, walking backwards and brushing out their tracks.

Vaughan halted at the water trough. "It's empty!" he wailed.

Donny shook his head. "We don't just let water run into it all the time. It would just evaporate in the sun and be wasted if we did," he replied.

He brushed his way over next to Vaughan and put his branch aside. Reaching over he grasped the valve wheel and went to turn it.

"Yow! That's bloody hot!' he yelled.

He let go and silently swore. He had known that and forgotten! Reaching into his pocket he took out his handkerchief and again grasped the wheel. It turned easily, as he knew it would, having been there two days before. Water began to spray and flow into trough.

Vaughan immediately reached out to wet his hands and face. Donny did not have time to warn him, did not even think he needed to. Vaughan at once cried out in pain and pulled his hands back.

"Aaargh! That burnt me!" he cried.

"Yeah well, you know bore water might be hot," Donny said, annoyed and not at all sympathetic. "Wait till it cools a bit."

Donny released more water until the long trough had about five centimetres of water in it. As he did, this he noted that that the cattle were watching and were starting to edge closer.

That will be good. They will obliterate our tracks, he thought.

He also kept looking around, particularly north-west along the line of the swale where the two ruts of a vehicle track led off toward the main station road.

Both boys were so hot and thirsty that they soon began testing the heat of the water, dipping their fingers in and splashing some over their faces, then their heads and shirts. That was bliss! Donny began to splash it all over his head, neck and shirt, enjoying the cooling effect of evaporation. Satisfied it had cooled enough to drink he unscrewed the cap of the plastic water bottle and dipped it carefully in and allowed it to fill. In the process a few of the floating particles went in but not many. He put the bottle in the shade to cool and went back to splashing himself.

Vaughan joined in but did not look happy. When Donny scooped up a handful of water and sipped it, he looked doubtful.

"What's that floating in the water?" he asked.

"Cow poo, of course," Donny answered. He had been gritting his teeth and trying to ignore it.

Vaughan looked appalled. "We can't drink that! It will make us sick," he cried.

Donny stared at him in disbelief. "So what? You might get an upset stomach and a bit of the runs but so what? You have to be alive to be sick. Now drink or you will be dead by tomorrow."

Suiting his own actions to his words, he proceeded to suck in as much water as he could. It took an effort to keep his face neutral as he felt the particles of 'matter' going down his throat, but he did grimace a bit at the hard, mineral taste of the hot, bore water. But he was used to that, had been drinking it all his life, so he managed. Vaughan made more of an effort of it, but Donny was pleased to see that he was actually drinking, though with lots of looks of disgust and mutters about the taste.

Both boys drank and splashed themselves and their clothes for several minutes. By then the water in the steel trough had cooled just to 'a still too warm' level for either comfort or taste but Donny didn't care.

We need to get away from here before any of those men think to come looking, he told himself.

As he thought this, his gaze scanned along the vehicle track, swallowing more water as he did. First, he noted that the cattle were edging in closer, obviously hot and thirsty. Then his eyes picked up a misty brown patch above the 'mirage' shimmer in the distance.

Is that dust? he wondered.

As he watched he felt himself gripped by fear. Out of the watery looking shimmer only a couple of kilometres away had appeared a vehicle. It was racing towards them, and he recognised it instantly as the station Land Rover. Sunlight glinted off its windshield and he was so afraid that for a few moments he had trouble speaking. Then he croaked and pointed.

"A vehicle!" he managed to say.

Vaughan spun round to look and his face paled under the sunburn. "Oh no, here they come! Let's get out of here!" he cried.

As he started hurrying away from the trough, Donny's mind clicked back into gear. "Not that way! They will see us. Go around the tank and keep that between the vehicle and us," he instructed.

After casting another quick glance at the rapidly approaching vehicle, he bent and scooped up the plastic water bottle and his leafy branch and hurried after Vaughan.

But even as he slid close around the side of the large water tank, Donny knew they had left it too late. It was at least a kilometre to the nearest trees or sand dune.

Those crooks will be here in a couple of minutes, he calculated. As his racing mind calculate this he glanced down and saw Vaughan's boot prints clear in the dust. *Tracks! Don't leave any tracks,* he thought. But that meant going backwards and even slower!

Seeing no other option, Donny began brushing out their tracks as he backed quickly around the curve of the water tank. Vaughen was crouched there, looking flustered and afraid.

"What will we do?" he wailed, gesturing to the vast open area beyond.

That sobered and steadied Donny. "Lie down in the bloody grass of course. Now get moving! Keep looking back to make sure you have the water tank between you and the Land Rover," he all but shouted, fear adding to his anger and contempt.

Vaughan did as he was told. Donny followed, brushing at the tracks and shaking his head in near despair. The grass nearby was very short, barely ankle to knee high and there were only a couple of slightly larger clumps of saltbush and spinifex.

Oh bugger! How can we hide in that? he fretted.

But there wasn't time to do much choosing! Already he could hear the vehicle approaching and he knew they had less than a minute or so to find somewhere to hide. So he kept walking backwards, brushing and gasping, his head swinging to and fro to look both ways. The only good thing he noted was that as he and Vaughan retreated the thirsty cattle were rapidly closing in on the water in the trough.

They will at least obliterate any tracks, he thought, clinging to every tiny hope.

And now time was up. Vaughan had reached the edge of the grass and turned to run but Donny called loudly.

"No! Get down behind those bits of saltbush. Get down!"

To his relief, Vaughan did as he was told and Donny now sprinted to join him, casting blurry, almost panicky glances back as he did. Next to Vaughan were another couple of small clumps of saltbush and a couple of slightly larger tufts of spinifex. It looked hopeless, but instinct warned him that to keep running was even more so. So he cast himself flat on the bare sand beyond the clumps. Ignoring the pain and discomfort of the hot sand, he lay flat and turned his head to look through the pitiful screen of vegetation.

The cattle that had hurried to the water trough gave him a few seconds warning when they started to scatter or back away, and then he heard the Land Rover's brakes and wheel sounds. The vehicle skidded and scrunched to a stop over on the other side of the water trough and Donny glimpsed its front just poking out past the right side of the water tank. Dust billowed and men swore as it engulfed them.

Bugger! It is those men, Donny recognised.

He tensed ready to run, determined not to give in.

Chapter 8

THREATS OF DEATH

The sand was so hot that Donny could feel it burning his bare skin. Near him Vaughan was muttering and letting out little whimpers of pain and trying not to lie flat.

"Get down! Lie as low as you can!" Donny hissed as the Land Rover's engine was switched off.

"But it's hot!" Vaughan wailed.

"Shut up and lie still," Donny hissed.

Remembering how distinctive a shape a hat was, he took his off and placed it under his wrists to shield them from the sand and then he lifted his head slightly to peer through the spiky grass.

Vaughan did the same. To Donny's surprise, he asked, "Why are all the cattle coming in?" he asked.

"Sssh! Quiet!" Donny replied in a croaking whisper.

But curiosity got him to lift his head to see what Vaughan meant. He saw that the cattle from hundreds of metres away were starting to converge on the water trough. Again, he shook his head at Vaughan's ignorance.

"Because we often bring the cattle a salt lick or molasses or hay. They associate vehicles with water and food. They are hoping for a treat," he replied.

Vaughan's face lit up with hope. "So these men might be just some stockmen then," he whispered.

Donny shook his head. "No. All our stockmen have leave over the holidays. And no-one is tasked with coming here today. It is those men. I recognise the vehicle. Now be quiet."

It was the men. Thug strode into view, the cattle scattering away from him. He stared in all directions and then went over to the water trough. That sent Donny's heart into palpitations of anxiety

Oh no! The water trough has got water in it. That will tell him we have been here, he thought, berating himself for such a mistake. But Thug just splashed it and then cried out.

"What?" came Ringer's voice.

"Bloody water's hot!" Thug replied.

"Of course it is! It's bore water, and it's been sittin' in the sun all day," Ringer replied.

He came into view and looked down into the trough. Donny went tense, thinking that as Ringer was a stockman he might twig to the fact that the tap had only recently been opened.

Ringer also splashed some of the water and washed his face. Thug just glanced, then bent to splash more water on his face. Then he cupped some in one hand and went to drink it.

"Oh yuk! That's bloody horrible," he cried.

Donny had to grin and got a sickly smile in return from Vaughan. Ringer began an explanation of why bore water tasted the way it did.

"Full of minerals and salts. Good fer ya," he said.

"Yeah well, let's look around anyway," Thug replied.

He now lifted a pair of binoculars that he had slung around his neck and once again scanned in all directions. Ringer joined him and began studying the ground, causing Donny to break into a sweat of anxiety over whether his brushing out of tracks had been sufficient. He knew his efforts would not fool a real tracker for a minute.

And Ringer's a bushman. He might have that skill, he worried.

Ringer must have thought he did as he stared off to the south-west and then began walking that way, scattering the cattle as he went.

"They would have to have come from that direction," he said to Thug. "So I'll just do a cast around to check."

Both men walked to the edge of the bare ground and Donny again tensed, ready to spring up and run. The two men were only a few metres to the right of where he and Vaughan had come onto the clearing and to Donny's relief they now turned right and began a clockwise search around it. That got his heart pumping hard again.

If they walk right around the circle they will almost step on us when they get to here. They can't help but find us, he thought.

The men went out of sight, away from them, causing the cattle to shuffle and back away. After the men had gone a few cattle bravely pushed forward to the trough and began drinking.

Poor buggers are thirsty, Donny mused. *And so am I!*

He ran his tongue over his dry lips and knew he needed more water.

Vaughan lifted his head to watch as the men vanished from view on the other side of the water tank. To Donny he looked very frightened. Then he really lowered himself in Donny's estimation by croaking in a harsh whisper, "Why don't we just surrender! They must find us."

Donny shocked. "No way! They haven't found us yet."

"But they might bash us when they find us," Vaughan croaked.

"Shut up! We aren't giving up. As long as we are free, we are upsetting Uncle James's plans. Now just shut up and lie under cover and don't you give us away or I'll bash ya!"

Vaughan looked resentful at that but subsided onto his stomach. Donny also lowered himself, but it took an effort to endure the baking heat from the ground. He began to sweat but that, he decided, was a very good sign. He also became aware that his leafy branch was sticking up and he slowly lowered it. The incongruity of the different leaves was apparent to him, but he hoped the men would not notice it.

There were several tense minutes before the men came into view again. to Donny's relief they stopped on the north-east side and stared out in the direction he and Vaughan might have gone. Donny tensed, worrying they would continue around the circle. But Thug now shook his head and walked back to the water trough, sending the cattle scattering away again. This time Donny wasn't worried. Enough cattle had trampled around the water trough to obliterate any tracks he and Vaughan might have left.

Thug now sent Donny's heart rate up again by clambering up on the corner of the tank stand. Up till now he had been worried that his bum and shoulders might be sticking up above the level of the grass and bushes, but now the man was much higher and Donny was sure he must see them if he looked down.

To his relief, Thug again raised his binoculars and scanned the distant sand dune and open country off to the south-west. Ringer stood below him, looking in the same direction.

Thug shook his head. "No sign of the little bastards. I dunno why the boss said to come and look here. We must be 20k from that other place," he said. He began climbing back down.

Ringer answered, "That was Bore No. 10, the New Lick."

"Where are we now?"

"Bore No. 8," Ringer replied.

"You reckon that those kids could have walked here in this heat?" Thug said.

Ringer shrugged. "The fat one couldn't, but young Donny could. He's a tough little bugger."

"Yeah, but could they even find this place? It all looks the same to me."

"It might look the same to you, but Young Donny lives here. He will be able to find his way cross-country." Ringer said.

Thug wiped sweat from his face. "Bloody flies! Yeah, maybe, but only if he leaves that fat one behind," he said.

Donny glanced at Vaughan and saw that he was blushing. And he could only agree with the 'bloody flies!' comment. The perspiration had attracted dozens of them and they were annoying him and Vaughan and neither could not move to brush them off. One even crawled up his nostril and he had to fight down the urge to sneeze as the tickling sensation became intense.

Worried about how Vaughan was coping with the flies, Donny swivelled his eyes to look, and then froze as a chill of real fear stabbed through him. Underneath the clump of spinifex only a half metre from Vaughan's right arm was a snake!

Horrified, Donny stared at it. *Bloody hell, a Death Adder! If Vaughan moves it might strike. Do I warn him or not?*

Trying to hide his alarm, he studied the reptile. It was a Death Adder alright. He could tell that from the shape of the head and the banding on the scales. It looked to be about as thick as his arm and was curled into the usual horseshoe shape with just the tip of its tiny tail sticking out. Worse still, it was looking intently at Vaughan, with its horrible, beady black eyes and its forked tongue was flicking out from time to time. To Donny that forked tongue was the worst. To him it looked truly reptilian and chilling.

Death Adders are ambush hunters, Donny told himself.

He was well versed in snakes and the danger they posed from many warnings by adults and from seeing them fairly frequently. He was sure that if Vaughan was bitten and the snake injected venom then he would almost certainly die.

We will never get him to a hospital in time, even if we surrender to these men, he thought.

But what to do? Torn by anxiety he decided not to warn Vaughan as he did not dare speak that loudly with the men so close. He began to will them to move away. Then his anxiety level shot up even more as Thug scanned all round again with his binoculars.

Go away! Go away! Donny thought. He found he was starting to tremble from being so tense.

Thug lowered his binoculars and shook his head. "Can't see anything," he said. "I doubt if those kids could have gotten this far. I reckon they will be lost out there in the desert, dyin' of bloody thirst."

"I hope not. That'll complicate things," Ringer replied.

"Little bloody troublemakers! If we find the little bastards, I reckon we should just shoot them and bury 'em in a sand dune. Nobody would ever find them out here," Thug said, sending waves of intense anxiety through Donny.

Ringer did not like that. He shook his head emphatically. "No you won't! Boss wants 'em alive as hostages so you keep your finger orf that bloody trigger. I don't want to spend another ten or twenty years in jail for murder. Anyway, they ain't here. Let's go and check the creek lines. The creeks are a more obvious route for a couple of kids if they are trying to reach the homestead."

To Donny's intense relief, the two men walked back around to the Land Rover, once again scattering the cattle, some of which kept looking towards him and Vaughan.

Come on you blokes, drive away! Donny thought. He was almost trembling with anxiety now, as the snake had curled up a bit tighter. *Getting ready to strike,* he decided.

To his annoyance, Thug came back into view talking on a satellite phone. Then Ringer briefly appeared before vanishing from view on the other side of the water tank.

"I'll just give these poor buggers a bit more water. Might be a few days before anyone gets out here again," he said, reinforcing Donny's notion that he actually was a real stockman who cared about cattle.

The sound of running water came to him, and after a couple of minutes the water noises stopped and Donny heard a vehicle door open and close.

Oh, thank God! he thought.

Then he glanced around and saw that Vaughan was getting ready to move. Appalled he shook his head vigorously and hissed.

"Vaughan, don't move! There's a snake near you."

Vaughan looked where Donny was pointing and blanched. He began to visibly shake.

"G… Get… Get it away from me!" he gasped.

Donny's mind raced and he shook his head. "Just lie still until those crooks are gone," he whispered.

Vaughan stared in horror at the snake and began to shiver and weep. "I can't! I'm scared."

"You must! Those men are just as dangerous. If you don't make a sudden movement and the snake doesn't feel threatened it won't bite you," he said.

He wasn't sure that was true but felt he had to say something to keep Vaughan calm.

"What type is it?" Vaughan asked, a distinct quaver evident in his voice.

Donny tempted to lie but decided honesty was the best policy. "Death Adder. You won't survive if it strikes. Just stay still till I get up and distract it, then go that way," he said, pointing off along the pipe.

Vaughan had gone very pale by this time and Donny could see beads of sweat forming and running down his face. It was evident he was under great strain.

He could crack at any moment, he thought.

He kept willing the crooks to leave. Then he heard another door open and shut on the Land Rover and he heaved a real sigh of relief. The vehicle's motor started and that caused the snake to pull its head back and turn it in that direction. Donny held his breath and bit his lip as the tension became all but unbearable.

Finally, after what seemed like minutes, the Land Rover started moving. It came fully into view and then swung away, accelerating as it did. Then it went roaring off back along the vehicle track. Donny shuddered with relief and then gathered up his thoughts to face the more immediate and deadly problem. He noted that the snake had again turned to watch Vaughan, who was now trembling and starting to sob.

Even so, Donny waited another minute. Then he carefully raised his head and tried to detect the Land Rover's position. But the water tank was in the way and all he could see was some dust drifting across. But he did note that when he moved the snake's attention shifted to him.

That's good. Now I have to distract it. He was sure he was too far away for the snake to reach him.

"Okay Vaughan, get ready. When I spring up you roll away and then get up and run. Ready?" he said.

Vaughan nodded but he looked very scared, and Donny wasn't sure if the older boy could act or not. *Oh well, nothing for it but to try,* he told himself.

Very slowly he got to his hands and knees and crouched ready to sprint. As he did, the snake kept its gaze fixed on him.

"Okay: one, two three, go!" he cried.

At the same moment, he sprang up and dashed across in the opposite direction he had told Vaughan to run in. As he ran, Donny saw the snake's head swivel to follow him and then swing back at an absolutely appalling speed towards Vaughan as he moved. Because Vaughan had acted. He had twitched and rolled away and was on his feet and running in an instant.

Donny stopped near the water tank, aware that his sudden movement had scared the cattle. They were scattering away from the trough in all directions. He skidded to a stop and peeked around the side of the water tank. His fear was that the crooks might have noticed the cattle moving; but to his relief, all he could see was a distant billow of dust. The Land Rover was now a kilometre or so away and travelling fast.

Donny now looked the other way and saw that Vaughan was nearly 50 metres away.

"Stop! Stop running you bloody idiot! It can't strike that far or catch you."

Vaughan ran a few more paces and then came to a gasping stop. He looked back and stood there, trembling and shaking his head.

Donny shook his head as well. "Now come here and lie down in the shade in case those men look back," he instructed.

Vaughan began walking slowly back, his eyes scanning the bushes and grass. "Is it still there?" he queried.

Donny didn't know so he cautiously made his way back towards the clump of spinifex the snake had been under. He was just in time to see the tail of the Death Adder slide from view another big clump of spinifex a few metres away.

"There it is. It's gone into that bush," he said, pointing.

Vaughan very reluctantly came back, his eyes darting around for any sign of another snake.

"Will it chase us and attack?" he asked, nervously eyeing the particular clump of scrub.

"No!" Donny said, annoyed now as the relief flooded through him. "They are fat little ambush hunters. They just lie in wait for their prey. You could easily outrun one."

He was sure of that from listening to the stockmen talk, and he was about to start a tale he had heard about men being chased by king browns and mulga snakes but then realised he didn't want to frighten Vaughan any more.

Vaughan made his way out onto the bare ground and into the shade. "What type was it?"

"A Death Adder," Donny answered.

"Are they dangerous?" Vaughan asked.

Are you a complete idiot! Donny thought but managed not say. Instead, he said, "Yes. That is why the word death is part of their name."

A trembling Vaughan lowered himself into the tiny patch of shade cast by the water tank and then lay back on the dust.

He needs a drink, Donny thought. *And so do I.*

Then he realised he had left his hat, water bottle and branch back in the long grass.

Bugger! We need them.

Chapter 9

BLOODY HOT!

Making a face to express his emotions, Donny said, "Just lie there for a few minutes and I will get you a drink."

After a careful look to check that the vehicle was not coming back, he made his way out to retrieve the items, his eyes also darting around for any sign of the snake. Thankfully he picked up his hat and dusted it and then put it on. Relief was immediate.

It felt like my brain was boiling, he thought, which got him worrying about how well Vaughan might be coping.

Selecting a spot on the eastern side of the water tank from where he could see along the swale and vehicle track, but which still offered a tiny patch of shade, Donny lowered himself down to lean back on the tank stand. Next to him, Vaughan now lay full length on the sandy ground. As Donny could feel the heat from the sand through his trousers, he wondered how Vaughan might be coping with the hot sand, but he looked so exhausted that he let him lie.

After a couple of minutes, Donny decided to drink from the water bottle. He unscrewed the lid and gulped down nearly half in one go. As he sighed with pleasure, Vaughan asked for a drink. The bottle was passed to him and emptied in seconds. Donny nodded with satisfaction and took the bottle back. Struggling to his feet, he made his way around to the trough. Stepping back into the direct sunlight felt like opening the door to an oven and he squinted against the glare. The braver cattle that were drinking mooed and shuffled and backed away. Donny ignored them and refilled the water bottle. As quickly as he could, he made his way back into the shade.

The water was still too hot to comfortably drink, and he had to refuse Vaughan's request for more. For a couple of minutes he stood there in the shade, leaning on the relative coolness of the water tank. As he did, his mind grappled with the problem of how to carry more water for the next leg of his planned journey. His gaze travelled back along the pipeline to the bore. A tiny bump in the grass reminded him of things he had seen a couple of years before when he had walked along the pipe with his dad.

There were old beer bottles there, he thought. His dad had said they had been discarded by the workers who had sunk the bore a hundred years before. *I wonder if I can find an old bottle we can use?*

Passing the water bottle to Vaughan, he stepped out into the sunlight again and started walking back along the pipe. Vaughan called after him.

Donny just called back, "Just looking. You sit there and drink."

Keeping a careful eye out for the snake, Donny made his way a hundred metres along the steel water pipe to the grassy mound. As he got closer, his questing eyes noted that his memory was good. There were old beer bottles. They were the big, brown coloured ones made of glass, much bigger than most contemporary beer bottles he had seen. They were half buried in sand and overgrown, but he soon uncovered a couple. But he had to go carefully as the first two he dug up were broken and had jagged edges.

I don't want any cut hands or fingers out here, he thought, recalling a time when he had suffered a big gash in the palm of his left hand a few years before, and his parents had to drive all the way to Golden Dawn to get it stitched.

Within five minutes, Donny had unearthed two big beer bottles that were unbroken. They were full of sand and rubbish but that didn't bother him. They could just be washed out. Then his eye lit on some clear glass, a square bottle, nearly buried.

A whisky bottle, he thought.

His grandad drank whisky, so he was familiar with such things. This was also carefully dug up and the bottles carried to the water trough, which Donny saw was now half full, and placed in to soak. He then retrieved the plastic water bottle, now empty, from Vaughan and refilled it. Standing it on the tank stand in the shade to cool, he again splashed water over his face, arms, and shirt and washed his hands and forearms. Feeling much better he then drank the entire 750ml of warm water from the plastic bottle. All the while he kept looking around, particularly along the vehicle track.

The old glass bottles were then carefully washed and rinsed out and filled. Donny puzzled for a while over a method of stopping the water spilling out and finally had to conclude there was no option but to just carry them carefully. Then he had another big drink and refilled the plastic bottle again. A pee was then needed, after which he again soaked his face and shirt. The plastic bottle was again passed to Vaughan who again drank it all. Donny refilled it and joined him in the shade.

Vaughan looked a bit better but was very sunburnt. He said, "What do we do now?"

Donny pointed off northwards. "Walk to Bore Number 5."

"How far is that?"

"Be fifteen kilometres," Donny replied.

Vaughan bit his lip and then shook his head. "I don't know if I can walk that far. I've got bad blisters and I am starting to get really bad chafe."

Donny already had some chafe, and it was hurting but he shook his head. "Too bad. You can't stay here."

Vaughan looked very thoughtful at that and then said quietly, "Thanks for warning me about the snake."

Donny shrugged. "It seemed to be the best thing to do. I didn't want you bitten."

"That is the first real snake I have ever seen," Vaughan admitted.

Donny, who had seen hundreds over the years almost gaped at him in astonishment. "You mean in the bush like?"

"Yeah. I had only ever seen one at the zoo, and it was behind glass and I didn't pay much attention," Vaughan commented.

"That one had my attention," Donny admitted.

"Mine too!" Vaughan replied. Then his face crumpled and he began to sob. "I... sob... I was so... sob... so scared! I thought I was going... to... going to sob... die!"

Donny was embarrassed to see the older boy crying and he sat and said nothing until the sobbing subsided.

"Anyway, we'd better get going and we might get to the next bore in daylight."

He estimated that it was after 2 o'clock. *Maybe closer to 3. That gives us about four hours. That's about 3 or 4K's per hour. We should be able to do that by dark.*

He knew that sunset was about 7pm at that time of year. But Vaughan was the problem. He was still sobbing and shivering.

Donny touched him and said, "Come on, Vaughan, let's get moving."

Vaughan looked at him with red-rimmed eyes filled with tears and shook his head.

"No. I can't do this. I hate it!"

Donny could only shake his head. "I'm not enjoying either, but we don't have a choice so let's go."

"We do. I can stay here. You will go faster without me," Vaughan replied between sobs.

Donny felt a surge of exasperation. "We've been over this! You can't stay. There's no food and we have no idea when someone, other than the crooks, might come here. We are better off together. Come on, we've got water and should be able to get there by sunset."

After a few minutes Vaughan's sobbing eased off and he had another drink. Donny didn't have a problem with that.

The more he drinks the better, and it will help replace those tears, he told himself.

But he was mightily unimpressed. He got to his feet and picked up his branch, and said, "I will just brush out my tracks. You refill that bottle and then head that way," and pointed North.

Without waiting to see if Vaughan did that, Donny worked back to where he had found the beer bottles and then started back towards the water tank. To his relief, he saw that Vaughan had risen to his feet and was refilling the plastic bottle.

When Donny arrived back at the water trough Vaughan was still there, splashing water on himself. He screwed the top back on the plastic bottle and said, "Who carries what?"

Donny pointed to the beer bottles and said, "You take those two and I will carry the plastic bottle in my pocket and the whisky bottle in one hand and the branch in the other. Now get going."

Reluctantly Vaughan obeyed, but he made a very awkward show of carrying the big beer bottles. Donny slid the plastic bottle into his pocket, picked up the whisky bottle and began backing away from the water trough, brushing out their tracks as he went.

When they reached the edge of the bare ground another problem immediately arose: Vaughan had stopped and was reluctant to walk among the clumps of salt bush and spinifex.

"There might be another snake," he explained.

"There undoubtedly are!" Donny exploded. He was hot, tired, cross and frightened too but still brave enough to risk it. "You've got boots on and long trousers. A snake bite is unlikely to get through all that. Oh, for heaven's sake! I'll lead."

With that he pushed past Vaughan and started walking quickly across the flat ground, keeping to the sun on his left to maintain direction north. Vaughan muttered and let out a few sobs before starting to follow. Now Donny silently cursed him. The thought of snakes, of that Death Adder, got him scared and he experienced a prickling sensation of fear that he imagined soldiers must feel when walking into a minefield. It took a conscious effort of will to ignore the danger and to keep putting one foot in front of the other.

As they headed diagonally across the swale, Vaughan pointed to his left. "Why don't we just follow this vehicle track?" he asked.

"Because it goes the wrong way. It goes north-west to the main station road. And if we walk along it, it will make it more likely we will get caught. I would have to wipe out our tracks all the way."

"Where did you say we are going to?"

"North to Bore Number 5."

"Is that shorter?"

Donny shook his head. "No, either way is two sides of a triangle. The homestead is north north-west, that way, and we are heading north. If we go along the road it comes to the station road and then goes north beside Burke Creek to the homestead. But that is where the crooks are more likely to look."

Vaughan did not look happy at this but shrugged and continued walking. To add to Donny's concern, he noted that Vaughan was starting to limp and also that he was walking with a peculiar gait, his legs a bit apart.

Chafe, he thought.

He was getting it himself and also under his armpits. But he didn't have any blisters although his feet felt very hot.

As they plodded along, Donny thought the heat might be about 38 or 39 C, normal for that time of the year. It was a real risk. If they had not had water, he would not have attempted the walk.

The sooner we are there, the better, he told himself.

So he strode on across a patch of gibber plain. As he did, the heat really hit him. The sun was reflecting up off the polished pebbles and the air seemed too thick to breathe. Visibility was also distorted, and they walked surrounded by watery mirage patches.

We might not see a vehicle until too late, he thought.

To add to his concern, Vaughan soon slowed down and Donny noted that he was continually sipping from one of the beer bottles. But all he could do was shrug.

No point in having a battle trying to get him to conserve water, he thought. *Anyway, it's better in him than spilt or evaporated.*

And spilt some of it soon was. They reached next dune and both came to a panting halt. Donny had a drink from his whisky bottle and looked up at the wall of sand and bushes. It seemed to loom above them like a mighty mountain range, even though his mind told him it was only ten or fifteen metres high. Vaughan had another drink and stood staring up as well.

Donny set himself to climb and only when he was about halfway up did he remember that he was supposed to go last to brush out their tracks. He stopped to let Vaughan go past and saw that the older boy was really struggling. He was gasping and sweating and kept crying out in pain at the hot sand.

"Come on, Vaughan! Once we are over this the crooks can't see us from the vehicle track and there are some trees," he said.

Or at least I think there are!

Vaughan continued to struggle up until he slipped. As he tried to steady himself, he tipped the beer bottle he was holding in that hand and water began to pour out.

Donny shook his head and cried out. "Vaughan! Vaughan! Keep the bottle upright!"

Vaughan stopped, gasping and heaving and staring stupidly back at him. Donny again pointed to the bottle and at last Vaughan understood and held the bottle up. But more than half the water had been lost. It was on the tip of Donny's tongue to call him a fool, but he resisted the impulse.

Getting over that dune was a real struggle. Vaughan complained and whimpered about how hot the sand was and how prickly the grass and bushes were. At the top he slumped down and wanted to stop and took a lot of urging to get him moving down the other side. And it didn't help that Donny had been wrong. There were no trees, just a vast gibber plain and areas of dry grass and small bushes, the distance lost in the heat shimmer.

"You told me there would be trees!" Vaughan cried accusingly.

"Sorry! I was wrong. It must be over the next dune," Donny replied.

He distinctly remembered there being trees in one of the swales close to Bore No. 5. He hadn't been across this particular bit of country except by air when his dad took him in a light aircraft the previous year.

"It's bloody hot!" Vaughan cried.

"It is, so we need to get across this next bit of country quickly," Donny said. "So have a big drink and let's get going."

Suiting actions to words, he drank the remaining water in his whisky bottle and started brushing out their tracks. Vaughan had a big drink from the half empty beer bottle but then just stood there swaying.

Donny gestured impatiently. "Come on, Vaughan, move!"

Reluctantly Vaughan did and they half slid, half staggered down the other side of the dune and out onto the vast flat area. As before, the heat hammered at them in waves and radiated upwards through their boots and into their faces, Donny made no attempt to brush out the line of boot prints where Vaughan's weight had crunched through the thin crust of cemented gibbers and salt. It was just too hard and would take too long.

He moved to the front and led the way across that vast plain. As he plodded along, Donny kept noting his own condition and glancing back to check on Vaughan. He realised that he had stopped perspiring and that the effort of breathing the hot, dry air was drying out his nasal tubes and throat. Even more unpleasant was that his eyes were starting to sting from the salt in his perspiration. The pain from his chafe was also burning, and his boots seemed to get heavier and heavier. And Vaughan was making really slow work of it, limping and obviously in pain from chafe

By then they were so far out on the plain that the sand dunes both ahead and behind were lost in the mirage 'water'. Vaughan stumbled to a stop.

"Have to stop! I can't go on!" he croaked.

"Yes, you can. You can't stay here. You will be cooked!" Donny cried, a feeling of apprehension rising up to tighten his chest and throat.

He began to fear he had made a terrible, possibly deadly mistake. *If Vaughan collapses out here, I will never be able to carry him to shelter,* he thought.

"Hot! Too bloody hot!" Vaughan cried.

"Have another drink, Vaughan," he said in desperation.

To his relief, Vaughan did, but then he just dropped the now empty beer bottle. Donny was annoyed as well as afraid.

"Don't drop that! Pick it up!" he snapped. "We will need it during the walk to the homestead."

Vaughan glared at him but reluctantly bent and picked the empty bottle up. Donny then had what seemed like a bright idea. He held out his leafy branch, now minus many of its leaves.

"Here, you carry this, and you will get a bit of shade. I will carry the bottle."

They swapped and Donny started walking again. The fear that Vaughan was going to collapse was now very real.

He's drunk all his water, or spilt it. We only have the plastic water bottle left, Donny thought.

Vaughan began limping along slowly, grumbling about blisters, heat and chafing. Donny kept glancing at him.

He's stopped sweating too and he's blinking a lot, he noted anxiously. *We have to get to some shade, or we are in real trouble!*

Chapter 10

BLOODY WEAKLING!

By an effort of sheer will power Donny kept plodding across that burning desert. Vaughan stayed with him but their speed was very slow. Donny began to get dots before his eyes and realised he was getting giddy.

Bloody hell! I'm getting heat exhaustion, he thought. He began to despair and wonder how to escape from the peril his notions had put them in. *I should have thought this out properly,* he thought bitterly.

Then the heat shimmer lifted for a few moments and he clearly saw the next sand dune only a few hundred metres ahead. That lifted his spirits, and he pointed and croaked at Vaughan to keep going. It took them nearly ten minutes to plod the distance and then another five to climb the dune. Luckily it was a fairly low one with what looked like a cattle pad running over a slow saddle.

Better still, the distance to the next dune looked to be only about a kilometre and the flat ground in between was mostly short, grey-coloured grass with a few clumps of saltbush or spinifex. Donny allowed only a minute to stand and have a drink and then he urged Vaughan to resume walking.

As they came down to the flat, the heat shimmer blotted out all but a vague dancing pink shape of the dune they were heading for. There were small patches of salt pan or claypan, both reflecting a blinding, white glare. Sweat trickled down both their faces and then quickly dried up. But the dampness had a cruel effect on the chafing under armpits and between their thighs. Even Donny was starting to feel that and was trying to walk with his legs further apart.

They had gone about half a kilometre when Donny noticed Vaughan didn't have his beer bottle. He came to a sudden halt and grabbed at Vaughan's arm.

Pointing down he snarled, "Where is it?"

Vaughan stared vacantly back and then shrugged. He shook his head but whether it meant he didn't know or didn't care wasn't clear. But it sparked Donny to teeth-grinding rage. He looked back and while he did Vaughan began to blubber.

"I just want to give up," he muttered.

"Well, you can't!" Donny snapped angrily. "There isn't anyone to surrender to and I'm not leaving you here in the desert to die. Now keep walking that way while I go back and get it."

Donny knew they would need that extra water carrying capacity to survive, but it was a fearfully long way back. He could just see the dune through the mirage water. Muttering words his mother would not approve of, he started trudging back. As much as he could, he gritted his teeth to ignore the pain from the chafing and strode back, very aware he had a dry mouth and had now stopped sweating.

That got him to pause and finish the small amount of water in his whisky bottle. The plastic bottle in his pocket was heavy and uncomfortable and he was sorely tempted to drink some of that, but he resisted it.

Vaughan might need it more, he thought. He was angry and upset and not impressed. *Bloody weakling!* he thought.

But that small drink refreshed him a little so he resumed walking as fast as he could manage back to the dune. By the time he reached it, Vaughan had vanished in the heat shimmer so he had no idea whether he had continued walking or not.

Luckily, he had no trouble finding the bottle as he had just followed their tracks back. It was lying on the sand and was so hot to the touch that he yelped when he picked it up. Blowing on it and his hands, he turned and hurried back onto the plain. Anxiety about heat and Vaughan kept him moving, and he pushed himself until he was panting and sweating again.

Slow down, Dumbo! he told himself.

That made it easier and he shielded his eyes against the glare as peered ahead into the 'mirage water' for any sign of Vaughan.

But when he saw him a surge of exasperation welled up to add to Donny's anger and frustration. Vaughan had walked only a few hundred paces and wandered off course. Muttering more swear words, Donny caught him up and thrust the bottle at him.

"And don't drop it again!" he snapped.

Vaughan looked at him vacantly and just walked with him. Donny tucked his whisky bottle under his arm and used that hand to grab hold of

Vaughan's sleeve. With energy fuelled by irritated anger and a growing feeling of dread, Donny pushed Vaughan and did not slow down until they reached the next dune. By then he was puffing hard, and Vaughan was gasping and staggering. And that dune looked the biggest so far. It towered up with a steep, sandy slope on their side. Donny swore and started up it, noting that Vaughan had lost his leafy branch somewhere.

It was fiercely hot, and the sand was loose and slid a lot and there was no breeze. Donny kept struggling up. He had to use the bottle in his left hand to help get a grip on the loose sand.

"Keep going to Vaughan, keep going!" he urged.

"I can't do it!" Vaughan gasped.

But Donny was determined so he shoved the empty whisky bottle under his armpit and used his free hand to help haul him up to crest. Ahead was another couple of kilometres of bare, open country and gibber plains. Half hauled and half pushed by Donny, Vaughan went down the other side and then out onto the flat. They set out across this, getting slower and slower by the minute. To Donny the glare was almost blinding, and dread was now clutching at his throat.

After about ten minutes Vaughan came to a stop. "I can't go on!" he sobbed. "I can't do it!" He crumpled onto the claypan they were on.

"You've got to!" Donny cried.

He hauled him up and they staggered along with him half holding Vaughan up. But it was very hard going and very hot. After another ten minutes of gasping, sweating effort they covered about a kilometre before Vaughan again collapsed.

"I can't do it! I just want to stop!" he waited.

Donny stood over him, disgusted, angry and afraid. "Oh, stop blubbering like a little kid who wants his mummy! Get up and walk," he snapped.

"No! Leave me alone."

"Get up!"

"You can't make me!"

"No, I can't. Oh, for God's sake! Get up you bloody weakling!" Donny cried, now starting to feel desperate.

Vaughan looked up, anger on his tear-streaked face. "You can't call me things like that!" he shouted.

Breathing heavily, his emotions boiling with anxiety and

determination, Donny stared down at him. "I just did, because that's what you are; a bloody weakling full of self-pity. I used to so admire you but now I just despise you and think you are a useless slug. Damn it! You are the big kid. You should be helping me up the sand dunes, not the other way around!"

Suddenly Vaughan could take it no longer and his emotions welled up to overwhelm him. A huge sob escaped, and he flopped down and began to blubber. The emotions were so painful Donny had to cry, even though he had little fluid for actual tears. And it was hot! He realised he was lying on a claypan: white, dusty clay that was baking him.

I must move! We can't stay here, he thought. But, oh, it was such an effort to even think of getting up!

With a conscious effort he slowed his panting breath and tried to calm down. It was difficult to do because his brain seemed to be all fuzzy and he realised he was dizzy. The sound of movement next to him caused him to roll his head sideways. His hat had come off and got in the way and he brushed it aside and found himself staring at Vaughan, who was glaring angrily back.

Then the heat and the glare became too much for Donny. *We will die here. I don't want to die! I haven't really lived yet,* he thought.

With an effort he rolled over and struggled to his hands and knees. He took out the plastic water bottle, with something of an effort as it got caught in his pocket. After unscrewing the cap, he took a sip and then held it out for Vaughan. Vaughan gave him a sulky look but then struggled into a sitting position and took it.

As he gulped the water down, Donny, who had calmed down a bit, said, "We need to keep moving. We are just baking here. The heat will kill us in hours."

In reply, Vaughan finished the remaining water and then looked into the empty bottle, his mouth turning down as he did.

"I'm not sure I can do it," he muttered.

That annoyed Donny again but he kept his tongue in check. "Well, you need to try. And if you don't want to make a bit of an effort to save yourself then do it for your mum and dad."

Vaughan looked hurt at that, and his face crumpled up again. "They don't care about me. They just ship me off to that bloody horrible boarding school," he said.

Oh you poor bugger! Donny thought.

But he didn't give up. Shaking his head he stood up and held out his hand for the plastic bottle.

"Well do it for my mum and dad then. They are going to be devastated if you die out here."

Vaughan looked resentful but handed Donny the bottle. Donny was annoyed that all the water was gone but also thankful.

He might make a couple more kilometres now, he reasoned.

"Come on, up you get and let's get off this bloody furnace," he said.

To his intense relief, Vaughan got to his feet. Donny did not want to push the situation any further, so he bent and picked up both beer bottles, placing one down the front of his shirt, and then wincing when the hot glass burned the soft skin of his stomach. Screwing the cap back on the plastic water bottle, he glanced at the sun to get his direction and started walking again.

As had happened before, the mirage water suddenly dispersed and the next sand dune came into clear focus. It was only a few hundred paces ahead. Donny started towards it and then realised he was not going north so changed direction to approach it at the diagonal. Vaughan muttered and whimpered but kept going and they reached the dune after about another ten minutes.

Luckily it was another low one, as Donny was determined to get over it before they stopped. He led the way, plodding slowly up, angling diagonally and finding that easier. With a huge sigh of relief, he reached the top and stopped.

Oh good! Trees, he noted.

The swale was only a few hundred metres across but was covered with grass, bushes and a scattering of trees.

"Let's get into some shade," he said, starting down the other side.

At the bottom, Vaughan stumbled to a standstill. "Just give me a few minutes rest," he croaked.

Donny shook his head and pointed. "Not here. Walk to that little tree over there."

So they both walked to a single straggly tree and flopped down in its shade.

I hope he will get up in a few minutes, Donny thought.

The sun was now well down, and they probably only had another couple of hours of daylight left to walk in. Once again, he wished he had a watch.

After five minutes, ants disturbed Vaughan and he sat up and swore, hitting at them and shouting, "Bloody ants! Bloody flies!"

Then his eyes met Donny's and he gave a sort of sickly grin and looked ashamed.

Donny stood up and pointed. "Let's go. We need to do a few hundred metres every five minutes."

They plodded on to the next sand dune, also a low one but thickly covered with grass and clumps of vegetation. The next bit of flat land was even better, with many more trees. Donny vaguely remembered that there was a feature nicknamed 'The Swamp' a few kilometres to their left near the road where rains had filled a gravel scrape and resulted in a thick belt of reeds, but he did not mention it. He was still wanting to go along the route he had selected.

We will go left to the main road if we get desperate, he told himself.

Seeing that Vaughan looked like he wanted to sit down again, Donny pointed and said, "We will walk to a bit of shade and rest. It is the hottest part of the day."

They set off and after a few minutes Vaughan pointed to a nice clump of trees not far ahead.

Donny shook his head. "No. Not them. Too obvious."

Instead, he led the way for a few hundred plodding paces more to a small patch of scrub. There was bare earth in the shade which looked to be free of ants. Groaning at their sore joints and muscles, the boys lowered themselves to the ground and lay flat, gasping and sweating.

Vaughan leaned back against the trunk of a tree and fanned his face and neck with his hands. "I hate this place! It is like hell on earth!" he said.

Donny shrugged and did not reply. To him was home and he actually loved it. "Bit hot at the moment," he agreed.

They lapsed into silence and Donny lay back and worried about parents and about Vaughan. He felt sick and sore physically and mentally he wondered if he had made a serious error.

Donny let them rest for what he calculated was about 15 minutes, until what he estimated to be about 4:30pm. He was now seriously worried that they might have at least five kilometres to go to the next water.

"That's long enough, let's go!" he said.

But it took some persuading to get Vaughan up. "How far to go?" Vaughan queried.

"Maybe five k's, certainly less than seven," Donny replied.

He actually thought it might be less but did not want to build up false hopes.

Vaughan looked dismayed. "We can't walk that far!" he cried.

"Yes, we can. My dad told me that soldiers can march 30 k's in a day, and that's when they are carrying their rifle and pack and so on. He says a person can walk a hundred metres in one minute, that's the length of a football field. So we can walk a kilometre in ten minutes. So we could do six k's in a bit over an hour."

"I couldn't," Vaughan replied.

"Never mind. We don't have a choice so let's try," Donny retorted.

He struggled up, groaning at his sore muscles and then stood waiting, swaying slightly and feeling very dehydrated. To his great relief, Vaughan also struggled to his feet. Donny took the opportunity to break off a low branch with plenty of leaves and he handed this to Vaughan. Vaughan also took one of the empty beer bottles. They resumed walking. Instantly the pain from sore muscles, sore feet, chafing, and blisters caused both to cry out. But the air was so dry Donny soon closed his mouth and just concentrated on putting one foot in front of another. He realised he had stopped sweating.

Every few paces Donny glanced at a very sulky looking Vaughan and was pleased to see that he was still plodding along. Reaching another sand dune, they crossed it and came to a swale that was nearly all gibbers but was only a few hundred metres wide. Better still, the sun was now so low to the west that the eastern side of the dune was now in shadow.

Flies, heat, and chafing continued to bother them but they kept walking. They crossed those gibbers in less than 20 minutes, the experience making Donny think of those stories about primitive peoples who did initiation tests of walking barefoot on hot coals.

They struggled over another sand dune and that swale was different again, mostly small bushes. In the distance there were some kangaroos which lifted their heads to look at them and then quickly bounded away. The downslope was all in shade and now reasonably cool. Donny agreed to a ten-minute rest and then urged Vaughan on. Because they were sitting on the downslope it was easy to get up, but the chafing still hurt! The boys plodded on. By then Donny was blinking and feeling dizzy.

They came to another dune, somewhat higher and covered with bushes. It became so steep they had to crawl. Puffing and feeling utterly drained, Donny reached the crest and stopped as soon as he could see over it. Then a shudder of relief ran through him. About a kilometre away to the left front was the water tank of Bore No. 5! But it was in the middle of a nice open, grassy swale with no cover. A few cattle were clustered at it or grazing nearby.

Made it! Donny thought.

Chapter 11

DARK

Some instinct stopped Donny from climbing up onto the top of the dune and he motioned Vaughan to stay down.

"What is it?" Vaughan asked.

Donny crept up behind a bush and looked carefully through it. "Not sure. I just have this feeling," he answered.

For the next few minutes he studied the whole area, moving slightly to get better views but being careful to stay hidden. As he did, he noted that many of the cattle were all looking towards where a vehicle track came from his left front beyond the water tank and windmill. That track crossed the next dune at a low point. There was another vehicle track going from the water tank north eastwards to cross the next dune almost in front of them.

Vaughan began crawling up. "What's wrong?" he asked.

"Don't know. I don't like the feel of the place," Donny answered. "Now keep down and be careful. Don't be seen by anyone on that next sand dune."

As he spoke he passed a dry tongue over his now cracked lips. Knowing that there was water just over there was a terrible temptation.

But it is already getting cooler. We will last a few more hours, he reasoned. It didn't make sense to take any risks after such an effort.

Vaughan joined him peering through the bush. "What am I looking at?" he asked.

"This is Bore Number 5," Donny replied. "It is almost exactly the same as the one we came from. There is the actual bore head over there." He pointed to where the stubby length of thick piping stuck up a few hundred metres to their front. "The cooling pipe runs across the flat to the water tank. You can see the troughs there. There are two here, one each side of the tank."

Vaughan nodded and Donny noted him licking dry, cracked lips. "Is that a road?" he asked.

Donny nodded. "Four roads come together here, which is why I am worried that the crooks might watch it. It is the most likely place for us to come for water."

Vaughan stared hard, squinting as the glare was still quick fierce, the afternoon sun reflecting off the opposite dune.

"Where do the roads go?"

"That one you can see going over the dune in front of us goes due east to Bore Number 6. The one to the left front goes north to Bore Number 2. There is a vehicle track, I'm not sure you'd call it a road, running right along the valley in front of us from off to our right to here. That road comes from Bore Number 9. It then goes on north-west until it passes the end of the sand dune country. It then joins the main station road about six kilometres north of the homestead."

"Oh, I see it now," Vaughan commented after studying the flat ground in front of them. "So how far to the homestead?"

"Fifteen kilometres," Donny replied.

Having travelled it many times he was sure of the distance. As he said that, images of the house filled his mind and he experienced a strong surge of what he thought was homesickness.

I wish I was there now! he thought.

Images of his mother and his bedroom and dogs all filled him with emotion and he became quite weepy.

"Why don't we just go down and have a big drink and then walk to the homestead?" Vaughan suggested. "There's nobody down there."

"Maybe not," Donny agreed. "But it doesn't feel right. See how all the cattle are looking off towards the road to Bore Number 2? If there is someone watching, they might be there."

Vaughan looked sceptical. "There are only three of those men. Surely, they wouldn't be able to drop one off here just to sit and watch."

"I would if I was them," Donny replied. "Uncle James needs to stop us getting to a phone or contacting the police. He could be guarding our dads while one of them drives around. In fact, I reckon there must be four or five of them."

"Why do you think that?" Vaughan asked.

"Uncle James said that our mums were being held hostage by two men so that means a fourth guy at the homestead at least," Donny replied.

Still Vaughan wasn't convinced. "He might just have said that, planning to take our mums prisoner when they got back to the homestead."

Donny conceded that was possible. "But I don't think so, just from the way he said it. I reckon they would want their hostages secure before they made their move at Bore Number 10. Now they've had time to drive here hours ago and put someone in hiding. I am worried it might be a trap. If we walk out in the open in daylight and a vehicle comes along we will never be able to hide in time. We will wait till it's dark."

"What if they've got night vision stuff?" Vaughan asked.

Donny knew about that as his father had a telescopic sight for one of his rifles that could see infra-red.

"That's a risk we will have to take," he replied. "So we wait."

To his relief, the older boy did not dispute his decision even though Donny could tell he was very dehydrated and thirsty. And waiting where they were was not pleasant as they were on the side of the dune which still had the sun on it. It was very hot and unpleasant, even as the sun sank lower and lower behind them.

"What time does it get dark?" Vaughan asked.

Donny thought hard before answering. From his memory he called up facts he had heard his parents using when arguing about the notion of Daylight Saving.

"It will be getting dark in Brisbane about 6:30pm," he said. "But we are a thousand kilometres west of there. We are almost in line with the South Australian border and their times are half an hour behind Queensland. So it won't get dark here until after seven o'clock."

"What time do you reckon it is now?" Vaughan queried.

Donny turned and briefly squinted through his fingers at the setting sun. "About six? I reckon we've got an hour or so before sunset."

"Bloody hell! I'm really thirsty," Vaughan added.

Again, he licked his dry lips and Donny noted that his eyes were red-rimmed and inflamed.

I suppose mine look the same, he thought.

Vaughan then surprised him by saying, "When was your dad in the army?"

"When he was young fella, a stockman. He was in the part-time army, the Army Reserve. He was in a mob called the 'Bush Rifles', the 49th Battalion I think it was. He said he had to only do five weeks training each year and that suited him," Donny explained.

"Did he have any rank?" Vaughan asked.

Donny shook his head. "Don't think so. He wasn't that interested. He did it with some mates and got paid during the off season. Then he got a job as a jackaroo on Glendowner station and didn't have time."

"Where's Glendowner?"

"Up north somewhere," Donny answered.

He fidgeted to get more comfortable, very conscious of those sun's rays that were still striking his back. Vaughan, he noted, was red and this got even more obvious as the sunset began and the sky started turning red overhead and to the west.

Oh, hurry up sun! Go down! he kept thinking.

Vaughan obviously thought so too as he muttered, "I'm sick of this sun! I wish it would go down. I think I'm getting very sunburnt."

"You are," Donny confirmed. "You look like a cooked lobster."

"Oh thanks!"

That caused Vaughan to sit in sullen silence for a while, only punctuated by an occasional swear word as he slapped at flies. Donny swore and brushed at them too and was only thankful there were no ants. Slowly, very slowly it seemed, the sun sank to the horizon and then below it. Was a typical western Queensland sunset, a blaze of crimson and red. The whole western sky had a ruddy glow long after the sun had gone.

"Thank God for that!" Vaughan said at last.

"We will wait another half hour, until it is fully dark," Donny said.

He was determined not to get caught, even though he was quite unsure if time was an important factor in the situation. All he was sure of was that he and Vaughan running away instead of becoming hostages must have thrown Uncle James's plans out.

At least I hope so, he fretted.

His objective remained the homestead, but he was quite unsure what he would do when he got there.

At last he decided it was as dark as it was likely to be. The sun had fully set, just the last shading of red remaining, low in the western sky.

"Okay let's go. No talking," Donny said.

Picking up his whisky bottle and beer bottle he stood up and then groaned as all his sore muscles protested. So did Vaughan and it took them a couple of minutes of movement before they warmed up and were able to work the stiffness out of their joints and muscles. And, to begin, with the chafing was nearly agonising. Slowly it developed into a sort of all pervading pain. Vaughan certainly did a lot of puffing and quiet whimpering.

The two boys made their way down the eastern side of the dune with Donny brushing out their tracks. Then he took the lead and struck off straight across the flat.

"Aren't we going to the water tank?" Vaughan asked.

"From another direction. If there is anyone there, they will expect us to come from the west," Donny replied.

Vaughan grumbled but accepted this, so Donny continued until he was reasonably sure they were out in the middle of the swale. Then he turned half left and continued until he came to the vehicle track coming from the south-east, from Bore No. 9. He then turned left again and walked parallel to it. This led them directly for the water tank.

"Slow down!" Vaughan hissed. "I can't walk that fast."

Donny shook his head. "You must. I don't know what time the moon comes up tonight. I want to be gone from the trough by the time it does."

He had never taken too much notice of the moon or its phases, but he did know that a bright moon in this open country made everything much more visible. But despite his feelings of urgency, he did slow down.

I don't want Big Sooky Boy to break down, he thought.

It took them nearly half an hour to reach the water trough. The last hundred metres they made very slowly, stopping to listen and allowing time for Donny to brush out tracks. At the same time, he was silently cursing the gentle breeze that has sprung up and made 'washing' noise around his ears and under his hat. And of course, the cattle became agitated at their approach and began getting up and snorting and snuffling. The herd began milling around and plenty of dust was stirred up. The cattle backed away from the vicinity of the troughs as the boys approached and that worried Donny.

If there is a watcher, he must notice all this noise and movement, he reasoned.

By the time they were close to the water tank, a black shape in the dark, Donny was almost gasping with thirst. Once again, he took the leafy branch and followed the precaution of walking last and brushing out their tracks, a process he found much harder to do in the dark. When he reached the closest water trough, Donny stopped and listened for a couple of minutes.

"What are we waiting for?" Vaughan whispered.

"Just listening," Donny replied softly.

Nothing. He then felt in the trough to check if it had water in it. *Dad and I filled this two days ago. It is probably due to be topped up,* he thought.

And he was right. There was just a muddy sludge in the bottom of the steel trough. Donny knew it wasn't really mud but he was too anxious and thirsty to care. Moving to the tap, a simple handle that was pulled around from closed to open this time, he started water flowing. The sound of the running water was louder than he expected and he at once turned the tap half back to slow it. And the sound of flowing water set the cattle all shuffling and standing up. The herd were mostly about 50 metres away or so, a grey, milling, snorting mass from which came an occasional low bellow.

Vaughan stared anxiously at the cattle in the dark. "Is there a bull?"

Bull! Donny thought in alarm, recalling the visit two days before, then shook his head.

"Not that I know of. Start filling your beer bottle. Here it is," he said, passing it to Vaughan.

Vaughan sensibly used the flow direct from the tap and Donny stood and waited, looking anxiously in all directions, his ears straining to detect any hint of danger as he did. Then he pulled out the second beer bottle from his shirt and handed it across to fill.

They quickly filled all four bottles and then washed themselves and their shirts. Perversely, Donny felt quite chilled when he splashed water over his face and chest as the slight breeze cooled him. He understood he was feeling sick from too much sun and over-exertion. Both boys then drank as much as they could. Donny drank three of the whisky bottles, forcing it in until he felt bloated and heavy.

We will quickly dehydrate, he told himself.

All the while he kept the tap open to fill the trough for the cattle, hoping the men would not notice but determined that the beasts would not suffer unduly. He also kept listening and looking around, checking for any sign of lights.

Satisfied they were as ready as they could be, Donny checked that the troughs were both full and then pointed which way he wanted Vaughan to go.

"I will follow and brush out tracks until we are back on the grass," he added.

Vaughan nodded in the starlight and then limped away, his awkward moments obvious even in the dark. Donny followed, their progress slow as he brushed at what he thought were their tracks.

The cattle should scuff out any I miss, he reasoned.

Once they reached the grass, Donny took over the lead. His first real problem was to find the vehicle track that led towards the homestead. This took a few minutes as three roads went out on the other side of the water tank area. In the starlight he had to stare hard, but he was able to make out the grey lines of the dusty wheel ruts and also the skyline of the dunes out on either side.

Vaughan had come to a standstill. "What are you doing?" he asked when Donny crouched down to better get the dunes silhouetted against the night sky.

"Making sure we are following the road to the homestead and not one of the other roads," Donny replied.

Satisfied he had the correct one, he began walking through the dry grass and bushes, keeping the track in sight a dozen metres to his right.

Vaughan followed but quickly began to grumble. "Ouch! Ow! This bloody spinifex hurts," he cried. "Why don't we just walk along the road?"

"Because then I'd have to brush out all our tracks and that would take a lot of time and effort," Donny replied.

He was still worried about the men arriving quickly by vehicle and felt the need to be well away from the track.

But walking hurt. Donny felt exhausted and the chafe was now agony at every step. And the muscles and joints all hurt until they warmed up and became just one huge pain. Vaughan was obviously hurting as well as he went slower and slower and had a very noticeable limp.

"Slow down!" he gasped. "I can't keep up. I'm buggered!"

So was Donny, but he persevered until they had walked about a kilometre. At that, point he detoured left to get further from the vehicle track.

Just in case, he told himself.

He was hoping to find some trees and bushes even though he knew there were none in that area. All he could find were some larger clumps of saltbush and spinifex. He made his way to the other side of these and kept walking until he found an area of claypan.

"We will rest for a while," he said.

He badly wanted to get to the homestead that night but understood that Vaughan might collapse if he pushed it.

Vaughan didn't collapse but he groaned and lowered himself to the dusty flat grey claypan.

"I hope there are no bloody ants!" he muttered. Then he lay back. "Oh, I so worn out, and hungry," he said.

Donny was too and was now very aware that his empty stomach was reacting to the large quantities of water and the small floating stuff in it. He sat and lay back, staring at the stars and trying to work out what time they might reach the vicinity of the homestead.

And with that came doubts. *I hope I haven't done something really silly by running away like we did,* he fretted.

To try to calm his anxiety, he replayed what he remembered of the conversation at Bore No. 10. That calmed him a little, but he knew his parents would be worrying about how he and Vaughan might be faring out in the desert.

And his parents will be really worried, he decided.

The temptation to just surrender and ease those worries came to the front of his mind. Then Vaughan began having muscle cramps. He cried out in pain, pummelled his calf muscles and then thigh muscles and sobbed. After each attack he lay trembling. Donny knew how he felt. He had suffered a couple of mild attacks and understood the horrible anticipation that at any moment another spasm of cramp might send stabs of agonising pain through him.

After a particularly painful bout, Vaughan lay back and sighed. "I can't take much more of this. I need a proper rest. How far do you think we have walked today?"

Donny did some quick calculations. "More than thirty, maybe thirty-five or -six kilometres," he replied.

"Bloody hell! That's not possible," Vaughan replied.

That comment surprised Donny. "Yes, it is! People run marathons which are about forty k's in about four hours," he replied.

"I'm not trained for that!" Vaughan retorted.

Donny, who had been training for his cross-country run, thought it no big deal but didn't say so. Instead, a glimmering of sense warned him not to humiliate Vaughan any more.

"So you did really well today," he said. "Across all those sand dunes too, and in the heat of the day."

That mollified Vaughan a little and he shook his head. "So how far to the homestead?"

"Fifteen kilometres, fourteen now, seeing we have walked about one to get to here," Donny replied. "We could be there by midnight."

Vaughan grunted and then said, "So give me a bit of a rest; and if we take it easy, I might make it," he said.

Donny nodded. "Okay, we will stay here for a couple of hours. Bloody hell!"

That last utterance because his stomach gave a big gurgle and then, as he went to lay down, he did an enormous fart. Embarrassed, he wondered if he should apologise.

But Vaughan chuckled. "You could propel a hot air balloon with that," he said.

"If we had one," Donny agreed.

He was embarrassed but also amused. So, he also chuckled and then gave a proper laugh. That seemed to ease the mood of both, and Donny certainly felt better.

Silence settled and Donny lay back, lamenting his now liquid and complaining stomach and staring up at the stars. He noted that it was very dark but that there was still no sign of the moon.

Vaughan also noted the stars. "I've never seen so many; or so bright!" he said. "This is fantastic!"

Vaughan half sat to get a better look. Donny certainly thought so too. He lay back and tried to relax, gazing at the thousands of stars that seemed to fill the entire sky, noting the clusters of them and dimly aware that he should have paid attention in school and to his dad when the various galaxies and so on were named.

Beside him Vaughan lay back and drifted into a twitching, snuffling sleep. Donny didn't think he would sleep but exhaustion took over and he slid into a restless slumber.

Chapter 12

LIGHTS

It wasn't the cramps or sore muscles that woke Donny. It was the cold. That did not surprise him as it was his home territory. But it did surprise Vaughan who also woke up shivering.

"Bloody hell! It's cold!" he moaned.

"Only about twelve degrees probably," Donny replied.

"This is a bloody desert! How can it get so cold?" Vaughan demanded to know. He was audibly shivering, his teeth chattering slightly.

"It always gets cold in deserts at night unless there are clouds to act as a blanket and keep the heat in," Donny replied. He had known this all his life and assumed everyone knew it. "You are lucky you weren't here a couple of months ago, in winter. It dropped below zero a few times and usually drops to about four degrees. Then it heats up quickly with the sun and can reach thirty or more during the day."

"Gawd, you are a bloody little know-all!" Vaughan retorted. Then he began rubbing his hands together and beating his arms on his body. "B... b... b... bugger! I'm freezing."

So was Donny, but after that insult there was no way he was going to admit it. Instead, he struggled to his feet, groaning at his stiff joints and sore muscles as he did. Then he began moving his limbs and walking slowly around to warm himself up. Vaughan noted this and went to get up, but suffered a cramp in his right calf muscle. This resulted in swearing and pummelling and only after it had subsided did Vaughan also get up and start to do some physical movements.

Donny was about to suggest they start walking when Vaughan suddenly stopped and pointed behind Donny.

"There's a light! I can see a light," he said.

A stab of fear had Donny facing that way in a second. His first thought was that a vehicle must be coming, but then he realised there was no light in the direction of the bore. Then his eyes noted lights off to his right and he froze and concentrated.

What the devil is that light? he wondered.

Blinking to clear sleep-gummed and dry eyes, he stared at where a distant light was showing above the crest of the dune. Even as he watched, he saw the light rise a bit higher and then go dull before suddenly glowing bright. Then it just vanished.

That can't be a vehicle's headlights, he thought. *There's nothing but desert in that direction. Those crooks wouldn't be driving around off the tracks at night, not unless they had seen us or our tracks.*

Which got him wondering if the crooks were somehow following their boot prints and were driving cross-country. But that seemed highly unlikely, and he shook his head in bewilderment. He had a good idea what he had just seen but did not want to lay himself open to more ridicule from Vaughan's tongue.

Vaughan kept staring intently. "Was that a vehicle, like the crooks in their Land Rover?" he asked.

"No. There is no vehicle track that way for twenty k's. You know that. We walked right across all that country," Donny replied.

"But I definitely saw a bright light," Vaughan insisted.

Donny thought he had also but held his silence, fearing being teased and put down. But then he saw another bright light suddenly rise above the skyline in the far distance. Vaughan also saw it and pointed.

"There! A light! Can you see it? It's moving."

"Yes," Donny agreed.

The light was brighter than any of the stars near it and certainly appeared to be moving. *It is,* Donny told himself. He had seen such lights before but knew many people ridiculed the whole idea and he was feeling a bit too down and uncertain to risk having the older boy laughing and sneering at him.

The distant light suddenly vanished. That did not surprise Donny, who had seen such phenomena before, but it did Vaughan.

"Where'd it go? It was just there," he cried.

Then another small light appeared. It seemed to shoot up and then stop and hover before suddenly becoming brighter and then moving sideways and then dimming before glowing again, a distant pinpoint. Donny found it impossible to estimate how far away it might be, but guessed several kilometres at least.

It looks like it is over past that sand dune, he thought.

Just as quickly as it had appeared the light vanished. Vaughan shook his head. "Where did it go? It was up in the air. Is it a plane do you think?"

"Not from the way it was moving," Donny replied. "More like a helicopter."

"Do you think the crooks have got a chopper?"

Donny wasn't sure. "Maybe, but... oh! There's another light."

Another light seemed to shoot up, but Donny noted that, like the earlier ones, it went no higher than a hand's breadth above the skyline. Vaughan stepped closer and gripped his arm.

"That looks just like a flare going up," he said.

"Flare?"

"Yeah, you know, like they shoot off boats that are in trouble, or like the army use at night," Vaughan explained.

Donny had never witnessed either of these things, but he had seen them on TV. "Have you seen them?" he queried.

Vaughan nodded. "Yeah, at an army cadet camp. But there can't be anyone from the army out there in the desert, surely?"

"Not that I have ever heard of," Donny answered.

That light also vanished but then two went up and both appeared to move to the left and then down again.

"What are they?" Vaughan queried, plainly anxious.

Despite his anxiety over Vaughan's probable response, Donny felt he had to reply. "Min Min lights probably," he said.

"Min Min lights! Don't talk nonsense," Vaughan retorted.

"Have it your own way," Donny replied angrily.

I knew he wouldn't believe, he thought unhappily.

"Rot! There's no such thing," Vaughan snapped.

"We see them all the time. Lots of people do," Donny replied as calmly as he could.

He and his family had seen such lights on at least a dozen occasions and so had many people he knew.

"They are just a fairy story to suck in tourists," Vaughan said with a sneer.

"This is the Min Min Shire," Donny retorted. "People have been seeing them for a hundred years or more."

There was a silence between them then and during it the lights vanished, only to shoot up again a minute later. Vaughan was obviously unsure as he asked again if there was an army exercise happening in that direction.

"No," Donny said. "They couldn't get here without us knowing. That is way at the back of our property. There are only the station roads."

"What if they flew in and parachuted down or came by helicopter?" Vaughan challenged.

"I still think we would have seen them or know about it," Donny answered.

But he was also worried and considered that a possibility. He had only seen a group of army vehicles once. That had been in Golden Dawn the year before and they were just doing a driver training course and were gone the next day, heading north along the main road.

"Could they be helicopter lights?" Vaughan asked as one of the lights got suddenly brighter before fading abruptly.

"Can't hear anything," Donny said.

"What's over in that direction?"

"A big salt lake, Lake MacAndrew, and then a hundred kilometres or more of nothing but desert," Donny answered. "No station homesteads, only a couple of water holes and bores, that's all. It's just desert."

"Is there anyone at this lake?"

Donny shook his head. "No. There is just a vehicle track to the south side. There are no buildings and no people. Usually, the lake is dry so there aren't even fishermen."

"And you reckon they are those Min Min lights?" Vaughan said as the lights again vanished. Then another light appeared.

"Yeah, I do," Donny said. "See how they don't rise very high? I mean they don't get above that sort of line of haze and dust just above the dunes. They don't go right up among the stars."

"And you've seen them before?"

"Yeah, and Mum and Dad, and the stockmen. Dad was talking to some roadworkers the other day and they said they had seen lights like that and had tried to take photos of them," Donny said.

"But what are they?" Vaughan asked, now obviously concerned.

"Nobody really knows," Donny replied. "Some people think they are static electricity, like when you comb your hair when its real dry. Others think they are glowing marsh gas, like the 'Will-o-the Wisps' they get in some places."

"Marsh gas! There aren't any marshes around here," Vaughan said.

"Oh yes there are! There are lots of small swampy flats that turn into marshes whenever there is a bit of rain. We walked across a couple. And all those claypans and salt flats. There's lots of gas under the ground. There are several big gas fields south of here. They pump it in pipes all the way to Brisbane and Mount Isa and to some of the mines up north."

That got Vaughan thinking. "Yeah, I've heard of them," he conceded.

Donny was relieved that he wasn't now being ridiculed, so he said, "Some people have suggested they might be like mirages, where a light a few hundred kilometres away is reflected, 'refracted' Dad said, through layers of dust, like through a prism."

He had seen a demonstration in a science lesson of light being refracted through a prism by Mr Prideaux on the last 'In reach'.

"They… they aren't ghosts are they? I mean like Aboriginal stuff?" Vaughan asked.

Hearing that quaver in Vaughan's voice gave Donny a little spurt of satisfaction. "Not that I've heard," he said.

The lights had stopped, and Donny again scanned in all directions for any other lights. He also looked to see if the moon was coming up. As he did, a dingo began to howl.

"What's that?" Vaughan cried, fear very evident in his tone.

Donny was tempted to say 'Werewolves' but instead just snorted. "Just a bloody dingo."

"Will it attack us?" Vaughan asked anxiously.

"Not very likely. They are scared of humans."

He had heard of dingos attacking people at coastal tourist places but understood that they were animals that were used to humans and weren't shot at or trapped like they were in this area.

"Stop worrying," he added, but then felt little stabs of fear himself.

Another distant howl from the dingo made Vaughan turn to stare in that direction.

"I heard they dragged a baby out of a tent and ran off with it," he said.

You're a baby! Donny thought, but managed not to say, although the temptation was strong.

"Yeah, but that was years ago, in the 80's. I heard Mum discussing it with Mrs Peabody. It happened out at Uluru but it was never proved," he said. "I've never heard of a grown boy being dragged off."

"But they are just dogs, and dogs sometimes attack people," Vaughan commented.

Donny did not want to discuss this. He had been bitten by a stockman's dog when he was five and that memory was still sharp. But the notion that a pack of dingos might act like a pack of wolves got him also staring anxiously in the direction of the sound.

They were both shivering, even while they jogged on the spot or stamped their feet. Vaughan looked around.

"I'm really cold. Why don't we walk? This open country looks easy enough to do it in," he suggested.

"Yeah, but that will mean following the road and that is further," Donny answered.

"What do you mean? You said it was fifteen kilometres," Vaughan countered.

Donny now felt he had to explain. "It is along the road. But that is two sides of a triangle. This road goes north-west for about nine k's to the main station road, and you then have to turn and go south along that for another six. It is much shorter if we go cross-country, only eight or nine k's," he said.

"So, we should go that way. It can't be any worse than walking in this rubbish beside the road," Vaughan answered.

That really stabbed at Donny's pride, and he felt quite ashamed. "That's a good idea but I didn't start going that way because I didn't want to get lost. If we go off course and can't find the homestead or a waterhole, we could end up dead."

Vaughan turned to stare at him. "You did bloody well all day. So all we have to do now is walk west and we should come to the station road somewhere near the homestead," he suggested.

Donny nodded and blushed, glad it was so dark. "Yeah, but I am not sure which way is west. I was waiting for the moon to come up," he admitted.

"Can't you navigate in the dark?" Vaughan cried, astonishment in his tone.

Donny blushed with shame and shrugged, "Not very well. The general trend of the sand dunes will help but if we are even a few degrees off course we will be in real trouble. We could go the wrong way entirely and find ourselves back out in the desert with no water. I stopped us because I don't want to get us lost. If we get lost and miss a waterhole we could end up very dead. It would be very easy to miss a small thing like a bore in the dark. We could walk past it and we wouldn't know that and could just go on out into empty desert."

Vaughan made a sneering noise which really stung Donny's feelings. Vaughan said, "Can't you navigate by the stars?"

Donny's emotions were now in turmoil, and he shrugged but boiled with resentment. "No, not really. Dad showed me some stars a few times but I didn't think I'd ever need that, so I didn't bother to learn them. I know people can do things like find south using the Southern Cross but I'm not confident and don't want to take that risk."

"I know how to find south using the Southern Cross. We were taught that at Army Cadets," Vaughan commented.

"Oh yeah! But we want to go west," Donny said, his voice tinged with angry sarcasm.

"Yeah, that's right! But if you know which way is south you can then work out east and west, Dumbo!" Vaughan said sharply.

At that, all Donny's anxieties, hurts and fears boiled over. "Don't call me names! You are the stupid idiot! We have wasted hours sitting here shivering when we could have been nearly at the homestead. We could have covered five or six kilometres," he snarled.

"Don't call me names! You didn't ask, and you didn't explain why we had stopped," Vaughan retorted.

"Bugger you! I want to save my mum and dad," Donny cried, hitting out at Vaughan.

Vaughan shouted angrily and hit back, pushing him away. Donny staggered backwards and fell hard on his bum in a spinifex. That really hurt and his temper flared.

Scrambling to his feet he put up his fists, ready to fight.

Chapter 13

NAVIGATION BY THE STARS

Vaughan was angry as well.

"Leave me alone! And don't call me names!" he shouted.

As he did, he stepped forward and Donny braced himself to fight. But Vaughan stumbled and then tripped. Regaining his balance with difficulty, he then fell over backwards, luckily for him into a saltbush, not a spinifex. With difficulty he struggled to his feet, Donny stepping back and allowing him to but ready to defend himself. Seeing his potential enemy suffer such a ridiculous fall eased Donny's mood and he even had the temptation to laugh.

Vaughan stood there in the starlight, swaying and breathing heavily. "God, I hate this place! I just want to go home!" he cried.

Then, to Donny's astonishment Vaughan began to sob. This turned into real blubbering.

Donny stared at him with a mixture of emotions: anger, contempt, resentment; dislike, definitely dislike. Unable to restrain himself, he shook his head and yelled, "Gawd you are a useless great slug! I've been carrying you all day and all you can do is whinge or cry and want your mummy! You are the big kid and you should be leading, not me!"

Vaughan looked shocked. He stepped forward and pushed Donny away. Donny stepped further back and lowered his fists, embarrassed now at the display of raw emotion. Neither spoke for a minute or so and then Vaughan made an obvious effort and stopped sobbing.

"Sorry," he muttered.

Donny saw the older boy's shoulders slump and he felt sorry for him, and also half regretted his hurtful outburst.

When Vaughan spoke again it was an almost normal voice. "It's alright for you. This is your home and you are used to it. But I'm not. And I'm not ready for this. I didn't want to come here for this holiday. I hate this place and I'm scared. I just want to get out of it."

That confession caused Donny to blush. *He is really hurting, poor bugger!* he thought.

"I'm scared too," he admitted. "But we are here, and this is real so we must try. And I want to help my mum and dad so tell me what to do."

"What do you mean?"

"Explain how to navigate by the stars and I will try to navigate," Donny replied.

"Will we start walking if I explain the stars?" Vaughan queries.

"Of course. You might be feeling sorry for yourself and maybe don't think you are important, but my mum and dad are and I am determined to help them. So how does it work? Tell me."

"My mum and dad are important too!" Vaughan cried angrily.

"Then let's go and save them! Tell me what to do!" Donny cried.

For a minute or so the two boys stood staring angrily at each other in the starlight, chests heaving. Vaughan took a deep breath and looked around, then turned his attention to the sky.

After a minute he pointed. "There! That's the Southern Cross."

Donny looked but could not see the familiar star pattern. "Where?"

"See those two really bright stars," Vaughan said, pointing towards the horizon. "They are the pointers. Now look down to towards the ground and you will see the Southern Cross. It is on its side."

"On its side!" Donny echoed.

"Yes, it is about to start setting," Vaughan answered. "See, the right-hand star of the Cross is almost on the horizon, I mean the skyline."

"What's the difference?" Donny asked, noting lots of stars but still puzzling over what the Southern Cross might look like on its side.

"Major Terrence explained it. A horizon is a straight line, and you only get that at sea or on flat land. The skyline is where there are hills and trees and things. Can you see it now?"

"Yes," Donny agreed. "But why is it setting?"

"Because it is rotating around the south polar axis or something," Vaughan said. Using his hands he demonstrated, first placing his fingers facing one way and then moving his hand up and across in a clockwise movement. "The Southern Cross, if it is up, may be visible lying on its left side or more upright, or, like now, lying on its right side. It depends on the time of year and so on. And sometimes it's not even up."

"Not even up! What do you mean?"

Vaughan gestured. "I gather that it isn't visible at night for three or four months of the year. I'm not sure. I didn't pay enough attention in the lesson. But definitely November, December and January I think, it does not come up at night. Never mind, there it is. Only just, so let's use it."

Donny agreed so Vaughan again pointed to the Southern Cross. "You can see its long axis? The short axis is across the arms of the cross. Sorry about all the teacher jargon. Don't know how else to explain it," he said.

Danny smiled at that. "That's okay. We do a bit of this stuff in class. Go on."

"Extend an imaginary line from the top of the cross through the bottom star and keep going for, I think, about four times that length. Maybe it is four and a half times the length of the long axis. Doesn't matter. This isn't precision navigating. It will make sure we are at least going more or less west and not south or north, and definitely not east."

"Too right!" Donny agreed. "If we wander off out into the desert and get lost, we are dead. So go on."

"Okay, from where that imaginary line reached drop a perpendicular to the horizon, I mean skyline. That is south. A perpendicular is a line that goes straight down," Vaughan explained.

"I know what a perpendicular is. We do this sort of stuff in Maths, and I like it," Donny retorted, resenting being treated as though he was ignorant. "I just never thought it would be any use in the real world."

"Sorry. Anway that way is south," Vaughen said, pointing. Then he put both arms together, pointing south. He then spread them to either side. "If I do this then my right hand is pointing west and my left hand is pointing east."

Donny copied this and then Vaughan did a right turn and extended his arms so that his left hand was pointing to south. Then he brought them together.

"That is approximately west. Now we pick a star and start walking towards it."

"Slightly north of west, say west north-west, would be best, as we are crossing the hypotenuse and it isn't an equilateral triangle. That will bring us to the main station road a bit south of the homestead," Donny replied, deliberately using the correct jargon to show Vaughan he knew something.

"Okay, I am aiming at that star," Vaughan said.

He pointed and then started to walk. Donny thought he knew which star so just walked beside him. As he did, he glanced to his left to note the location of the Southern Cross and thought, *If I keep that first star of the Southern Cross on my left, I must be going the right way.*

It was easy walking and just enough starlight to avoid the clumps of spinifex and saltbush. That added distance of course but Donny felt very much better, except that the chafing began to return quickly until the pain just became a blur.

After ten minutes they came to the sand dune they had been walking beside, except this time they had to cross it. Donny told Vaughan to lead on: "Go diagonally," he instructed.

He followed, trying again to use his branch to brush out their tracks in the dark. Because both the sand and the air were cool it was much easier. They were soon on top and stopped.

Both had a drink from their bottles then turned to look south. "That right-hand star of the Cross is just going out of sight," Donny commented.

"Doesn't matter," Vaughan replied. "Even when it is all gone the Pointers will still give us a guide."

"Pointers?"

"Those two very bright stars up to the left of the cross. They are called the Pointers as they seem to aim at the Cross," Vaughan explained. "And you can use them for another way to find south."

"Oh yeah? How?"

"I will use schoolteacher words again," Vaughan cautioned.

"Suits me. I like Geometry," Donny replied.

"Well join the two pointers with an imaginary line, and from the midpoint of that line erect a perpendicular towards the Cross and extend it until it intersects the imaginary line through the long axis of the Cross."

To Donny it sounded as though Vaughan was deliberately trying to show off but he had no trouble with either the words or following the instructions. "What then?" he commented.

"Drop another vertical line to the horizon. That is south."

Donny did that and then compared it with the first method and was satisfied both vertical lines went to the same place. "That's good! Okay let's get on," he said.

Vaughan checked his star and resumed marching. They went quickly down the other side of the dune and Donny brushed after him and then caught up. "Which star are you aiming for?" he asked, having lost track of it as he worked.

"That one now. The first one has set," Vaughan answered.

"Set?"

"Yes, all the stars set in the west. They appear to go down but actually it is the rotation of the earth as it rolls away from them that makes it look that way," Vaughan replied. "So you have to be very careful and remember to keep checking your star and to have another one ready. It only takes about fifteen to twenty minutes for a star that low to sink out of sight."

That was all fascinating to Donny and he mentally filed the information. *Knowledge certainly is power,* he thought, remembering his teacher saying that. *And she said: 'Knowledge is a light burden'. And that's true too!*

Feeling much more confident he caught up with Vaughan and ignored his aches and pains to keep striding across the flat, a wide extent of gibber plain and salt pan that was easy going. So, apart from feeling tired and hungry and very stiff and sore from blisters and chafing, he felt good. Vaughan kept up and, except for an occasional whimper, seemed to be going well.

Then they came to an area of spinifex and saltbush and some long grass. Vaughan stumbled a few times but mostly they were able to avoid clumps of spinifex. It seemed they were going well and Donny estimated they had covered a kilometre or more before Vaughan stopped.

"Do you think there might be more snakes?" he asked, his voice obviously quavering.

Donny had been trying to push that fear to the back of his mind but now it took centre stage. "No. I think it is too cold. They are cold blooded reptiles. They will be curled up in a burrow," he replied, but had to summon up his courage to start walking again.

Bugger Vaughan! he thought.

Now every step took a small amount of courage. Placing his boot down on the narrow strip of sand between clumps of grass had him fretting that a snake might be there and suddenly strike from the side.

But if I am going to rescue mum there is nothing to be done but ignore the fear and walk, he told himself.

After a time the worry subsided as other anxieties took its place. And at least Vaughan was following. The boys tramped on in silence for another five minutes.

"What time do you think it is?" Vaughan asked.

Donny could only shrug. "Be after midnight I reckon," he replied.

He was feeling better but was now worrying as the two stars marking the long axis of the Southern Cross had now vanished below the skyline and only the last star and the Pointers were still showing.

We need to get on, he thought. *We need to get as far as we can before we lose direction.*

He kept glancing behind, hoping for some sign of the moon coming up but there was none, and Vaughan had no idea what time moonrise might be.

Some kangaroos springing up and bounding away frightened them next and so did the thumping of an emu as it ran away. Donny was amused by Vaughan's cries of alarm but managed to not comment. A cool, dry breeze that dried the eyes began, coming from the south-west.

They came to another dune and at the top Vaughan stopped. "I need a rest," he said.

Donny did not want to stop. He calculated that they had covered at least two kilometres. "We need to get as far as we can before the Southern Cross is gone completely," he said.

He pointed to where the last star of the Cross was almost resting on the skyline. It was partly obscured by a hazy band of dust in that direction.

"The Pointers will be up for another half an hour or so," Vaughan said. "If we push it, I am liable to break down and then we won't get anywhere. So, give me five- or ten-minutes rest."

Donny had to concede the logic of that, so he sat down when Vaughan did. Both had another drink. Moodily Donny watched that last star vanish. And it took only a few minutes for their perspiration to chill in that breeze. Getting unsteadily to his feet he looked down at Vaughan.

"Come on, I'm getting cold again," he said.

Vaughan nodded and then groaned as he got up. Donny understood why. All his muscles had gone stiff and he also groaned when he started to use them. The boys hobbled slowly down and only then did Donny remember he was supposed to be wiping out their tracks. He swore at himself and sent Vaughan on ahead and started brushing.

The next flat was luckily open and Donny again took the lead, glancing continually at the Pointers and then at his chosen star ahead. As the Pointers sank closer to the horizon and no moon made its appearance, he became more and more anxious. A feeling of dread gnawed at him as he worried about what might be happening to his parents and what might happen when those stars were gone.

By an effort of will power they pressed on for just over half an hour until Vaughan begged to stop for a rest.

"Slow down! I won't make it if I break down. I'm not as fit as you," he called.

Very reluctantly Donny agreed. "Okay, but we need to be at Burke Creek by daylight. We won't survive another day out in the open desert," he said.

Gripped by a sensed of impending doom he lowered himself to the sand, his limbs trembling with the over-exertion and his heart gripped by dread.

We have only come three or four k's, he thought and knowing that they still had five or six to go dismayed him.

They both sat down and Donny kept glancing at the last Pointer, which was now low on the skyline. Vaughan battled a cramp and then muttered a bit before saying, "Let's do what we did on cadet marches."

Donny was intrigued. "What's that?"

"Soldiers march for 50 minutes and cover five kilometres and then rest for ten and then march for another fifty. Our Cadet OC used to make us go slower and only do three k's in 45 mins and then rest for 15."

"That's sensible. Let's do that," Donny agreed.

He was afraid but also pleased that Vaughan hadn't just given up. *He is at least starting to contribute.*

After another drink they got to their feet and started marching. All the time Donny kept looking left and watching that last Pointer sink out of sight. As it did, he kept selecting stars ahead of him so they could keep direction for a while afterwards.

Then it was gone. "We will have to stop soon," Vaughan commented.

Donny knew that but was torn by the urgent desire to keep walking and the knowledge that, if they went badly off course and got lost, they would be in real trouble.

We won't survive a second day like yesterday, he thought.

Very reluctantly he came to a stop and looked anxiously east for any sign of the moon.

Chapter 14

FEAR

Donny had another drink and that finished the water in his whisky bottle. By then his muscles had stiffened up and he felt the cold starting to get at him. Partly it was that dry breeze but there was nowhere to shelter from it. And the cold gave him the need to do a pee. With an effort he got up and walked away a few paces to do that. Having relieved himself he came back and sat down again. Vaughan sat in silence, but it was obvious he was cold as well.

After an hour of this, Donny was very worried. Part of it was anxiety over what might be happening to his parents (and Vaughan's). Another part was anxiety over their physical survival but that was more about Vaughan than him. But the last part of his worries was over still being out in the open country when the sun did come up.

We need to be under cover by then, he thought. There was the temptation to keep walking, to cut down the time they might be exposed in daylight. But Donny shook his head. *We need to be certain, not sorry.*

Vaughan stood up and began moving his limbs rapidly to warm up. As he did, he said, "What are you planning to do at the homestead when we get there?"

Donny shook his head. "I am going to play it as it comes. I had hoped to get there tonight so I could creep in and find out what was happening. But if we can't make that then we might have to lie in hiding somewhere and watch all day and go in tomorrow night."

"There might be no-one there," Vaughan suggested.

"So then we know to look elsewhere. And I can probably use the phone to call the police," Donny replied.

"Uncle James said people would get hurt if the police were contacted," Vaughan reminded him. "That's what hostages are for."

Donny knew that but wasn't sure if he believed it. But he did think they needed adult help and quickly.

"I was thinking that if we could find my mum, and your mum, we could rescue them and hide."

"Risky," Vaughan said.

"Maybe, but we need to go and look before we can make any real plans," Donny agreed. Then he turned and looked up.

"Oh! When is that bloody moon going to come up!"

"It may not come up," Vaughan commented.

"Not come up!"

"No. That's right. Some nights the moon does not come up at all, or it only comes up for a short time close to dawn."

Donny was going to say: 'I don't believe you!' but the way Vaughan said it caused him to say, "Are you sure?"

"Of course. We've done night exercises at army cadets, and we had no moon. And anyway, Major Terrence told us that," Vaughan replied.

Donny was shocked, by his own ignorance as much as by the dismaying notion that they might be there until dawn.

"So we are stuck here?" he muttered, shivering and clasping his arms around his body.

That got his mind racing, tossing various unpleasant options and possibilities around. He was sure he could run those five or six kilometres in an hour as soon as the sun showed enough to give him clear direction.

But what about Vaughan?

It got so cold Donny began to shiver. He struggled to his feet and began marching on the spot in an attempt warm up. As he did, his stomach gurgled loudly and both boys chuckled at that.

"Bloody hungry!" he commented.

"Me too!" Vaughan agreed.

Donny looked around and then up at the sky. "Aren't there any other stars we can use for navigating?" he asked.

Vaughan stopped jogging and also looked then shook his head. "Only the Milky Way," he replied, "and it's not a very reliable guide."

"Which one is the Milky Way?" Donny queried. He thought he knew but wasn't sure.

Vaughan looked at him, his astonishment evident even in the starlight. Using both arms he made a great sweep across the whole sky.

"This great belt of stars that goes from horizon to horizon. But it's only a general guide. It runs roughly south-east across to north-west."

Donny blushed as he had been correct. "But we could still use it," he commented.

"We could, but as I said, it is only a general guide and not reliable," Vaughan replied. "And you'd want to be sure you were going the right way or you would go 180 degrees the wrong way."

A spasm of doubt flicked through Donny as he stared up at the millions of stars. He thought he knew which way north-west was but there was a little niggle of doubt.

"That way," he said, pointing.

Vaughan nodded. "I reckon, but it is a real risk."

"We might walk a bit further, but we can't miss the main station road or Burke Creek if we go roughly west."

"Do you think it's worth the risk?"

Donny nodded. "I do. The less distance we have to go in daylight the better."

Vaughan looked doubtful but then shrugged. "Maybe."

But now Donny was impatient to be moving. "What if we go for one kilometre and then stop. That will warm us up at least."

As he said this, he did a huge fart.

Vaughan chuckled. "That should warm you up too," he said. Then he smelt it and waved his hand under his nose. "Oh, psshaw! Speaking of marsh gasses!"

Donny flamed with embarrassment but had to chuckle as well. "Okay, let's go. Don't leave your bottles behind."

Both boys bent and picked up their bottles, mostly now empty, and then started slowly walking. As they trudged slowly along, weaving among the clumps of grass and spinifex, Donny felt a mixture of relief and anxiety. Continually glancing up at the stars, he hoped they were going the right way. Worry about his parents and about whether his actions had been very dangerous and foolish or not also added to his stress. But he was not concerned about getting into trouble from his parents for doing what they had. He had been in trouble too many times in the past for various escapades for one more to matter!

"How will we know when we have gone a kilometre?" he asked.

"Count paces. That's what we used to do in cadets," Vaughan replied. "A kilometre on flat ground is about fifteen hundred paces for a cadet. So, we will both count and check each other every few hundred."

Donny began counting, holding his hands clenched and opening one finger every hundred steps. That meant gripping the empty whisky bottle under an armpit but that was easy. He found it a real relief to be up and doing. At three hundred he called out the number and Vaughan agreed a few seconds later.

"Stop at five hundred," he added.

So they did and Vaughan drank some water from his remaining beer bottle. Donny had a sip of his as well and then they resumed walking. It was still cold and the breeze remained chilly. The walking at least warmed them a little and also improved their morale. But the walking still hurt and took a conscious effort to do. The chafing, blisters, and sore muscles all added up to a total feeling of pain all over.

They did another stop at a thousand and then stopped at fifteen hundred. Vaughan looked around and up at the sky.

"I reckon we should stop for a while. If you are right, we only have four or five k's to go."

So they found a patch of bare claypan free of ants and sat down again. As before, Donny wished there was some shelter from the breeze but he was still glad to sit and ease his legs and chafing.

"Are you still in the army cadets?" he asked.

Vaughan shook his head. "No. I did two years, had to because every kid at my school has to be in the cadets in Year 8 and Year 9. But I got sick of being bossed around by a lot of little Hitlers."

That notion bothered Donny, who was a very independent soul. "Is there a lot of bullying and shouting?"

"Not shouting. The army cadet policy is strongly against that. I mean, it's against the bullying too, and to be fair most of it is just a carry-over of the school culture. The older grades pick on the lower grades. It's not supposed to happen, but the older kids, the prefects and so on who are supposed to stop it, are often the ones doing it."

"Don't the teachers stop it?"

Vaughan shrugged. "They are supposed to and sometimes they do but usually it happens when they aren't around, and it's not considered good form to dob."

For the next half hour, they discussed boarding schools and what went on in some of them. To Donny it was vaguely disturbing as he knew he would have to go to a boarding school when he reached Year 7.

Suddenly, Vaughan scrambled to his feet and stared into the distance. Donny joined him.

"What is it?"

Vaughan pointed. "See those three stars in a line just coming up above the horizon? I think that is Orion's belt."

"What does that mean?"

"It means we have another star constellation that I know and can use to navigate with," Vaughan answered.

"How does it work?"

Donny could see the three stars clearly but the pattern was not clear.

Vaughan pointed. "Those three stars are Orion's belt. This is ancient Greek stuff you understand. I think he was one of their gods but I'm not sure. Now you might see that there are three more stars just up to the right of his belt?"

Donny indicated he could. Vaughan went on, "That is his sword. Now this will get a bit tricky to describe. It would be easier if I could draw it on a notebook and show you, but we are trying to find his shoulders and his head. So, look on our side of the belt and sword and you might be able to pick out two stars that mark his knees and two more that are his feet. If you go the other way, there are two stars that mark his shoulders and a tiny one that is his head. Major Terrence said that he must have been a pinhead."

Donny stared and thought he understood. Vaughan pointed again and went on, "Remember that he is upside down to us. This was all worked out in the northern hemisphere, if you know what that is."

"I know!" Donny snapped. He was feeling ashamed of not knowing more but he had learned that!

"So, be careful if you see a diagram in a book. Most books are published in the northern hemisphere and show Orion right way up, but to us he must be viewed upside down. So I have worked out his shoulders. Now I put my arms out in line with them and that gives me roughly east to the right and west to the left. It's not that accurate, more south-east and north-west. I'm sure which is east because that is the direction the stars are coming up from. Get it?"

"Yes. So that is north," Donny said, pointing in the direction he thought was correct.

"That's right. So we can turn left and start marching. Just keep in mind it is only approximate," Vaughan said.

"So, let's get moving!" Donny said.

He was both angry at lacking the knowledge and at being belittled and ashamed. Suiting actions to words, he snatched up his drink bottle and branch and set off with Orion behind him. Vaughan followed without argument.

As before, it hurt to get going, but once they were warmed up the pain was easier. The going was flat for ten minutes and then they encountered yet another sand dune. They plodded slowly up over this at a diagonal again and Donny went last to brush out tracks.

Down on the other side was another of those little incidents that punctuated their march. Several small birds suddenly took flight from the grass almost right under their feet. The sudden explosion of movement and whir of wings caused them both to start and jump back. Donny found his heart hammering even as he tried to pretend he hadn't got a fright.

"Only a couple of quail," he commented.

On they went, going progressively slower as they became weaker from lack of food and drink. It seemed that the energy just slowly drained away. And the chafing and sore muscles got worse. For Vaughan this also meant blisters and he began to limp so badly he was hobbling. Donny was hurting too but there was no way he was going to admit it.

"We are lucky Orion came up," Vaughan said as they walked. "It is like the Southern Cross. Some months it doesn't come up at all and in other months it comes up at different times."

Hearing that made Donny realise just how little he knew about the stars, and he resolved to make a real effort to learn more.

Then Donny was cheered even more. A lightening paleness in the sky to the east became apparent. Vaughan pointed to it.

"That will be the moon coming up. Now it will get easier. We can navigate west just by keeping it behind us," he explained.

And it was the moon. As a sliver of crescent moon began to lift above the skyline, he felt positively cheerful. It was only a new moon, a slither, and did not cast much light, but it all helped.

At Vaughan's suggestion they walked as quickly as they could for a kilometre, which he estimated took about 15 minutes. They then had a ten-minute break. Donny wanted to keep going but had to concede Vaughan's point and allow a rest. Then it was on, this time across a flat that had a few clumps of small trees but was mostly just gibber plain and salt flat.

Three kilometres were covered in this way and at each halt Donny noted that the constellation of Orion was higher above the horizon and easier to understand.

Good! he thought. *Only two or three k's to go.*

Then he noticed a bright light on the skyline directly behind them. "A light!" he cried. As he did, he experienced another stab of fear.

Vaughan turned and looked, then shook his head. "Is it a vehicle?" he asked.

"Don't know! Let's look for some place to hide," Donny answered.

He turned and began running, jogging anyway, through the clumps of saltbush and spinifex. Vaughan ran with him but within fifty paces began to fall behind.

Donny could hear him gasping and had to slow down to stay with him. As he ran, he kept looking around in the darkness and behind to check on Vaughan and the light. That light puzzled him.

If it's a vehicle, how is it driving over the sand dunes? he wondered. He was both puzzled and frightened. But the light did not seem to be moving. *It's only one bright light. So, it can't be headlights or there'd be two. Is it a torch?*

Vaughan came to a gasping stop and also looked back. "That's not a car," he observed. "Is it a helicopter?"

That notion sent a shiver of fear through Donny. But it didn't look right. "No. It's right down on the skyline."

"No, it's not. Look, it is just above the skyline," Vaughan said, still panting to get his breath back.

Donny looked, then rubbed his eyes and stared. Squinting in the cool dry air he saw that Vaughan was right, the light was definitely in the air. He was about to suggest that it was a Min Min light when Vaughan began to laugh.

"What? What are you laughing at?" Donny cried, worry adding a sharp edge to his tongue.

"It's the planet Venus, or maybe Jupiter. No, it will be Venus," Vaughan said. Then he took several shuddering breaths and shook his head. "Bloody hell, that gave me a fright."

Donny was too ashamed of having been afraid to appreciate the humour of the situation and Vaughan's next comment sent new stabs of anxiety through him.

Vaughan said, "You only see Venus early in the evening or just before dawn, depending on the time of year. Sometimes it is called the Evening Star and obviously now it is the Morning Star."

As the implications of what Vaughan had explained sank in, Donny looked back at Venus.

Morning Star! That means daybreak isn't far away.

He stared hard at the sky behind him and thought he could detect a faint lightening above the dark line of the last sand dune. Another stab of fear went through him.

"We need to be off this open country before daybreak. Those men will be driving around then looking for us. Come on!"

Chapter 15

BURKE CREEK

For a few seconds Vaughan just stood there while Donny set off running. When Donny realised he was not being followed, he stopped and gestured urgently.

"Come on! Stop standing there and move! We need to be off this open country before it gets light," he cried.

To his relief, Vaughan started walking, fast, but not running. Donny had to restrain his impatience and walked with him. It only took a few minutes of this before Vaughan began panting and then grumbling. Donny fumed about that but could not think of any argument he had not already used to get the older boy to make more of an effort. And it was an effort. Sore muscles, lack of energy, and pain all added up.

Despite that, they did keep moving at a steady walk. Donny had started counting paces but soon lost count as his mind kept running over options or his thoughts were concentrated on keeping direction. They pushed on for what Donny guessed might be twenty minutes before they came to another sand dune. This one was quite low and that cheered him up as he thought he knew where it was.

As before, he sent Vaughan on ahead and made an effort to brush out tracks. Once again, Vaughan stopped on the crest and Donny had to nudge him to get him moving again. But he then stopped and looked around. Behind him he noted what was obviously the first glow of dawn. Then he looked ahead and almost cheered with joy. In that half-light he could see a long way and he saw that ahead of them was a wide, flat plain which ended at a dense line of real trees.

"Burke Creek!" he cried, his voice cracking with relief. But it was more than a kilometre away and it was rapidly growing light! "Come on! Keep going! It is starting to get light."

He started striding down the side of the dune and then remembered he was supposed to be wiping out tracks and had to turn and go back up a couple of paces. But he was now gripped by apprehension and that added a sharp edge to his emotions. When he saw Vaughan stop at the bottom he hurried down, placing his empty bottle under his left armpit and swapping the branch to that had so he could grab at Vaughan's shirt with his right.

"Come on, run!"

Vaughan swore at him and struck his hand off. "Stop pushing! I'm going alright!" he snapped.

"Then run. It's only to those trees," Donny retorted.

He took the empty bottle from under his arm and started running. Luckily the going was easy, mostly short, dry grass with only a few tufts of spinifex. Behind him he heard the thud of rapid footfalls and a glance over his shoulder showed Vaughan running as well.

But he could not keep it up for long. After about a hundred paces, Vaughan slowed to a gasping walk. Donny shook his head, very aware of his chafing but annoyed that the older boy could not run any distance. "Come on! Keep trying!" he called.

But Vaughan shook his head. "You go on. I will try to keep up."

"No! Keep going, you bloody weakling!" Donny snarled, his anxiety fuelling his dislike.

"Stop calling me names, you scrawny bloody squirt!" Vaughan gasped back. "Or I'll rearrange your ugly face and make it even uglier."

Donny realised he had really hurt Vaughan's feelings, so he clamped his mouth shut and kept striding across the flat.

If I have to I will leave him to get caught, he decided.

He was sure he could do better on his own. So he kept running, only to pull up suddenly. Just in time his eyes had detected a black, vertical line in the half-light.

Donny's spirits soared. *A fence! Must be the Horse Paddock,* he thought.

"What is it?" Vaughan gasped as he ran up to join him.

"Watch out! Barbed wire fence," Donny cautioned. "We are close to the homestead."

He cast an anxious look around to check but nothing to alarm him was visible. *The homestead must be just behind that big clump of trees to our right,* he thought.

The need to be under cover as quickly as possible got him down on hands and knees and he began crawling under the bottom strand of the three strand, barbed wire fence.

"Argh! Ouch!" he cried as a barb snagged his shirt and then tore the skin on his back.

Cursing and swearing softly, Donny lowered himself some more and dragged himself under.

"You should go under fences like this on your back," Vaughan said.

"What?" Donny asked.

He stood up and began dusting his hands and knees. The plastic water bottle had worked its way out and he picked it up and thrust it back into his pocket.

"We were taught in army cadets to go under fences like this one on our backs," Vaughan replied. "Watch me. You lie down beside the fence and take hold of the bottom strand between two of the barbs. Then you twitch your legs under and then your shoulders. That way you can see the barbs and hold them away from yourself."

As he explained this Vaughan followed his own instructions and then rolled onto his hands and knees and stood up beside Donny. Then he bent to pick up the bottles he had placed under the fence first.

Donny was not impressed with being told. Having lived all his life with barbed wire fences he thought he knew better, but he had to concede that what Vaughan had said and done seemed to work better. His sore back testified to that!

"What about when the enemy are shooting?" he argued.

Vaughan shook his head. "This isn't for getting through barbed wire obstacles on a battlefield. They are different. This is just to safely get under cattle fences in Australia."

Donny did not feel like arguing so he set off at a fast walk, very conscious that the sky to the east was rapidly turning pink.

The sun will be up soon!

Vaughan strode along with him, both boys looking around for any sign of the men or vehicles. Then Donny put his arm up in a signal to stop. He could see what he had been expecting. Pointing he said, "The main station road. We will cross on the clumps of grass. Don't leave any foot prints."

This was done and by then it was light enough for Donny to check that they had left no obvious sign of their crossing before heading off again. The trees along Burke Creek were only two or three hundred metres away by then, two or three football fields was the way he estimated that.

"Let's run. We need to get out of sight quickly," he said.

He started to run and heard Vaughan also running close behind him to his left. The going was easy, and Donny was feeling almost elated.

I know exactly where we are and we are nearly there, he thought.

As he ran, Donny kept looking back to his right and left, dreading to see a vehicle come into view. Now he was determined to get under cover quickly and he gritted his teeth and ignored the pain from his chafing. But then he was dismayed at how quickly he seemed to get tired. His energy just seemed to drain away.

Probably because I haven't eaten a few meals, he decided.

Despite his weakness he managed to make himself keep running. To his relief, and surprise he saw that Vaughan was also making a real effort, his face contorted with pain and determination and his breath coming in great gulps and gasps. But above the sound of their laboured breathing and thudding of their boots Donny heard a noise.

Motor vehicle? he wondered.

Then he saw the dust. It was drifting up above the trees in the direction of the homestead.

"Vehicle coming! Lie down!" he croaked.

They were only a hundred paces from the trees, but Donny could see that they would not reach them in time. Picking a large clump of saltbush, he stopped and turned around before lying carefully on the sand. There were some burs there which hurt but he reasoned there was no time to find a better spot. Vaughan had not questioned his orders and lay down nearby behind some spinifex.

"Keep yer bloody head down!" Donny hissed as he moved to be able to peek around the side of his saltbush.

Just in time! he thought as a vehicle came racing into view from behind the trees. It was the station Land Rover and was going fast. *Have we been seen?* he wondered.

But the speed of the vehicle indicated it was not about to stop. It went racing past at high speed, trailing the usual plume of dust. Donny peered intently at it and tried to see who was in it but all he could detect that there were men in the front. Then the land Rover was past and the dust began slowly spreading and settling over the area where the boys lay.

"Did you see who was in it?" Donny asked.

Vaughan raised his head and shook it. "Not really, but I think it was our two friends from yesterday. I didn't recognise Uncle James. I wonder where it is going in such a hurry?"

"Looking for us I suppose," Donny surmised. He watched while the vehicle stopped about a kilometre away.

"What are they doing? Why did they stop?" Vaughan asked.

"Gate," Donny replied. "We are in the homestead Horse Paddock."

"Do you know where we are?"

"Exactly. We are about a kilometre south of the homestead. We must have wandered a bit off course."

Just as well though, he thought. *Otherwise we would have come over that last sand dune with the rising sun behind us and anyone awake at the homestead would have seen us.*

The Land Rover moved a short distance and then, once the gate was closed, went roaring off to the south. Donny waited until it was lost in the distant dust cloud before getting to his feet. As he did, he noted a big snake track in the sand near Vaughan, but as Vaughan was already up and picking at prickles in his hands he said nothing. Muttering swear words he turned and started walking again, plucking out the burs as he went.

That last hundred paces were hard. Donny found he was gasping for breath, and he hurt so much he realised he was hobbling. So was Vaughan but the older boy had a determined look on his face and kept limping as fast as he could. Then they were on a slight sandy rise among the trees and Donny stopped and pointed where he wanted Vaughan to go.

"I will brush out our tracks. If anyone walks along the creek searching for us that is what they will be looking for," he explained.

Which is what he did while Vaughan limped up over the rise and then stopped.

"Bloody hell!" Vaughan muttered.

"What?"

"Water," Vaughan replied.

Donny had been expecting that and was surprised that Vaughan was surprised. "Yeah, we had a good fall of winter rain about three weeks ago," he said as he moved up to join Vaughan on top of the creek bank.

From there it was quite a steep slope down among trees and bushes to where brown water filled the creek bed in a pool ten metres wide. Donny pointed out the route he wanted them to go along and then followed, brushing carefully as he went. The route took them to the right, northwards for a hundred paces or so until the pool narrowed and they could walk down a sandy slope pockmarked by horse's hooves. Here they were able to cross to the far bank on some rocks covered with dry mud. Donny now led the way up in among a clump of trees and bushes where they had view back across to the road through gap in the trees.

"This will do for a short rest," he said.

After a careful check for ants and burs, he lowered himself down and sighed with relief as he stretched out his legs. Vaughan followed his example, leaning back on a tree trunk. Donny drank half the water remaining in his plastic bottle, and, having noted that Vaughan had no water left in his two beer bottles, handed him the bottle.

"You drink what's left," he said.

Vaughan did so and then looked around. "What do we do now?" he asked.

"Have a short rest and then move to where we can see the homestead," Donny replied.

Just thinking of the homestead made him yearn to be there. Then his stomach grumbled and he had strong images of sitting in the kitchen eating fried eggs and bacon. He salivated and wondered if he could somehow get them some food.

His thinking was interrupted by Vaughan crying softly in pain and rubbing at his left calf muscle.

"Cramp!" he groaned.

He thumped it with his fist and then hit harder, tears coming to his eyes. After a few minutes the cramp eased but it left Vaughan trembling an anxious.

"I don't know if I can walk much further. How far is it?"

"Only about a kilometre," Donny assured him. "You can stay here while I go and have a look."

Vaughan made a face at that suggestion. He did not say so, but Donny surmised he was not keen on being left alone, even that close to the homestead. Then Donny's stomach gurgled again and despite his best efforts he did another loud fart.

"Bloody hell!" Vaughan cried. "They will hear that at the house!"

"I'm hungry!" Donny retorted, stung by embarrassment and the worry that his stomach was actually feeling very liquid.

I hope I'm not getting the runs, he thought.

Then the first rays of the rising sun lanced through gaps in the foliage and drove him to move. The air began to rapidly heat up.

At least we've got plenty of water, he told himself.

Then a crow arrived to study them from atop a nearby tree. It cocked its head from side to side and began making loud *caaarck* noises. Donny waved his fist at it.

"Go away, you bloody thing!" he cried as loudly as he dared.

"Why does the crow matter?" Vaughan queried.

"Because it could give away the fact that we are here," Donny replied.

"How?"

"Just by sitting there staring down at us and making that crow noise," Donny replied. "You wouldn't notice it, but my dad and all the bushmen and stockmen would and they would wonder what it was looking at."

"Is Cousin James a bushman?" Vaughan asked.

"No, but that Ringer bloke is. He might notice."

"What can we do about it?"

"Nothing. All we can do is hope it loses interest. But I reckon we should move closer to the homestead before it gets too hot," Donny suggested.

Vaughan nodded. Donny stood up and picked up his bottles and branch. "Don't leave those beer bottles. We might need them," he said as Vaughan also got slowly to his feet.

"I need a drink now. I'm getting very thirsty," Vaughan said.

As Donny began walking, he gestured down at the muddy water in the creek.

"We may have to drink that."

Vaughan looked disgusted. "We can't drink that! It will make us sick."

Donny shrugged. "As I said yesterday, you have to be alive to be sick. If you don't drink you die," he said. "Anyway, we will find a better spot where it is easier to fill the bottles without having to get stuck in that mud down there. I will lead now. You grab yourself a new branch and come last and brush out any tracks."

Vaughan did as he was told and Donny began moving very slowly from tree to tree, scouting as he went, eyes and ears open.

Chapter 16

THE HOMESTEAD

At first Donny worked his way along the west bank of the creek. Out to his left extended kilometre after kilometre of flat, almost bare land, all the way to the horizon. Along the top of the bank was a thicket of trees, mostly gnarled and stunted mulgas and gidgees. There was some undergrowth of spinifex and saltbush and a few large bushes but mostly the ground was bare sand and that was a problem because it meant they left very clear tracks. So he went slow enough to allow Vaughan time to brush most of them out. To Donny's eyes, the fact that the sand had been brushed over looked very obvious but he hoped that either the Thug or someone equally inexperienced at bushcraft might be the person to search the area.

Vaughan was conscientious enough but looked very tired and it obviously suited him to go very slow. That suited Donny too as he did not want to blunder into any problem. Very carefully he scanned ahead and on each side before moving to the next bit of cover. Already the air was hot and the sun so bright that the shadows were important. It was a real relief to be moving out of the direct rays of that blazing sun.

As they crept along from tree to tree, Vaughan looked with distaste at the muddy slurry in the creek bed.

"This Burke Creek, does it have anything to do with those 19th Century explorers Burke and Wills?"

"Yeah. They came through here," Donny replied.

"Did they die somewhere around here?"

Donny shook his head. "Nah! They died down on Coopers Creek, that's a few hundred k's south of here."

Vaughan looked out across the flats where a heat shimmer was already starting and made a face. "I can see why they died!' he muttered.

Donny was a bit affronted by that insult to the country he loved. *We could have died too, but I knew where to find water,* he thought, dislike of the older boy surging in his emotions.

Then they came to a large pool and when he went around it to the left

Donny found he had difficulty seeing through the gaps in the foliage on the other bank.

We need to change back to the other bank, he thought, knowing that the homestead was on that side. But he did not want to waste time or energy back-tracking, so he continued on.

Vaughan caught up to him. "Do you know where we are?" he whispered.

Donny nodded and pointed down at the 25-metre-wide pool of muddy brown water. "Yes. This is the Skeleton Hole," he replied.

"Skeleton?" queried Vaughan, glancing anxiously around.

"Yeah, some joker died here back in the early days," Donny replied casually.

He had known the story all his life, so it had no particular meaning but the idea obviously worried Vaughan.

Vaughan looked at the water. "I really need a drink, but I don't think I can drink that. Is there another water trough or bore we can go to?"

"Only at the homestead. But we won't be able to go there in daylight," Donny answered. "There's a smaller pool a bit further along which usually has better water in it."

They continued slowly on and encountered another of those little local dramas with wildlife that left them startled and pretending to each other they hadn't got a fright. A huge monitor lizard, a Perenti, largest of the goanna type, suddenly erupted from a bush and scuttled up a tree. As it went up it vanished from view by climbing up the trunk on the side away from them. When up in the branches it stopped and peered down at them, its dappled skin almost perfect camouflage against the mottled bark.

Donny forced a grin for Vaughan's sake and continued, detouring away from that tree. He kept moving slowly and after a hundred paces came to another dilemma. The creek narrowed and would be easy to cross but it also curved away to the right and made a big curve. Donny knew that it swung back again a few hundred metres ahead and that it then ran straight for a while at the next big waterhole. The homestead was just past that.

Do we cut across this flat open area to take a short cut? Or do we stay under cover and have to go further?

It was a decision he had to make and he opted for safety, even though it meant walking a few hundred extra metres. He did not explain the problem to Vaughan as he did not want an argument. To do this, he made his way down the steep bank to a rocky bottom and across to the east side again. Vaughan followed without any protest.

Up on the other bank Donny stayed close to the lip of the bank to keep as many trees as possible between him and the open country on their right.

The road is just out there, and the house will come into view soon, he thought.

It was now hot going, and the flies came to really annoy them. The ground was more broken up, and Donny followed a thick trail of hoof prints down to where water was collected in small rock pools.

"This will be the best we will find," he said as he crouched to refill his whisky bottle.

Vaughan stared at the pools askance and shook his head. "Can't we wait?"

"No. It will be after dark before we can risk trying to get water at the homestead," Donny replied.

He lifted his bottle and tried to ignore the muddy mixture swilling in it. To prove his point, he summoned up his bravado, put the neck of the bottle to his lips and drank, and nearly gagged at the smell and taste.

Vaughan saw this and made a face. "You will get sick," he said.

"And you will die from heat stoke if you don't get liquid into you," Donny retorted.

With that he forced himself to drink more, opting to gulp rather that sip. It almost worked but it was hard going. The muddy taste wasn't too bad, but the smell was vile.

Vaughan licked his lips and looked anxious. He shook his head but after Donny had drunk the whole bottle empty and began refilling it he finally crouched and filled one of the beer bottles. But then he looked at the water in the bottle and shook his head. Donny forced another big gulp of the horrible liquid down and then poured some over his head and shoulders. The water was warm but then the faint breeze gave it a refreshing, cooling effect. Vaughan opted to do that as well. Only after Donny had drunk and refilled his bottle again did Vaughan at last start sipping. And that was all drama, pulling sour faces, sniffing, coughing, muttering, and grimacing. But at least the water went down.

Donny refilled his bottle and then took out his small plastic bottle and filled it before kneeling to splash more water over his head and shoulders. Vaughan at last took a few big gulps and, with an obvious look of distaste on his face, forced the rest down. Then he also filled both his bottles.

It was very hot and airless in the deep bed of the creek, so Donny slowly made his way up to the shade of the trees. He really wanted to strip off and wash his body, especially the chafing, but he felt inhibited by Vaughan's presence. And now he needed a pee. So he went behind a bush and did so. To his dismay, he noted that his urine was dark yellow.

As he was peeing Vaughan came up beside him, causing him to falter and blush. Vaughan glanced and then said, "That's not good! I suppose mine will be the same."

He proceeded to pee as well, and he was right. His was also dark yellow. He shook his head and said, "Our cadet instructors said our urine was supposed to be pale yellow, like straw. That colour means we are not drinking enough, and the salts will build up in our kidneys."

That was interesting to Donny but he was embarrassed so he gestured back down at the pool.

"Well go on, go back and drink your fill," he replied.

Vaughan just shrugged and finished peeing, obviously not fazed by doing such a thing in public. Donny now led the way slowly along the bank to where it started to curve back to the left.

Pointing to his right he said, "The road is just out there a hundred metres or so, so we need to be careful."

They were. Moving from tree to tree they continued, and bit by bit the homestead and its outbuildings came into view in the distance. These were up on a distinct rise about half a kilometre from the trees along the creek. On the flat between them half a dozen horses were grazing. Donny smiled as he recognised his own saddle horses, including his favourite: Minnie.

The boys continued until the creek curved back to the right and they came to another big water hole, 25 metres wide and half a kilometre long.

"Yabby Waterhole. This will do. If we go any closer we could bump into people coming down to do things to the pump."

"Suits me," Vaughan agreed, hobbling slowly along as he continued to brush (not very effectively) at their tracks.

Donny found a shady little space among the trees and bushes where they could observe the homestead and then lowered himself to sit. He sighed with relief and tried to physically relax. But he was at once assailed by more pain as all his chafing and blisters began to throb and itch. Within a couple of minutes, he became aware of an almost overwhelming tiredness.

"We had better take turns watching," he said, knowing that he felt exhausted and was liable to drop off to sleep.

Vaughan agreed. "Hour on, hour off then?" he suggested.

Donny nodded. "I'll go first," he said and then stared out at the homestead.

As it had been his home all his life, he knew every bit of it intimately, so he now looked for any changes or movement. Clonargh Station homestead was very typical of its type. The focus was the actual homestead building, one story with wide verandas, just visible behind its garden fence and wall of shrubbery and greenery. To the right of that were a couple of sheds: two old and one new, that contained workshops, storerooms, and a vehicle garage. To the left of the house were old stables and several buildings including the old wool store (It had been many years since the station had run sheep), stockmen's quarters and their cookhouse. A few hundred metres further to the north and still up on the rise were a set of old wooden fences and the corrugated iron shape of the old sheering shed.

Vaughan looked as well and then said, "I didn't realise the house was so far from the creek."

"It needs to be," Donny replied. "When the floods come all this flat country is covered."

Images of the vast flood two years before filled his mind, and Vaughan gave him such a look of disbelief that he got annoyed.

How is he so ignorant? He's been here before!

He said, "The last flood came almost up to the old stables there, just above where those horses are grazing."

That seemed to settle that, so the boys studied the place.

No sign of anyone, Donny noted. That got him worried. *Are Grandad and Mum there? Is anyone there?* he wondered. Doubts about the whole escape and evasion escapade again came to torment him. *Maybe I have made a terrible mistake and none of this has been necessary? Mum and Dad will be beside themselves with worry.*

Vaughan asked the same questions, but Donny could only shrug. There was no way he was going to risk being seen by walking across all that open ground. Then that bloody crow joined them and began to *caaark*!

"Bugger off!" Donny hissed.

He looked around for a stone to throw but here were none. All he could do was swear and fret. Then another cramp hit Vaughan and that distracted him. Another bird arrived, some sort of finch and it looked at him, cocking its head from side to side before flitting off into another tree. Then more birds, a whole flock, all chirping and tweeting.

"Bloody Happy Jacks! Bugger off birds!" he muttered.

Then he heard a soft snore and saw that Vaughan had gone to sleep slumped against his tree. The older boy looked so exhausted that Donny felt a twinge of pity for him. He eased his own sore and seemingly heavy limbs and squinted into the glare, and promptly fell asleep himself.

It was the cockatoos that woke him, or rather brought him back to full wakefulness as the ants, flies, and heat had been nudging him. Donny felt awful. He had a disgusting taste in his mouth and his whole skin seemed to itch and feel gritty and dirty. Rubbing sleep-gummed eyes he looked around and then realised what they had both done.

Oooh bugger! I went to sleep. We both did. I wonder if anything has happened?

A pulse of shame made him sit upright and study the homestead. As he did, Vaughan snuffled and groaned then woke up, slapping at ants that were crawling on his skin.

"Bloody things!' he snarled. Then it was the flies. He rubbed his eyes and glared at Donny. "Anything happening?"

Donny shook his head. "Nope. No sign of any movement and no vehicles."

"What time is it?"

Donny glanced up and was surprised to note that the sun was almost directly overhead. "About midday, I reckon."

He was astonished to realise they had been asleep for three or four hours. The sun had moved so much that both boys were no longer in the shade, so they moved to new positions and resumed watching.

After a time Donny said, "So every kid at your school has to be in the army cadets, Vaughan?"

Vaughan nodded. "Yeah, in Years 8 and 9. That's why most parents send their kids there. So, I'm in Year 10 and didn't have to be in them this year."

"What did you do in army cadets?" Donny asked.

He had very briefly met a teenage girl from a station out along the Donohue Highway who had been a cadet at her boarding school in Charters Towers, and she had obviously really enjoyed her cadet experience.

Vaughan shrugged and made a face. "Oh well, we learned lots of things like map reading, First Aid, radios and stuff. And a lot of drill, well, not really. We did a bit of drill in our recruit training and then getting ready to march on Anzac Day and a fair bit at the end of the year for a ceremonial Passing-Out Parade."

"Did you get to fire rifles?"

Vaughan nodded. "Yeah. In our First Year we only fired at the WTSS, that's a computer system where you have a rifle that fires a laser beam and the computer tells you what you did right and wrong. As Second Years we fired live ammo at the rifle range."

"You any good?"

Vaughan so obviously hesitated that Donny guessed he wasn't, but the reply was, "Average."

"Did you get any rank?"

At that, Vaughan looked defiant but sheepish. "Nah! I could'a but I chose not to. I qualified for lance corporal."

"It all sounds okay to me," Donny said. "Anyway, what you learned about navigation was a real help to us."

He was about to say more when he heard the sound of an approaching vehicle. The boys moved to watch, lying flat among the bushes. It was the station Land Rover, and it came from the south and went out of sight in front of the homestead, where it stopped. Donny had seen two men in it, but they had just been dark shadows.

"Ringer and Thug?" he suggested.

"Looked like it," Vaughan agreed.

"So there might have been someone at the homestead," Donny added.

He was relieved, having spent all those hours hiding just in case. *I hope Mum and Dad are there,* he thought.

He began considering how he was going to approach the place in the dark and what options they might have. Then another sound caught his attention, a distant vibrating tremor to the north that grew rapidly louder and closer.

"Helicopter," Vaughan said.

It was. Into view swept a small mustering chopper, just big enough to seat two people. It went almost directly overhead and then circled around to land out of sight in front of the homestead.

"Only one person in it," he said.

"Uncle James I think," Vaughan agreed.

The helicopter's motor was switched off and there was then a long period during which nothing happened that the boys could see or hear. The sun went over to their backs and sweat began to trickle. The boys kept edging around to stay in the shade but finally Donny had to move to a new tree. By then he was feeling quite upset in the stomach. Despite that, he forced himself to drink most of another bottle of the creek water.

Then squelching in his lower stomach and bowels told him he had to go to the toilet quickly.

Or I will do it in my pants!

Embarrassed and also annoyed that Vaughan might be proved right in something, he quickly explained and then made his way back down into the creek bed and across behind a big log that hid him from view. Just in time he got his trousers and underpants down and then squirted liquid filth even as he squatted. It was smelly, messy and extremely embarrassing. Worse, he had no toilet paper and had to work his way out to a small puddle and use the muddy water to wash himself. He was still engaged in that unpleasant task when he heard the helicopter start up.

Bloody hell! I'll get caught out in the open with my duds down! he thought anxiously.

He nearly was. He just had time to wash and pull his pants up before he heard the helicopter's engine noise change as it took off. He only just got under a big bush before the machine came buzzing towards him.

Have we been seen? Donny fretted.

But the helicopter just flew low overhead, still turning, and went off south following the creek line. Now worry that their tracks might be obvious caused Donny more anxiety. To his relief, the helicopter flew on southwards and vanished in the distance. Still feeling anxious about his stomach and bowels, he did up his belt and hurried back up to where Vaughan was still watching.

As he hurried up the bank, Donny heard the Land Rover's engine start. Vaughan briefly glanced back at him but made no comment about what he had been doing.

Instead, he pointed. "There goes the Land Rover again," he said.

They watched in silence as it drove off south again. They heard it stop at the gate to the Horse Paddock and then listened until the sound died away in the distance.

"I think they are looking for us," Donny said.

Vaughan nodded. "I reckon. And they must be very worried. Having two dead kids lost out in the desert will upset their plans. They won't be thinking straight because it will mean real trouble if they are caught. Hey!"

The cry because a man had suddenly appeared at the back gate of the house and he was carrying something. The sound of dogs yapping and barking carried across the flat and the boys saw the man drag two dogs secured to leads out through the gate. The man clipped the leads to the back fence and then put down an object Donny deduced to be a water bowl. The dogs crowded around it lapping and the man went back through the gate and shut it.

"Bugger! That's how I was planning to go in," Donny muttered.

"Are they your dogs?" Vaughan asked.

Donny squinted to look in the afternoon glare and shook his head. "No. I can see a big Alsatian that is definitely not one of ours. I think I can hear ours barking around near the old stables."

"Should we just get out of here. If they come looking for us with dogs we have no chance," Vaughan said. "We can just follow this creek north to the highway, can't we?"

"We can, but I'm going to see if my mum and dad are in the house first. So I am waiting. You can go if you want."

Vaughan looked very anxious but then shook his head and settled again in the shade.

"I'll guard. You have a sleep."

That was easier said than done. The soil was a gritty mixture of sand and fine, grey clay and it had found its way inside their clothes to itch and irritate. But Donny was really tired and after watching the ants for a while he dropped into a fitful sleep, frequently roused by those same ants, or by flies and birds.

He was again woken by cockatoos. A flock of them settled in the trees above them and set up a screeching and cackling that was not only very loud but which Donny felt sure would attract the attention of the man at the house. A glance towards the sun told him it was now late afternoon and that was something. He lay there, pretending to sleep for a while but actually thinking hard. He was scared and knew that hurrying to the highway to make contact with other adults was probably the right thing to do. But there was that niggling fear of the threat of what would happen if they went to the police.

The sound of Vaughan moving got him up. Blinking and yawning he saw that Vaughan was moving away.

"Just going to the dunny," he explained.

Remembering his own embarrassing situation, Donny pointed. "If you need to do a crap, go down to the water so you can wash yourself later," he said.

Vaughan nodded and went away. Donny sat up, washed his face and rinsed his eyes and then forced another half bottle of water down. He began to perspire immediately.

I will refill them with clean rainwater from the homestead tanks tonight, if I need to, he told himself.

Half an hour later an unhappy looking Vaughan returned, and Donny guessed that he also had an upset stomach. But the subject was so shameful he made no mention and merely kept looking towards the homestead.

Another hour went by and then the sound of the helicopter came again. Both boys crouched in hiding but it went past following the road and this time landed near the garage. There were a few drums of aviation fuel there and the machine was landed near them and the engine switched off. Uncle James got out and moved a hose from the nearest drum and began hand pumping fuel. As he did, the man from the homestead appeared, and now he was carrying a gun. The man strolled over to chat to Uncle James until the refuelling was done. Donny studied their body language and gestures intently to understand what they were saying. And he didn't like it.

Uncle James seems to be indicating something over in the direction we went, Donny surmised. *I hope he hasn't found our tracks and is following them.*

Half an hour later the helicopter, now refuelled, was started up and

Uncle James flew it away again, to Donny's dismay in a south westerly direction.

They might have found our tracks. That is the direction of Number 8 Bore.

But there was nothing else they could do but endure the heat, flies, ants and birds. To his relief, the cockatoos moved away but then the 'Happy Jacks', Apostle Birds, returned, to flit around chirping. Both Vaughan and he dozed a bit, but it was too uncomfortable to sleep properly. Both drank a bit, but Donny was sure Vaughan wasn't drinking much and was hoping to get good water later. He knew he was.

Very slowly the sun sank lower. The western sky took on a ruddy hue and the breeze picked up and the flies eased off. Then, just as the rim of the sun touched the western horizon, the sound of the helicopter came to them. It came buzzing in along the creek line and both boys hunched behind bushes as it clattered overhead. It landed and was again refuelled. The man with the gun appeared and he went away and came back with a strange dog on a lead. The lead was secured to the helicopter's skids.

"Not taking any chances," Vaughan commented.

Seeing that done worried Donny. *Does Uncle James suspect we are alive and in this area, or is it just a normal precaution?*

It was dusk by then and both men walked off towards the homestead. Donny took that as his cue, and he eased his cramped muscles and stood up.

"What we going to do?" Vaughan asked.

"I'm going to sneak in and try to find out what is going on," Donny replied.

"What do you want me to do?"

"Come with me to the stables and refill our water bottles while I try to find out who is in the house and what is going on," Donny replied.

"Be a bit risky."

"This is my home! I know every nook and cranny," Donny retorted. "You can stay here if you like and if I don't come back by about midnight try to get to the highway."

That idea obviously did not appeal to Vaughan as he shook his head vigorously. "I'll come."

Donny bent and picked up his empty bottles and then feeling scared, weak, and nauseous he started walking.

Chapter 17

MY HOME

Satisfied it was now too dark to be seen from the buildings Donny carefully made his way out onto the open grassland. There he turned left and began walking slowly along just on the edge of the trees.

Vaughan followed but hissed at him, "Where are we going?"

"Further around, away from those dogs," Donny whispered back.

He had considered the direction the light breeze was blowing in and did not want any risk that their odours might waft towards those dogs! Behind them the ruddy glow of the sunset faded, and Donny was confident that, with the dark line of trees between them and the sunset, they were invisible.

Unless the crooks have some of those see-in-the-dark gadgets.

He walked slowly along the edge of the field, counting paces and continually glancing to his right towards the buildings. There were lights there and that made it easier to keep direction but harder to see what or who was there. At 500 paces he stopped and Vaughan came up close beside him.

"Why have you stopped?" he whispered.

"I am going to start angling up towards the stables now," Donny said.

"Isn't that really risky?"

"Yes, but the crooks won't expect us to do it so it's a fair risk," Donny answered.

He set off across the flat, using a star to guide him. He had only gone a hundred paces or so when what he was expecting happened. There was the sound of horses: snuffling, hooves thudding, and some neighing and whinnying. Dark shapes appeared and then one came right across towards them.

Donny was touched. It was his favourite pony Minnie, and she had obviously detected his scent on the gentle breeze. She was cautious until he called her name softly and clicked his tongue a couple of times. The pony then walked right up to him and nuzzled him with her muzzle. Donny rubbed her nose and ruffled her ears.

"Sorry girl, I haven't got a treat for you," he said as softly as he could.

Donny loved horses and knew they liked him. He had been riding since he was a toddler, held on by his mother or father, and now he pressed his face into the pony's neck and inhaled.

Oh, I love that horse smell! he thought, and gently stroked Minnie's throat as she rubbed against him.

Vaughan came closer. "Is that your horse?" he hissed.

"Yes, she's my favourite pony. Her name's Minnie, short for Min Min," Donny replied.

"Won't those dogs hear the horses?" Vaughan suggested anxiously.

"For sure, but they will expect that. The horses have been somewhere in this paddock all day," Donny replied. He noted that several other horses were now coming closer. He patted Minnie again and shook his head. "I'll bet you poor fellows haven't had any treats today," he murmured.

He wasn't worried about water for them as they could just go down to the creek at any time. Then what he thought was a brilliant idea came to him.

We can escape on horses, he thought.

He moved to get closer to Vaughan's left ear. "After we have rescued our parents, we can escape on the horses if we have to," he muttered.

"Sorry, no. I can't ride a horse," Vaughan admitted.

Donny was astonished and disgusted. "Your dad owns a cattle station and you can't ride a horse! Well, that blew my plan," he said.

"What is your plan?" Vaughan asked, obviously upset.

"I am going to sneak in and find who is there. If our parents are, and we can rescue them without the crooks knowing, then we will try to get to the highway by daylight. If we can't rescue them, I will still try to find out what I can and I will get us some food," he said.

"Okay," Vaughan agreed.

Donny rubbed Minnie's nose some more and then gently pushed her away. "Not now Min Min."

He then continued on across the field. The pony walked with him, but he did not mind that. She would provide good cover and mask their scent from those dogs. Several of the other horses walked with them but the others either lay down again or wandered off into the night. After a few minutes, Minnie also lost interest and returned to cropping grass. The horses were left behind.

The boys progressed until they reached the bottom of the gentle rise the buildings were on before Vaughan tugged at Donny's sleeve.

"Vehicle coming!" he hissed.

Donny now also heard the faint sound of an engine and he glanced towards that direction. In the distance to the south he saw the loom of headlights.

"The Land Rover coming back probably. Come on, let's get up to the stables quickly."

Donny had been scared from the very start but now he was anxious they not fail by being caught out in the open. So he hurried up to the left end of the stables. As he reached them, he heard more dogs growling and tugging at chains. Luckily the barking of these dogs was mixed in with the arrival of the Land Rover. The strange dogs at the helicopter and back gate also began barking and that covered the sounds even more.

A man began shouting at the 'bloody dogs' to shut up! *That sounds like the man with the gun,* Donny thought. *And he sounds like he is outside. Now, where is he?*

A quick peek around the north wall of the stables showed three dogs chained there and Donny sighed with relief, they were the station dogs and knew him well. There was no-one in sight and he could hear the Land Rover doors being slammed and voices at the front of the homestead, so he hurried across to the dogs and began to pat them. In response they stopped barking and growling and began whining and licking. These were working dogs, not house pets but they still liked a bit of attention and liked him.

"Sssh! Quiet you mutts," he whispered.

Then they set up barking briefly when Vaughan joined him, until they recognised his smell as well. There was a rainwater tank on a low tank stand at the end of the stables so Donny passed Vaughan his two bottles and showed him where the tap was.

"Fill all the bottles and have a big drink yourself, and give these poor dogs a drink too," he instructed.

"You be careful," Vaughan whispered.

"See you in half an hour or so," Donny replied.

He was very keyed up and afraid by now, but he was also very determined. To add to his emotional state was outrage that the men were in his home. So he ghosted along the open front of the stables, relishing the scents of leather polish and dubbin (and even horse manure) as he went. Carefully he slipped from stall to stall, his eyes questing for any sign of the man with the gun.

Close on Donny's left was the main station road, and 25 metres beyond were two old timber and corrugated iron huts that were no longer in use but had been built in the long-ago for people like boundary riders and shepherds when the station had employed such people. His mother was planning to have them renovated to offer city people holiday 'farm stays', but the work had not yet begun. There was no sign of anyone there and Donny continued towards the south end of the stables.

The last stall was lit by the flicker of coloured lights, but he was expecting that because in there was a bank of solar-powered batteries, recharged by a large array of solar panels on the roof, one of his father's innovations. It was one Donny knew his mother really approved of as it meant that the big diesel-powered KVA generator in its little shed over beyond the garage only had to be switched on in an emergency. A quick glance showed Donny no-one there, so he slid on to the end of the building. There was a large pepper tree and he enjoyed the scent of its leaves as his eyes probed the bushes and trees in the garden of the homestead 50 paces away.

Ten paces over was an old tractor, half hidden in weeds. Normally Donny steered well clear of it in case of snakes but now it offered him cover so he slid into its shadow. And he was just in time!

There's the man with the gun!

The man had strolled into view from the front of the house where the Land Rover was now parked outside the front gate. Donny noted several other vehicles also parked there. The veranda lights were on at the house and lights showed in several windows but there were so many bushes, flowers, and shady trees in the garden (His mother's particular place of enjoyment) that it was hard to see.

Donny now crouched in cover, willing his stomach to stop gurgling as the man with the gun looked towards the stables. Even to Donny's inexperienced eyes it appeared that the man was bored, as he then strolled on along the side of the garden and around the back, where the chained dogs at once set up a barrage of barking at him. The man yelled at them and the noise subsided.

Move now! Donny told himself. *Before the man comes back.*

Despite being very scared, dry throat, rapid heartbeat, sweaty palms, Donny moved, hurrying across the dusty ground to the side gate of the garden. When he reached it, he found his breath was coming in rapid, hot gasps and the thudding of his heart made it hard to hear. His main fear was that the man with the gun might actually shoot. Knowing that the side gate squeaked, Donny opened it very slowly. By lifting it at the same time he managed to get it open without making any noise. For the next minute he crouched in the shadows cast by some crotons by the lights at the house. Seeing no sign of anyone, Donny slowly and carefully closed the gate again.

Can't leave it open or that bloke might notice, he reasoned.

Then he went down to his hands and knees, crunching a few dead Croton leaves as he did. Realising his hat was a problem when creeping, he took it off and placed it in the garden bed. Then he listened again. Still nobody and no sounds, so he crawled out from the garden bed and onto the lawn. And it was a lawn, real, soft green grass that his mother cared for to make the homestead a little oasis in the desert. Donny crouched, mouth dry with fear and his vision hampered by the lights in the buildings in front of him. He listened and stared in all directions trying to locate the man with the gun.

There were three buildings. Directly in front of him was the main station homestead, a large, single-storey structure built of timber on low stumps. Wide verandas surrounded it on all sides and a couple of rainwater tanks made it look bigger than it actually was. The building was more than a hundred years old and was the only home Donny had ever known. Connected to it at the rear, to Donny's right front, by a five-metre-long covered walkway, was the kitchen. Over beyond that and only partly visible were what had been the servant's quarters ('In the "Good Old Days" of Great Grandfather Mortimer, when wages were lower and workers more plentiful,' as his grandad often said). These were now guest accommodation. There were more water tanks and trees over there as well.

Hearing and seeing nothing, Donny hoped the man with the gun was now over on the far side of the house so he took a deep breath and hurried forwards silently across that lovely, soft lawn (Which all the horses and goats wanted to get at!). He went directly to a short set of three steps that led up to the side veranda. The veranda lights were all on and he felt very exposed, so he went straight to the nearest door, and got a shock. The door was locked!

Donny stared at the door handle in surprise and then tried again. The handle would not open the door. Never in his life had he known that door to be locked. It was closed in the hot months to keep in the air-conditioning his mother had insisted on, but never locked. The door had decorated glass panels and Donny pressed his face to one and then used his hands to cut out the glare from the veranda lights to look in. A long hallway went right across to the other side of the house, crossing another at right angles in the middle. There was a single light on at the crossing and a glance showed Donny there was nobody in there.

Then his gaze noted the reflected light coming from the glass front of the gun cabinet just inside. He studied the scene, his mind racing. Quite clearly visible were the lovely, polished wood stocks and the shiny metallic gleam of the oiled barrels and working parts of the six guns he knew were there.

There's my rifle, he noted, his eyes taking in the details of a new .225 Savage bolt action. A fearful temptation welled up. *If I can get a gun those men will regret it,* he told himself.

He wasn't sure how he would go about it, but he tried to visualise forcing the men to surrender. But first he needed a gun!

Donny could see that the gun cabinet was locked and knew that the key would be in a locked drawer in his father's office, which was one of the front rooms. For a few moments he contemplated breaking one of the glass panels of the side door to get into the hallway, but then shook his head. He had heard of criminals, burglars and so on, breaking glass to get in but he knew it would make a noise.

And I don't know how they do it silently, he lamented.

Recognising that he had neither the knowledge nor the skills, he dropped that idea. And there was still the problem of ammunition. That was also locked in a cabinet in his father's office.

I've got a box of ammo and a full bandolier in my room, he remembered.

But that caused a surge of guilty shame as he knew that he should not have them and had not told his parents. And his room was at the front at the far corner.

To his left a few paces away was a door that led into his parent's bedroom. It connected through to the office. There were no lights inside, so he hurried to it and tried to open that door. It was also locked. For a few seconds or so he was so flummoxed by this unexpected development that he just stood and gaped.

Then he moved to his left to peek around the corner to his right. From there he could see all the way along the front veranda. It looked normal, with its usual clutter of armchairs and small tables and pot plants, this was where the family gathered for morning and afternoon teas on the shady southern side of the house during the summer months, but all the doors were shut! Donny had only ever seen that when there was a dust storm. And he knew it would be a terrible risk to walk along there if, as he estimated, the man with the gun was patrolling counterclockwise.

He could appear at any moment.

Now almost in a fluster because his initial plan had been thwarted, Donny turned and hurried back along the veranda to the far end. There was another door there and just beyond it a lighted window. Inside was the lounge room and Donny peeked in. Nobody there.

So where are the crooks? he wondered. Suspecting they might be in the dining room or kitchen he moved further to his right. *Maybe having dinner?* he thought.

Feeling he just had to know, Donny stepped across the back veranda and swung himself down under the wooden railing onto the lawn, avoiding one of his mother's flower gardens as he did. Once there he proceeded on hands and knees to the corner and then left around it and towards the brightly lit walkway from house to kitchen. It wasn't much cover but better than walking along the back veranda.

It was just as well he did because the screen door of the dining room suddenly swung open and a man with a gun came out. It was Thug. He turned and held the screen door open and luckily did not glance sideways, giving Donny time to duck in against the nearest bush. It turned out to be a rose bush and he had to stifle a yelp as several thorns dug into him.

Ow! I keep telling mum not to plant things with bloody thorns or spikes, he thought.

It was an ongoing argument; his mother being pulled by old cultural values to try to make an English garden versus common sense that suggested that dry-climate plants might be better in a desert!

Biting his lip to counter the sharp little pains, Donny tensed ready to run. But Thug just held the door open. To Donny's astonishment a teenage girl wearing jeans and stockman's shirt and with her hair pulled back into a ponytail, walked through the doorway and along the walkway. In the lamplight her hair glowed a brilliant copper colour. She was carrying a pile of plates. Then he recognised her.

Sharlene Sanderson from Glen Morris, he thought. *What the hell is she doing here?*

He had met her a few times at School of Distance 'in-reaches' and knew who she was, but she had gone to boarding school a couple of years ago. She walked along the walkway and used one hand to open the screen door of the kitchen.

The girl stood holding the door and Donny understood that there were more people to come. But his mouth literally fell open when the first one to appear was his mother. She was also carrying plates and bowls. Donny's heart turned over and he felt a frantic urge to rush forward to rescue her.

Oh, I wish I had that gun now! he thought.

His mother walked across and into the kitchen. She was followed by a tubby woman with red hair Donny guessed was Sharlene's mother. Thug closed the screen door to the dining room and walked across to the doorway to the kitchen. His heart hammering from a combination of fear and excitement, Donny just lay in the shadows of the rose bush and endured the pin pricks from the thorns. There was the clatter of crockery and tinkle of cutlery and women's voices and then Sharlene reappeared with some bottles in one hand and walked across to re-open the dining room screen door. She was followed by her mother and then Donny's mother, both carrying large plates in both hands. Thug closed the kitchen door and followed and then Sharlene followed him into the dining room.

For a few seconds Donny lay there amazed and afraid but also aware that this might be an opportunity. For what he wasn't quite sure, but he determined to try.

I'll get closer. I might be able to overhear what they are saying, he decided.

Acting on that he quickly crawled along beside the back veranda until he reached the walkway. There he hesitated. He could just see in through the closed screen door but could only see the back of a man, Ringer, he thought. There was the murmur of voices and the sound of cutlery, but he could not make out any words. And the thought of food made him salivate. His stomach churned in response to his hunger. A loud, liquid gurgle resulted.

Bloody hell! They'll hear that, he thought.

Then an idea came to him: crawl up under the dining room and try to eavesdrop. He acted on it at once, partly out of anxiety at being caught out on the open lawn by the man with the gun. But he had to overcome a few fearful memories before he moved. Several times over the years he had been under the house; usually chasing soccer balls and the like, but he had also seen several snakes slide in under there. The most recent a few weeks before had been a big tiger snake that had eventually slid out on the far side and been shot by his father.

In underneath it was dark, dusty, and unpleasant and there were cobwebs, but Donny ignored the discomfort and worry about spiders and made himself move. The house was almost at ground level at the front but here, at the back, he could just crawl on hands and knees. So he made his way into an area of almost complete darkness, lit by the brightness all around. Then he listened. All he could hear were the murmur of voices and the occasional thud of a boot or scrape of a chair.

"No good!" Donny muttered, as nervous reaction at his fear and frustration and irritation fuelled his emotions.

Then his stomach gurgled again. *I'm going to fart!* he thought.

For several seconds he struggled to suppress the urge, and failed. The resulting emission was not loud but was very smelly. For a moment or two Donny feared he had given himself away if the people above also smelt it. But then, being after all an imp of a boy, he imagined what the people in the room above might be doing. He pictured Ringer glancing sideways at Thug, who would be glancing back. The situation brought a grin to Donny's lips.

That will give them something to puzzle over while they all look sideways at each other, he thought, remembering such a reaction among his peers during lunch at an in-reach the previous year.

Then another idea came to him: *I will get some food.*

He had decided there was no realistic way of rescuing his parents, so walking to the highway to get help looked to be the next best option and he knew that both he and Vaughan needed food to give them energy.

Squirming around he made his way back out to where a short flight of steps led up to the side of the walkway. From what he had seen he decided that the crooks had just eaten a main meal and were now having desert.

I'll have to be quick, he told himself.

He lifted his head to look towards the screen door of the dining room. Then he looked around. Still no sign of the man with the gun. He decided he would risk it, but he knew it was a real risk as the kitchen had only the one door and both windows were sliding glass with insect screens on half and he wouldn't be able to leave through either of them.

For perhaps a minute Donny hesitated, breathing fast and heart hammering, and then he berated himself for being a coward and stood up. In three steps he was up on the walkway in the bright light and after three more he was at the kitchen screen door. Having often snuck in for a snack he knew exactly how to open that door silently.

A few seconds later he was inside. All the while his mind was racing with what type of food to take. Donny knew that he would not have attempted what he was doing if he had not known every intimate detail of what was inside. But this was his home, and he did know. On the right was a walk-in pantry and on the left a walk-in linen cupboard. Then there was the actual kitchen with a big refrigerator and freezer on the left and along that side wall benches with pots and pans and the sink. On the right was a set of cupboards and drawers with knives, forks, spoons, plates, cups, and so on. In the middle of the room was a kitchen table that often doubled as the breakfast table for the family and beyond that was the stove, a nice new gas one which had replaced the old wood burner that Donny had actually loved, as it kept everything warm on those cold winter nights when temperatures dropped below freezing.

Sliding open the pantry door, Donny made his way in, his eyes scanning the shelves. These were laden with cans, bottles, packets and bags of food. Quickly he spotted what he wanted: cans of ham and of corned beef. He grabbed a couple and then realised he needed something to carry it all in.

And one for Vaughan.

He cast his gaze around and located what he wanted, the shopping bags his mother took with her on the monthly trip to town. He had just picked up one of these when he heard the kitchen screen door being opened. He had been listening for the sound of anyone coming along the walkway but hadn't heard anything. And now someone was coming into the kitchen! Silently he cursed himself.

I didn't slide the door shut!

His heart leapt into his mouth and something close to panic surged as he looked frantically around for a place to hide in that tiny space.

Chapter 18

TENSE MINUTES

There was nowhere!

Donny tensed, ready to leap out and knock the person aside and try to get out. Then into the doorway stepped Sharlene. She was looking into the pantry! Donny saw her eyes go wide and her mouth open in surprise. Not knowing if she was with the crooks, he shook his head and put his finger to his lips.

For a tense few seconds the pair stared at each other. To his intense relief, Sharlene did not cry out and was alone.

With a wry smile, she said softly, "Hello Donny. Those horrible men in there were just making bets on whether you were still alive."

That 'horrible men' comment eased a lot of Donny's anxiety about whether she was friend or foe.

"How many men are there?" he whispered.

"Three, and there's another one wandering around on guard outside," she answered. "Your Uncle James seems to be their boss and there's a guy they call Ringer and another horrible brute."

"You won't tell on me?" Donny asked.

Sharleen shook her head. "No fear! They have taken my mum and me hostage and are making us do all the work. Look, just wait a minute while I take them back some cream. That's why I came. Then I can help you."

Donny could only nod and Sharlene came into the pantry, studying the shelves. Donny pointed up.

"Third shelf," he said.

Sharlene reached up and took a can of cream and nodded thanks before vanishing back out the door. As she went back through the screen door, Donny was assailed by doubts.

If she really is with the crooks, she has got away and can just call them, he thought.

In which case the best option was to run, now! But something about her attitude and body language calmed him and despite being very anxious he stayed. But he did not waste the time.

144

Condensed milk! he thought. *Vaughan will like that.*

He knew he did. One of his most enjoyable treats was to be allowed to open a can of sweetened condensed milk and to eat a spoonful or two!

But cans are no good. Once we open one, we will have to eat the entire contents at once.

From having done just that he knew how sick that might make them feel, however enjoyable to start with! But he knew there were also tubes of condensed milk. These were taken by the stockmen so they could make a brew when out on the run. And there they were. Donny slid his cans of meat into his bag and then grabbed four tubes and slid them in as well. Then he looked around for what else he could quickly take. Some small tins of peaches and fruit followed.

As he was doing this, he heard footsteps on the walkway and again tensed. But it was Sharlene. She came in and looked at him.

"What are you doing?"

"Getting some food. We haven't eaten for two days," Donny replied. His stomach reinforced this by making gurgling noises.

Sharlene grinned. "The ugly guy reckons you and your mate are both dead out in the desert. Your Uncle James isn't sure and that Ringer bloke has bet them that you are alive. But they don't think the other kid would make it. Did he?"

Donny nodded but did not want to say any more. "Is my dad here and Uncle David?"

Sharlene shook her head. "Neither. Your Uncle David was allowed to drive away but they said they would shoot your dad if he went to the police. I think your Uncle David has gone to Sydney to get some ransom money. I don't know where your dad is."

"Could my dad be in one of the other buildings here?" Donny asked, his mind doing a quick inventory of possible hiding places.

Sharlene shrugged. "Don't know. But if he is we haven't taken him any meals."

That was bad news for Donny, and he felt a real stab of anxiety. "What about my grandad?"

"Yeah. He's here. He's locked in his room. And he's very upset. I just took him his dinner a while ago," Sharlene said.

He would be, Donny thought. *He must be very disappointed in Uncle James.*

He said, "Do you think I can rescue you all: my mum and Aunty Beryl and grandad and you and your mum?"

Sharlene shook her head. "Not easily. They've all got guns, and all the doors and windows are locked except the back door. Here, give me that bag and grab another. Come in to the kitchen and I will get some stuff for you."

Donny was not keen on leaving the pantry but, after a quick glance along the walkway, he hurried through into the kitchen. He followed Sharlene left to the fridge and freezer.

She opened the big freezer in the corner. Lifting the lid, she said, "I told them I was coming back for ice cream. I'll just take it through, and you grab what you want, a loaf of bread to start with."

She hurried away carrying a 4-litre plastic bucket of ice cream and Donny did as he was told. Leaning in he took two loaves of bread and shoved them into the second shopping bag.

They won't noticed they are gone, he thought.

The station bought loaves of bread by the dozen every week or so and they were put in the freezer to keep fresh. Again, he looked into the freezer but could not see anything else that might be useful. There was lots of frozen meat, hams, mince, sausages, chickens and so on, but there was no way he was going to try to cook anything.

Now very anxious to be out of that room, he closed the freezer and turned to the big floor-to-ceiling refrigerator beside it and opened a door.

Ah yes! Some cheese and there's some cooked sausages we can eat cold. And I'll have those two left-over rissoles.

His gaze roamed around the interior of the big fridge, noting butter, vegetables, a whole array of bottles of chutney, sauces, gherkins and so on. But his mind rejected anything that needed to be kept cold. Then his eye lit on several large bottles of Coca Cola in the door.

"Ah, yes!" he muttered.

The idea of having a cold drink of Coke had instant appeal. He lifted one out that was partly empty and hastily unscrewed the lid. Putting the neck of the bottle to his lips he took a gulp, and nearly coughed as the gasses and sharp cold of the liquid hit the back of his throat.

Easing it back he then took a slower sip. *This might help settle my upset stomach too,* he thought, remembering something he had heard about sugar killing the germs that cause such embarrassing ailments.

As he took another drink, he heard Sharlene returning. She let the screen door slam and then looked around the open door of the fridge.

"What are you doing? Oh, you grubby boy! Use a glass like a civilised person. Here, give that to me and grab another full bottle and take it. It will be good for energy and hydration in the heat tomorrow."

She took the open bottle and turned to the sink. Donny reached in and pulled out a full bottle and slid it in beside the bread. As he did, he heard footsteps approaching along the walkway. Sharlene was busy filling a big glass with Coke, and she looked over her shoulder in alarm.

"Behind the fridge door, quick!" she hissed.

Donny obeyed at once, moving to his right around the right-hand door of the fridge and trying to press back into the tiny space between the fridge and the freezer. By then his heart was hammering and he was tensing ready to run.

The screen door squeaked open and the footsteps came through past the pantry. Then the man with the gun appeared just past the other side of the left-hand fridge door! To Donny's surprise, Sharlene went to meet him, moving as though to return the Coke bottle to the fridge and holding the full glass in her left hand.

Cool as could be, she said, "Your tea is there on the table, under that dish. And if you want any ice cream or lemon meringue tart, you'd better get into the dining room quickly before those other gutses scoff it all."

The man pointed to the glass of Coke. "Can I have some of that?"

Sharlene handed it to him. "Here. Now wait a moment while I get you a knife and fork."

Donny was filled with admiration with how she just handed the man the glass and then walked out of sight past him and started rummaging in a cutlery drawer. The man had hefted his gun, a pump action shotgun he noted, to his other hand and now tilted his head back and quaffed half the glass of Coke in one go.

If he glances back he will see me, Donny thought, his heart racing as the adrenalin surged through him.

He was sure his lower legs and boots must be visible below the bottom of the fridge door. The man was just finishing the drink when Donny heard more footsteps approaching and the screen door open again.

I'm sunk! he thought, fearing that another member of the gang was going to come into the kitchen.

Then his Uncle James spoke from the other side of the fridge. "What are you doing here, Reggie? You are supposed to be out there on guard."

"Just getting me tea," Reggie replied in an aggrieved and slightly rebellious tone. "Besides, I can't see anything out there and I think it's a waste of time. Those kids will be dead out there by now."

Uncle James spoke sharply back. "I don't think so. We have tracked them all the way to Number Five Bore. That means they got some water and they could be heading this way."

"They couldn't walk that far! They're only young kids, aren't they?'

"Donny's a tough little bugger, the cheeky brat! He might, but I dunno about the other one. He's a city kid and doesn't look very fit. We will go and follow them in the morning."

"Maybe, but even if they come here, they can't do much. We can just lock up the house and let the dogs loose and they can't get in," the man, Reggie, replied.

"Well, I'm the boss," Uncle James snarled, "And I'm payin' ya. So eat that food quickly and get back out for a bit longer."

"Yes, boss," Reggie answered.

He handed the now empty glass to Sharlene, who handed him a knife, fork, and spoon in return and then turned to pick up the covered plate on the table. She removed the cover and Donny was instantly hungry.

Roast beef and baked potatoes with gravy! he noted.

Uncle James obviously stood aside while Reggie turned (Luckily away from the fridge) and went towards the door. Then he said sharply to Sharlene, "And what are you doing here, girlie?"

"I was getting him his dinner and now I am going to wash up," she retorted angrily.

As she did Donny noted that she was taller than him and possibly stronger, and then, being a normal male, noted that she was just developing a lovely womanly shape.

And under all those freckles she is actually quite pretty.

He was particularly taken by the way her hair glinted under the light, reflecting a lovely copper-coloured sheen. He certainly admired her self-control.

Uncle James snorted but obviously accepted this as he turned to follow Reggie. "Make sure you don't go outside, girl. We've got some savage dogs out there."

Sharlene made no answer to this but did scowl as Uncle James turned away. Donny found his heart was pounding so hard there was a swashing, thudding sound in his ears. He heard the screen door open and bang twice and the footsteps receded towards the house. Sharlene looked at him and then gave a theatrical silent sigh.

"That was close!' she murmured.

"I'd better get out of here," Donny replied.

"Have your glass of Coke first," she replied, reaching in to grab the half empty bottle.

While she refilled the glass, Donny looked quickly around the kitchen. He was trembling now as the reaction set in, but his mind was busy working.

"There's some fruitcake in that tin. I'll cut a slice while you grab a few biscuits," he said.

Stepping out from behind the door, he hastily opened the cake tin on the bench and then grabbed a knife to cut it. Sharlene handed him the glass and said, "You'll need knives and forks."

"And a spoon," Donny added as he sliced off two generous slices of fruitcake.

Sharlene hurried across to the cutlery drawer and came back with these items. "And a can opener, and salt," she added.

These quickly wrapped them in a tea towel, and they were placed in the other shopping bag. Donny noted a roll of paper towel. Remembering his humiliating problem of cleaning himself down at the creek, he stepped across and grabbed it.

"Instead of dunny paper," he explained, blushing as he did. He knew there was no chance of them going to a toilet inside the house to get any toilet paper.

Donny now grabbed the glass of Coke and began drinking, pointing up to the biscuit cupboard (one of his favourite places).

"Packet of biscuits please," he managed to say between gulps. Sharlene reached up and placed a packet of Orange Slice in his bag, which was now feeling quite heavy.

"Where will you go?" she asked.

Donny was thinking to the highway, but he did not want to say that in case the crooks somehow got the information out of her. Instead, he said, "Please don't tell my mum we are alive and well," he croaked.

He knew the uncertainty would be causing her a lot of pain but feared her attitude would then unconsciously transmit a message to the crooks.

Sharlene nodded. "I'll just tell her what your Uncle James just said, that they have found your tracks at the Number Five Bore. That will cheer her up and give her hope."

"Thanks. I'd better be going now," Donny said.

He placed the empty glass down and picking up the first shopping bag. It had two cloth handles but also a longer strap that he was able to put over his head to carry it slung. On an impulse he picked up an apple from the bowel of fruit on the bench and shoved it in his pocket. Picking up the other bag by its handles he moved towards the door.

Sharlene shook her head, closing the fridge door, and said, "I'll go first and block them if they see you."

That really impressed Donny. As Sharlene went towards the screen door, he peeked around the corner and then, seeing none of the crooks, followed. A few seconds later he was outside on the walkway. He was surprised when Sharlene kept walking.

"I'm going to get the dirty dishes. That will distract them," she murmured. "Good luck!'

By then they were at the steps going down the side of the walkway and Donny fled down them silently, casting an anxious glance back over his right shoulder as he did. Now trembling with reaction, he hurried away across the well-lit lawn towards the side gate. He heard Sharlene open the dining room screen door and speak but there was no angry shout to indicate he had been seen.

Made it! he thought. *But they are on our trail. Can we get away before they track us down?*

Chapter 19

INTO THE NIGHT

Dry in the mouth with fear, Donny hurried back out into darkness. A few seconds later he was across the lawn and at the side gate. Carefully he opened it and stepped through. As he went to close the gate, he remembered his hat and had to step back into the yard to get it.

I'd look a goose getting cooked tomorrow without it, he thought.

After closing the gate, he made his way at a quick but quiet walk across to the stables and along to the water tank where he had left Vaughan. Vaughan had heard him coming and hid until he saw who it was.

"What have you got there?" he whispered.

"Food. Come on, let's get away from here so we can eat and talk," Donny replied.

There was a minute of delay while the full bottles of tank water were carefully slid into the bags and Donny then handed the one without a strap to Vaughan to carry.

"Bloody hell! It's heavy!" Vaughan cried as he picked it up.

"It won't be when we've had dinner and a big drink," Donny retorted.

Reaction was now setting in and he found he was shivering as though he was freezing. The boys started walking across the open yard towards the buildings that normally housed the stockmen.

As they walked, a horrible thought came to Donny. *The crooks have tracked us to Number 5 Bore. And we have just walked all around the stables and across to the yard and back and made no attempt to brush out our tracks!* For a few moments he felt sick, and then angry with himself. But then he just shrugged. *There are probably a lot of other boot prints there and they might not notice, not until they track us from the creek tomorrow, and then the hunt will be on!*

Vaughan walked beside him and, as they passed the first building, a nice old bungalow with a few trees on the north side, he said, "Where are we going?"

"To the highway I reckon. The crooks have found our tracks and have followed them to the Number Five Bore," Donny said.

"How did they do that? I thought we were very careful."

"We were, but I suspect the pattern shows up more clearly from the air. And we must have missed a few footprints. And out in all the open country we just walked along," Donny replied. He was annoyed by that 'we', remembering how little Vaughan had actually done.

"So they will catch us tomorrow."

"Not if we move fast enough," Donny said. He then clenched his jaw with grim determination.

"What did you... argh! What's that?" Vaughan cried.

"A horse. It'll be my pony, Minnie," Donny replied.

It was. Out of the darkness came the pony, snuffling and then neighing happily. She came hurrying over to Donny and he put out his hand to pat her forehead. Then he remembered the apple. Minnie was the reason he had snatched it up. Quickly he took it out and held it near her muzzle.

"Here you are, Minnie, old pal," he said.

The pony daintily took the apple in her teeth and began to crunch on it. Donny stopped and patted her.

"Sorry old girl. I will give you a proper rub down and we can have a good gallop in a few days."

Then he felt a surge of resentment. *If stupid Vaughan could ride a horse we could have one now, and be at the highway by sun-up!*

He resumed walking northwards past the buildings. Vaughan walked with him and so did Minnie until they came to a barbed wire fence that ran across their route.

"Top end of the Horse Paddock," Donny explained. "Well, goodbye for a bit old horse."

He patted Minnie and felt his heart tighten up with emotion. Knowing his mother was a hostage back there and that his father was a prisoner somewhere unknown got him all teary. He managed to suppress this, not wanting Vaughan to sneer.

After a gruff goodbye to the pony, he followed Vaughan's example and lay down and rolled under the bottom strand. That put them out on more open country with the main station road not far to their right. That was too close for comfort for Donny, so he led the way slightly downhill until they were again close to the trees lining Burke Creek.

It was easy walking, even in the starlight, as there was very little vegetation. But it was starting to hurt. The sore muscles and chafing all began to add their protests to each step and Vaughan groaned or whimpered from time to time although he gamely kept up. When they had gone about a kilometre, they came to a vehicle track that ran east to west across their route. Donny turned left and walked through the grass beside it.

From behind, Vaughan called, "Where are we going? Where does this road go?"

Once again, Donny was astonished, knowing that Vaughan had been to the station on several holidays and even along this particular road.

"It is the road to Number Four Bore and Number One Bore, and there is a branch to Glen Conner Station," he said.

"Are we going there?"

"No. I am going across to the west side of the creek and we will then walk north. That puts all the trees along the creek between us and the main station road," Donny explained.

He was going to add thoughts on the danger of the crooks using spotlights, but did not bother. *He can work it out for himself why that is safer.*

They were in among the trees along the creekbank by then and had to go very slowly as the bank was very steep, almost vertical, and Donny had no desire to get a sharp stick in his eye. He knew they could have just walked down the graded cutting along the road but was still determined to make tracking them difficult. At the bottom, however, he did step up onto the low concrete floodway the station had constructed to stop vehicles bogging in the wet. This was easy walking and then it was uphill. Here Donny switched across to the right-hand side of the concrete and then made his way up the steep bank through some long grass and prickles that got them both swearing.

"Bloody hell! Can't you find a better way?" Vaughan grumbled.

"You bloody lead then!" Donny snapped back.

I've just about had enough of Vaughan, he thought.

He then had to use his hands on a tree trunk to haul himself up a steep section. On top he turned right and began weaving north-west through the trees and bushes until he came out into open country again.

Even then he did not stop, despite a few requests from Vaughan. He plodded on for another half a kilometre and then stopped at a clump of trees that offered plenty of cover.

"This will do. Let's have a feed and I will tell you what happened," Donny said.

He eased off the shopping bag and carefully set it down against a tree. The two boys seated themselves and Donny began to extract food that could be easily eaten from the bags. The big bottle of Coke was an instant hit with Vaughan. He could hardly wait to unscrew the cap and put it to his lips. Donny smiled with satisfaction and then took a turn having a drink. He did not mention he had already had a big drink in the kitchen.

Donny groped in his bag and found one of the cooked sausages. "Here, have this," he said, passing it to Vaughan. Then he said, "Stop! Put salt on it." He dug around until he found the wrapped-up saltshaker and passed it across.

As Vaughan sprinkled salt on the sausage, he said, "Salt is what we need. We have been sweating salt for two days now. If you drink too much you wash out more salt and then your nerves don't work properly and you get cramps."

Donny half-believed that so took the saltshaker when Vaughan had finished with it and used it on the second sausage. Even before he bit into it, his palate was telling him he really did need the salt. That first mouthful was almost bitter but oh!...

Vaughan went on, "Our cadet instructor said most people get it all wrong about heat and dehydration. They drink too much and that makes them sick. You've got to eat as well and include salt. They learned that the hard way when some champion athletes dropped dead doing endurance runs over the Kokoda Trail in New Guinea."

"I know that, in Papua," Donny replied gruffly. He had learnt that at the last Anzac Day ceremony in Golden Dawn.

"Yeah, that's right. Anyway, these guys all drank and drank and then just had heart attacks. It took the medical people a while to work out how such healthy athletes could just keel over. But it was because their heart muscles cramped. So you need some salt," Vaughan said.

Donny could only agree, his mouth now full of chewed sausage. That was swallowed and he then had another drink and dug into the bag to find the two rissoles. One was offered to Vaughan and he ate the other. While they sat eating, Donny described how he had crept in to listen and then into the kitchen before being sprung by Sharlene.

"Who's she?" Vaughan queried.

"She's a girl a few years older than me, twelve or thirteen. She lives on Glen Morris Station," Donny explained.

"How do you know her?"

"She did Distance Ed until she went to High School and she was on a few of our in-reaches," Donny explained. "Now she goes to boarding school in Charters Towers."

"How come she and her mum are here?"

"They were on their way to spend a few days in town but dropped in to say hello as they went past," Donny explained. "The crooks just stuck them up and made her mother phone her relatives and say they were staying here for a few days as my mum needed some help."

The fruitcake was brought out after more Coke was drunk. There was no way to measure the Coke, and Donny suspected Vaughan was drinking a bit more than his fair share but he did not object, having had a good guzzle in the kitchen. He explained what he had overheard and puzzled over where his father might be.

"I don't think he is in one of the buildings back there or they would have had to guard him, and feed him and the guard. Sharlene was sure there were only four crooks there."

"So there might be a fifth one somewhere else if your dad is a prisoner some other place," Vaughan suggested.

Donny could only gloomily agree, and he began to puzzle over where that might be. At least two places came to mind, but he had no way yet of checking on them. "So I am going to tell the cops," he said.

Vaughan was horrified. "But those men said they would shoot your dad if anyone went to the police!" he cried.

Donny's stomach churned with apprehension at that, but he shook his head. Despite having strong doubts, he said, "I don't think they will. That would get them into far more trouble than just the kidnapping and robbery. I doubt if the other gang members would allow it, and I didn't think Uncle James hates Dad so much he would do such a thing. I think it is just a threat to scare us."

"Plenty of brothers have killed each other," Vaughan said gloomily.

Donny shrugged, and said, "I am walking to the highway as fast as I can." He did not say 'we' as he was determined to go alone if Vaughan was a problem.

"How far is it?"

"About thirty k's," Donny replied. "We can knock over twenty tonight at least and should get there mid-morning."

Vaughan groaned at this. "Which way is it? How do we navigate?" he asked.

"Easy, we just walk north beside the creek here and it takes us there. I don't even need the stars. Anyway, you can hide here if you don't want to come. Just don't tell those men what I am doing if they catch you," he said.

"I'll come with you," Vaughan replied. "Can I have some more Coke please, that has really lifted me up."

Donny was secretly very pleased. *I can just leave him at a waterhole if he breaks down,* he told himself as he passed the Coke bottle to Vaughan

The Coca Cola bottle was soon empty, so Donny carefully emptied one of the big beer bottles into it and then screwed the cap back on. He then placed the empty beer bottle in the bag as well.

As he did, Vaughan slapped loudly at his other hand. "Bloody mozzies!" he cried.

There were, a lot. They were buzzing and biting. It gave them incentive to pack up and stand up. Both needed a pee by then and Donny realised he was now feeling goose bumps from the night chill.

"Let's start walking. It will warm us up," he said.

As before, it hurt to get going but once they were plodding along the aches and pains seemed to subside into one general mass of misery. The going was easy, flat and with very little grass and almost no spinifex. Donny was sure he was going the right way but when they stopped for a moment he looked around for the Southern Cross, just to check. Remembering Vaughan's diagrams, he soon found the Cross, lying on its side and starting to set. It was directly behind them.

Good! he told himself.

They did not stop for more than a few minutes as the cold breeze had sprung up and walking helped warm them. Donny knew he was sore, but still had not developed any blisters but could see that Vaughan was definitely hobbling. But now he wasn't worried about leaving him as they were beside the creek. He did not know if there was water in that section of it as they usually went past further out on horses or motorbikes, and he had never actually walked along the bed of the creek, particularly as it frequently broke into two or three channels. But he did know there were two permanent waterholes between there and the highway so he was sure they would be able to find water.

But despite the food and soft drink, he was feeling very weary. The sleep during the day had been one of exhaustion and had not left him feeling very refreshed and he knew he was tiring quickly. Gritting his teeth he doggedly kept putting one foot in front of the other.

As they walked, the boys encountered the usual night problems of prickles, animals, birds, mosquitoes, and other annoyances. There were a few cattle, and Donny made a note of them as he did not think there should be any in that area at the moment.

They must have wandered. I'll tell Dad, he told himself.

That notion brought tears to his eyes and he snuffled a bit, not wanting Vaughan to notice in the starlight.

After a bit, Vaughan stopped and said, "Let's be practical. I'm not as fit as you. So let's walk for the count of 500 paces and then stop for the count of five minutes, then walk another five hundred.

"Okay, Donny agreed. He was actually glad to stop for a few minutes, despite having that driving urge to push himself on.

I'll be no use to Mum and Dad if I just push myself till I collapse, he rationalised.

After that they moved steadily but slowly on. A small creek with a few scattered trees along its course wriggled its way in across the plain and was difficult to cross as it was too wide to jump and steep-sided. Luckily the bottom was dry. There were a few patches of saltbush and spinifex that they had to weave their way through, and with the fear of snakes returning every step took a little toll of courage. There were also stretches of gibbers and claypan. They were easy to walk on but there was a niggling fear that they might be leaving boot prints that were very visible from the air.

Donny tried to keep track of time by the speed at which the Southern Cross vanished below the skyline, but he knew it was very approximate. He estimated he had been in the kitchen at about 8pm so now decided it was close to midnight. Keeping track of the distance was much harder. He thought they had covered between 5 and 7 kilometres when it was time for another rest stop. He knew he needed to rest as his muscles were now starting to tremble and felt drained of any energy.

With a groan he sat down on a claypan they had found. Vaughan sat down and then took off a boot and a sock and rubbed and tended to his feet.

"I've got a few blisters," he muttered. Then he was hit by cramps in his thigh muscles.

So was Donny and he cried in agony and pummelled at the knotted muscle tissue until the pain eased. Vaughan lay back sobbing and rubbing before putting his sock and boot back on. Then he had a drink, lay back and stretched out. Donny did likewise. Staring up at the stars he shivered from a mixture of cold and anxiety.

Oh, I hope Dad is alright! he thought.

His eyes closed and he slid into a sleep of exhaustion. Next to him Vaughan also slept.

A cramp woke Donny, and he hit at it and sobbed in pain. As he did, he opened his eyes and looked around, half stupid with sleep.

"Where am I? What's going on? On no! We went to sleep!" he muttered.

Rolling to his hands and knees he saw that Vaughan was snoring beside him. He began shaking him, realising as he did that both he and Vaughan were shivering from the cold. Vaughan took a minute or so to rouse and then was just as disoriented.

"Wha? Wha'sa matter?" he muttered.

"We went to sleep! Come on, get up! We need to get moving!" Donny cried.

He struggled to his feet and stared around anxiously and then looked up at the stars. To his horror, he saw that the Southern Cross was now completely gone. And when he looked to where he thought north was, he found he was quite unsure. A little stab of shame and panic lanced through him and he shook himself and again stared at the stars.

Then he saw three bright stars close together in line. To his dismay, they were high in the sky.

"Is that Orion?" he cried, grabbing at Vaughan to get him up.

Vaughan stood and looked. "Yes."

"Bloody hell! We've been asleep for hours!" Donny cried. He was angry with himself and dismayed at the mistake. "Come on, grab your gear and let's go!"

To his relief, Vaughan did, and the boys resumed their weary plod. Donny was furiously angry with himself as he had planned to cover 20 kilometres at least, but he now suspected they had not even done half that. Sick at heart he began walking as quickly as he could. His dismay grew even more when he detected a faint lightening in the sky off to their right. Looking hard at it he wondered what it was.

That's east. Surely that's not the sun coming up? he wondered.

It wasn't. It was the moon, a pale sickle of moon with the dark portion just visible.

Vaughan noted it too, and said, "Must be about four or five o'clock. The sun will be up soon."

That idea added to Donny's sense of mounting alarm, and he tried to walk even faster but Vaughan complained and told him to slow down.

"You will exhaust yourself. Take it easy. Remember the tortoise and the hare," he said.

Donny was in no mood for nursery rhyme parables so just snorted but he did concede the logic and slow his pace. Moodily, he watched the moon climb up, causing the stars to mostly disappear and even making Orion difficult to see. For another two hours or so they plodded slowly on, resting as much as walking. It became a real test of endurance.

Then the sky to the east began to lighten and start to turn pink. *Dawn!* he thought. A feeling of sick failure churned in his stomach. To try to keep his spirits up, he told himself that they probably had a few hours yet. *If Uncle James flies back to the Number Five Bore and tracks us to the homestead, then that will take a while. We should reach the highway if we keep pushing on.*

The boys trudged on and Donny became more anxious as it rapidly became light. Then the sick feeling shifted to his gut as a sinking feeling of despair and failure as the faint tremor of helicopter rotors came to him on the still air!

Chapter 20

VAUGHAN

The sound of the approaching helicopter sent a chill of fear through Donny. For a few seconds he just stood and stared back in the direction the sound was coming from.

"The helicopter! How did they know to search here so soon?" he cried. Feelings of defeat and despair almost overcame him.

"Saw our tracks at the house or the stable probably," Vaughan suggested, and grabbed at Donny's sleeve. "Come on, get under cover!"

Both boys started running towards the trees along the creek. Except that this section of creek was wider and divided into three or four channels of varying depths, with more long grass than trees. Plus the trees were mostly isolated and stunted. But that was all the cover there was so the boys each chose a tree and hunched in under the sparse foliage.

"Don't look up!" Vaughan cried. "Our cadet instructors told us that. If you look up at an aircraft your face reflects the light and is very obvious. So don't."

Donny nodded and hunched against the trunk of his tree as the sound of the helicopter grew rapidly louder. He found that not looking at the thing was hard to do. Every part of his being seemed to quiver with uncertainty, and he had to control an almost overwhelming urge to look at the object of his fear. To stop this, he pressed his face into his sleeve and tried to use his ears.

Then the helicopter swept low overhead. At that, Donny just had to risk a glance, thinking no-one in it would be able to look back and down. He was just in time to see the helicopter buzz away from him.

They haven't seen us, he thought.

But then the helicopter suddenly turned with a clatter of rotors. It swept around to the left and came heading back. Donny gaped at it in alarm and then remembered to hide his face.

But he had seen people in the helicopter peering down and realised he needed to have moved around to the other side of the tree. Movement beside him told him that Vaughan was doing just that.

As he did, Vaughan called to him, "Too late! Don't move now! Don't look up!"

To Donny's horror, the helicopter buzzed low overheard just out over the open country and then began to swing left again to come across behind him. He risked a glance under his left arm and was dismayed to see Uncle James apparently staring at him.

"I think they have seen us," he cried. It came out almost as a sob.

"They have," Vaughan agreed. "So take off your bag and get ready to run."

"But we might need the food and water," Donny replied as he watched the helicopter circle around behind him and then come clattering down in an obvious landing attitude.

"If we don't outrun them, you won't need it," Vaughan retorted. "Maybe we can fool them and circle back to get it. Now hurry!'

Donny was very reluctant to part with that bag of food and water but, as the helicopter clattered low overhead, he realised Vaughan was right. As the helicopter settled about 50 metres out from the trees, he lifted the strap over his head and placed the bag in the long grass under the tree.

"They might have guns," he shouted above the roar of the helicopter's engine.

Vaughan shook his head. "Maybe, but I don't think they'll use them. They want us alive, not dead. Now get ready and run when I say so. Follow me."

As the helicopter's skids settled on the flat ground and the rotors flung up a swirling mass of dust and sand, Vaughan stood up.

"Now!" he cried.

A moment later he was running away from the helicopter and down into the first of the creek channels. Donny gaped and noted that Uncle James was the pilot before springing up and following.

The boys slid and jumped down into a dry gully about ten metres across and half that deep, and then went scrambling up the other side to where a line of trees marked the other bank. By the time he reached the top, Donny was already puffing and so was Vaughan. But the older boy just glanced back as he reached the trees and then ran on, still directly away from the helicopter.

As Donny scrambled to his feet at the top of the bank, he also looked back and through the thin screen of trees he saw that Uncle James was looking at them and pointing. Then he saw Thug appear at the front of the helicopter, his head swivelling around as he looked for them. To Donny's relief, the man had no gun.

Oh good! I reckon we can outrun him, he thought. He turned and raced after Vaughan.

By then Vaughan was ten paces ahead and already slithering down the steep sides of another gully. The ground was covered with fairly long grass, still green from the recent rain. The bottom of this gully was only three or four metres deep, but it was too wide to jump so Donny slid down into it and braced himself to lean out against the other wall when he hit the bottom. Vaughan was already clawing at the other bank, but it was too steep and for a moment Donny feared they had made a real mistake. Vaughan gave up and turned to run to his left along the dry bottom. After a dozen paces he found a place where they could scramble up and up he went.

Donny followed, and as he clawed his way up using the long grass and its roots he heard the helicopter engine rev. As his head came above the ground level, he saw the helicopter lift off.

Is he just going to chase us in the air? he wondered.

Then he saw that Thug was not in the helicopter. The man was running towards them and was just reaching the line of trees they had been hiding under. As Donny got to his feet and resumed running, the helicopter banked low overhead, its rotors make a distinct 'thwaking' sound. It was very low and Donny glanced up in fright. His eyes locked with Uncle James's as the man leaned out of the side of the helicopter. Uncle James was glaring at him and shouting but what he was saying was lost in the machine noises.

The helicopter was so low that the rotor downdraft set the grass and leaves thrashing and some dust flew up. Donny stopped and looked up in fear. As he did, Vaughan came back and grabbed his sleeve.

"Run! He can't land here," he shouted.

Donny nodded and understood. *If the rotor blades hit a tree it will crash,* he told himself.

Ashamed at having stopped, he ran with redoubled effort. They reached a third flood overflow channel. It was only a couple of metres wide and about the same deep and Vaughan took it at the run, jumping straight across. Donny followed. But as he landed on the other side his foot caught in the long grass and he pitched headlong. The fall was bruising but did no other harm. And there was Vaughan, grabbing to help him up. As Donny got to his feet, he saw Vaughan looking behind and he also glanced back and saw that Thug was just appearing out of the first flood channel. Thug's face was red and he looked angry.

That spurred Donny into running even faster. They came to the fourth flood channel and it was much bigger, ten metres across and deep, with steep sides and a few muddy pools in the bottom.

The main channel, Donny told himself.

Vaughan had not waited but was already halfway down the steep bank. He was going so fast he slipped on the grey clay, which crumbled under the impact of his boots. Down he went! A moment later Vaughan was rolling in mud at the bottom.

Donny followed, risking the same fate by running diagonally down across the eroded bank. Twice his boots started to slip but he was going so fast that, by the time the ground gave way, he was onto another patch. He reached the bottom in a run so fast he almost went tumbling as he over-ran himself. Aware that the helicopter was still hovering above him, he turned and rushed across to grab at Vaughan's shirt. His own boot slipped in the mud, but he just dug the heel in and managed not to fall. Changing to a better grip, he hauled Vaughan out onto the dry creek bed.

"Thanks!" Vaughan gasped as he rolled over and got to his feet.

He glanced up at the hovering helicopter and set off running northwards along the dry creek bed. Donny followed, very aware that they did not know how close Thug was.

He could be catching up by running along between the creeks, he thought.

Knowing that Thug had the helicopter to guide him as to their location induced a nightmare feeling of almost despair. Vaughan continued to run north along the creek bed. This led them in under some overhanging trees, but a glance upwards showed Donny there was not sufficient foliage to hide them from above. The helicopter was still flying just behind, and Uncle James was obviously tracking their every move. Then they came to another muddy pool. The sides were too steep to run along, and Vaughan was baulked.

"Up the bank to the right," Donny shouted.

Vaughan nodded and set himself at the steep slope, grabbing at exposed tree roots to help get up. It took a few seconds of scrabbling, slipping, and clawing to get to the top. By then Donny found he was gasping and sweating and wondering how much longer they could keep it up. At the top he looked back and saw a very angry Thug only 25 metres away and on the other bank. He had done what Donny feared, but he was now blocked by the muddy pool and had to keep running along the top of the other bank.

Vaughan raced through the line of trees and bushes and out onto the edge of the open country. The helicopter swung out overhead and just behind them. Vaughan glanced back at it and then across at Thug, who was now running almost parallel on the other bank. As he ran, Vaughan made a rude gesture at Thug and then increased speed. Donny felt a mix of emotions at that.

We have really stirred Uncle James and that Thug bloke up, he thought. *They will be really angry if they catch us.*

Anxiety at being hurt or hit helped pump more adrenaline and he ran on. And after a minute or so, during which they covered at least a hundred metres, Donny's earlier assessment was proved correct. They were running faster than Thug who was falling noticeably behind.

But how do we escape the helicopter? Donny wondered.

Vaughan was obviously thinking the same thing, but it did not slow him, just kept him looking around. Then the helicopter gave them a new situation to cope with. Instead of hovering and following just behind them, it suddenly swooped forwards, the wash of its rotors sending both boys to a crouch as it passed very low overhead.

What's it doing now? Donny wondered.

He got the answer a few seconds later. The helicopter was landing about a hundred metres ahead. Vaughan turned his head as he ran.

"He's going to try to cut us off," he shouted.

Donny could only nod agreement. His mind raced in an attempt to come up with a solution. Then Vaughan gasped at him, "We are going back across to the other aside. We need to run really fast to keep ahead of that Thug bloke. Now go!"

He suddenly swerved back through the line of trees to the creek bank. Donny followed, noting as he did that the helicopter was still settling and its rotors still spinning.

Uncle James will be a fool if he gets out before the rotors stop, he thought. He had seen many helicopters land and understood the problem. And that gave him a surge of hope. *Uncle James didn't land far enough ahead!*

Vaughan had run diagonally down into the main creek bed, so Donny followed. As he went down, he noted that Thug was still running along the top of the other bank and was about 50 paces back. Knowing it would be a very close race sent pulses of anxiety through Donny but now he was determined.

They might catch us, but they will bloody well earn it, he vowed.

Down in the creek bed once more, in a thankfully dry section, Vaughan kept running north. Donny followed. He was really gasping now, and he could see that Vaughan was too. Sweat was staining his shirt and Donny could hear his laboured breathing. Glancing anxiously back he got a glimpse of Thug's head and then Thug stopped running and leaned out to look into the creek bed. He saw them immediately and at once came skidding and sliding down into it.

"H... H... He... He's in the cr... creek be... beh...behind us!" Donny gasped.

Vaughan glanced back and at once went left and up what looked like a cattle pad in the creek bank. Donny agreed with that plan and at once followed. As he started up, he saw that Thug had managed to slide down without falling and was now running along the bed of the creek and was only 20 or 30 paces behind. The man was furiously angry, red in the face and gasping.

That gave Donny more incentive to stay out of the man's grasp and he dashed up that cattle pad so fast he caught up with a labouring Vaughan. Donny pushed at him.

"Run! Run! He's just behind me!" he cried, panic starting to well up and choke him.

Vaughan glanced back and then made an obvious effort to run. He crashed through a bush and out onto the grassy flat. As he did, he let go of a branch he had pushed aside and it sprang back, nearly knocking Donny over as he clawed his way through the entangling bush and out into to open. By then Thug was only a few paces behind, his hands starting to reach out in claws to grab at him. Vaughan took one glance and redoubled his efforts. He ran diagonally across the grassy flat to the narrow channel. As he reached it, he swerved away and then ran in a sort of semicircle to leap over it. Donny followed his lead, now only metres in front of those grasping hands. Thug was so close he could hear his laboured breathing and muttered swear words.

The channel was a bit wider than Donny would have wanted to jump, but spurred by fear he ran at it and sprang as hard as he could. Anxiety at stumbling or tripping churned in his stomach but, to his relief, he landed running and kept going. There was a thud behind him and he glanced back and saw that Thug had also managed to leap across.

Bugger! Donny thought.

Vaughan had run on diagonally and Donny approved of that. It meant that Uncle James was now two creeks away and he could not even see the helicopter because of the intervening trees and bushes. But meanwhile Thug was close on their heels and all Donny could do was summon up the will power to force himself to keep running.

They came to the next flood channel and again Vaughan ran long beside it, looking for an easy way across. Donny saw that the bank was just too steep and the bottom was a muddy pool. And running in that longer grass was harder and with the threat of it tripping them at any second. Donny could feel the beginnings of a stitch and he wondered how much longer Vaughan could keep it up. And Thug was still close behind, though audibly gasping.

Suddenly they came to the end of the grass. Vaughan vanished from view and Donny's brain registered that they had been running on a sort of dry island and had come to the top end of it. Beyond was the first creek and Vaughan had gone racing down a narrow cattle pad into the bed of it. But he didn't stay there. He ran straight up another cattle pad, pushing through some branches overhanging the track as he did. Donny, now almost sobbing with the effort of sucking in enough air, followed.

At the top, Vaughan let go of a branch he had pushed aside. Luckily, Donny saw this and was just close enough to grab it so it did not strike him. Instantly an idea came to him and he acted on it, pushing the branch right back as he pushed past it, and then letting it go just as Thug came panting up the path. The branch struck Thug hard and he had to grab it and wrestle it aside.

"Little bastard!" he snarled.

At the top Vaughan had run out onto the open country to the west of the creeks. Donny, maliciously pleased at his little ploy, followed. And so did Thug, but a hasty glance showed Donny the man was a bit further back, maybe ten metres?

He's not as fit as us, Donny thought.

"Keep going, Vaughan," he managed to gasp.

Vaughan did, turning right to run along the west bank of the creek. As they ran, Donny kept glancing to his right, wondering where Uncle James had got to and dreading to see him suddenly appear in front.

Then Uncle James called out from among the trees over to their right! "Hey Benny, where the hell are ya?"

Thug was too winded to call back, so he lumbered to a gasping stop and tried to answer. But he was so puffed he had to take several deep gasps before he could call, "Over here! Hurry up! The little shits are gettin' away!"

We are too! Donny thought, his hopes climbing as Thug started after them, but now 20 metres behind.

Vaughan was obviously hurting but gamely kept going, despite an obvious stitch. They ran on for another hundred paces, but as soon as Thug slowed to a gasping walk Vaughan slowed as well. Donny copied him. The two boys strode along, gulping deep breaths and wiping stinging sweat from their eyes. Both kept glancing back and Vaughan kept the pace fast so that Thug was soon 50 metres behind.

"Okay, let's see if we can lose them," he gasped.

He turned right and plunged down into the first creek bed again. This provoked a shout from behind them and then a distant cry from Uncle James that caused Donny a sardonic smile. The creek bed was luckily dry and was mostly hard clay, but after fifty metres they came to an area of rocks and sand that slowed them. Then the creek divided again and Vaughan took the right hand one.

"We might be able to double back and wreck that helicopter," he croaked.

What a good idea! Donny thought.

"Let's try it," he gasped in reply.

Chapter 21

FIELDCRAFT

Donny was now so annoyed, irritated and upset that the idea of striking back really appealed to him.

"Let's do that," he agreed.

"First we have to hide from these guys," Vaughan replied. "That will take a bit of fieldcraft."

Hearing that really boosted Donny. *Oh good! Big boy is finally taking the lead,* he told himself.

"What's fieldcraft?" he gasped.

"Creeping and crawling and camouflage and concealment and that sort of stuff," Vaughan answered between gulps of air. He wiped sweat and looked around, studying the ground.

Donny looked back but could see no sign of either man. "We'd better be quick," he gasped.

They had just run out of a patch of scrub and bushes and onto an open grassy flat 50 metres across. The whole area had been trampled by cattle and was dotted with hundreds of cow pats. But there were still plenty of tufts of taller grass. Vaughan led the way across it, running and continually looking back. They came to the small, narrow gully and jumped and a dozen paces on came to a shallow waterway, only half a metre across and the same deep. Vaughan jumped this but then stopped and looked back. Donny had jumped by then and was anxious they keep running, knowing that Thug or Uncle James could appear at any moment.

Vaughan pointed down. "In here, quick!"

Donny looked at the shallow ditch, just grey clay with grass hanging over the edges and right out in the middle of the open area.

"Here?" he cried in astonishment.

"Yeah, here," Vaughan replied, jumping down into the ditch as he said it. "Always hide somewhere unlikely and this is as good as we will find. Now get in and lie down facing away from me. If we are spotted just get up and run and we will split up. Now down!"

Donny was reluctant to concede that the shallow ditch was a good hiding place, thinking that in among the thick bushes on the far creek bank would be much better. But he did as he was told and lay down.

I hope there are no snakes in this long grass! he thought.

When he was down, Donny lay on his front with his hands under his chest and one leg drawn up so he could lift into a sprint if he had to. He was very scared and his heart was hammering from fear as much as the exertion. And his breath was coming in rasping, noisy intakes.

Calm down! Get your breath back and get ready to run, he told himself.

Now he could hear the men! First, he heard Uncle James call from further away and then he heard Thug much closer. From the sounds, Donny deduced that Thug had stopped at the edge of the open area and was waiting for Uncle James. He would dearly have loved to lift his head to look and it took a real effort of will power to just lie there, his breathing and heart rate slowly easing.

Then he heard Uncle James much closer, obviously talking to Thug. "Well, where are they?" he snapped.

Thug answered. "Somewhere ahead of me."

"You were supposed to catch the little buggers," Uncle James snarled.

"Yeah, well, they are younger and can run faster than me," Thug replied.

"Which way did they go?" Uncle James asked.

Donny could picture them studying the crushed grass and for the first time he thought Vaughan had made a good decision.

"Straight across I think," Thug answered. "They were just running flat out through here when I last seen 'em."

The voices came closer, and Donny heard the thuds of the men jumping the first small gully. He cringed, heart hammering in anticipation of being discovered. But then the men stopped only a couple of metres away.

"Can't see them," Uncle James commented.

"They'll be hiding in all those bushes along one of these gullies," Thug answered.

Uncle James swore. "Well, we'd better get looking," he said.

"You'd do better to get back in that chopper and look from that. Two of us on foot are gunna have a real problem searching all these channels," Thug replied.

"Yeah, I guess," Uncle James said. He sounded quite unsure, which cheered Donny up a lot. But then Uncle James said, "I think we better rethink all this. I'll go back and get Ringer to come and join you with that Land Rover. Have a quick look here, with Ringer doing a bit of tracking. Then you two head for the highway and watch that."

"You reckon them kids can get that far? It must be thirty or forty k's."

"Thirty-five from the homestead and we are already ten north of there. Yeah, I reckon they can, that little bugger Donny for sure," Uncle James said.

"Yeah, he's a wiry little bastard and he can run, but I dunno about that other kid," Thug said.

"Dave's kid? Yeah, he looks a bit of a slug," Uncle James agreed.

That comment made Donny blush in sympathy with Vaughan, even though he actually agreed with it.

Thug spoke next. "Ya reckon they know which way ter go?"

"Yeah," Uncle James answered. "Young Donny knows all this country well and he will know his north and south, but that other kid wouldn't know shit from clay."

That comment caused Donny very mixed emotions because he had no doubt that he and Vaughan would have been in real trouble if Vaughan had not known how to find direction from the stars. Then Uncle James's next words got him really thinking.

"So you go and watch the highway with Ringer. I'll have a look ahead of you here, but then I gotta go back and refuel. I should have done it last night, and when Ringer found them tracks at the stable at daybreak I didn't wait to do it. So I'll go back and do that and brief Ringer along the way. You better get over closer to the road or he won't see you and you'll have to walk all the way to the highway."

"Bugger that!" cried Thug. "So what do we do if those kids do get to the highway? How ya gunna keep the cops out of it?"

"I'll get Reggie to move all the hostages at the homestead over to his place and I'll be at Clonargh with a story ready. But we don't want that, so we'll work hard at catching them," Uncle James replied.

"What about yer brother? Ya gunna move him?" Thug asked.

"Nah! No casual search is going to find him," Uncle James replied. "But we need to catch these bloody kids. And maybe this time they can get permanently lost out in the desert,"

That 'permanently lost' and all it implied sent shafts of terror stabbing through Donny. He lay there sweating and hoping they would not be discovered. To his relief, the two men started walking east towards the main creek and station road. Donny waited a minute or so until he was sure the men had moved away and then very cautiously raised his head, only to have a bar of sunlight stab right into his eyes.

Bloody hell! The sun is just coming up now! he thought in astonishment.

Squinting he managed to get a glimpse of the two men as they vanished to cross the next creek. As they did, Vaughan also lifted his head.

"Did you hear that?" he whispered.

"Yes."

"Then as soon as they go down into the main creek let's get moving. We need to get ahead of them," Vaughan said.

But Donny had another idea. He had just remembered who Reggie was. "No. We are going south-west to Glen Conner Station," he said.

"Why? Where's that?"

"That Reggie bloke who was the guard last night, I just remembered how I know him. He's the caretaker for Glen Conner. If that is where Mum and Dad are being taken that is where I'm going," Donny said.

In the front of his mind was the notion that there might be fewer guards there, so a rescue might be possible.

"Okay, but we need to stay here a bit longer," Vaughan said. "Wait till that damned helicopter has gone."

Donny saw the sense in that, so they lay in the ditch, perspiring and hoping they weren't seen from the air when the helicopter was again airborne. But they weren't. Ten minutes later they heard the helicopter start up and then lift off. Donny hunched in close to the side, remembering the warning about not looking up. To his relief, the helicopter flew north just over the east side of the main creek. That made sense to him.

The pilot is on the left and can see better from there, he told himself.

Which meant that when it came back it would be over on the other side, following the western flood channel from just out over the open country. And it was, when it came back five minutes later. As it went past a hundred metres away, the boys stayed low and then very cautiously peeked out, searching for Thug. The sound of the helicopter engine receding into the distance was music to Donny's ears.

Now to find Mum and Dad and rescue them!

After a few minutes of looking without seeing any sign of the man, a task made more difficult as the rising sun was in that direction, Vaughan said, "We will have to risk it. Let's crawl back over to the big creek on the western side and go back and get our bags of food and water,"

Donny agreed, even though the idea of crawling in that grass did not appeal. He thought of snakes and then ticks, but what they actually encountered were numerous cow pats, some very new and sloppy. They had to crawl around these but did not manage to avoid all trickles and splashes of the manure; and when sweat and dust were added, they were two very hot and grimy boys when they slid into the western creek bed.

"Try not to leave any tracks," Vaughan commented as they started walking quickly south along the dry creek bed.

Which was easier said than done. Donny would have dearly liked to detour to one of the muddy pools they passed to wash his face and arms but realised he had to put up with being dirty. Finding their gear was a bit tricky too. They had run so far and in such a state of anxiety that the exact location was only found by getting up on the western bank and weaving through the trees and bushes until they almost stumbled over the bags.

Donny had been pleased that Vaughan had been showing some initiative and leadership, but he now had a plan.

"I reckon we just walk quickly south for ten minutes and then strike out south west into the open country," he said, pointing to the vast open plain that extended to the horizon on that side.

"We risk being seen," Vaughan argued.

"Not if we separate and if we go fast enough," Donny replied. "That Thug fella should be over on the eastern side of the creek with lots of trees in between. The only other choice is to wait here until that helicopter comes back and then hope we don't get seen. It will only take about an hour for Uncle James to refuel and get back. It would be better to be three or four kilometres away by then."

Vaughan nodded. "Okay, let's go."

"Not yet. Let's have a big drink and refill these bottles again before we do," Donny suggested.

So they did that. Vaughan emptied his beer bottle, and Donny drank the contents of both his whisky bottle and the plastic water bottle. Then they walked south until they found a suitable pool and very carefully edged out on rocks to refill them. Donny took the opportunity to rinse the sweat and grime off his face and hands, then did what he could to brush out their tracks as they retreated up the bank.

Wouldn't fool an Aborigine but it might be enough to baffle Ringer, he told himself hopefully.

By the time they set out into the open country the sun was well up and the air was already hot. There wasn't a cloud in the sky and Donny was apprehensive about crossing all that desert. Vaughan looked anxious too.

"How far is it?"

"From here? Probably about thirty k's," Donny replied.

"What about water?"

"I am aiming for a little oasis Dad showed me once," Donny answered. "But it's a risk."

"Yes. We could get lost and just die out there. But it is flatter country and fewer sand dunes than what we walked across the last few days. And if I can't find the oasis, we can walk west another few k's and we will come to King Creek, which is like this. Then we will be alright. We can't miss it as it also flows north to south right across the next property," Donny explained.

Vaughan licked his lips and looked apprehensively out at that vast, flat plain where the heat shimmer was already starting.

"Okay, let's go."

Donny was really pleased that Vaughan had agreed to his plan, and he was now determined to rescue his parents without involving the police.

Then we will get the cops, he told himself.

As he and Vaughan walked out from under the shade of the trees, he called, "We will walk a few hundred metres apart so we don't leave an obvious set of tracks," he called. "Just stay in sight of each other."

Vaughan nodded and veered off to the left. Donny angled to the right, keeping the sun behind his left shoulder to get the direction. He walked a quickly as he could, very conscious that Thug was back there somewhere and might see them, and of the time ticking quickly by.

That bloody helicopter will be back soon! he fretted.

Soon the two boys were several hundred metres apart and Donny could see that Vaughan was walking quickly, limping a bit but obviously pushing himself. He suspected that his pride had been stung by the men's comments.

Good! It might make him lift his game, he thought.

As he hurried along, Donny kept glancing back and then to the south, ears listening. He found it particularly pleasing to note how the trees along Burke Creek grew more distant and were becoming rapidly harder to see as the mirage effect of the heat increased.

And it was hot! He found himself sweating so hard that drops trickled down his forehead and into his eyes, the salt stinging and irritating. The salt in his perspiration had the same effect on his chafing and he found he was grimacing and even gritting his teeth in an effort to ignore the pain. He pushed himself to get away from that creek as quickly as he could.

Then there was that vibration in the air. "The helicopter!" he called, but not loudly.

He did not want to shout and hoped that Vaughan had the good sense to just stop and lie down. There were no bushes to hide behind, just a thin cover of short, dry grass. Donny lowered himself and let out an involuntary cry of pain as the sand and pebbles where so hot that it really hurt. Glancing sideways he saw Vaughan had also gone to ground and was just a tiny bump in a vast landscape.

Twisting his head around, Donny looked for the helicopter and then remembered he shouldn't do that. So he just tucked his head under his hat and looked under his arm. But he did not see the helicopter go past. The sound told him it had, and he then heard it buzzing around the creek line behind. But it was so far away that when he did get a glimpse it was just a tiny black dot in the heat shimmer.

We can't just lie here much longer, Donny thought. *We will fry like an egg!*

But they had to endure another ten minutes of that blistering sand and baking sun before the sound of the helicopter receded northwards.

As soon as it did, Donny got up, dusting his hands as he did. He now found that he had forgotten to keep his bag upright and that nearly half the water in his whisky bottle had leaked out. He swore at himself and then took the whisky bottle and emptied it, gulping the nauseating muddy water but thinking it better to have it in him than to risk spilling it again.

I hope Vaughan hasn't spilled his beer bottles, he worried.

It was now obvious to Donny that the heat was going to be a life and death issue. He began to question whether his plan was a good idea. But a streak of stubbornness set him walking again, aiming for a tiny blob on the distant horizon. To his left he saw Vaughan also get up and start walking.

After a time that tiny blob resolved itself into a large bush. It was mostly lost in the heat shimmer, which gave a real mirage effect. Donny aimed for it and after a while decided Vaughan must be doing the same thing as they were getting closer to each other. He was. The boys came together at the bush, a huge clump of spinifex growing in a ring and which offered no shade. Making their way to the west side of the bush they stopped.

"Bloody hot!" Vaughan offered.

"Yes. We'd better find some shade and rest until things cool down a bit," Donny suggested.

"Is the country like this all the way?" Vaughan queried. He already looked very sunburnt and red in the face.

"Mostly. There are a few scattered trees but only one creek like that one back there," Donny said. He pointed to where a lone tree stood up like a tiny model in the far distance. "What about we walk to that?"

To his surprise, Vaughan shook his head. "No. Bad fieldcraft. It is so obvious that it will attract attention. We need to keep away from anything like that."

While they each had another drink, Donny looked out into the heat haze and pointed. "You see that little bump of a hill? We will split up again and meet up there."

"Okay, but not on the hill. Aim a hundred metres to the left," Vaughan agreed. "We don't want to skyline ourselves."

So the walk continued, soon to become a sweaty slog as the heat grew. There wasn't a cloud in the sky and no breeze to give relief. The ground changed to a mix of gibbers and grass, now so hot Donny could feel the heat reflecting up in waves and his feet begin to feel like they were on fire. He began to blink and found his vision going blurry.

Maybe this wasn't a good idea? he worried.

Chapter 22

TEST OF CHARACTER

It took nearly twenty minutes of painful plodding in ever-increasing heat for Donny to reach the place Vaughan had indicated. That was about a hundred metres or so south of the small rise and Vaughan stood there waiting. There was no shade of any sort and Donny was now worried he had made a real mistake.

Vaughan had a drink from a beer bottle, then held it upside down. "Out of water," he said.

"We will drink the Coke bottle then," Donny answered.

But he did not want to. He wanted to keep it as a reserve for emergencies, but then looking at the shimmering heat all around he decided this was the emergency. He shrugged off the bag and dug out the bottle.

As Vaughan finished a drink from it, he said, "Is there any more water ahead of us?"

Donny looked south and squinted. "You see that little cluster of black on that rise down that way?" he said, pointing.

Vaughan took another gulp of water and looked, then nodded. "Yeah."

"That is Number Four Bore. Those are cattle and you can just see the water tank," Donny explained. "But I don't think we should go there as the crooks are certain to look, and they might find our tracks again."

"They'll find our bloody skeletons!" Vaughan croaked.

Donny looked at him and noted that his lips were starting to crack and that his eyes looked bloodshot. He said, "I think it is about five k's away. I'd rather push on and find some shade and wait till it is cool."

"It's a real risk," Vaughan said.

He took another gulp and passed the now half empty Coke bottle to Donny. Donny had a big drink and then screwed the lid back on and placed the bottle back in his bag.

"So where is the next water?"

"In Camel Creek, on the next property," Donny replied. He was very anxious now but still determined.

176

"How far?"

"About twenty k's," Donny answered.

"Bloody hell!"

"Theoretically we could do that in four hours," Donny commented. "But I reckon we stop in the first bit of shade we find, even if it is a lone tree."

"Okay, Vaughan agreed, glancing again at the distant Bore Number 4. "Do we split up again?"

"Yes. Aim for that clump of saltbush or whatever it is," Vaughan said.

He lurched into motion and Donny gritted his teeth to ignore the pain and made himself move.

The next hour was what Donny imagined hell might be like. The terrain was easy, mostly gently sloping gibber plains with a few clumps of bushes and a couple of straggly trees. Vaughan kept pace with him, a tiny figure almost lost in the mirage shimmer. What added a cruel twist was seeing Bore Number 4 in the distance, then losing sight of it in the heat haze and behind a long gentle rise of higher ground. It was the temptation of knowing it was there and that they were walking away from it that particularly tested Donny.

They aimed for a low, flat hill, with Vaughan again warning him not to walk up onto it and skyline himself. They met on its southern slope in sweltering, blinding glare.

As they came together, Donny gave a sigh of relief. About a kilometre ahead were some scattered and stubby trees and more grass. He pointed to them as Vaughan plodded over to join him.

"We will stop in those trees. And we won't separate for this bit."

They began walking and Donny noted that the soil had changed back to sand with small tufts of dry grass and a scattering of bushes. A glance behind showed they were leaving a trail, but he was too hot and tired to find the energy to do anything about it.

As they walked, Vaughan said, "This all reminds me of a joke I heard at cadets. It's about the French Foreign Legion." Donny wasn't in the mood, but he nodded to continue. "Well, these two legionnaires were lost in the desert and were very hungry. They looked everywhere for something to eat. One of them says, 'Let's split up. You go that way and I'll go this way, and we will meet up later at that little hill over there.' So they do and the other guy finds nothing. But after a while he sees all these vultures circling over in the direction his friend has gone. So this legionnaire thinks that maybe his friend is in trouble so he heads that way. It is very hard going as he has to crawl up sand dunes and so on. As he does, he sees more birds arrive and start circling and some even go down to land. He crawls up a sand dune and finds a big claypan and his friend is lying on his back out in the middle. There is a circle of vultures around him and even as the legionnaire looks one of the vultures hops closer and looks like it is going to peck out his friend's eyes. To save him he races down the sand dune and onto the claypan shouting, 'Shoo! Shoo!'. All the vultures flap away and as they do the legionnaire lying down suddenly sits up and shakes his fist at him. 'Oh bugger you!' he shouts. 'I nearly had one then!'

It took Donny a few seconds to understand the joke and then he chuckled, his lower lips splitting painfully as he did.

"That's good," he said.

Vaughan gave a tired smile in return. "Some food would be nice," he said. "You've got some in that bag, haven't you?"

"Yes. Let's get in this shade and we will have breakfast," Donny agreed, leading the way in among a small clump of spindly trees.

"More like lunch," Vaughan commented, glancing up at the sun which was now high in the sky. He put his bag down and eased himself to the ground. Donny took off his bag and dug in it. First, he pulled out a loaf of bread.

"Plenty of bread," he commented.

"Bit dry. Have you got anything with liquid in that bag?"

Donny dug out a big tin of peaches. "Yes, here."

"Oh, good man!" Vaughan commented, reaching out to take the can.

Donny extracted the second can of peaches and then the can opener and spoons. Vaughan praised him for that as well and he felt a real glow of appreciation.

The cans were opened and the liquid drunk. It was a bit sticky but to Donny tasted heavenly. Then he sat and spooned the sliced peaches into his mouth slowly.

"We have to eat them all. We can't take the can with us," he said.

"We've got plenty of time," Vaughan replied. "I don't think we should be walking out in that sunlight. And it will be hard to navigate too as the sun is now so high up it is hard to get the right direction."

Donny nodded and settled to enjoying his peaches. When they were all gone, he took out a slice of bread and found it still moist in the middle. He happily munched on that, and Vaughan joined him. Between bites Vaughan asked if he had anything to put on the bread.

Donny mentally slapped himself for forgetting and then grinned and took out a can of ham. This was sliced up with a knife and added to bread to make sandwiches. In a few minutes it seemed the ham was all gone, and they boys had each eaten two sandwiches. Between them they ate half a loaf in half an hour.

Donny held up the cans of corned beef. "We can have these for tea," he suggested.

"Oh, you have done well," Vaughan praised. Then he nudged the bag and said, "What's that big can in here?"

"More peaches, or maybe pears, I think," Donny replied.

He reached in and pulled out the can. Then he blushed as he saw the label.

"Pears my bum! That's a can of beetroot!" Vaughan cried. He burst out laughing. Donny had to join in. Vaughan shook his head. "We will save them for supper," he said.

Having eaten and had another drink, which lowered the quantity of water to just a few mouthfuls, they lay back in the shade. Stretching out to relax caused a few more twinges and small cramps and then Donny had to go to the toilet. Now he thanked his foresight in taking the paper towel and Vaughan praised him again. He found it a real challenge to go back out into the blazing sun and embarrassing to go behind a nearby bush to do his business, but it was also a real relief. It was even more of a relief to find he was not as runny as he had been. Carefully he covered the paper with sand.

Don't want the helicopter spotting that!

He rejoined Vaughan, who had gone to sleep despite the flies and ants. Finding his shade had moved, Donny shifted to a new spot and sat down. He would dearly have loved to take off his boots and socks to cool his feet, but the sand was so hot he decided against it. But he did take off one boot and sock at a time to cool and check his feet. It was a temporary relief and pleasing to note that there were red spots but still no blisters.

Good boots, he thought. *Dad is always careful about making sure new boots fit.*

Then he sobbed as anxiety about his father and mother welled up. Exhaustion took over and he slid into a deep sleep. For the next five hours or so they both rested, sometimes deep in dreamland but mostly experiencing a restless slumber as they were continually disturbed by flies and ants. And then a crow arrived and perched nearby and let out its horrible *craaark*.

Donny sat up and looked around. It took him a few seconds to realise where he was and to ungum his sleep-stuck eyelids. But there was nothing to see except the shimmering glare and miles of empty desert. He brushed away some flies and tried to swallow. He found he had a disgusting taste in his mouth and that his skin felt hot and dry.

Not good, he thought, listing heat exhaustion as the cause. A headache seemed to confirm this.

Vaughan also woke up and took himself off to relieve himself. When he came back Donny took out the Coke bottle.

"We will finish this," he said.

Vaughan agreed so they drank the last of the water. "How far have we come, do you reckon?' he asked.

"I'd say more than ten k's," Donny replied. "It must be only a couple of k's to the property boundary."

"What time do you reckon it is?"

Donny studied the sun through slitted fingers. It was now low in the west. "I reckon between four and five o'clock," he said. "Still too hot to walk. We will wait another couple of hours. I think we should eat while it is still daylight."

Vaughan did not dispute this, so they sat with their backs to the sun in what little shade they could find and ate. The corned beef sandwiches were hard to swallow but the juice from the beetroot can helped. As he drank some of this, Vaughan grinned.

"We will be doing purple poo now," he quipped.

Donny had to grin. The food was good, and he enjoyed the beetroot as well as the sandwiches. Then he held up the biscuits.

"Might save these for tomorrow," he said. The condensed milk he was saving.

This was agreed to, so they sat and talked until they estimated two hours had gone by. It was definitely cooler by then, so they checked their feet and then stood up and Donny hoisted on his now almost empty bag.

"What about these cans?" he said.

Vaughan shook his head. "Just hide them in the spinifex bush there. It will take too much effort to bury them."

So that is what they did. By then the sun was low and almost shining in their faces but Donny was now feeling refreshed and anxiety spurred him into wanting to move.

They set off, and after the usual period of aches and pains as they warmed up they were able to stride along at almost normal pace. The country remained gently undulating or flat and varied between sand and grass, gibber plain, and claypans. As they walked, across a rock-hard claypan Donny remembered the joke about the Foreign Legion and had to smile.

A dark lump appeared ahead and as they got closer Donny saw it was a dead cow beside a three-strand barbed-wire fence. He had seen plenty of dead beasts over the years and took no particular notice of this one other to observe that it was still putrefying, with empty eye sockets and obvious signs that the scavengers had been at the carcass.

Vaughan wrinkled his nose in disgust. "What's this fence?" he asked.

"Boundary fence between our place and 'Glen Conner'," Donny replied. "Don't leave any boot prints in those wheel ruts," he added, indicating the vehicle track that ran along beside the fence.

They stepped carefully across and brushed out a couple of prints in the sandy soil and then crawled under the fence. As they stood up, Vaughan pointed to the nearby carcass.

"That reminds me of another joke," he said.

"Well, tell me," Donny asked as they resumed marching.

"The same two Foreign Legionnaires are still lost in the desert, and they are starving," Vaughan explained. "As they are walking along, they see this black, shimmering thing ahead. As they get closer, they see it is a dead camel with a swarm of flies buzzing around it." He glanced at Donny and smirked. "Bit like that," he added, jerking his thumb back at the dead cow.

"Go on!" Donny replied, not amused that Vaughan seemed to be testing him.

"Well, they walk up to it and see that the reason it looks like it is moving is because it is a squirming mass of maggots. The flesh has all rotted and is slimy black and green. Anyway, they stand looking at this for a while and then the first legionnaire says, 'Well, we've gotta eat or we die.' So he digs his hands into the rotting flesh and scoops out a big handful and eats it."

As he said this, Vaughan made motions of eating and added chomping, slurping sounds.

Donny shook his head. "Fair go!" he muttered, feeling his stomach churn with nausea.

Vaughan grinned and then clutched his stomach and acted as though he was throwing up. "As the first legionnaire goes to spew, the second one whips of his kepi and catches the vomit in it. Then he lifts it up and looks into it and then reaches in and begins scooping the mess into his mouth. 'Ah!' he said. 'That's better. I like my food warm!'

"Vaughan!" Donny cried. "That is revolting."

"Good joke though, eh?" Vaughan replied. "Tell it at the dining table next time you have something like creamed rice."

At which Donny had to laugh. The boys trudged on, and Donny found he was bending his head forward to so that the brim of his hat kept the setting sun out of his eyes. To him, Vaughan just looked like a boiled lobster.

It'll be dark soon, Donny thought. *We have a chance!*

Chapter 23

SPOOKED

As the sun sank from view, Donny looked around and was heartened to see the Southern Cross. It was already starting to set but was clear enough to work out south-west from.

"You might not have enjoyed being in the army cadets much, Vaughan, but you certainly leaned a lot of useful stuff," he commented.

Vaughan's response was grunt and non-committal shrug. "It had its moments. Some activities were better than others," he said.

Donny did not pursue the subject. Instead, he looked ahead and noted in the rapidly fading light that the country ahead appeared to be flat and open, with a few small rises. He had never been in that part of the neighbouring property and hoped they would not encounter some unexpected obstacle.

As it got dark, Vaughan again asked how far they had to go. "I'm feeling a bit worn out," he admitted.

"So am I," Donny said.

Already his muscles were feeling tired, and he had blurry vision and a real headache. A tight little fear was now gripping his heart, worry over finding water before either became a heat casualty.

"I think we have about another fifteen kilometres," he said.

He actually thought it might be a bit further but did not want to dishearten the older boy. Then, right on dark, they got the first fright of the night. From out of an unexpected dip in the ground ahead, a family of kangaroos sprang up and went bounding away into the darkness.

"Bloody hell! They gave me a fright!" Vaughan said.

Donny could only agree. His own heart had leapt and took quite a few minutes to slow down again. It quickly began to get cold again. There was no breeze and not a cloud in the sky and the only sound was the crunch of their boots on the sand and pebbles and their breathing.

We are a long way from anywhere, Donny thought. *I hope nothing goes wrong.*

But he kept his worries to himself and concentrated on staring ahead and putting one foot in front of another. From time to time, he counted paces as he tried to keep track of both time and distance. Not being on his own place gave him a peculiar feeling he could not quite define. Then it came to him.

Like a soldier being in enemy territory, he thought.

By agreement they walked 500 paces and then found a place to sit down to the count of 500.

"We've got all night, haven't we?" Vaughan asked.

Donny nodded. "Yeah, I reckon. We can't do much without a good look at the place."

He had been to the Glen Conner homestead several times but had never been particularly interested as the people there had been old and not very friendly.

Another 500 paces and rest. Then another. It was as much as Donny felt up to. He was worn out and needed a proper rest and food but was willing to keep pushing himself until his parents were safe. Vaughan had stopped muttering and grumbling all the time but Donny could tell he was still hurting. He was limping and obviously had chafe between the thighs.

But he is doing better, he conceded. *And another 500 so we can sit for a bit.*

Luckily the ground stayed almost flat and almost devoid of any vegetation, so the walking was safe and easy with barely a stumble. Another 500 and sit. Donny was happy that they had now travelled at least three kilometres from the fence. But while they sat there another problem developed.

Vaughan pointed and said, "There goes the last of the Southern Cross. We only have the Pointers now. We'd better make the most of them."

Donny could only agree and, while he would have liked to rest a bit longer, he made himself get up, groaning aloud at the pains. Then it was off across the desert at a steady walk. This time they pushed it until the second pointer vanished below the distant skyline. In that time Donny estimated they had covered another three kilometres. But then they had to sit.

Vaughan and he scanned the sky but there were no other stars he was confident to use. Vaughan again marvelled at how brilliant the stars were and how many they could see.

"Just using the general pattern of stars setting in the west will make sure we are going roughly that way, but it is not as accurate," he said.

Donny stood for a moment staring around and then he stopped and rubbed his eyes and stared to the east.

Is that a light? he wondered. "See there, Vaughan, what's that?"

Vaughan stood beside him and studied the skyline and then shook his head. "Might be a vehicle's headlights, I mean the glow or loom of them with the vehicle out of sight over the horizon."

Now that he looked more carefully, Donny agreed. There appeared to be the glow of possibly two beams of light.

"Definitely moving," he said.

"Maybe the crooks driving along that track beside the fence?" Vaughan suggested.

They watched as the glow moved from right to left and then vanished. Ten minutes of staring in all directions revealed nothing more. Then something howled behind them!

"Dingo!" Vaughan breathed hoarsely.

"Long way away, somewhere along Camel Creek," Donny added.

The howl had set the hairs on the back of his neck standing up, but he did not want to admit he was scared. Luckily the howl died down and silence settled again, an eerie silence devoid of any normal sounds.

Both boys tried to sleep, but it rapidly became too cold for sleeping so they sat and talked. Mostly it was by Vaughan about his boarding school. That was not a topic Donny really wanted to hear about, although he knew that in four years' time he would have to go to one. What particularly bothered him were Vaughan's tales of bullying and silly pranks.

No-one had better bully me, or they will regret it, he vowed.

Then he had a good idea. Digging in his bag he extracted the tubes of sweetened condensed milk.

Passing one to Vaughan he said, "Dessert in the desert!"

Vaughan was very appreciative and said so. For the next twenty minutes they sat and quietly sucked on the tubes, savouring the sweetness and the tiny amount of liquid. It certainly had the effect of lifting Donny's spirits. After consuming half a tube, he felt sick from all the sweetness so screwed the cap back on and put it away for later.

Then suddenly Vaughan sat up and pointed. "Lights!"

Donny joined him and stared. There were faint glows in the haze off to the south. He stared, rubbed his dry eyes and stared again. So did Vaughan.

"Not moving, are they?"

"Just sort of shimmering and going up and down a bit," Donny said.

"Are they some of those Min Min lights?" Vaughan asked, the quaver very clear in his voice.

"Might be, or another vehicle a long way away," Donny replied.

After a few more minutes of watching the tiny lights suddenly glow and fade, Vaughan muttered, "Oooh! That is spooky!"

Donny could only agree but said nothing. The two boys stood and stared but the tiny, distant lights flickered and then faded. For another ten minutes or so the boys stood watching but nothing more appeared. Then Vaughan swung and pointed to the east.

"Orion is starting to come up. We can move."

"Thank Christ for that. I'm getting bloody cold," Donny replied.

"Yes, we can thank Christ, or at least God," Vaughan replied in a censorial tone.

That surprised Donny as he had not known that Vaughan had any strong views on religion. Picking up his bag he set off beside the older boy, renewed hope now welling up.

It must be after midnight, but we still have time to get to the crook's hideout, he thought.

For the next hour they walked slowly with short rests. Donny told himself they had covered another three kilometres.

Must be past halfway, he told himself.

Then they heard the mournful cry of a curlew.

Vaughan shook his head. "I hate that sound! It is really spooky."

"Just a curlew," Donny replied.

He really liked them. A family of them had been nesting in the homestead garden all his life and he thought they were nice birds.

Then they encountered cattle, a whole herd that got spooked by their approach and went stampeding off. Vaughan swore but Donny thought it was a good sign.

"We must be close to water," he suggested.

He knew there were some waterholes along Camel Creek but not exactly where. Five minutes later, just as they were sitting down for another short rest, Vaughan pointed back over Donny's shoulder, south.

"A car!"

Donny looked and saw that the glow of headlights was moving east to west a few kilometres to the south.

"On the road from our place to Glen Conner," he said.

As the vehicle was almost certainly being driven by one of the men, he watched it with deep anxiety. Suddenly a beam of light sprang out from the moving vehicle and swept across the flat desert.

"Spotlight!" Donny cried.

He had been out many times with his father or some of the men when they went 'spotlight' shooting for rabbits, foxes, dingoes, and other feral pests. He was also aware of just how deadly it could be. Most of the men were able to hit a small animal several hundred metres away with just one shot.

"Down!" he said. "And whatever you do, do not look at that beam if it shines on us."

He proceeded to explain the problem to Vaughan. Suddenly, just when the car looked to be well past them, the headlights swung towards them so that Donny could see both lights. It began heading north towards them, the spotlight beam sweeping around on both sides.

Vaughan gasped. "Coming this way! Have they seen us?"

"Don't think so. It is going to pass well ahead of us," Donny replied. "There must be a vehicle track there."

He dimly remembered seeing a track when being driven along that road and had wondered where it went. Then the spotlight beam lit up a line of trees, grey in that light, a few hundred metres beyond the car.

"Camel Creek," he muttered.

Then the beam swung to their side and swept across the flat desert.

"Down! Close your eyes," Donny cried.

But he did not obey his own safety instruction. He dipped the brim of his hat but kept one eye open behind his open fingers. But he was scared and knew it. That word 'permanently' flitted across his mind.

If they shoot us and hide our bodies out here nobody will ever find us, he thought, then trembled.

The beam swept over them but, to his intense relief, did not stop. The vehicle continued driving and was soon crossing in front of them and two or three hundred metres away.

It's on a track alright, Donny noted, seeing both the speed and the trailing dust. *It looks like our Land Rover.* Then a ghastly idea came to him. *If we had walked a bit further before sitting down, we would have been right near that track and not even known it was there!*

As the vehicle drove on, the noise of its motor and juddering as it hit ruts and potholes sounding loud in the still air, Donny watched it, shivering with cold and fear. But his mind was moving just as fast.

"As soon as it is past, we are going to get up and run. See those trees? That is the creek. Don't stop until then," he said.

He then dragged his bag to him and looped it over his shoulder and got ready to sprint. When the car looked to be about half a kilometre away Donny called, "Now!" and sprang up.

Vaughan did likewise and the two boys dashed forward across the flat desert. After a couple of minutes, Donny started to get winded but he could just make out the sandy ruts of the vehicle track in the starlight.

"Jump the track," he commanded, and both he and Vaughan did.

As he ran, Donny kept glancing to his right at the taillights of the vehicle, just visible through its trail of dust. He was worried it might stop and start back, but to his relief the glow and probing beam just kept moving away. But now they were both puffing and slowed to a jog and then to a plod. The line of trees got closer and closer and then they were among them.

Donny stopped and found he was on top of another typical Channel Country creek line, steep banks and a dry bed, very visible in the starlight. He moved over the crest and then stopped.

"Get our breath back," he croaked.

Vaughan was happy to do that, and the boys lay on the bank where they could just see the lights of the vehicle. These were still receding into the distance.

"Made it!" Vaughan gasped. Then he gave a sort of a choking grunt. "Oh bugger! That vehicle is turning around!"

Donny crouched behind cover and watched it come back towards them. He was sure they hadn't been seen but he still felt stabs of apprehension. As it got closer and the spotlight beam began sweeping along the creek line, he and Vaughan both crouched below the bank. After it was past them, he peeked over and watched. Then he nodded. The car was doing what he expected. It had turned right about a kilometre away and vanished from view among the trees.

"It must be going to the Glen Conner Homestead," he said as the lights re-appeared behind them.

Both boys stood and watched until the lights vanished over a rise in the distance. Vaughan then looked at him.

"That's good news, isn't it? Oooh! Bloody hell! What was that?" he cried, 'that' because some creature, bat or bird, had just swooshed very low over their heads with very audible flaps of its wings.

"Owl," Donny replied, trying to pretend he hadn't got a fright as well.

Vaughan swore then muttered, "Do you think we might find some water? I'm really dry."

"Not sure. I seem to remember there was a pool near the road. Let's look," he said.

So they started slowly trudging along the top of the bank, weaving around the trees. There weren't as many trees as there had been at Burke Creek and in places there were large gaps between them. The soil was sandy and that worried Donny as he knew they must be leaving tracks, but in the starlight he could not see how clear they were.

Starlight? he stopped and looked around and then pointed.

"The moon," he said.

The sky to the east had a distinct lightening and the first view of a rising moon at first cheered him and then chilled him.

That means we don't have much darkness left, he thought. His plan was to get to Glen Conner before daylight.

"Must be about four o'clock, or four thirty," Vaughan commented.

"How do you know that? I thought it came up just before daylight," Donny replied.

"It comes up between 45 and 55 minutes later each day I think," Vaughan said. "Sometimes it comes up in the daylight. So sun-up is about six or so."

"That only gives us about two hours to go six or seven k's," Donny commented.

As he wove a route through the scattered trees he kept glancing back at the moon. He had never really studied the moon before, just taken it for granted. Now he noted that the part lit by the sun, which was still below the horizon, was a bright silver crescent but he could clearly see the dark section.

Amazing! he thought.

Suddenly Vaughan stopped and gripped Donny's sleeve. "Wh... What's that?" he whispered.

Donny's gaze followed his pointing finger, and it took him a few moments to work out what he was looking at. But when he did, he almost cried with relief. In the middle of a sandy area stood a large pile of stones. Surrounding it were four posts in a rectangle. A chain connected them.

"That's the Camel Driver's Grave," he replied.

That means we are only a few hundred metres or so from the road and the pool of water.

But the sight had an entitle different effect on Vaughan. "Camel Driver's Grave?" he echoed.

"Yeah, some guy who died back in the 19th Century when camels were the main form of transport. He was found here with a dead camel and buried. They think he might have been an Afghan or Arab so it's not a Christian grave."

"Oh, it's spooky in the moonlight," Vaughan said, a slight tremor evident in his voice. "Let's keep moving."

They did, finding water soon after that. Getting the water was a challenge as the banks were steep and muddy and Donny did not want to leave too many tracks. After ten minutes of searching, he managed to find a dry patch of creek bank with rocks where he could lean out and not sink to his ankles in mud.

All the bottles were refilled and they both had a drink. The water tasted very gritty but did not smell too bad.

"Still going to give us upset stomachs probably," Vaughan predicted gloomily.

By the time they left the pool, slapping at the huge mozzies that now attacked in a swarm, Donny saw that the moon was already a hand's width up into the sky and he began to fret. So he pushed it. Disregarding Vaughan's grumbles, he climbed the far bank, turned left and walked quickly to the vehicle track that connected the two homesteads. After looking and listening for a minute, he then crossed straight over. After brushing out tracks with a branch he broke off, they walked out into the flat desert, still heading south-west.

"We need to push it," Donny said. "If that vehicle comes back, we are right near the road. We need to get away from it and find somewhere to hide for the day."

"What about this Oasis you talked about?"

"That is what I am aiming for," Donny said.

He was now confident as he knew where he was. He strode on across the desert, only slowing because there were numerous clumps of spinifex. Vaughan strode along beside him, limping but not complaining. The water had refreshed them both, even if it was half mud.

Then Donny noted a change in the skyline and muttered a few swear words. A sand dune. But it actually sent his morale right up as he knew the Glen Conner homestead was in among dunes.

They struggled up the dune, brushing out their tracks as they did, and then paused on top among numerous clumps of spinifex and saltbush.

"A light!" Vaughan cried.

Donny's spirits soared. "Glen Conner Homestead," he said.

Chapter 24

OBSERVATION POST

"So what are we going to do when we get there?" Vaughan asked.

"I was thinking we need to hide in a place where we can watch in daylight. I reckon it's too dangerous to just try to sneak in tonight," Donny answered.

"Okay, an OP. That sounds like the best plan," Vaughan replied. He turned to face Donny. "Okay, I know what to do. During our annual cadet camp last year, I did what they call Tier 2 training, for older cadets with no rank. We spent five days in the field doing a Reconnaissance Course and we had to do two Observation Post exercises. One went all night and the other went for a night and a day. What's the layout of this joint?"

Donny listened to this with a mix of astonishment and relief. At last Vaughan was doing something to live up to his reputation! For a moment he was at a loss for words.

"Oh bugger! It would be easier if I could draw a map in the sand," he said.

"Well, you can't, so describe what you can. What are the main features?"

That made Donny gather his thoughts. "Well, um, well, it's... I mean, there is this sand dune and then another one, same as all the others. The homestead is set right below the next one. I guess we can see that light through the gap where the road from the highway goes through."

"And what about cover on these sand dunes?"

Donny nodded. "Yeah, they have lots of small bushes on them like the ones we have been crossing," he explained.

"Any trees or bushes?"

"Not many just on the other side of the next sand dune. But there are lots along King Creek which is just the other side of the homestead," Donny said.

"Will there be water in King Creek?"

"Sure to be," Donny replied. "Might be a bit sludgy and muddy but that is why the homestead was built there, for the permanent water hole."

"What about this famous oasis you have been promising me?" Vaughan asked.

Donny pointed in the darkness. "Just over there, about a kilometre or so. That dark clump. It's actually a gravel pit they got stone out of to build up the road on the sand. It has filled up with water and trees have grown up around it. It is much better water because it fills up from rainwater and run-off from the dune. It's a bit salty but much clearer. The cattle really like it because it's got a solid ramp leading down into it."

"So it'll be full of cow poo too!" Vaughan commented.

"It'll be okay. Better than what we've been drinking anyway," Donny explained.

"Any other water? I mean like a bore or windmill or whatever?"

Donny shook his head but then remembered and said, "There's another old gravel scrape on the other side of the dune opposite the homestead turn-off, but it is mostly a swamp and has only a few bushes and a couple of trees."

"That sounds better," Vaughan said.

"Shouldn't we hide up on top of the dune where we can see the whole homestead?" Donny queried.

"Be good if there was lots of cover but no, being on a skyline is bad. You can be silhouetted against the sky and seen, and people are more likely to notice," Vaughan answered. "An OP needs to be where it can see but not in an obvious place. For similar reasons I don't like the idea of the river. It is too obvious, and they are likely to look there. Anyway, we had better move as it will be daylight soon, so follow me," Vaughan said.

He set off down the dune, brushing out his tracks as he went. Donny followed, also brushing out tracks. As they went downwards, the light went out of sight and the lightness of the moon and approaching dawn marked the crest of the dune behind them as a stark skyline. At the bottom Vaughan did a half-left turn and went off across the flat heading almost south.

Donny caught him up. "You are off course, the oasis is over there," he said, pointing to their right.

"I know," Vaughan agreed. "But I think it is too risky. It is close to the road and is the sort of place the crooks will search because it has both water and good cover. We are going over this dune away from the homestead and will get water from the swamp," he replied in a tone that brooked no argument.

Donny had been really looking forward to showing off his little secret place and was at first sharply disappointed. But then he thought about it and had to accept the force of Vaughan's explanation.

So for fifteen minutes they plodded across a grassy flat and then carefully scaled the next sand dune, once again being very careful to wipe out any tracks. At the crest, Vaughan went down and crawled up and over, then crouched behind a clump of spinifex to look out on the other side. Donny joined him and the lights at the homestead at once came into view.

"Like Christmas down there!" Vaughan commented.

Donny could only agree. The whole homestead area seemed to be lit up by spotlights and many buildings had lights in them. The boys looked out and scanned what they could see in the moonlight. Out to the south was just flat, open desert; fairly grassy but desert all the same. A faint ribbon of the gravel road ran off across this to the south.

"Where does that road go?" Vaughan asked.

"Just to the airstrip and on to the southern boundary and a couple of bores," Donny replied.

Further to the south-west began the distant line of trees that marked King Creek. The tree line ran northwards and went around behind the buildings and was lost to view behind the sand dune. Donny pointed.

"The creek goes around the far end of this big sand dune. Between us and the homestead is a low saddle or pass where the main road goes through and there are a couple of big water tanks up on the next part of the dune."

"What's on the north side of the dune on the other side of the road?"

Donny knew that. "Their wiener paddock. It is kept well grassed by irrigation and has a barbed wire fence around it." Then he glanced behind him and was shocked to see a bright light on top of the dune they had just left. "Uh! A light!" he croaked.

Vaughan swung round to look and then shook his head. "Not a light. Venus coming up, the Morning Star,"

Donny felt embarrassed at having made the same mistake twice but now he saw that the light had actually risen a bit above the crest of the distant dune.

"Sorry," he croaked, but the notion of the 'Morning Star' suddenly felt like a good omen.

We will be alright now, he told himself.

Vaughan faced the front again. "Where's this swamp? Oh, I see it. Okay come on, it is getting light fast. Make sure we don't leave any tracks," Vaughan said.

He then set off down the side of the dune, sliding and crawling to keep low among the bushes. Donny followed, impressed by the older boy's caution.

As he went down the slope, he saw that the swampy gravel scrape was almost full of muddy grey looking water among reeds. Most of the swamp had been fenced off and the few cattle there lifted their heads and watched them with no obvious concern. He also noted that tracks would not be a problem as the whole area was well and truly trampled by the cattle. Along the base of the dune at the edge of the swamp were a few small clumps of bushes and a couple of small trees. Vaughan headed for them, moving on the grass out from the dune until he was closer.

The barbed wire fence ended halfway up the steep slope of the dune, but Vaughan rolled under the fence and moved along the edge of the swamp towards the clumps of bushes on the lower slopes of the dune. Donny did not like that.

"There'll be snakes," he cautioned.

And there were. They saw two slithery, greeny-brown things that slid off into the reeds at their approach. Donny shuddered but kept moving. They came to a little dip where recent rain had eroded a small rill down the side of the dune. At the bottom was a small area of water clear of reeds, a puddle rather than a pond, but still big enough to refill all their water containers while standing on some grass.

By then it was starting to get light and the glow at the homestead lights was much less obvious. Then the barking of a big dog startled them and sent them scurrying in among the bushes.

"They've brought their dogs," Donny said.

Vaughan nodded. "I reckoned they would have." He then pointed up. "Just up this little dip and in among those bushes I think will do us."

The boys crawled slowly up about ten metres, obliterating their tracks as they went. Here they cautiously made their way in among the bushes and found a small open area shaded by a couple of small trees. It was less

195

than halfway up the dune but allowed them an overview of the whole area, including all the buildings of the homestead.

"Made for the job!" Vaughan said as he put down his bag.

Donny eased his bag off. From there they could see clearly where the main road crossed the low saddle in front of them and all the way along the south side of the continuation of the dune. A big steel water tank stood out on a bulldozed flat at their end of the next dune and overlooked the saddle.

Vaughan had a drink and then pointed around. "This is good. It is not obvious. We can sleep here, and if we have to we withdraw down that little dip and back the way we came. We go to the toilet back the other side of the bushes but make sure you can't be seen from the homestead and that everything is buried. Now, let's have breakfast and go to the toilet and so on before it gets fully light."

Even as he said this, the lights at the homestead, now looking quite dim in the early light, suddenly went off. The dogs started to bark again, and a man shouted from near the main house. But nobody appeared and silence settled, broken only by a crow that settled in a nearby tree and *caarcked* at them. A rooster began to crow over beyond the homestead.

Donny crept away to relieve himself and then returned to share the last of the bread. It was a curious mixture, half as stiff as toast from drying out in the desert heat, and half mouldy. Ignoring the unpleasant taste, Donny forced it down and followed it with the last of his tube of sweetened condensed milk and a big drink of water.

Vaughan then said, "We will take turns, hour on, hour off, as near as we can estimate. I'll go first. You get some sleep."

Donny was happy with that arrangement and made himself as comfortable as he could, scrooping out a small level area on the steep slope of the sand hill. He did not think he would sleep but, to his surprise, he drifted off, only to be woken half an hour later by Vaughan.

"What is it?" Donny muttered.

"Two people. One is a woman and the other looks like a girl. They have come to the side of the house and are feeding one of those bloody dogs."

Donny groaned and stretched and then sat up. Moving to where he could peek through a small gap in the leaves he stared at the homestead. He saw a solidly built woman in a shapeless floral dress and a slim person who even at that distance (half a kilometre, he estimated) was definitely a girl. The woman carried a shotgun, and the girl was throwing food to the dog.

"That's Ma Baker," he said. "Or that's what my dad calls her anyway."

Vaughan chuckled. "Ma Baker! That's good!"

"Who's Ma Baker?" Donny asked, annoyed by the mirth which seemed to encompass his relative ignorance as well.

"She was a gangster or bank robber or something in America back in the last century," Vaughan explained. "She used a shotgun or a sub-machine gun of something."

"That's actually Reggie Benson's wife. He's the caretaker, and she's got a shotgun," Donny replied. He had only ever met the woman twice and disliked her intensely. "She will know how to use that shotgun," he added.

"What about the girl?"

"That's Sharlene Sanderson, the girl who gave me the food at home," Donny replied.

As he looked, the first beams of sunlight lanced through the gap in the dunes to light up the homestead area. In that sun, Sharlene's hair shone like burnished copper. The two people vanished around the back of the house and silence again settled. Donny was in no mood to talk, being now satisfied that his mother and David's were almost certainly in that house, along with his grandad and Sharlene's mother.

But how many crooks? Two for sure, he deduced.

Donny settled down again but this time could not sleep. His mind was too busy and he was too worried. He took over from Vaughan, who lay down and promptly went into a deep sleep, do so deep that he began to snore and Donny had to wake him up. Just as he as was doing that, he heard a vehicle.

It was the Land Rover with Ringer and Thug. It came from the north along the road and through the saddle and then turned into the homestead yard, pulling up in front of the house. This set up a barking frenzy from at least three dogs, and then Ma Baker appeared and greeted the men. They all vanished inside and silence settled again.

"They didn't look happy," Vaughan commented.

"No, probably been out all night looking for us," Donny said.

That notion caused them both to grin at each other. Vaughan lay back down again and Donny resumed his watch. The sun rose, the air heated up, insects began humming or clicking or buzzing. Flies arrived, but blessedly no ants. The crow *caaarcked*. Time passed slowly and the air grew hotter and hotter.

In the shade the boys did not feel it too much. They drank and rested and watched. At least two hours after sun-up they heard the helicopter. It flew low overhead and then landed out from the homestead near a long shed that was obviously a garage. There were fuel drums at the far end. But only diesel, Donny noted.

"No aviation spirit there," he commented.

They watched Uncle James climb out of the helicopter and walk to the homestead, being held at bay by one of the savage dogs until Ma Baker came and led him in. An hour later he left again, walking out to the helicopter, which was started up and flown away along the line of King Creek heading northwards. Soon after that, Ringer and Thug came out, refuelled the Land Rover from one of the drums, and then drove off northwards.

That put Donny in a real quandary. His aim of rescuing his parents remained unchanged but he could not see how. He wondered if a reconnaissance along the line of King Creek to study the back of the buildings would be any use. He put this to Vaughan, who shook his head.

"We can't get there without walking across a lot of open country. Maybe tonight," he replied.

So they settled down to watching and waiting. The day dragged slowly on. The sun moved to vertical and Donny saw the moon clearly in the blue sky halfway down in the west. He was embarrassed to realise he had never known it was often up during the day.

I never noticed, he thought ruefully. Then he farted, a long, wet sounding blast.

Vaughan turned to frown at him. "Bloody hell Donny! That will set those dogs barking!"

Donny blushed, and then realised that it really smelt as well. Vaughan wrinkled his nose and then shook his head.

"They will smell that at the house and think a beast has died over here."

"Sorry. It's the water I suppose," Donny mumbled. He had a sip of water settled down to watching again.

Next was seeing Ma Baker and Sharlene go to a set of small buildings over near King Creek behind the house. Faint cackling sounds came to them.

"Feeding the chooks," Donny surmised, and watched as the pair returned to the house.

Their water was all gone by mid-afternoon, when the sun was blazing down on their side of the dune with relentless intensity, but they were at least in the shade. Donny noted Vaughan running his tongue over dry lips. Glancing at the swamp, so tantalisingly close nearby, he told himself they would have to wait.

Then a man appeared near the last building closest to the dune. He had a gun, a dog and a pair of binoculars.

"Who's he?" Vaughan asked.

"That's Reggie, the caretaker," Donny answered. "I think he and his wife are just managers minding it for a bank after the old couple died. Some problem with their will, Mum said. It hasn't been sorted out yet."

Donny dredged up bits of talk he had overheard from his parents and not cared about at the time.

"Where do you reckon he's going?"

"Up to that water tank," Donny suggested, indicating the huge steel tank on the end of the dune just across the road.

He was right. Reggie walked up a bulldozed vehicle track that led to the flat area at the water tank. Here he began to carefully scan the surrounding country with the binoculars.

"Looking for us," Vaughan suggested.

Donny agreed, apprehension clenching his chest and stomach. "I wonder if they think we are in the area?" he said.

Vaughan could only shrug and the boys crouched low and hoped. Then Reggie turned and walked towards them and out of view into the saddle at the main road.

Both boys looked at each other, anxiety on both their faces. Donny slung his bag with its empty bottles in preparation for flight. He kept looking along the dune and up at the crest above them, but half an hour of tension went by with no sign of the man. To their enormous relief, Reggie suddenly reappeared walking south along the road through the saddle.

"Where's he been do you think?" Vaughan whispered, the man being only a couple hundred metres away.

199

"Just looking around I reckon," Donny answered.

He thought, but did not say, that Reggie had probably been to the oasis to check it. *Just as well we didn't go there,* he thought.

In his mind Reggie was a thoroughly disagreeable character and quite likely to shoot. To their relief, Reggie cut off along a side track and back to the homestead, setting another dog barking as he did. He vanished back into the house.

"Well, I reckon our mums are in that house," Donnie said.

"Yeah, but how can we rescue them with those bloody dogs at front and back?" Vaughan said.

"Don't know, but when it gets dark I am going to try to sneak closer."

He actually had an idea involving those fuel drums to make a diversion, but he did not want to voice it yet.

And I haven't got any matches!

Then, just as the sun was sinking into the trees along King Creek there was a sudden eruption of poultry cackling. All the dogs began barking and growling. A couple of minutes later, Ma Baker, shotgun at the ready, appeared at the back of the house and went towards the area where the noise was coming from. She vanished from view and a few minutes later the distant cackling died away. Suddenly there was the loud bang of the shotgun and another outburst of cackling. Soon after that, Ma Baker became visible walking southwards among the trees. She poked around for a while and then went back the way she had come.

"I wonder what that was all about?" Vaughan said.

Donny, who had participated in many such scenes at home over the years just shrugged.

"Something getting at the chooks," he suggested.

"How would they know at the house?" Vaughan queried.

"By the way the chooks make noises and cackle," Donny replied.

He then made a very good but soft imitation of the '*carck!*' hens make when danger threatens. There were no further shots or noises, and they didn't see Ma Baker return to the house. A few minutes later, all the lights around and in the homestead suddenly came on, making the sunset even more obvious. Donny hadn't realised how dark it had become, his eyes having adjusted as the light decreased.

"Nearly time to move," he said.

"What do you plan to do?" Vaughan asked.

"First I'm going to try to distract those dogs somehow," Donny said.

"How?"

Donny shrugged. "I was thinking of tipping over those drums of diesel and then somehow setting fire to them. Then, when all the crooks run out to see what is happening, go to the house from the other side," he replied.

"You mean split up? One of over this side and one over there?" Vaughan queried, anxiety evident in his voice.

"Something like that," Donny agreed.

"What if the crooks just let the dogs loose?"

Donny had no answer to that, but he felt he had to try something. "Let's get closer and see what we can find out," he said.

"Refill our water first," Vaughan said.

So they did. They went back the way they had come, down to the pond and used it to have a huge but muddy drink and then to refill all their containers. Having done that, and rinsed the sweat and salt off their faces and arms, they crawled under the fence and made their way across the muddy paddock to the southern corner of the fence. As they did, they encountered a few cattle and some kangaroos that had come in to drink. These moved away without any noticeable disturbance.

The boys moved forward at a crouch until they reached the road just near the homestead turn-off.

"No tracks," Vaughan hissed.

So they ghosted across, brushing behind them and then lay down in the dry grass near the station mailbox. Donny was already feeling very afraid and worried because the homestead lights were lighting them up to a noticeable degree. Then he heard a peculiar but familiar noise and saw a dark shape silhouetted against the lights.

"Down!" he whispered to Vaughan.

Vaughan at once lay flat in the short grass and Donny lay next to him, his eyes straining to see into the bright lights.

What is this coming? he wondered, fear gripping him tight.

Chapter 25

SHARLENE

"We should have crossed further away from the road," Vaughan whispered. "What if the crooks come along with their vehicle?"

Donny berated himself for not thinking better. But it was clearly too late to move as the sound, a person's boots crunching on gravel, were getting closer. Then, when the person was about ten or fifteen metres away, they took a course so that they did not have a bright light directly behind them. He saw that it was a person pushing a motorcycle.

What the hell? he puzzled.

Then, when the person was only about five metres away and almost level with them, Donny saw that the person was Sharlene.

What the hell? Is this a decoy or a trap or something? he thought.

His mind raced with options: was she secretly an enemy? Was she sent out to locate them? But instinct and logic both told Donny that she was not one of the gang.

Or she would have dobbed me in two nights ago.

Acting on this, he called softly, "Sharlene!"

She gasped and at once halted and stared towards where he lay. "Who's that?"

"Me, Donny."

"Donny! Oh, thank God!"

The tone of her voice finally convinced him. Donny got to his feet and hurried across to her. Vaughan followed. As he reached her, Donny whispered, "What are you doing?"

"Running away. I'm going to get the police," Sharlene answered.

"Are my mum and dad in that house?" Donny asked.

"Yes, well, your mum is but not your dad. Ssssh! Not so loud. We need to get right away from here before those horrible people realise I have gone," Sharlene said.

She at once resumed walking, pushing the motorbike. Donny understood instantly. She had not started the bike up because of the noise it would make.

The three of them reached the turn-off and Sharlene turned left. Donny understood she was aiming for the Min Min Highway and probably Golden Dawn. Vaughan began to whisper, asking about his own parents, but Sharlene at once shushed him.

"Wait till we are over this sand dune and there is no chance anyone will hear us. Noise travels a long way on a still night."

So they strode along in silence, except for the crunch of their boots and of the motorcycle tyres. Donny kept glancing to his left at the lit-up homestead area, expecting at any moment to hear shouts or vehicles. He was also gripped by the anxiety that other crooks, like Ringer and Thug, could suddenly appear in front of them with their headlights and spotlights.

Sharlene walked so fast up the slope to the saddle in the sand dune that Donny found he was both puffing and perspiring. But he made the effort to keep up. Now that Sharlene was with them, he wanted to talk to her and that meant getting right away from the homestead area quickly. At every step he felt safer. As the trio reached the crest and went over it and there was nothing but darkness ahead, he heaved an actual sigh of relief.

As they started down the other side, Donny on her left and Vaughan on her right, Sharlene said, "Well, I'm Sharlene. Donny, I know from school camps but who are you?"

"I'm Vaughan MacAndrew," Vaughan replied.

Sharlene nodded in the starlight. "You must be the one they call the fat kid.

"I'm not fat!" Vaughan protested. By the hurt tone in his voice Donny could tell that the name had stung.

Sharlene looked at him and said, "Sorry, but that was what they called you. A couple of them were making bets that you would just die out in the desert. They were very surprised when they saw you over on Burke Creek a couple of days ago."

A couple of days ago! Donny thought with surprise.

But when he did think about the situation it seemed to have gone on for ever. He said, "Do you know what this is all about?"

"Yes," Sharlene replied. "They don't stop talking when I am serving food or taking plates to wash or anything. Your Uncle James and his little gang are holding my mum and your mum prisoner for ransom."

"Who is at the house?" Donny asked.

"My mum, your mum and a hoity-toity lady who talks with a plum in her mouth and complains a lot. She is a real pain."

"That will be my mother. She can be a bit of a trial," Vaughan answered, obviously embarrassed.

"Sorry."

Donny spoke next. "What about my grandad? Is he there?"

"Yes. He is locked in a side room. I did hear your Uncle James discuss putting him with your dad, but they haven't done that yet."

That was bad news to Donny and increased his anxiety. "Do you know where my dad is?"

Sharlene shook her head. "No. But I did hear your Uncle James say that no casual search will find him. Sorry."

"How many crooks are there? How many at the house?"

"There were five of them this morning, six if you count that horrible woman who lives there," Sharlene answered.

"Ma Baker," Vaughan commented.

At that, Sharlene let out a real peal of laughter. "Ma Baker! That's good! I was calling her the Wicked Witch except she hasn't got a pointy hat and she has a shotgun instead of a broom."

"What was that shot down at the creek just on sunset?" Vaughan asked.

"A fox getting at her chooks."

"What were you doing?"

"I've been everybody's dog's body. I've been cooking, washing up, feeding the dogs, feeding the chooks, you name it. But I just had to get away. That horrible Reggie was leering at me and making disgusting suggestions and hints, but never when his ugly wife was around."

"You should have told her. She might have put a poison in his food then," Vaughan suggested.

"I did tell my mum," Sharlene replied.

"Can we rescue our mums?" Donny asked.

Sharlene shook her head. "I wouldn't try. They are locked in the main bedroom and that horrible couple are in the next room and they have guns."

Vaughan spoke next. "Could we get a gun?"

Again, Sharlene shook her head. "No. The gun cabinet is locked.

Oh, please don't try! I don't want anyone hurt. Let's just go and get the police."

"I'd still like to try," Vaughan said. "We've come a long way to get here."

"How did you get here?" Sharlene queried.

"We walked," Vaughan replied.

"Walked! Where from?" Sharlene cried in astonishment.

"Clonargh."

"Oh, you did not! That's at least forty kilometres away and all desert," Sharlene said. She plainly did not believe them.

Donny had been feeling excluded and now spoke up quickly. "We did. Now we need to get to where we can contact the police. Is there a phone in there?"

"Yes, but no good. That horrible couple have a satellite phone and have put the radio in their room. The landline doesn't work. The line is down somewhere I heard."

Donny was disappointed but then had to smile. "How did you get past those bloody dogs? They were what was worrying us."

"I've been feeding them for three days, so they've stopped barking at me. So I just waited until things were quiet and then lifted the bike keys from the key rack in the kitchen and took the dog at the front some more meat. As soon as it started eating, I just walked over to the garage and got this bike."

"Can you ride a motorbike?" Vaughan asked.

"Of course I can!" Sharlene snapped back in an offended tone. "I live on a cattle station. I ride bikes all the time. Can you?"

"Yes, I can ride a motorbike," Vaughan replied, his voice sounding very defensive.

Sharlene looked hard at him in the starlight then said, "Yeah, good. And I know little Donny here can ride bikes 'cause he's a station kid too. But the question is: what do we do now?"

"Go and get the cops," Donny replied at once. "I don't believe those crooks will actually shoot anyone."

"I agree," Sharlene replied. "But what are you guys going to do?"

"Can we come with you?" Vaughan asked.

"There are three of you. We can't fit three on a little bike like this," Sharlene replied.

Donny now spoke, "I don't think you should try to go on your own. Those other crooks, Ringer and Thug, they are probably waiting at the gate on the highway, and when Ma Baker and horrible Reggie discover you have gone they will come driving."

"And Uncle James in his helicopter," Vaughan added.

Sharlene looked troubled and they trudged on in silence for a minute or so. By now they were down on the flat and Donny could just make out the dark clump of trees marking his secret oasis. He was aware that every minute counted and that they should be moving much faster, instead of walking speed while they talked.

Vaughan then spoke. "What if you take one of us and we go along the road on the motorbike, then drop them off and come back for the other one. And if you run into the crooks just take off cross-country and leave us. We will survive okay."

Donny now spoke. "No, you go, Vaughan. I will be alright. Those crooks won't catch me. I want to go and look for my dad and grandad."

"No!" Sharlene said firmly. "We all go. I will take one of you five kilometres and drop them off and come back for the other one. That way we are never too far apart if something does happen."

"That's a better idea," Vaughan agreed before Donny could even open his mouth. He went on, "And the person waiting starts walking. They can cover nearly a kilometre in the time it takes you to do a round trip."

"Good idea," Donny managed to put in. "You two go now. If you have to hide or cut off into the bush, go to the left of the road."

"How far to the highway?" Sharlene asked.

Donny answered. "About forty k's I think."

"I don't know how much fuel this bike has got," Sharlene said.

"If we run out, we just walk," Vaughan replied.

Donny was so surprised by this comment that his mouth fell open. *He's just trying to impress her,* he thought with annoyance.

"Right, let's stop talking and get moving. Who's first?" she said.

Donny said, 'Vaughan,', at the same moment Vaughan said 'Donny'.

Sharlene snorted. "Donny, you are the youngest, get on! Vaughan, you start walking."

She swung her leg over the bike and kicked the stand up, then switched on the ignition and kicked the engine lever to start it. To Donny's relief and surprise, the motor started first go and Sharlene called on him to get on. Donny had rarely been a pillion passenger on a bike and certainly not one driven by a girl. Very diffidently he climbed on, but didn't know where to hold. He was very aware she was girl and did not want to offend her. First, he put his hands forward on her hips and was even more aware of her gender.

Sharlene turned her head. "Grab hold of my belt," she said.

Donny did so. He was just big enough to see over her shoulder. He was also very conscious of the feel of her back and of her scent. That caused him a sudden wave of anxiety.

I hope I don't smell too bad, he thought, very aware now that he had not had a bath for days and had been sweating a lot.

Sharlene let in the clutch and accelerated and they were off. To Donny's surprise, she did not turn on the headlight and then thought that was a good idea.

If we see the crook's headlights coming the other way it will be too late to turn ours off, he reasoned.

In the starlight it meant going fairly slow, by motorcycle standards. There were a few bumps and the cool night air quickly began to chill him but Donny found the whole experience exhilarating. The proximity and feel of Sharlene added an unexpected spice to the thrill of the ride. Donny was not yet at that age when girls were that important to him, but he was filled with admiration for her spirit and ability.

It was a bumpy ride on the gravel road but Donny had expected that and had no trouble hanging on. The only real issues were going up over the succession of sand dunes, each about half a kilometre apart; and him keeping his shopping bag balanced behind him. As she approached the crest of each one, Sharlene slowed the bike so that she just had control, ready to suddenly stop or turn. But at each dune there was nothing but blackness ahead, so she glanced behind and then went on over the top and down the other side.

Suddenly the bike came to a stop and Donny noted a tiny light over at the front. "What are you doing? What's the problem?" he asked, wondering if they had run out of petrol.

"Just using the light in my watch to check the distance," Sharlene replied. "Another couple of hundred metres will do."

She revved the motor and set the bike in motion again. Just before the next sand dune, clear to see in the starlight, she pulled the bike to a stop.

"Okay, Donny, off you hop. Start walking. I will go back and get that other kid, but when I come back I will pass you and go on for another five kilometres. That's leapfrogging rather than being like a caterpillar," she said.

Donny slid off and she at once swung the bike around and set off back. He watched for a minute or so and then remembered he was supposed to be walking. So he started striding along, very conscious of his stiff muscles, chafe and tiredness. But he was so relieved to be going fast to get help and determined not to have Sharlene think badly of him that he ignored the pain and pushed himself.

Not having a watch himself, he could only guess at the time it took before he heard the sound of the motorcycle engine come from behind. But he thought it was probably between fifteen and twenty minutes and he was sure he had covered a full kilometre by then. He had crossed two dunes and was in the middle of wide, treeless flat when Sharlene and Vaughan reached him. So as not to be run over in the dark, Donny stood at the side of the road and waved.

Sharlene saw him in the starlight as she pulled the bike to a stop and said, "I'll be back for you in a few minutes. Keep walking."

Then the bike accelerated off into the darkness leaving Donny feeling very much alone and conscious that he was now at the back. Which got him looking continually back over his shoulder as he strode along.

About 20 minutes later he heard the motorbike returning. Sharlene did not waste either time or words. She saw him, skidded to a stop and swung the bike around.

"Get on!"

Donny did and a second later they were away. More bumps, a sandy stretch that gave a few steering and traction problems, another dune and then another vast, treeless flat. He glimpsed Vaughan standing there beside the road and then it was on for another five kilometres.

As the bike came to a stop, Donny nodded with satisfaction. *That is eleven or twelve k's. We are doing well!*

He did not wait to be told but jumped off at once, settled his bag more comfortably and resumed walking. Sharlene just swung the bike around and set off back for Vaughan. Just knowing that it was less than 30 kilometres to the highway sent Donny's spirits up. After the last few days, it seemed no distance at all.

Sharlene returned and Donny climbed aboard. He was glad of the lift as he was starting to feel tired and the aches and pains were very wearing. Just being close to Sharlene was nice too.

She can certainly handle a bike! he thought.

They passed Vaughan again in an area with a few scattered but stunted trees. Another five kilometres further north Donny was dumped again, and now he began to feel positively optimistic. He had been expecting to have to hide from the crooks long before this and wondered if they had even discovered that Sharlene was not there. By his calculations they were now only about 17 kilometres from the highway.

Half an hour later it was his turn again. He had walked another kilometre or so and by then was feeling both chilled and positively worn out. He had drunk the contents of the whisky bottle and was still feeling thirsty. To be able to sit on the motorbike and zip along felt like absolute luxury by comparison.

But this time when he got off, only about six kilometres from the highway, Sharlene told him not to walk.

"This thing is nearly out of fuel. If it runs out, me and your chubby mate will have to walk, and if you keep walking we will never catch you up. We should be less than ten k's from the highway I reckon."

"Six or seven," Donny replied.

He was glad that he didn't have to walk, and he unslung his bag and sat near a bush that offered some cover if the crooks came driving by. He was also maliciously pleased that Sharlene thought Vaughan chubby. He listened to the sound of the motorcycle receding southwards and then had another problem. His eyelids seemed to droop down of their own accord.

"Don't go to sleep!" he told himself.

He pictured Vaughan and Sharlene walking past and not seeing him in the dark. *And if I go to sleep on the road the crooks might run me over!*

So he stood. To help keep awake he studied the stars, noting that the Southern Cross was almost down again and that Orion had not yet come up. Then he looked both ways for the loom of any headlights.

After about ten minutes he began to worry. There was no sound of the motorcycle and no other noises. Just silence and feeling all alone in that vast immensity. After another five minutes he really began to worry.

"Something's gone wrong," he said aloud, needing the comfort of his own voice.

Chapter 26

BOARDING SCHOOLS

After another ten minutes, Donny was sure that something serious had occurred. He hoped it was just the bike running out of fuel but feared that they had been captured by the crooks. But there was no real option but to stand and wait. As he waited, Donny's mind explored the possibilities, dredging up ever more horrible possibilities: a crash that had injured one or both (How could he look after them and still escape?); a meeting with Ma Baker who used her shotgun when they refused to stop (He was certain Sharlene would try to get away).

More time dragged by. Donny noted its passing by the movement of the stars; and just standing he soon got cold and had to jog on the spot and do a few small star jumps in an attempt warm himself. All the while a feeling that was a mixture of fear and despair began congealing in his stomach. His high hopes of an hour before slumped. He did a pee and then opened his plastic water bottle and drank.

How long do I wait before starting out on my own? he wondered.

There was even a temptation to walk back to try to find out what had gone wrong. But a minute of mathematics told him that would be the wrong thing to do.

I might walk three or four kilometres and would then have to walk three or four back.

In his current state of near exhaustion that idea had little appeal. So he waited, and it seemed an age before anything changed. But finally Donny heard a low murmuring and then the distant crunch of boots on sand.

Is that them? he wondered, hope surging again.

Two dark figures appeared in the starlight against the paler tone of the gravel road. They obviously saw him at about the same as he heard a soft hiss of warning and they stopped. Vaughan's voice came quietly.

"Is that you Donny?"

"Yes," Donny replied, and they hurried forward to join him. "What happened?" he asked when they were close.

Sharlene answered. "Bike ran out of fuel. I was only about two k's from picking up Vaughan here but that took me a good half hour to walk and then we had to start this way."

"What did you do with the bike?" Donny asked.

"Just wheeled it off into a bit of scrub and dumped it," Sharlene replied.

Donny worried that it might be easy to see from the air but could not think of any other easy option and did not want to criticise Sharlene, so he said, "What now?"

Vaughan answered. "We walk."

Sharlene asked, "How far?"

Donny answered. "Maybe only six or seven k's, ten at the most to the highway, and then we flag down a vehicle."

Vaughan gave a chuckle. "With my luck I'll flag down the crooks!"

Sharlene answered. "Have to risk it." She looked at her watch. "We should be able to do that in two or three hours."

"More like three or four," Vaughan said. "What time is it now?"

"23:15. Bugger! I was hoping to be in Golden Dawn by midnight. Have you guys got any water in those bags? I didn't get a chance to sneak any out and I'm getting a bit dry."

Donny was puzzled by the way she said the time but immediately went to get the Coke bottle out. But Vaughan beat him to it, pulling out one of his beer bottles.

"Here, we need to empty this before any more gets spilt."

He passed it to Sharlene who took a gulp and then pulled it away. "Aw yuk! That's horrible. What is it?"

"Just water from the swamp near the homestead," Vaughan replied in a defensive tone.

In the starlight Donny saw Sharlene grimace and then drink again. She handed it back and Vaughan emptied the bottle in several gulps and then placed it back in his bag.

"Okay, let's start walking, but not on the road. You okay with walking through the bush, Sharlene?"

"Sure. I do it all the time in army cadets."

"Are you an army cadet?" Vaughan asked, surprise in his voice.

Despite that, he started walking, heading off the road and onto a vast flat covered with short grass.

211

"Yeah. I'm a second-year cadet, a lance corporal," Sharlene replied. "I just finished a week in the bush on our Annual Field Exercise before I came home a few days ago. Are you a cadet?"

Vaughan obviously hesitated before answering. "I was. I did two years but I'm not in cadets this year."

"Did you get any rank?" Sharlene asked as they walked.

Donny was anxious for them to walk faster, to get away from that road as there was almost no cover if the crooks with the spotlight came along. He was also a little bit resentful at being exclude from the conversation and so just trailed behind.

Vaughan again hesitated before answering, giving Donny a little spurt of malicious satisfaction.

"No, I was only a cadet. I did qualify for lance corporal at the end of last year but didn't stay on, so they didn't promote me."

"How big is your cadet unit?" Sharlene asked.

"About four hundred. There are six hundred boys at the school, and you have to be in cadets in Years Eight and Nine," he replied.

"Boys? No girls?"

"No, all boys," Vaughan answered.

"That's not good. You go to some posh boarding school near Sydney, don't you?" Sharlene said.

"The Duke of Glenshire's College, Dukes for short. It's one of the oldest boarding schools in the country. It's near Sydney. What school do you go to?"

"I go to the Northern Goldfields College in Charters Towers. We've got about four hundred kids there, about half and half boys and girls. It's a really nice place and I like it."

"Is you cadet unit part of the school?" Vaughan asked.

"No. It is based there but kids from other schools can attend. About half our cadets come from the State High School. There are only twenty of us and three Officers of Cadets," Sharlene explained.

"That's a bit small," Vaughan commented.

"It is very nice, thank you. They are a great little group, and we get a lot done. And we meet up with other cadets on some activities. But usually we run our own program as the normal units in North Queensland do their camps and courses in the school holidays, which is when all us boarders have gone home."

"Same with us," Vaughan said.

As Vaughan spoke, Donny noted that he kept glancing around. Donny guessed what he was looking for and pointed.

"There's Orion just coming up," he said.

"Thanks," Vaughan replied. He stopped and looked around.

Sharlene also scanned the stars. "What direction are we going?"

"At the moment north-west, but I'm not sure if that is best."

Donny thought for a moment and then spoke. "North-west will be good. That will take us well away from the station road and the junction where it joins the highway and we must come to the highway eventually."

"But it will be a bit more than your six- or seven-kilometres Donny," Sharlene commented. She thought for a moment and said, "It is the hypotenuse of a triangle and will be about eight or nine."

"I know what a hypotenuse is!" Donny replied, a bit hurt by the way she had assumed he knew nothing. To show his displeasure, he started walking and took the lead, using Orion to aim north-west.

As they walked, Sharlene and Vaughan resumed discussing their boarding schools and their cadet units. Donny listened gloomily, already half familiar from hearing others, about their dormitory arrangements; what time they got up; class times and teachers; then after-school activities such as sports and when cadets was.

Vaughan said, "Every Thursday afternoon for three hours we do cadets. One hour is school time and two hours is in activity time."

"What do people do who don't do cadets?" Sharlene asked.

"They have chores, like cleaning sports gear, weeding, painting, and that sort of thing. What about you?"

"Our cadet unit meets every Tuesday afternoon in term time from 3:45 to 5:45. That allows time for kids from other schools to get here and then time for boarders to get back to their schools for the evening meal."

That started a long discussion on boarding school food which Donny listened to with foreboding. Food wasn't a big issue with him but there were things he really liked and others he did not like, and he suspected he would not get many of his favourites at boarding school.

I wish they'd stop talking about food, he thought. *I'm bloody hungry now!*

As if on cue, his stomach grumbled and the other two chuckled.

Vaughan then said, "I'm in Year Ten. What grade are you in?"

"Nine," Sharlene replied.

Donny heard this and shook his head. *Vaughan wants to know how old she is. He's trying to impress her,* he thought.

Then he had to listen while they discussed various teachers and their foibles and odd behaviours. Donny had enough experience of teachers to follow this, but he had liked all his teachers and did not want to get shamed by saying so. He did try to join in the conversation a couple of times but the two older kids seemed to ignore him, so he lapsed into a hurt silence.

After walking for about half an hour (Donny estimated two kilometres), they came to a sand dune. Donny told them to go up and brush out their own tracks as they went. As he didn't have a branch, he followed and used his hands. On top Vaughan suggested a ten-minute rest, so they all sat and Vaughan's second beer bottle was brought out and emptied, each taking a turn to drink from it.

Suddenly Vaughan pointed into the night. "What are those lights? Is that the homestead we came from?" he cried.

Donny looked "No. Couldn't be. It is too far way."

His first thought was that it might be the men in the Land Rover but then shook his head. He could see a tiny ball of light, but it appeared to be just above the horizon.

And it is the wrong direction for that road. Is it the helicopter? he worried.

"Is it the highway?" Vaughan asked.

Donny sneered and said, "No, you are looking south-west, and the highway is to the north."

Sharlene stared, and then said, "Just a Min Min light I reckon."

"Do you believe in them?" Vaughan asked.

Sharlene sounded surprised and then annoyed. "Of course! We see them all the time. It is the Min Min Highway we are heading for, and this is the Min Min Shire. Haven't you seen them before?"

"Yes, during the last two nights," Vaughan admitted.

Sharlene nodded. "We sometimes just sit and watch them from our back patio. And there's a bunch of road workers who see them from their camp all the time and they say they have tried to take videos of them."

Donny stared at the distant, flickering ball of light that seemed to hover just above the distant horizon.

Yes, a video! That's a good idea. I must try that. That will shut up all those people who think it is all just made up.

They then began a discussion on what caused Min Min lights until Donny got tired of Vaughan trying to impress her.

"We'd better keep moving. We want to reach the highway as quickly as we can," he said.

They stood up, but Sharlene then said, "No we don't. There is almost no traffic on this highway at night. Some nights there isn't a single vehicle."

Donny knew that and blushed and to cover his hurt set off down the dune. "Brush out your tracks," he called gruffly.

The next flat area was half claypan and half gibber plain. The walking was easy in the starlight, but Donny did wonder what sort of tracks they might be leaving.

Uncle James will be up in his helicopter at first light, he fretted.

The trio trudged along in silence for a while and then Vaughan started talking about boarding schools again, obviously trying to impress Sharlene. That irritated Donny some more and he was glad when they encountered some cattle. Then there were the usual night incidents of kangaroos, emus, and some sort of indeterminate little hopping creature.

I hope we don't meet a snake, Donny thought, remembering that Death Adder.

Now they could time their progress better by using Sharlene's watch. Vaughan suggested they walk for 45 minutes and then rest for 15, and that is what they did. They come to a small clump of mulga forest and Sharlene checked her watch, very carefully shielding the light as she did.

"Nearly Zero One Hundred. Times up," she said. "Let's have a break."

They stopped and Donny unslung his bag and put it down. He badly needed a pee but was too embarrassed to say so with a girl there.

Vaughan helped by putting down his bag with the two empty beer bottles, and saying, "I need a drink, I know that."

"And I need a pee!" Sharlene said. "You boys go that way and I will go that way," she added, pointing in the starlight.

Vaughan looked worried. "Will you be alright?" he queried.

Sharlene snorted. "I grew up in this country. Of course I'll be alright. I'm only going to do a pee in the bush! And we do it all the time in cadets when out on a night navex or patrol."

Donny was obscurely pleased that she had snapped at Vaughan like that and grinned as he walked off the other way until he was on the other side of the clump of trees. Vaughan moved to nearby and the boys stood with their backs to each other while they relieved themselves. As they did, Vaughan grunted and then did a loud fart. Donny chuckled.

"Just as well you did that now. Sharlene won't be impressed by them," he said.

"Bite yer bum!" Vaughan retorted, obviously annoyed.

The boys made their way back to their bags and sat down, Donny still chuckling. He dug out the Coke bottle ready to drink. When Sharlene returned, they shared half of the bottle.

"That's all the water we have. Go easy in case it is a while before a car comes along to give us a lift," he said.

Suddenly Vaughan's stomach gurgled, and Donny had to laugh. Vaughan wasn't amused.

"I'm hungry," he said in an aggrieved tone.

Donny's own stomach then churned, and he realised he was going to fart. Desperately he tried to will himself not to. To no avail. There was a loud *Frrffrt!* sound and he blushed in the darkness.

Vaughan said nothing but Sharlene did. Waving her hand in front of her face she cried, "Oh Donny! That is deadly! Oh pssawh!"

Donny blushed even more. "It is the water we've been drinking," he tried to explain, hotly aware that Vaughan was quietly sniggering. "And the only food we've had in days is what you gave us at the homestead."

"Oh, you poor boys," Sharlene said.

Feeling his stomach churning again Donny stood up. "Time we got walking," he said, anxious to avoid embarrassing himself again.

"You are right," Vaughan agreed, also standing up.

He picked up his bag and looked at the sky to check the stars. As he did, there was a streak of light across the sky, high up to the north.

Sharlene cried, "Ooooh! A shooting star! Make a wish."

"Meteorite you mean," Vaughan corrected her.

Silly boy! Donny thought. *She won't like being corrected.*

But he could not help taking a jab at Vaughan. Remembering what one of the stockmen had said one night, he said, "More likely to just be some space junk, an old satellite or something."

"They are still the most beautiful stars," Sharlene said.

They set off walking. It was getting chilly, so Donny was glad to warm up and he also noted that his muscles and chafe weren't bothering him as much. He also noted that Vaughan was no longer walking in an odd way or limping.

We must be getting fitter and more used to walking, he decided.

Feeling better, he easily kept up with the other two. But he was also aware that his energy was draining rapidly before each rest, from lack of food he presumed.

They walked for another 45 minutes, crossing a vehicle track and coming to a barbed wire fence. Vaughan went to tell Sharlene how to do that, and she just sniffed and said, "Captain Ross taught us how to get under barbed wire fences safely, thank you!"

She then demonstrated that he really had, and they continued, going slower and slower as they wore out. It became colder. Then 03:00 passed and they halted for another rest among clumps of spinifex. Donny calculated that they had walked between six and seven kilometres and that kept his hopes up.

We should get to the highway in the next hour or so, he told himself.

So he stretched out on the sand and tried to ignore his upset stomach and to avoid farting again.

The walk then became a plod. Donny noted that Sharlene was very fit but seemed to be limping a bit. He guessed she was developing blisters. Vaughan continued to be all attention to her and Donny not impressed. There was another rest stop at 04:30 and then they plodded on. Not long after they had started walking again Donny noted a lightening in the sky to his right. It clearly outlined the crest of another of the long sand dunes.

What is that? he puzzled.

The answer came to him as they slowly made their way up and over the dune. It was the moon coming up, now a very clear crescent and just past the New Moon stage. It was so bright it made walking very easy but also bothered him.

It will also make us very easy to see! he thought.

They sat and watched the moon come up, then continued walking. After about half an hour, they came to another dune and crawled up, making a half-hearted attempt to erase their tracks. Without any word the came to a stop on top.

Then Vaughan cried out and pointed. "Lights! What are those lights?"

Chapter 27

THE MIN MIN HIGHWAY

The trio, shivering slightly in the chill breeze, stood on the crest of the dune and stared at the distant lights. Donny was puzzled.

"Is that Kiruna Homestead?" he asked. Then he shook his head and answered his own question. "No, it couldn't be. That is way over to the east near the Diamantina Crossing."

As he looked, he suddenly saw a glow in the haze just above the skyline but then it vanished. The others saw it too and Vaughan pointed.

"What's that?" he asked.

Then the glow showed again, nearer and clearer this time and then there was a momentary flash of light before the glow faded. It was Sharlene who answered.

"That is the loom of a vehicle's lights on the highway," she said.

"Loom?" Donny asked.

"Yeah, where lights are reflected by dust or something," Sharlene explained. "Where my cadets unit does some of its bivouacs, they are weekend camps, at a place called Sandy Ridge at Macrossan, we can see the loom of Townsville's lights in the dust and clouds over the city. And Townsville is about a hundred kilometres away from there. Look, it's a vehicle."

Two distinct beams now showed in the dust haze that hung in the lower air. Then two pinpoints of bright light, obviously vehicle headlights, appeared. As the beams dipped and the headlights vanished, a row of tiny red lights followed and then were gone.

"A semi-trailer," Donny commented, now understanding that the vehicle had gone up over one of the sand dunes along the highway.

The semi came into view in the distance, now running on almost level ground, the red lights along the side of its trailer becoming larger all the time as it got closer.

Vaughan spoke next. "How far away is the highway, do you think?"

Donny wasn't sure, but Sharlene answered at once. "Be at least three kilometres and may be five."

"We should be walking," Vaughan said. "That might be the only truck all night."

But the trio did not move. It was obvious they had no chance of getting to the road before the truck had passed. So they stood and watched as it crossed their front and then went past the cluster of bright lights which were to their left-front on the other side of the highway.

Sharlene pointed to the lights. "I know what that is. That's the roadworker's camp at the junction with the road north to Min Min National Park."

Donny knew she was right and was ashamed he had not remembered. It had been there on his last trip to town a few weeks ago. His impression of the world was that there were always roadworkers somewhere along that road on every trip.

They move their camp to be near their work site, he thought.

The lights of the semi-trailer vanished up over a very long rise to the west. Donny looked in all directions and saw no other lights or even the loom of any. He even looked hopefully to the west to see if the loom of Golden Dawn's lights was showing in the night sky. But there was nothing, particularly as the moon was now well up and was almost a half-moon. Its brightness was obscuring many of the smaller stars. Then he shook his head, knowing that the few lights in a tiny town of less than 200 people would not produce a glow in any way comparable with a city of 200,000.

"I can hear another motor," Vaughan said.

They all listened and, sure enough, the vibration of an engine came faintly to them. It was Donny who realised what it was.

"That will be a diesel generator at the road camp to make electricity for them," he said.

Sharlene looked at her watch and said, "It's coming up to five o'clock. We'd better keep moving."

So they started down the side of the dune, and only when they were near the bottom did Donny remember tracks.

"Tracks! Rub out your tracks," he called.

They did the best they could, but nobody had the energy to go back to the top and wipe out those marks in the sand. At the bottom they were on a very long, gentle downslope covered with a few clumps of mulga, the odd larger bush, and lots of spinifex and saltbush. It was painful and awkward to walk through and meant a lot of weaving around and sometimes just trampling painfully through. Fear of snakes rose to dominate Donny's thoughts, but he was careful not to mention that, partly because he did not want them to think he was a coward and partly because he did not want to slow their progress.

"That might have been the only truck all night," he commented.

"Oh, shut up Donny!" Sharlene said with a laugh. "There'll be more."

"Might not be," Donny replied, stung by her response. "Dad says the Min Min Highway is the least used in the whole of Queensland. Some days there is no traffic at all."

"Certainly the worst," Vaughan agreed. "It seems to be mostly dirt."

"It is getting better," Sharlene answered. "Every year they make more of it bitumen. I think the bitumen starts just west of here."

"It does," Donny agreed. "It starts just after the Government Bore."

"That's what those road workers will be doing here," Vaughan suggested.

"Probably."

"What will we do when we get there? Do you think the roadworkers will help us?" Vaughan asked.

Sharlene snorted. "Of course they will! And they will have a radio so they can call for medical help. They can use that to contact the police."

They walked on in silence for a while. Donny ignored his sore feet, aching muscles and thirst, the lights ahead seeming to beckon him on with hope of many good things. He had expected another sand dune but instead the ground sloped on down to a small streamline, really just a dry gully, which was hard to scramble across and which had only a scattering of stunted trees along it. The trees were clear to see as darker lumps in the moonlight.

As they reached the creek, the lights of the road worker's camp went out of sight and it was only as they trudged up the long slope on the other side that they came back into view.

"Bloody hell!" Vaughan grumbled. "How far is it?"

"Not far now," Sharlene said. "I can see people walking around."

Donny realised he could as well. He could even see the detail of a person through a lighted window. The camp, he now saw, was made up of half a dozen demountable buildings.

"We'd better get a move on," he suggested.

"Why?" Vaughan asked. "What are they doing up at this God-forsaken hour?"

Sharlene answered. "They get up early to get to the worksite so they can start work as soon as it gets light. It is still cool, and they can then knock off and have a rest in the heat of the day."

No sooner had she said this than the sound of a big engine starting up came to them. Then more engines started up, and clearly on the night air came the banging of vehicle doors and distant shouts. Donny felt a stab of anxiety and increase his pace. Then a vehicle came into view from behind the buildings, going left and then swinging towards them on what was obviously a side road. Headlights showed towards them, but they were still one or two kilometres away so did not light them up. The headlights stopped at the junction with the highway and then swung left again and the vehicle accelerated eastwards across their front. A second vehicle appeared behind it.

"What's going on?" Vaughan asked.

Sharlene answered. "They are going to work. They must start at six o'clock," she said.

The group began hurrying forward but the saltbush and spinifex were so thick it was impossible to run, and they soon came to a panting halt. They stood and watched as more vehicles came out of the camp: two white 4WD work vehicles with orange flashing lights on top, two graders, and two big trucks that Donny said were water trucks. These all drove off eastwards, each leaving a trail of dust and vanishing from view over the first sand dune in that direction.

"What will we do now?" Vaughan asked.

"Still go to the camp," Sharlene said. "There might be someone there like the cook or an office person."

So they resumed walking, taking more care again to avoid the prickly bushes as much as they could. Suddenly, Donny saw a light in one of the demountable buildings go out and he stared in dismay. Another light went out.

"There is someone there, but they are switching off the lights," he cried.

That got them walking fast again, but to no avail. Before they had gone another two hundred paces, all the lights were out and the muttering of the diesel generator had stopped. A minute later, a white work utility came out from the buildings. It also drove off eastwards. Donny felt a stab of defeat as they were still more than half a kilometre away. That so disappointed them that they again came to a stop and stood there staring into the night, chest heaving and breath coming in gasps. Donny found he was perspiring.

I'm very thirsty. I hope there is water there, he thought.

With that hope, and in the hope that there might be an adult there who could help them, he resumed walking. They continued on, threading their way among the tufts of saltbush and at last came to a barbed wire fence 50 metres from the bare ribbon of the highway. It took a minute or so to crawl under the fence and then they walked forward to the edge of the highway. Donny now saw that the buildings were a hundred metres further north and the grey ribbon of the side road led up past it on the western side.

As the highway was gravel, he said, "No tracks," and proceeded to scuff out his own as they padded across. Still hoping there was someone there, they continued on, through more saltbush. As they got closer, Donny noted that the whole camp consisted of six demountable buildings set up on short steel frameworks. The buildings were arranged in a hollow square (He knew to call it that from a maths problem he had failed at school!). There were two buildings on the south side of the square, closest to the highway, two more on the right or eastern side, and two on the northern side. The area had been scraped clear of vegetation and a layer of gravel covered it all, but the weeds and saltbush encroached up to the outside of the buildings. There were three big plastic water tanks, one at right hand end of both the far buildings on the north side of the square, and one at the right rear end of the closest building in the eastern row. No vehicles were visible but there was a big box trailer parked at the end of the east row. All the lights were out.

In the bright moonlight the camp had a spooky, eerie look, but Donny knew that was ridiculous. A few minutes before it had been full of shouting workmen hurrying to work. Despite that, he was feeling very anxious and really wanted to approach cautiously, but Sharlene and Vaughan just walked through the saltbush to the gap between the two buildings closest to them.

As they came to the front of the buildings, more details came into view and they stopped. Opposite them was the graded open area, and beyond that a radio mast and satellite dish in a little fenced compound. It was obvious that the vehicles had been parked around the central square. They looked in all directions but all Donny could see were closed-up buildings with shut doors and lights.

Vaughan shook his head, and said, "I hope it's not all locked up."

He and Sharlene went left to the front door of the building closest to the road. A sign beside the door proclaimed it to be the 'Office'. Vaughan knocked and when there was no response, tried the handle. Then he shook his head.

"No good! Locked," he said.

That was sharp disappointment! Sharlene led the way to the right to the first of two doors. A sign said: 'Store'. It was locked, which to Donny was no surprise. The next door was labelled 'Workshop' and it was also locked. His hopes continued sliding down.

They hurried across to the first of the eastern row of buildings. Beside it was the big square trailer, and behind it on their right, a water tank. Donny's eyes scanned the tank, and they quickly found what they were searching for, a tap!

"Let's get some water anyway," he said.

Vaughan shook his head. "Let's see if there is anyone here first."

He led the way back past the big trailer, which Donny now realised was some sort of mobile freezer. Sharlene went up the three steps to the first door and tried it. There was no sign on the door. To their relief, the door swung open, outwards.

"A kitchen!" Sharlene cried.

They crowded up the steps and into the kitchen. There was enough light from the moon for him to see that there was no-one there and while Donny was disappointed at that he was very pleased to be in a place that might have food. A glance to his left showed a passageway and open roller door on a serving bench through into a dining area. The kitchen itself had a long bench on the other side with a sink and taps and underneath a dishwasher. To the right of the door were a stove and an oven and various cooking appliances. On the side near the door were two big refrigerators and two floor to ceiling freezers.

"Food!" he cried. *But first a drink.*

There was a coffee cup upside down on the draining board, so he snatched it up and held it under the tap. With a hand that trembled he turned the tap.

"Oh water!" he cried, almost overcome with relief.

He quickly filled the cup and then drank it down in a couple of huge gulps. It was bliss!

"Proper town water," he commented.

He refilled the cup and stepped aside to let Sharlene in to fill a glass she had found. Sipping the second cup more slowly, Donny looked around the darkened kitchen and found he was shaking and on the edge of tears. It was all so reassuring, so normal, such a change from days of lying in the dirt and drinking cow poo and mud!

Vaughan found a cupboard with cups and also began drinking. "We'd better refill all our containers while we can, in case we have to suddenly leave," he suggested.

"We should be alright now, surely?" Donny said, confident the road workers would look after them and keep them safe.

Sharlene put her glass down and moved to look in the first fridge. As she opened the door, the light streamed out and Donny blinked. She reached in and then held out a clear plastic bottle of water.

"Here, stick this in your bag, just in case," she said.

Donny did so and then refilled his cup for a third drink. Sharlene had another drink and then looked in the next fridge.

"Ah! Here's what we want, food!" she said, taking things out and placing them on the bench.

"Won't we get into trouble?" Vaughan asked, putting his cup down and moving to look at what she was placing there.

Sharlene shook her head. "I doubt it. There's a lot here. The men may not even notice. Anway, our parents can pay for anything we take."

Donny moved to also look. The first thing he noted was a packet of sliced bread on the bench near the servery.

"Fresh bread!" he cried as he opened it.

"Some of the workers probably go into Golden Dawn every day, or at least every couple of days," Sharlene suggested.

"How far is Golden Dawn?" Vaughan asked.

"About a hundred k's from our front gate. There is only one station, Craiglie, and it is near the junction with the highway going north," Donny said. He was embarrassed that he could not remember the name of that highway, but the others did not seem to notice. "It is ten kilometres from the junction to the town," he added.

The next half hour was taken up with eating and collecting food or drink bottles. The old beer bottles and the whisky bottle were placed in a rubbish bin out of sight and replaced with clear plastic water bottles with lids. Donny refilled his own and the Coke Bottle. The whole time he was busy chewing or stuffing food into his mouth, slices of smoked ham, bread, cheese slices, some fruitcake. Some was added to his shoulder bag until it began to bulge and weigh him down.

Sharlene looked at it and said, "We may not need any of this. The workers may come back for breakfast or at lunch time. We can just wait here until they do. Anyway, we should be safe here."

Vaughan looked out through a window that faced east, and said, "It's getting light outside."

Sharlene looked at her watch. "Yes, 6:10. Be dawn soon."

During all this time they had been standing around the kitchen, eating and looking at things in the fridges, but now Donny saw a larder beside the doorway to the dining room. He opened it and discovered some muesli bars, so he pocketed a couple and then saw that there were bottles of peanut butter and pots of honey.

"I might have a peanut butter and honey sandwich," he said.

He dug out a plate from a drawer and then a butter knife from a drawer and took out a slice of bread from the now almost empty packet on the bench. He had just opened a tub of butter which he took from the fridge when they heard a vehicle coming. It sounded like it was coming from the north which surprised him.

As the vehicle sounds got louder and closer, Vaughan looked through the open doorway and the others joined him. A brown SUV came into sight on the road from the north. It was towing a long, grey camper trailer and trailing the usual plume of dust. It went driving past at such a speed Donny didn't think it would be able to stop at the T-junction with the highway. But it did, with a grinding skid of tyres on gravel. The vehicle was briefly engulfed in the trailing dust and then turned left and accelerated off eastwards along the highway.

Vaughan turned to Sharlene. "That wasn't the crooks."

"No," she agreed. "I think it was just a tourist who's come from the Min Min National Park."

"We should have run out and flagged it down," Donny said.

He felt quite foolish for not thinking of that and saw by their expression that the others thought so too. He moved to butter his bread.

Sharlene moved to watch the vehicle through the windows facing east. "It is going the wrong way for us. It will be going to Windorah and that is a couple of hundred k's," she said.

Vaughan went back to the second fridge and found an apple tart. He cut a slice and began eating, dropping a few crumbs on the floor.

"Careful!" Sharlene snapped. "The workmen will know we have been here if we have to leave early."

She snatched up a cloth and bent to wipe up the mess. Donny saw Vaughan blush and look unhappy and that caused him to smirk mentally.

Vaughan moved to stand over the sink. "Sorry. Anyway, I thought we were just going to wait here until the workmen come back."

Donny answered that while spreading butter on his slice of bread. "What if the crooks turn up first? They must be looking for Sharlene now. They are sure to check places like this."

It was not what he wanted, but he had become very wary over the last few days. He finished buttering his bread and started spreading honey on it. Sharlene put the lid back on the butter tub.

Then another vehicle sound came to them, this time from along the highway to the east. Vaughan stopped eating and moved to look out the window and then stared.

"It's a green Land Rover." he said.

Donny was just moving to put the butter and honey back in the fridge but now turned and looked out. What he saw instantly sent stabs of icy fear through him.

"It's the crooks!" he cried.

Chapter 28

HIDE!

Donny stared through the window, aghast.

Oh no! They will find us, he thought.

"Quick, outside and hide!" he cried.

He hurried across the room and grabbed the carry bag. A glance through the window showed him the crook's Land Rover was now only a minute or two away, only 200 metres from the turn-off. He was about to run to the door when he remembered his buttered bread.

If I leave that it will be noticed, he reasoned.

He turned to get it but ran into Vaughan, who had also grabbed his bag and was hurrying for the door as well. Both boys collided and nearly fell and there was an outburst of swearing. Vaughan shoved Donny aside.

"Out of the way, squirt!" he snarled.

Donny hit the cupboards but managed to keep on his feet. He snatched up the piece of bread and then dithered over the butter knife, peanut butter and honey. But Sharlene beat him to them.

"Go!" she cried. "I'll put them away."

"You'll get caught," Donny gasped, but he obeyed.

Something like panic was now rising in him as the Land Rover was almost level with the camp and would be there in seconds rather than minutes. Determined to escape he bolted to the doorway and then down the three steps in one bound. Behind him he heard a knife tinkle in the sink and Sharlene slam the fridge door.

Vaughan was standing a couple of paces away, looking frantically in all direction, obviously unsure which way to go or where to hide. To Donny, expert at 'Hide and Seek', there was only one practical option in the time available.

"The water tank! Get round the back of the water tank!" he cried.

Without waiting to see if his advice was acted on, he turned and ran. As he did, Sharlene came through the doorway and at once stopped, reached back and swung the door shut. By then Donny was running between the end of the building and the parked freezer trailer. By the noises behind he knew Vaughan was following. What he was afraid of now was that the men in the Land Rover might be able to see their legs through the half metre or so gap under the buildings to his right. He could only hope that the wheels of the trailer hid them.

Donny's next fear was that he would run out past the end of the building on his right before the Land Rover had passed on the other side, but his ears told him that would not happen. Already the Land Rover was slowing and turning up the side road. Only seconds to hide!

He was going so fast as he came to the water tank that he skidded on the weeds that had grown up since it was placed there. The water tank was large, several thousand litres, made of dark green plastic and placed on a low but solid, concrete base. Weeds were growing up around it. The water tank was much taller than a man. For a fleeting second Donny thought of climbing on top to hide, but he rejected that and instead skidded to a crouch on the eastern side. Vaughan came around the curve of the tank so fast he ran into him.

Donny was knocked over, sprawling out onto the weeds past the other side of the water tank. As he went down, he was aware that Sharlene had come racing from the hut to join them. From his position on hands and knees down in the weeds, Donny was able to see right through underneath the building and was appalled to see the Land Rover turning right into the gravel quadrangle. As it was driving straight towards him, he left his hat where it had fallen and pressed himself flat in the weeds.

Can they see me? he worried, dimly aware his piece of bread was scrunched into a sticky mess in his right hand.

The Land Rover stopped about ten metres from the door of the kitchen. That meant that the upper body and windscreen of the vehicle were out of sight above the base of the building, but Donny stayed down, gasping for breath and tensing, ready to run. He watched as the Land Rover's engine was switched off and both doors swung open. Out of each side stepped the men: Thug on the office side and Ringer on the north side.

The Land Rover's doors were slammed shut and Thug shouted, "Ahoy! Anyone here? Anyone home?"

There was no answer, but in the relative silence Donny was aware that his own heart was hammering very loudly and his breath was rasping.

Thug then said, "Ringer, you see if those doors are locked. I'll look over here."

Donny saw Thug's boots and lower legs move south towards the office building while Ringer's came almost straight towards him. Glancing up he saw that anyone in the kitchen who look down would see him, so he reached out to grab his hat and then wriggled back behind the curve of the tank. In the process his slice of bread broke into pieces, and he was left clutching less than half of it. But he was too scared to care. Vaughan and Sharlene were both crouched there, each looking a different way around the tank.

"Keep back!" Donny hissed.

Dropping what remained of his piece of bread he wiped his hand on the grass and weeds and then got to his hands and knees and adjusted the carry bag so he could run. A glance showed Sharlene's face looking very determined and that she had gone pale under all her freckles. Vaughan on the other hand just looked scared.

Thug now banged on the office door and tried it, with no luck. Ringer went to the kitchen door and found it unlocked. Donny heard him call out, then heard his boots go up the stairs and into the kitchen. A few moments later he glimpsed movement at the small section of window that he could see. Worried about being seen, he backed around the tank, bumping and pushing Vaughan.

"Stop pushing!" hissed Vaughan.

"Shh the pair of you!" whispered Sharlene.

Donny glanced back at Vaughan's angry face and then saw Sharlene get down on hands and knees to peek around the other side of the tank.

"That man is looking under the office," she said.

There was the crunch of boots on gravel and then the thud of them going up the steps of the kitchen.

"Anyone in here?" Thug called.

"Nope, but there's some food," came Ringer's reply, just audible.

"Leave it alone! We got to check this place out first," Thug replied.

"You look. I'm hungry," was Ringer's response.

Thug swore and stomped off into the dining room. There was the sound of a door opening as he went down the steps of the dining room. Donny went lower, putting his hand on the greasy grass as he did. He swore under his breath and then peeked under the building. He saw Thug's boots go across to the other buildings on the north row. He heard doors being banged and then glimpsed Thug kneel to look under the building.

229

Just as well we didn't try to hide under there, Donny thought.

He edged back a bit so as not to be visible from the windows as Thug came walking back across to the kitchen. Donny heard him go up the steps and then his voice but could not make out what he was saying.

But he did hear Ringer's whining reply: "Makin' meself a bloody samwich, eh? I'm starvin'."

Then Donny heard something else and went all tense. It was the sound of another vehicle and it was coming from the east, from their exposed side! He swung his head to look and saw a white work utility heading towards the camp along the highway!

"Bloody hell! You guys get down!' he croaked.

But they had already heard it and joined him lying flat in the grass.

Oh, I hope the person driving that didn't see us before we got down, Donny fretted.

But all he could do was lie there, blinking into the rising sun which was just peeking over the skyline beyond the approaching vehicle. There was nothing for it but to wait and sweat with anxiety as the white vehicle went past and vanished behind the southern huts. Donny hoped it would continue on, but to his dismay he heard it slow and then turn up the side road and then into the camp. Now he just had to know so he curled around and looked around the other side of the tank, where he couldn't be seen from the kitchen window. This put him beside Sharlene.

The vehicle stopped and a man in boots and blue safety trousers with reflector rings on them got out. As the man began walking towards the kitchen door, he called out to Thug and Ringer.

"Hey! Who the hell are you blokes? What are you doing in our camp?"

Ringer answered, sounding as though he had a mouthful. "Just lookin' fer some bloody trouble makin' kids."

"What the hell! Is that food from our kitchen?" the man snarled, obviously angry but equally sounding wary.

As well he might, Donny thought. *He's all alone and there are two strange men, and they could harm him easily.*

"Aw, sorry mate," Ringer replied. "Give us a fair go. We been up all bloody night searchin' and I'm starvin'."

Thug now spoke. "No worries, mate. Sorry! We'll pay for it if ya like. We've just had a real long night. Ya haven't seen any kids around here, have ya?"

"It's council rations that. You'll have to pay at the Shire Council office in town," the man replied.

He had stopped out in the yard and Donny saw both Thug's and Ringer's boots come down the steps to join him. The man was still obviously very wary.

"What's this about kids?"

Thug answered. "Aw, some teenage ratbags. Three of 'em, a girl and two trouble-making boys. They stole some stuff at Clonargh a couple of nights ago and last night they stole motorbikes at Glen Conner homestead."

"Where are they from?" the road worker asked.

"Dunno," Thug replied.

Donny glanced at Sharlene beside him to see how she was taking it and then his gaze lingered. The first rays of morning sunlight were striking her hair, and it seemed to have a brilliant sheen.

Like polished copper, he thought. Then another thought came to him. *She's actually very pretty under those freckles.*

Then he transferred his attention back to the men. The road worker was speaking.

"So what makes you think they might be in this area. We haven't seen any bikes on this road for weeks."

"Our boss has found one of the bikes. He's in a helicopter and he called us up on the satphone and told us he was trackin' 'em from the air and it looked like they was headin' this way," Thug said.

That appalled Donny and he could only shake his head and think that was very bad news. It made him suck in a deep breath and tense for running. Up till now he had been gripping his hat in his hand, and he glanced down and saw that his greasy fingers had left grimy marks on the felt where the melted butter had soaked in. A little spurt of anger stung Donny as he remembered how Vaughan had run into him. Silently swearing, he put his hat on and prepared to run.

Worse quickly followed. From what he could overhear, Donny decided that Thug was using the satellite phone to talk to Uncle James.

Damn! That helicopter will be here soon, he deduced. So where to hide from it?

"Are these kids dangerous, you know, violent or armed or anything?" the road worker asked.

"No," Ringer answered. "Just bloody cheeky troublemakers."

"So what…?"

The voices stopped and Donny understood why. The tremor of helicopter rotors causing their characteristic vibrations had reached his ears. He looked around frantically.

Where can we hide? he worried.

Lying out in the weeds as they were he was sure they would be instantly spotted from the air. The only place that seemed to offer even the shred of a chance was either under one of the buildings or inside one. There was clearly no way to get inside any of them, so he decided it must be underneath.

But that seemed a hopeless choice! All the buildings were set up on a steel framework on bare gravel and from any distance it was possible to see right through underneath them. But now he could hear the helicopter's engine and by turning his head in that direction he spotted the tiny black speck in the sky to the south-east. It seemed to be hovering over that last sand dune and Donny swore again. He knew they had not brushed out their tracks very well as they had come across it. Then the tone of the engine changed to a definite buzz and the helicopter began heading rapidly towards them.

"Under the building," he hissed. "Go to the right of the tank and keep it between us and the chopper."

"But…" Vaughan began.

"No other option. Go!" Donny hissed.

He then set the example and crawled quickly around the tank, his heart now hammering as the adrenaline was pumping. He was hotly aware that anyone in the kitchen would see them or that if any of the three men bent down to look they would be seen!

As he crawled around the tank, Donny again felt that slimy buttered bread and honey and experienced another little spurt of annoyance. But no time for irritating trivia! He kept crawling, so that he was at least on the other side of the tank from the approaching helicopter. A few more metres of rapid crawling and he was in under the building below the sink area. The gravel was sharp on his hands and knees, and he had to stifle an involuntary cry of pain. To his intense relief, both the others followed him and they all lay flat, Sharlene on his left and Vaughan on her other side.

A minute later the helicopter clattered very low overhead, directly over where they had been lying at the tank. It went on over the buildings and, by the engine noises, Donny knew it was going to land. It did, blowing out the usual billows of sand and dust as it settled. To Donny's dismay, he found he could see nearly all of the helicopter out beyond the vehicles.

If the pilot looks under here, he might see us, he fretted. *And of course there are bloody ants!* Little black ants, crawling and nipping around his hands and wrists.

There was another delay as the helicopter motor was switched off and then the wait till the rotors had stopped spinning. Donny saw Uncle James step out of the pilot seat, but he could not see if there was anyone else in the machine.

I just knew it would be Uncle James, he thought bitterly.

He was certainly not his favourite uncle! Donny was relieved to note that he could only see the lower three quarters of his uncle and the closer he got to them the less was visible.

Uncle James walked over to join the group just outside the kitchen. As he reached them, Donny heard him say, "G'day! My names Jack Reagan. Glad you are here."

The road worker introduced himself and then wanted to know what was going on. "These guys tell me there are three kids in the area stealing things. Do you want me to contact the police on our satphone?"

"No thanks," Uncle James replied. "This is actually just family business, and we don't want the embarrassment of it being made public. When we catch them, we will sort it out."

"You sure?"

"Yes, very sure," Uncle James replied. "But we would appreciate you keeping an eye open and letting us know if you see them." There was short pause, and then Uncle James said, "Here's my number. Please call."

"Where are these kids then?" the road worker queried.

"Not sure," then, "Have you blokes found any sign of them?" Uncle James asked, directing the question to the two crooks.

Thug answered. "No. We searched around here and there's no sign of 'em."

"You sure?"

"Yes boss, I'm sure!" Thug snapped. "I looked under the buildings and the only one unlocked is this one and we went in there and there's nowhere to hide."

The roadworker now spoke. "These men were taking food from our kitchen when I arrived."

"Were you?"

"Aw, yes boss. Sorry boss," replied Ringer. "We been up all night and I'm really hungry."

"Bugger! Look mate, I'll settle this with the right people if you let me know who they are."

Thug now asked, "Where do you reckon these kids are, boss?"

"I tracked them from where I found a bike and I thought I saw their tracks on that last dune over that way. So if they aren't here, they must be hiding somewhere close. I might go and have a good look along that creek line back down at the bottom of the slope."

"What'll we do?" Thug asked.

"You stay here till I come back and pick you up. Ringer, you drive up and down the highway from there to the station gate and back. I'll call if I need you," Uncle James instructed.

The roadworker now spoke up. "I'm only here to collect the morning tea. You can't stay in any of the buildings. I have to lock them. I dunno why this one was left unlocked."

Uncle James spoke. "That's alright, mate. You just get on with your job. My worker here will just sit in the shade and phone me if there are any problems. Ringer, give him your satphone."

Donny saw Ringer's legs move towards the Land Rover and the roadworker's towards the steps. The roadworker clumped up into the kitchen and began moving around, muttering while he did.

Then Donny farted. He desperately tried to stop it by clenching his buttocks, but it came out with an obvious and audible *pufffrrrt!*

Sharlene gave him a disapproving look, then her face crinkled up as the smell hit her. She began waving her hand in front of her face.

"Oh Donny!" she whispered.

Vaughan also wasn't impressed and gave him a glare. For a few seconds Donny feared his social indiscretion might have been heard. But when it obviously hadn't, he started worrying about the people smelling it, because it really did smell!

And the three crooks were just there at the steps!

Chapter 29

WHAT WILL WE DO NOW?

To Donny's horror, Ringer had just walked back with the satellite phone and said, "Here's the bloody phone. Jeeze, Benny, you stink! It smells like somethin' dead."

"It wasn't me!" Thug cried.

Donny had a flash of insight and decided that Thug (Benny), did not want to name his boss but obviously thought Uncle James had done it.

Uncle James wasn't amused. "Stop your bloody nonsense! Just get on with the job."

Ringer replied, "Aw yeah, but boss, he's been doing that fer days now. He stinks the whole Rover out."

"It's that bloody bore water or somethin'," Thug said, obviously embarrassed and annoyed.

Donny grinned. So did Sharlene, but Vaughan clearly did not approve.

Then Thug said, "Hey boss, don't you think it might be time we gave this up as a bad job? If those bloody kids have reached the highway here, they might contact the cops."

"No!" Uncle James replied angrily. "There is too much to lose. And you blokes are in it with me, so we keep tryin'. My brother is due back this evening with the money, and we can split then."

"But boss, I don't like it," Thug said.

"Too bad! You are being well paid. Now you watch here, and Ringer, you go back and tell those roadworkers near Sandy Crossing the same story and make sure they report the kids to us, not to the cops."

Ringer grunted and turned to walk back to the Land Rover. Thug muttered and grumbled. "Okay, boss, but you better organise some food for Ringer and me. We missed dinner and haven't had any breakfast."

"Yeah, I'll get onto it," Uncle James promised. "Now stay here and don't go to sleep!"

With that, Uncle James turned and strode off back to the helicopter. By the time he was in and had the engine going, Ringer had driven the Land Rover away. This left Thug standing outside the kitchen.

The roadworker called, "Hey mate, can you give me a hand to carry this stuff to my ute?"

Thug did. Donny watched them carry an eski, a large box of cake, a hot water urn, and some sort of big container to the utility. The roadworker then said, "Thanks. You can have some morning tea if you want while I check all these other doors are locked. It's there on the bench."

"Thanks," Thug said and went up inside.

Donny and his friends then lay and watched the legs of the roadworker as he went from door to door checking them and then locking them if he had to. He then came back to the kitchen and went up inside.

"Lazy buggers!" he grumbled. "Leaving doors unlocked."

The two men talked quietly for a few minutes and then both came back out. The roadworker locked the kitchen door, and said, "Sorry, mate. Good luck with your search."

"You let us know if yer see these bloody kids, eh?"

"We will. See ya!" The roadworker climbed into his utility, started up and drove away.

Donny nudged Sharlene, and whispered, "Back to the other side of the water tank."

Gesturing with his head, the trio began to crawl slowly so as not to make a sound as Thug had seated himself on the kitchen steps. It took a couple of minutes for the group to return to the outside of the water tank. Donny found it an unpleasant transition from the shade under the building to being out in the blinding sunlight. He was also busy wiping and scraping at his hands and wrists to remove the little black ants that were now all over them.

As he crept past the mashed remains of his sandwich, Donny noted that every small piece appeared to be alive with more ants. Usually he liked ants, and so did his father. His father thought they were a sign of a healthy environment and even fed them in the kitchen, but his mother ruthlessly sprayed and wiped.

At least these aren't bull ants or meat ants, he thought.

But out in the weeds the bush flies arrived, doing their usual trick of landing on the face to get at the moisture in the corners of the eyes and up the nose.

But now they had a real dilemma. Uncle James was busy flying his helicopter back and forth along the shallow gully on the south side of the highway, and Donny was afraid that at any moment he might swing back around and come over before they had time to get back under a building. He and the others kept anxiously watching it, ready to scuttle away.

During that time, three vehicles went past on the highway. A big truck that looked like it carried fuel came from the west and went off to the east; a car towing a huge caravan came from the east and went west; and then an SUV towing a camper trailer went east.

Any one of them would have done, Donny thought, *even the fuel truck. We just need to get proper adult help.*

But as long as Uncle James was flying nearby and Thug was in the quadrangle, they were pinned down.

Sharlene voiced it. "What do we do now?"

"Get to the highway and flag down a vehicle," Donny replied.

"Probably be our mate Ringer in the Land Rover!" Vaughan said.

"We are trapped here for the moment," Sharlene commented, lifting her head to look outwards. "There is very little cover."

It certainly looked that way to Donny. As far as he could see, there was hardly any bush. Most of the ground was covered with small bushes that were barely big enough to hide behind lying down and offered no cover from above. The ground near the highway was particularly bare, especially to the west where it was just a mixture of short grass and bare sand on a very long rise to a wide crest.

Ten minutes went by with the situation unchanged. The air grew hotter as the sun rose higher and the flies and the ants began to move from irritants to bloody nuisances. The sound of footsteps got Donny peeking around the side of the tank. He saw Thug's boots as the man strolled around the quadrangle. But he did not go far as the only shade was on the western side of the two eastern buildings, the kitchen and some sort of accommodation block. After a few minutes, he moved back and sat down again. But his nearness got Donny and the others tense as there was always the chance the man would just stroll out between the buildings and be able to see them.

At last, at 09:30 by Sharlene's watch, the helicopter flew away eastwards, zig-zagging low as Uncle James searched a wide strip beside the highway. The friends watched it until it was just a speck in the distance and then sat up to have a drink. Donny farted again and this time Vaughan punched him.

"Little bugger! You nearly gave us away then," he hissed.

It wasn't a hard punch and Donny grinned. "Just trying to use gas warfare to knock the enemy out," he said, using an expression he had heard his father use when his mother berated him for being smelly.

That conjured up images of his father and mother that got him instantly anxious and weepy. *I hope they are alright. They must be terribly worried about us,* he thought.

"Vehicle!" Sharlene warned.

It was coming from the east, trailing the usual cloud of dust. They shielded their eyes and squinted into the sun to study it.

"I was right," Vaughan said as it got closer. "It's the Land Rover."

They lay down and sweated from the sun and anxiety as the Land Rover drove in from the highway. It came to a stop in the quadrangle and the friends lay with beating hearts, tense and ready to run but ears focused.

They heard Thug's boots on gravel and then his voice. "What's the go? Any luck?" he called.

"Nah! No sign of the little bastards," Ringer replied.

"Any chance of breakfast? It's after ten," Thug asked.

"Yeah, here's a packet of sandwiches: corned beef and pickles. Reggie drove out to the gate wiv 'em," Ringer answered.

"Bloody Reggie and that witch of a wife! I don't trust either of them," Thug exclaimed.

"Yeah, he's a grumpy bastard," Ringer agreed. "He was grumbling 'cause he has to drive for several hours to take food and water to the boss's other brother."

That got Donny speculating, but Thug's next words sent his hopes up even more.

"I reckon we should give this up as a bad job and get out of here while we have the chance. It'll be a hard place to get away from if the cops are warned."

"Yeah, it's hundreds of kilometres; hours of driving in any direction; to get to the next town and the cops will have time to set up roadblocks," Ringer agreed.

"And I don't trust the boss. He says his brother is bringing the money this evening, but we might be lucky to see any of it if we aren't right there."

"Yeah, maybe. But we better keep lookin' till then, but then organise to get to town," Ringer replied. "Anyway, I'll do another lap of this bloody highway. See ya in an hour or so."

The Land Rover sped away back east along the highway. Thug sat down on the steps again. By peeking in under the building, Donny could see the back of his legs and his boots. He also noted that the strip of shadow on that side of the building had shrunk to only a few metres.

When it gets past midday, the shade will be on this side of the building, he reasoned. Now that was a worry! *We need to get away from here.*

No sooner had the Land Rover gone from view than Donny heard the buzz of the helicopter again.

"Back under the building," he hissed.

By the time they moved the helicopter was already visible in the distance and it turned into a bit of scramble for them to get in out of sight. Donny was worrying that Thug might hear them, but his initial problem was quite different. To get under the building quickly he had angled to his right, to make room for Sharlene, so he went under in a different place.

As he did, he felt a sharp sting and realised he had been stung by some insect. It was so unexpected he almost cried aloud but managed to stifle the impulse. Then he saw them: what his mother called paper wasps. Usually they did not bother him, but now he saw he had brushed one of their small nests that was hanging down from the steel framework. Worse, the wasps also stung the others, drawing sharp exclamations from Sharlene and swearing from Vaughan. The only thing that saved them from being heard was the clatter of the helicopter as it flew low overhead.

Donny saw Thug's boots and legs as he walked out into the quadrangle. The helicopter did a complete circle, which got Donny fretting in case their boots or legs might be visible. Uncle James did not land but obviously spoke to Thug as there was a conversation on the satellite phone, but the words were mostly lost to Donny in the engine noise. Then the helicopter flew away. To Donny's surprise, it went westwards along the highway.

As it went, Sharlene tugged at Donny's sleeve and jerked her thumb to indicate moving back. Donny complied, his neck and wrist still hurting from the wasp stings. The friends moved back to the outside of the water tank as the sound of the helicopter died away. Donny saw that Sharlene had been stung on the left cheek, forehead and throat. The stings were now red and swollen.

"Sorry about the wasps," he whispered. "You aren't allergic, are you?"

Sharlene shook her head. "Hurts a bit. No. Look, we need to get away from here before the shade moves to this side of the building. That fellow will come around here, and we can't possibly hide then."

"I agree," Donny answered. "But I don't fancy crawling all the way to the highway through that spinifex."

What he was really worried about was a needle leaf from the spinifex puncturing someone's eye.

"There'll be lots of prickles and bindis too I suppose," Sharlene agreed. "But we have to try."

It was obvious they could not just get up and walk those 200 metres without being seen as Thug was strolling around and looking out through the gaps and from time to time bending to look underneath.

Vaughan had been listening. "Well, we can't stay here. We are starting to fry, and we will get found. So we must at least get further away."

"What if the helicopter comes back?" Sharlene suggested.

Donny shook his head. "I reckon he's gone to Golden Dawn to refuel. He's been up since before dawn and must be low. That gives us a couple of hours."

"Okay, let's crawl," Sharlene agreed.

They all had another drink. The sun was sweltering by then and perspiration was soaking their clothes and trickling down their foreheads. Vaughan set out on his stomach.

"Leopard Crawl," he whispered.

Donny did not know what that meant but after watching for a few seconds he got the idea. Sharlene, as an army cadet, knew exactly what to do.

"Take that hat off, Donny, and hold it in front of you. Otherwise it sticks up above the bushes and is very obvious," she whispered.

It was very slow, and, as Donny had suspected, quite painful. There were lots of prickly bushes and little burrs and an occasional sharp little rock, testing both nerves and muscles. Down in the weeds the air was stifling and there was no let up from the flies or the ants.

I just hope we don't meet a snake, Donny thought, picturing one striking at his face. But he did not mention the possibility and comforted himself by knowing he was last in line.

Their progress was directly towards the highway and that had the disadvantage that when he looked back Donny could see Thug's legs through the underneath of the two southern buildings. It was such slow going that in twenty minutes they only covered a very painful 75 metres. They came to a stop in a tiny dip. To add to their mental stress, they heard a vehicle coming from the west but did not dare stand up and walk so it went past and vanished to the east.

"A truck," Vaughan commented.

They resumed crawling, Vaughan still leading. But they had only gone a few metres before the sound of another vehicle reached their ears. This one was coming from the east. Vaughan lifted his head to peek.

"Damn! It's the Land Rover," he said.

That got them lying flat. Donny sweated and brushed at the ants, which still found the stickiness on his hands attractive. As he expected, the Land Rover went past and then turned up the side road and into the workers' camp. It was only there a minute or so before he heard it drive out again. He did not dare lift his head to watch but had to depend on his ears. So, when it turned right at the T-junction he was surprised. Then he did look.

"Going west!" he commented.

"Is that Thug fellow in it do you know?" Vaughan asked.

"Didn't see," Sharlene answered.

They all looked but could not see him. That left them with a terrible dilemma: if he was, they could get up and walk; and if he wasn't they might be seen and caught! They lay there for a couple of minutes, sweating and brushing at flies.

"What will we do?" Sharlene asked.

"Keep crawling," Vaughan said in a very firm voice, much to Donny's surprise.

So they did. Now the tension began to ratchet up.

Uncle James could get back here at any minute, Donny thought.

He was now getting very agitated and really wanted to get to town as quickly as he could. Just before noon they arrived close to the highway and lay among the small bushes. Now the sun was a real problem, and Donny saw that both Sharlene and Vaughan, neither of whom had hats, were very red in the face.

"Which way should we go?" Vaughan asked.

Sharlene answered. "It doesn't really matter, as long as we can get word to the police," she said.

But Donny didn't like that. He was determined to go to Golden Dawn. He knew it well and knew the people there.

"No," he said. "Windorah is about two hundred k's. Golden Dawn is less than a hundred."

"Vehicle," Vaughan said. The sound was coming from the west.

"Only one person watch. Get down, Donny," Sharlene ordered.

It was Vaughan who peeked. He took one look and then lay flat. "Bloody hell! It's the Land Rover coming back," he said.

"Make sure you are hidden. Get your bum down, Donny," Sharlene said.

That comment annoyed Donny because he was sure he was lying as flat as he possibly could. But he did look sideways to check that he had a couple of good bushes between him and the highway. Once again, he tensed, ready to spring up and run.

The sound got rapidly closer, and he expected it to turn into the camp but instead it just went racing past. As it did, he tried to see who was in it but it was too quick. Then it was gone, leaving them coughing in the dust trail.

"Did you see who was in it?" Vaughan asked.

"No," both Sharlene and Donny replied.

"So we don't know if that Thug bloke in still back in the camp, or east of us in the vehicle, or west of us somewhere," Vaughan said.

That was a really worrying problem. Donny had a suspicion but just shook his head.

"We will just have to take a chance," he said, feeling driven to get to the police but also angered and itching to hit back.

More minutes dragged by and the sun continued to beat down. There was not a cloud in the sky and Donny became both thirsty and hungry. Worry about Uncle James returning in the helicopter and finding them began to gnaw at him.

Then another vehicle sound came to them, this time from the east. Vaughan lifted his head to look.

"It's a Four-Wheel Drive towing a caravan. Tourists," he said.

"What will we do?" Sharlene asked.

Chapter 30

TAKE RISKS

"We have to take risks," Donny said. "We can't stay here. We must get to the police."

"Okay, I'll flag it down and hope," Vaughan said, dusting himself as he stood up.

Donny and Sharlene stood up as well. As he did, Donny stared anxiously at the roadworker's camp.

If Thug is still there, he can see us now. We could be on the run in a minute or so.

Then he switched his attention to the highway in both directions and to the 4WD and caravan approaching. It was a white Toyota Prado towing a very ordinary looking Jayco caravan.

"I hope the people are helpful," Sharlene said, mirroring Donny's thoughts.

Vaughan now put down his bag and stepped out onto the edge of the gravel highway. Here he held up both hands in an appeal to stop. Sharlene stayed where she was and did the same, but Donny just stood, looking around for danger and ready to bolt.

As the Prado got closer, Donny saw that there were two people in the front. He could see their faces looking at them. For a few seconds he thought it was not going to stop, but then it began to slow and finally came to a halt with a sharp skid of locked wheels on gravel. He then saw that the two people were an elderly man and woman.

Grey nomads, he thought.

The woman was driving and the man in the passenger seat waited until the dust cloud had billowed past and dispersed, before winding the window down.

"Yes, can we help?" he asked.

Vaughan spoke. "We need help. Please take us to the police."

"The police! What's the problem?" the man queried.

"Some men are trying to kidnap us," Vaughan replied, gesturing with his arms.

Sharlene added to this by stepping closer. "Please, horrible men who have taken our parents as hostages. Please take us to town to the police."

The man frowned and stared at her. "You look like you've been in the wars a bit," he said. The woman just looked worried.

Donny thought they looked like they were nice people. He stepped closer and said, "Please! We have been on the run for four or five days."

He paused to try to count how many then just shook his head and, to his great shame, burst into tears. The two people both stared and ran their eyes over them. Their struggle to make a decision was evident on their faces. Donny understood.

It is a very isolated place, and they are probably afraid they are going to be robbed, or worse.

He had heard of occasional murders on lonely outback roads, nearly always by strangers, not locals. An idea came to him as he saw the elderly couple look at each other, obviously trying to make their mind up. Wiping away his tears, he stepped forward.

"Just take one of us. Sharlene, you go. Vaughan and I will keep on hiding. We will be alright."

Vaughan nodded. "That's a good idea. Donny and I will be fine. Sharlene, you go and get the cops. If you people will take her that is."

Sharlene was horrified. "I can't leave you!" she cried.

"Yes, you can!" Donny replied with heat. "We were on our own for four or five days before you joined us."

He had been astonished and pleased by Vaughan's answer. *He's grown up a bit in the last few days,* he thought.

The elderly couple listened with evident astonishment. "Who are you young people?" the man asked.

Vaughan answered. Pointing he said, "This is Sharlene, and she lives on Glen Morris Station, which is back that way about a hundred Ks; and this is young Donny MacAndrew. He comes from Clonargh Station, which is over that way. And I'm Vaughan MacAndrew, his cousin, from... from Sydney."

"So what's the problem?" the woman asked.

Vaughan glanced at Donny as though to get guidance about how much to tell, then said, "We don't want to put you in danger by telling you too much but my uncle James and a gang of crooks are holding our parents as hostages in return for money."

"Ransom money," Donny added.

As he stood there, he was fidgeting with impatience, fearing to see Thug or the Land Rover or the helicopter appear at any moment.

Both elderly people frowned. The man shook his head. "So what are you young people doing out here?"

Donny answered. "Vaughan and I ran away from the crooks and have been hiding and trying to find our parents so we could rescue them."

The man looked around. "Out here? In those buildings over there?"

"No!" Donny replied. "That's just the roadworker's camp. We just came here to try to get help but... but..."

He stalled, trying work out how to keep the story simple. He was going to say that there was no-one there but wasn't sure if Thug was still there or not.

Vaughan took up the tale. "Oh, please take Sharlene to town and get the police. The crooks could come back at any moment."

"These men, are they dangerous?" the man asked.

The friends all looked at each other with evident uncertainty. Donny shrugged and replied, "I think Uncle James might be, and a couple of them have guns. But the others, not really. Oh please, take Sharlene and get going!"

The man looked at the lady and then at them. "We can take you all, but we will have to shift some of the gear in the back."

He indicated the rear seat and back of the vehicle, both of which were piled high with luggage and camping gear.

Vaughan pointed to the caravan. "Just put us in the van," he suggested.

Both adults shook their heads. The man said, "We can't do that! It is against the law."

"Oh please!" Donny cried, anxiety gnawing at him. "You won't get into trouble. We need to get moving quickly."

"If we're going to the police we could get into trouble," the lady said.

Donny shook his head. "No, you won't! Constable O'Grady knows us, and we will explain."

The man looked worried then looked at the lady again. To Donny's intense relief, she nodded. The man climbed out of the car and said, "I'll open up. You kids just sit on a seat or on the bed and don't touch anything."

He walked to the side of the van pulled out a folding step. Donny followed, then Sharlene and then Vaughan, who detoured to pick up his carry bag. The man used keys from his pocket to unlock the door.

"Up you go," he said.

Donny had never been in a caravan so let Vaughan and Sharlene go first. As he stepped up inside, his first impression was of stuffiness and then of what a relief it was to be out of the sun and glare. The windows, he realised, were tinted. On his right, along the rear of the van, was a stove and then cupboards with a sink and washing up area. Turning left he found he was in a short passageway with a refrigerator on the left and a table with bench seats either side on the right. A large bed took up the front of the van. There were various lockers and small doors, but the overall impression was of pleasant comfort.

Vaughan seated himself on the first bench seat near the fridge and Sharlene slid into the second. She went to move across, but Donny went past her and stood at the end of the bed. The man followed them up, pointed to the sink and said, "There is water in that tap, but I have to turn on the pump. It is not supposed to be on when the van is being towed."

"We've got water, thanks," Vaughan answered. He indicated his bag.

The man nodded. "Good. But I will still turn it on because you might need it. Sorry, there is only that portable toilet there. Not very private but okay for a married couple."

He pointed to a small plastic Portapotee in the space between the bed and the left side of the van. Donny blushed but Sharlene said, "It will be fine. It is only an hour or so to town."

"Where do you want to go?" asked the man.

"To Golden Dawn, to the Police Station," Vaughan replied.

"Do you know where it is?"

Donny smiled at that. "It is our local town. It only has two streets. You will find it easily."

"Alright. But we don't do much speeding on gravel roads so it might be more like two hours."

"That will be fine," Sharlene replied. "Please just start going."

As the man turned to go down the steps, Donny called, "We might meet the crooks along the way. They are driving a dark green Land Rover. And they have a helicopter."

"Okay, the man replied, looking very thoughtful. "What if they ask us to stop?"

"Just leave the door unlocked so we can get out quickly please," Vaughan answered.

The man nodded and stepped down. The door was swung shut and, to Donny's relief, not locked. He heard the steps being swung up and then the crunch of boots. There was a window on the left beside the bed and through it he saw the old man walk back to the vehicle. Taking off his carry bag, he turned and sat on the end of the bed.

A minute later they began to move. Donny nearly burst into tears with relief. At last it seemed that their problems were over!

For the next few minutes, they sat and looked out the windows. The van went up over the long, bare hill and Donny saw a familiar vista open up, nothing but short grass and flat land as far as the eye could see. But they were out of sight and out of the sun and rolling along in comfort at 50kph! He grinned, and after a few minutes of looking out, Vaughan offered Sharlene a drink.

"And some food please," she added.

The thought of food made Donny salivate and his stomach gurgled again. Sharlene twisted around, and said, "Don't you fart in here, Donny!"

Donny blushed with shame and nodded. Digging in his bag he took out a drink bottle and emptied it. *I'll refill that in a minute,* he told himself.

But food was more the priority. From the bottom of the bag he dug out several badly squashed slices of fresh bread, some cheese and slices of smoked ham. These were shared out, Sharlene having discovered some plastic plates in a drawer. The food was rapidly consumed and more water drunk. Sharlene took the empty bottles and refilled them and Donny and Vaughan placed them back in their bags.

"Just in case," Sharlene explained.

Donny looked out again. It was all familiar from many trips to town, but he could not have named the place. The van bounced and swayed a lot, but the road had been recently graded and Donny knew his dad usually drove at 100kph on it with no problems. But having eaten he now felt very sleepy. He wriggled backwards on the bed and went to lie down.

"Donny! Don't you put your boots on that bed," Sharlene snapped.

Donny almost replied, 'Yes Mum!' but the thought of his mother and the rebuke added to his anxiety, which made tears come again, to his shame. So that Vaughan and Sharlene should not see them, he turned his head away and lay flat.

Sleep claimed him within minutes. But it was restless sleep, disturbed by bumps and bounces and by Vaughan and Sharlene talking but he only surfaced some time later when the van came to a stop. Groggy with exhaustion, Donny sat half up and muttered, "What's up?"

Sharlene came and bent down to look out. Because the front window had a stone guard they could only see dimly through that, so the side windows were all they had to look out from.

"Oh, I know this place. What's it called?"

Donny shook his head and stared out the right-hand side. A fenced-in clump of trees stood at a road junction. Nearby was a huge iron pipe sticking up beside a rusty old steam tractor of 19th Century vintage. Beyond them was a large gravel car park, shelter shed with picnic table and a public toilet.

"The Government Bore," he said.

"Oh, so it is!" Sharlene agreed. "We stop here sometimes so Granny can go to the dunny."

"Not far now. We hit the bitumen soon," Donny said, his hopes soaring.

"Should we stop and use the phone at Craiglie?" Sharlene queried.

Donny thought hard, remembering distances and times: *30 kilometres to Craiglie homestead, then another five to the highway junction, that highway that runs all the way up western Queensland from Birdsville to Mount Isa. 1000 kilometres long. Bloody hell! What's its name? We go along it all the time!*

Then he shook his head. "No. It's only another ten k's to town from the junction," he said. "We will be there quicker."

What he didn't say was that he did not like the McPherson's. To his surprise, Sharlene agreed.

"Good! I don't feel like explaining it all to the McPhersons. I don't like them," she said. "They think they are a cut above everyone else, particularly the old lady." She then changed to mimic an upper-class accent, looking down her nose as she did. "Oh, you know! My mum says she thinks she's the great lady of the squattocracy! As though they were the first pioneers instead of us and you MacAndrews!"

Donny laughed. It was a sentiment frequently aired in his family. But he did not mention the rude comments he had overheard his father using about what the old Mrs McPherson thought didn't stink!

Craiglie is only a thousand square kilometres bigger then Clonargh, he thought resentfully.

Once again he remembered his parent's comments about how many of the properties in the shire had been settled back in the 19th Century by very determined and tough Scottish pioneers. It did not occur to him until many years later that he must have inherited a good measure of their quality in his genes!

There was the crunch of boots, and the old man came to the door. "We just stopped to look at the bore and to go to the toilet. Is that okay?"

"Of course," Vaughan agreed.

Donny would have preferred to just keep driving but knew they could not begrudge the old couple a short comfort break. So they drove in next to the toilet and they all took turns at scuttling across and using it. That was a relief and saved a lot of embarrassment, so Donny was happy with that. While they waited, they described some of their adventures to the old couple, who introduced themselves as Mr and Mrs Ross from Townsville. He was a retired schoolteacher and she had been a teacher aide.

Sharlene explained about the bitumen and Craiglie while they were waiting. Then it was on again, the door closed, and steps put up. Donny went back to bed but Sharlene came and hit at his boots.

"Move over Donny. I want some bed," she demanded.

Donny did and was very pleased. He was now smitten by her and very jealous that Vaughan was making an obvious play to impress her.

The road was still good gravel, so good that Donny hardly noticed when they bumped onto bitumen.

Oh, thank God! Won't be long now, he thought, and dropped back into a deep sleep, to be shaken awake by Sharlene in distress.

"Wake up Donny, wake up! It's the helicopter!"

Chapter 31

THE WASHAWAYS

Donny jerked awake and sat up.

It hadn't been a nightmare! That vibration was real! There it was, flying low only 50 metres away. Even as Donny watched, the machine buzzed out of sight ahead of them. He sprang off the bed and snatched up his bag.

"He will land in front of us and stop us," he cried. "Get ready to run."

Already he could feel the caravan's brakes slowing it down. Donny looked out through both windows but could see no sign of the helicopter.

"He's probably landing on the road to block it," he suggested.

"But can't they just drive around it?" Vaughan said.

Donny looked out and saw a long line of trees not far ahead on both sides. On both sides there were cattle standing around on dry mud. He groaned, "No! We are at The Washaways. If he lands on the road there it is on a causeway with mud on both sides. They will have to stop."

He did not think the old couple would try to do anything else. The car and van came to a stop and Donny paced up and down the short passageway, feeling like a trapped animal. His emotions began to boil. All those days of being hunted, of being sore and thirsty, of painful experiences! Now they all seemed to mount up to one huge irritant, one intense desire to end things and to strike back. A feeling of hatred mixed with rage at Uncle James filled him.

There he was! Uncle James was pushing the old man back along the side of the road towards the door of the caravan. Donny noted that the old man was looking distressed and that Uncle James was holding a gun in his right hand, an automatic pistol, and a satellite telephone in his left.

He kept shoving the old man. "Get it open!" he shouted as they passed below the side window.

Donny glanced out to confirm where they were. He saw that they were indeed on a causeway that dropped down to a wide area of mud, much of it dry and dotted with dozens of cattle. Ahead there was a wide sheet of water.

It is The Washaways. We must get across, he told himself.

"When I get Uncle James out of the way, get off and run around the back of the van and then go left and across the bridges. Don't stop to help, just run!" he told Vaughan and Sharlene, both of whom were now standing as well.

But first there was Uncle James to deal with. Donny was now too emotional to be thinking clearly as rage and determination mingled. He was so roused that the sight of that gun was no deterrent. Then a plan just came to him.

He stepped across to the doorway just as the door swung open. There was Uncle James! Donny hurled his bag with the four full water bottles in it with all the strength he could muster and then sprang out, shouting his hate as he did. Uncle James had just pushed the old man aside and was about to step up, but the folding step wasn't out so it was quite a distance, so the flying bag took him completely by surprise. It struck him full in the chest, and he staggered back. Then Donny collided with him, his full 60 kilograms moving at speed.

But in his haste, Donny had miscalculated. The causeway was higher and steeper than he had noted; and while the bag caused Uncle James to stagger back, Donny's full weight hitting his stomach and chest completely overbalanced him. He let out a cry of surprise mingled with pain and then went over backwards, sprawling and tumbling down the rocky sides of the causeway, all the way to the bottom where he ended up upside down with his head in the mud and feet up the slope. In trying to protect himself, Uncle James had dropped the satellite phone, but the pistol was still gripped in his right hand.

Donny had tumbled down with him and was momentarily dazed and bruised. He rolled off a stunned Uncle James and lay beside him.

There is the gun! Donny noted.

Frantic to get it and get away, he grabbed at it and pulled. No good. Then he remembered what his father had said: *'If you want to break someone's grip just pull their little finger, until it breaks if necessary.'*

So that is what Donny did, semi-aware that he was snarling and swearing at the same time. Uncle James's eyes opened and he stared in horror at Donny and yelled, but his hand had twitched convulsively and the gun had fallen onto the dry mud.

Donny snatched it up and sprang back away from Uncle James,

who was both winded and stunned. *What will I do with the gun?* Donny wondered.

He did not know how to use it, other than what he had seen on TV, and he did not want to get involved in shooting anyone. On an impulse he stood up and hurled the gun as far as he could out onto the wet mud. Then he turned and went scrambling up the steep bank.

Both Vaughan and Sharlene were standing beside the old man. They were gaping in horror at the whole incident. Donny's anger flared again.

"Run you two! Run I said! Go!" he said, and pointed the way he wanted them to run.

Stung by his savage tone of command, they did. As he scrabbled up the slope, Donny was aware that his bag was at the bottom behind him but he just kept going.

We can do without water. It's only ten or fifteen kilometres to town and this creek goes all the way, he told himself.

At the top, Donny stopped to glance back down and then turned to the old man, and said, "Sorry Mr Ross. Try to get away if you can."

Then he bolted, following the others around the back of the van. Now he was using local knowledge. The Washaways were four braided streams that were tributaries of Eyre Creek, one of the huge network of streams that made up the vast area called 'The Channel Country'. They meandered for many kilometres across the flat country, joining up and then separating again.

In places the streams spread as huge swamps, usually dry. At others there was a single deep channel, and Donny knew that the recent winter rains had filled that channel.

We need to cross here, or we will have to go for a long way to cross, or we will have to swim, he thought.

By then he was around the back of the caravan and now turned left to run forwards past the car. He saw that Vaughan and Sharlene were both passing it. As he reached the front of the caravan, Donny saw that the old lady had gotten out and had hurried around the front of the car to see what the disturbance was. She was looking shocked and frightened.

"Sorry!" Donny gasped as he raced past the vehicle.

Ahead of him for the next 200 metres stretched the causeway and four concrete bridges. All the channels of The Washaways had water in them but the last one was the widest. In between were mud banks. To the right, the creeks all curved away to the west but to those on the left went straight for a long way, to vanish among trees and marshes. The far bank was lined with a dense growth of tall reeds and large trees. The helicopter had landed on the first bridge, completely blocking the road.

Vaughan and Sharlene ran past the helicopter, both continually glancing back to check. Donny made urgent gestures to keep going.

"Keep running! Get across and then go right! Go North!" he yelled.

Donny ran to the helicopter and then dithered. He would have dearly liked to stop it flying somehow but did not know what to do. For a few seconds he considered trying to push it over but when he tried it was too heavy. As he did, he glanced back and saw that Uncle James was stumbling out over the mud to where he had thrown the pistol.

I should have brought it with me and thrown it in the water, he thought.

Something like panic surged. "Oh God! We must get away," he croaked.

Then movement on the highway in the distance behind the caravan caught his eye. He focused and then gasped.

"The Land Rover! Oh no!"

Fuelled now by another spurt of fear, as well as more adrenaline, he turned and sprinted for the far end of The Washaways. Running faster than he had ever run in the school sports, he dashed across those concrete bridges, glancing back a few times. That kept him informed that Uncle James had the gun and was trying to wipe mud off it as he struggled back towards the vehicles. Remembering his father's advice, Donny told himself that Uncle James would be a fool to try to fire that gun without first cleaning it. That was some relief.

And it's only a pistol, not a rifle, he thought, knowing well that rifles could kill at many hundreds of metres range.

To his annoyance, he saw that Vaughan and Sharlene had stopped at the end of the last bridge and were staring back at him.

"Go right, go right!" he shouted, making sweeping motions with his right arm as he did.

He was nearly up with them before they nodded, turned and started running. There was a dense belt of tall reeds in the shallow water there and then a thicket of trees, but a dirt vehicle track went off just beyond that. A road sign said: BIRD HIDES. Vaughan turned and ran out of sight along that track, followed by Sharlene.

When Donny reached it, he also paused to look back. To his horror, he saw that Uncle James was back up at the caravan and was waving the gun at the old people. Worse still, the front of the Land Rover was just showing past the caravan.

"Bugger!" he muttered. "We will have to outrun those bloody crooks again. I hope Sharlene can run."

Worry about her fitness redoubled when he dashed off the bitumen highway and along the dirt vehicle track and found her and Vaughan both standing there gasping for breath.

"Keep going! The crooks will be after us in a minute," he croaked.

Without waiting he dashed past them and continued along the track, immediately confronted with choices. Dirt vehicle tracks seemed to lead off everywhere. He had been there only once, when his mother had wished to visit. But none of the family were avid birdwatchers so they had never been again and that had been several years before. He knew that some of the tracks led to little timber huts, bird hides, which overlooked the creek and surrounding swamps, and that other tracks led to places where tourists could camp with their vehicles and caravans. But which ones?

The whole area was a maze of tracks amid cane grass and reeds that were taller than a person. Donny made a choice, suspecting it might be wrong. He saw one track go off to the right and knew it went to a hide overlooking the causeway area. The one he had chosen led to two more hides hidden among the trees along the creek bank. He came to a standstill looking down a steep bank at what was obviously deep water. Frightened ducks with lovely shiny green necks went paddling and skittering away.

"That way!" Donny cried, pointing to his left as Vaughan and Sharlene caught up with him.

He was now in such frame of mind that he was prepared to just leave them if they could not keep up. He went running off along another track, followed by the other two. Several camp sites were passed and two more bird hides that overlooked a wide bend in the creek. On the other side of the creek was an area of marsh, mainly reeds and grass growing in water. They came to another bird hide and the vehicle track ended at a campsite among some trees.

"Where to now? Where are we going?" Vaughan asked. He was gasping for breath and red in the face. So was Sharlene.

"To town," Donny said.

He looked frantically for an easy way through the tangle of reeds and bushes ahead of him. He noted a faint foot track and headed for it at a jog, then slowed to duck and weave through the bushes.

"How far is it?" Vaughan asked as he puffed along close behind.

"A bit over twelve k's I reckon," Donny replied.

From the back Sharlene called, her voice punctuated by gasping breaths. "Should we now try to reach Craiglie homestead. It will be closer."

Donny considered this but then shook his head. He pushed aside more low branches and trampled into long cane grass.

"No. It's about five k's still and we would have to go along beside the road and that is all open country," he said.

"You said the town is ten kilometres north of the junction near Craiglie," Vaughan said.

"That's right. So we have another one of those triangle problems, except we might have to detour and duck and weave."

Then he swore as a branch brushed his hat off. He snatched it up and held it in his hand.

"Twelve or thirteen k's then?" Sharlene said.

"Might be a lot more if we have to hide all the way along the creek," Donny replied.

He had now come out in an open of reeds and only a cattle pad made it possible to proceed quickly. Fifty metres ahead were more trees; and at that point the creek began to swing around to the north-east, reinforcing his comment. To get across the open ground before the helicopter could get airborne, he jogged.

As they arrived at the trees, the sound of the helicopter starting up came to them. Donny came to a panting halt and peered through a gap in the trees. He found he could just see the Prado and caravan but had to move a few more paces to get a view that included the Land Rover and helicopter. A single glance gave him all he needed to know. Uncle James was in the helicopter, Thug was getting into the Prado, and Ringer was shepherding the old couple back to the Land Rover.

"They've taken the old people hostage as well," he said, pointing.

Even as he watched it, the helicopter lifted off. Then the Prado and caravan drove forward across the causeway and went out of sight behind the trees where the bird hides were. The Land Rover followed.

Where are they going? he wondered.

Curious to know their plans but also driven by the urge to get away, Donny turned and resumed pushing through the undergrowth. He knew he needed to stay under the trees as the helicopter was now up and looking for them, flying low backwards and forwards over the bird hide area. As it did, it disturbed hundreds of birds. These flew up in all directions, the helicopter almost colliding with some.

"We need to get right away from this area as fast as we can," Donny croaked.

A branch scratched his hand and leaves brushed his face, but he pushed on as fast as he could, thankful that the trees along this section of bank were a real thicket. Glancing back to see what the noise was, saw that Vaughan's bag kept getting caught by branches.

"Leave it, Vaughan. We will just take one water bottle each. We need to run," he said.

So they each grabbed a water bottle and Vaughan dropped the bag under a bush. Then the helicopter was overhead and they had to crouch under what cover they could find. The helicopter was very low and several times Donny glimpsed it through small gaps in the foliage, but it seemed that Uncle James could not see them as he moved on northwards. But they still could not move without being spotted.

Donny took the opportunity to peer back across the bend in the creek and the large swamp that took up most of the big curve beyond to look at the causeway area. He was just in time to see the Land Rover drive back eastwards along the highway.

"Now where is Thug with the Prado and caravan?" he asked.

"Maybe he has parked it back there at those bird hides?" Vaughan suggested.

"That's what I think," Donny agreed. "So now he will be after us on foot."

But how to get clear? Out to their left was a huge open area of grass, at least two or three kilometres across and quite devoid of cover. To the right was the creek and swamp! The only option at that moment was to push on northwards along the creek, even though it was curving north-east at that point, so further from town.

Donny began slowly pushing through the thicket, when every instinct was to run. Then they had to stop and crouch under bushes again when the helicopter came back towards them. Once again, Uncle James kept them pinned while Donny pictured Thug tracking them from behind.

But once again the helicopter went by and then hovered about a hundred metres further south, near where Donny thought the last of the bird hides was.

"Talking to Thug I reckon," he said. "Let's take a risk."

He stood up and forced his way out to the edge of the trees, using his hat and water bottle to help. When he got there, he directed a hard look to his left at where the helicopter was hovering and then turned right and began hurrying along right on the edge of the trees and bushes. The others followed.

Vaughan crouched next to him, sucking in deep breaths but looking determined. "That Thug bloke must have still been at the roadworker's camp and saw us get into the caravan," he said.

"I reckon. Okay, when we run, we are doing the cross-country, five kilometres in twenty-five minutes. As soon as we get a chance, and even if we don't, we go straight across this big open area to those trees over there where the creek bends back again. If the helicopter lands, then we split up. I will deal with Uncle James. One of you guys should make it to town to get the cops."

The other two both looked scared at this but nodded. Then they had to hide in under bushes as the helicopter came clattering back, again flying very low.

Thug will be following our tracks now. He must be only a hundred metres or so behind, Donny reasoned. It was all starting to look pretty hopeless, but he was determined. *I'll do a marathon run if I have to,* he told himself, then amended it to a half-marathon.

The helicopter had moved just far enough away for them to resume pushing through the trees. In this way they covered another hundred metres before it came buzzing back. Once again, they hid. It was very sweaty and unpleasant with leaves and grass down the backs of their shirts and stuck to their skin. He saw that various rough leaves and prickles had scratched them so there were little trickles of blood mixed with the sweat.

As the helicopter moved on southwards, Vaughan had a drink and then offered Sharlene a drink. She shook her head.

"I've got my own bottle," she said, holding it up.

Vaughan smiled. "It's okay. I can drink the creek. You drink this. You don't get an upset stomach," he said. "You don't want to be doing farts like Donny."

Sharlene's face dimpled into a grin and then she went all prim-and-proper and said in a very ladylike voice: "Ladies don't fart thank you! They occasionally experience emissions of colonic miasma."

Despite being initially hurt and annoyed by Vaughan's comment, Donny had to grin at Sharlene's reply. Then he grinned again to himself.

Vaughan has certainly picked up since he's had a girl to show off to! he thought.

Sharlene accepted the drink and then they began moving again, slowly because of the helicopter but very aware of the possible appearance of Thug behind them. They recovered their breath, and drinking kept them hydrated. But Donny fairly itched with impatience. In half an hour by Sharlene's watch, they only moved about half a kilometre.

At this rate it will be tomorrow morning before we get there, if that Thug character doesn't catch us first.

Chapter 32

THE BURNING SUN

It was 1:15pm before they moved (1315hrs by Sharlene's watch as she had it set on 24-hour time, which Donny realised he probably needed to understand). They crept cautiously through the thicket, looking behind as much as keeping track of the helicopter. Even in the shade of the trees it was very hot, and a heat shimmer caused mirage effects out on the open plain to their left.

It was glancing at this that something else caught Donny's interest, a pale thin line right on the horizon. He stopped and squinted in the glare and then nodded. It was the next line of sand dunes. That cheered him up. He knew that these dunes ran almost north-south. There were three dunes before the homestead of Craiglie Station, then Western Creek, one of the many channels off the creek they were following, and then two more long dunes that ran all the way to town with the highway on the far side of the second one.

They continued for another hundred metres and then the situation suddenly changed. The helicopter came back and landed only about a hundred metres to the south of them. The friends crouched under cover and watched as its engine was switched off. As the rotors swished to a standstill, Thug appeared from the tree line behind them. As Donny had feared, Thug had a shotgun and the sight of it chilled him. Thug went over to the helicopter and he and Uncle James had a conversation. Thug was obviously getting orders as he did a lot of nodding. Then he turned and began walking back to the trees and the helicopter started up again.

"That looks like trouble," Vaughan suggested.

"I agree," Donny said. "They have some new plan I reckon."

"Let's get further away while we can," Sharlene suggested.

So they started walking again. But the effort of weaving through the thick scrub was very wearing and Donny was determined that, at the first reasonable opportunity, he would start running.

I will leave these guys to follow in their own time if they can't keep up, he thought.

A glance at Sharlene's watch told him it was 1345hrs and that meant that time was getting short. That comment about Uncle David arriving back this evening was now gnawing at him, as he suspected the crooks would then flee. But what would they do to the hostages before they did? Several options came to mind, and he felt so apprehensive he felt sick.

The helicopter lifted off and, to Donny's surprise, did not resume searching for them. Instead, it flew off northwards towards the town. Donny watched it until it was out of sight, and then said, "Now is our chance. I am going to run across this big open field. I am going to run for twenty minutes by your watch Sharlene, if you can keep up."

"Don't get cheeky!" Sharlene retorted.

They burst out of the cover and started racing across the grassy plain. The grass was a bit longer than usual and made running difficult, but Donny had the incentive to get out of shotgun range as quickly as he could. So, as he ran, he kept glancing back to his left rear for any sign of Thug. But he saw no sign of the man. Now he concentrated on his running, not wanting to shame himself in Sharlene's eyes by appearing weak. Not after that last comment!

But he was not as fit as he would have liked, and within a couple of hundred metres he was puffing and by another he was panting and feeling the strain. At 400 metres he had the beginnings of stitch and was perspiring and his heart hammering. But so were the others and they were falling behind so he slowed down. Then Vaughan slowed to a jog and Sharlene stayed with him. Donny relented on his earlier resolution and slowed to stay with them.

Looking back gave him real satisfaction. He calculated that they were half a kilometre or more from the tree line and already it looked very distant. But he was also very conscious that they were right out in the middle of a big open area.

If that helicopter comes back now, we will stand out like flies on a white ceiling, he thought.

At his urging they pushed it, jogging and walking fast; and after ten minutes was up, Donny estimated they had covered a kilometre and a half. He looked back to check if Thug was following and was gratified to see no sign of him. He also noted that the trees along The Washaways were now looking very distant and were starting to vanish in the mirage shimmer. That was good.

A movement out to the south-west caught his eye so he stopped to study it while allowing the other two to catch up. The moving object was mostly obscured by the heat shimmer, but then he saw it was a big truck, heading to his left.

That is a truck on the Min Min Highway, he reasoned.

As he watched it go out of sight among the trees where the creek bent at the bird hides, a white car towing a caravan came into view going the other way. Donny stared at it as it headed west. Vaughan and Sharlene joined him and also stared. Vaughan pointed.

"Is that the old people's caravan, do you think?"

Donny shook his head. To him all caravans looked the same. "I don't know," he replied, but he suspected that was. Anxiously he watched the caravan vanish into the heat shimmer.

Vaughan thought so. "I reckon that Thug bloke has been ordered to take it to town," he said.

"But why?" Sharlene queried.

Vaughan answered, voicing Donny's suspicions. "I reckon they have given up trying to catch us out here and are going to set a trap to catch us as we try to get into town."

"I think so too," Donny agreed. "Oh, come on, run! We need to get there before they are ready." He turned and started running.

"Donny! Donny, slow down! You can't beat them. It is still nine or ten k's to town."

"Seven or eight," Donny replied through clenched teeth.

He did not care. He felt driven. So he kept on running. The other two reluctantly began running behind him. He pushed himself for another ten minutes until he thought he had covered at least another kilometre and a half and was gasping and sweating so much in the heat he had to slow.

While he stood there with chest heaving, waiting for the others to catch up, he looked back and noted that the trees along the creek behind him were very hard to see. The ones at the bend that he was aiming for now looked to be only a kilometre ahead. He had a big drink and as soon as the others caught up, resumed walking.

The others protested but Donny was adamant. "We rest in those trees," he said firmly.

They accepted this so they strode on, the grass now so long in places that it impeded walking. It also meant they could not see where they were putting their boots and fear of snakes began to build up in Donny's imagination.

Sweating and puffing, they reached the trees and flung themselves down in the shade. "What time is it?" Donny asked.

"1430 hours," Sharlene answered.

Vaughan gestured out to the open country and blinding sunlight. "Which way do we go now. This creek is curving away to the right."

"We need to go north-west," Donny said.

"Which way is that?" Sharlene queried. "Can you trust the sun? It is a bit too vertical over head for any accuracy, isn't it?"

"I'll show you," Vaughan said.

He finished having a drink that emptied his bottle then picked up a short stick and stood up. He pushed the stick into a crack in the clay out in the sun. Then he placed a small stone on the end of the stick's shadow before walking back into the shade.

"Tell me when ten minutes has passed."

Donny did not want to waste ten minutes. *We could walk another kilometre in that time,* he thought impatiently.

But he also understood the others needed the rest and his need was to be sure of direction. So he had a drink and fidgeted until the time was up.

Vaughan then went out and placed another small stone on where the shadow had moved to. It was only a few centimetres.

"You need to do this a couple of times and for fifteen or twenty minutes, each time," he explained. "But the line from one to the other stone is approximately west to east." He pointed that way. "So that is east." Swinging around he spread his arms and brought them together for north and facing that way he then put his left arm out. "That must be about north-west."

That was good enough for Donny. He stood up and started walking. The others grumbled but did likewise. But striding out into the burning sunlight was a shock. It was so fierce it seemed to cut through clothes, and he quickly clapped his hat back on. Looking ahead into the heat shimmer, he picked a spot on the sand dune that had now become quite a feature of the middle distance. The dune cut diagonally right across their route.

Despite the heat they walked quickly. But it was an effort. The air was so hot that breathing it in felt like sucking in some boiling liquid.

The only breeze was from their own movement and a glance upwards showed only a few scattered cumulus clouds. Not enough to provide any shade. The ground was dried out as well and the grass became shorter and sparser until they were back to walking on gibber plain again.

But they were making progress, and ten minutes of this had the sand dune only a kilometre or so ahead. It had emerged from the mirage and taken on a pink tone, mottled by the white flowers on the small bushes that dotted its slopes.

As they got close to the dune, Sharlene pointed upwards. "Look at all those birds!" she cried.

Donny looked and saw that dozens of hawks and eagles were circling in the distance ahead of them. "Must be something dead," he suggested.

"It will be us if we keep pushing it!" Sharlene retorted, wiping perspiration from her forehead.

Vaughan chuckled. "That reminds me of a joke," he said. "There were these two French Foreign Legionnaires lost in the Sahara Desert, and they were very hungry...." He proceeded to tell the joke about the vultures.

Donny wasn't sure if Sharlene would be amused but she positively shrieked with laughter when he finished.

"Oh Vaughan! That is a very good joke."

That hurt. Donny fumed with what he did not want to name as jealousy while Vaughan and Sharlene chatted about cadet jokes. Donny gritted his teeth in frustration, knowing he was being unreasonable; that no high school age girl would ever consider a primary school boy for a boyfriend.

But oh! She is so wonderful!

They walked on, the heat from the ground reflecting upwards and seeming to burn through the leather of his boot soles. The air also came in alternating waves of hot and very hot. He understood that it was a risk walking in the open in such heat, but he shook his head.

The sooner we get there the better.

It was close to 1500hrs when they reached the base of the dune. As they got closer, the heat reflected off the sand and made his face feel hot and dry. Donny did not think it worth the effort to try to obliterate their tracks, so they just plodded and scrambled up, only pausing to peek through bushes before stepping up onto the crest.

They came to a gasping, sweating halt. Donny drank the last of his water and so did Sharlene. What he saw in front both cheered and depressed him. It was what he had expected to see, another wide, bare plain of two or three kilometres and another creek line. The plain was covered with clumps of saltbush, tufts of dry grass and spinifex with a few darker green areas that he suspected were swamps. The creek line was only a wandering thread of trees, and not very many. Another kilometre or so beyond that was another sand dune.

"That is Western Creek," he explained, "And the airfield and town are over past that next sand dune."

He wanted to push on immediately, but Sharlene insisted they rest for ten minutes. As they sat there Sharlene pointed off to their left.

"That black thing is what has attracted the birds," she said.

Donny shielded his eyes and squinted. "Dead beast I think," he suggested. He found it a bit far to see the details.

"Probably," Sharlene agreed. Like him he knew she had seen plenty of dead animals over the years.

Vaughan looked and then said, "Definitely a dead calf or something like that," he said. Then he grinned. "That reminds me of another joke."

He proceeded to tell the joke about the French Foreign Legionnaires and the rotting camel.

Sharlene listened with an obvious mixture of amusement and horror. "Oh Vaughan! That is disgusting!" she cried.

But then she laughed, sending more little stabs of envy through Donny. He had sat there fretting and wanting to get on, so now he stood up and led them down the other side and out onto the flat. Direction keeping was no problem as the sun was now low enough to be right in their faces, adding to the discomfort. It quickly turned from being an uncomfortable plod to a real ordeal. The heat waves shimmered and reflected sunlight had them squinting and gasping, and both Vaughan and Sharlene got even more sunburnt as they had no hats. Donny began to watch them with some anxiety, noting that he was still sweating but feeling really hot. Sharlene in particular was starting to limp and looked exhausted.

The creek was reached at 1530. It was only a single narrow stream with steep sides of dry mud and a few muddy pools in it. There were easy places to cross where the cattle had, but it was harder to find a place to refill their water bottles without stepping into the churned up and glutinous mud. Donny did not really want to drink any of the water, particularly as he now estimated they were only about 5 or 6 kilometres from the town, but he made himself. It was hardest for Sharlene. She carefully filled her bottle and looked askance at the objects floating in the muddy water.

Donny made himself gulp down a big mouthful and then said, "It's only cow poo, Sharlene."

"It looked disgusting!" she cried, curling up her lip and shaking her head. "It might make us sick."

"Might make you fart like Donny," Vaughan added with a grin.

"Oh, poo to you too!" Donny cried. Then he grinned and said, "You could drop from heat stroke if you don't get more liquid in you. You've stopped sweating. The worst it will do is make you sick."

Sharlene did a lot of grimacing and muttering but finally drank. "Aargh yuk! That is vile!" she said, turning her head away and making a sour face as she did so.

But then she made herself drink some more. Donny applauded and then drank more and refilled his bottle. So did Vaughan. Then they sat in a small patch of shade for another ten minutes.

Donny pointed along the creek bed. "You could follow this creek all the way to town if you want. It joins The Washaways about two kilometres east of the town. But it will be longer to walk."

"What are you going to do?" Vaughan asked.

"I'm going the shortest route, straight across country," Donny replied.

"We will come with you," Vaughan said. "We are still good for a few more k's."

Donny looked at him and shook his head with a mixture of admiration and concern. "You've come a long way in the last few days," he admitted.

Vaughan shrugged. "Our Cadet OC said that on a field exercise it takes about four days for people who aren't used to walking in the bush to get fitter, and after that they go like a train."

Donny turned to Sharlene. "What about you Sharlene? You look a bit bu... er... (He struggled not to use the swear word 'buggered') er... worn out."

She nodded. "I am, and I'm getting blisters and starting to chafe," she admitted. "But I am good for another couple of k's. To that next sand dune anyway."

With that, Donny led them up an easy cattle pad and out into the blazing sunlight again. They headed across the next kilometre of flat to a sand dune that appeared to dance in the heat shimmer. As he walked, Donny kept listening for the first tremor of the helicopter and kept looking in all direction for any sign of it. To be caught right near the end would be so maddening!

The heat was fierce, and Donny could see Sharlene wilting as she walked. Her limp got worse, and he started to worry she might collapse as she was so red in the face.

Just as well we had that drink back there, he thought, anxiously aware that his mouth had already gone dry again. And the bloody flies had arrived to annoy!

Just on 1600hrs they reached the next sand dune. They all came to a swaying stop at the bottom and it took an effort to start and to plod up it. This time though Donny was more careful near the crest. He stopped the others and crept up the slope, glad he had that water bottle to put on the scorching sand instead of his bare hands. He peeked over and let out a little gasp of triumph.

The airfield!

He beckoned the other two up and they crouched gasping among the bushes there while he pointed to the main features. About two kilometres to his left were the buildings at the airfield, a small terminal building, a couple of sheds, and a small hanger. The flat strip of bitumen that formed the runway was just visible and hot air was shimmering above it. There were no aircraft, vehicles or people in sight.

"The highway is another half kilometre or so over beyond it," he said, pointing while scanning for any sign of vehicles or the men. "That line of trees in front of us is Eyre Creek and the town is on the other side of it. There are lots of waterholes, but you can easily find a place to cross. See that radio mast sticking up above the trees? That is near the hospital. If you aim for that you must hit the town. It has lights on it at night."

"Why are you saying that?" Vaughan queried.

"Because I am going to ask you to stay here with Sharlene and go slowly while I run to town," Donny replied. He had made his mind up about that and was now determined. "It's only a couple of k's and I can be there in half an hour."

"We can go too," Vaughan said.

"No. Please. Sharlene looks ready to drop. Have a rest here for half an hour in the shade." He pointed behind them to where the eastern side of the dune was now in shadow. "Then go to the creek near the highway and hide there until I call for you. If I haven't done that by 8pm it will mean I have been caught. Then it is up to you to sneak into town and try to find some adult to help."

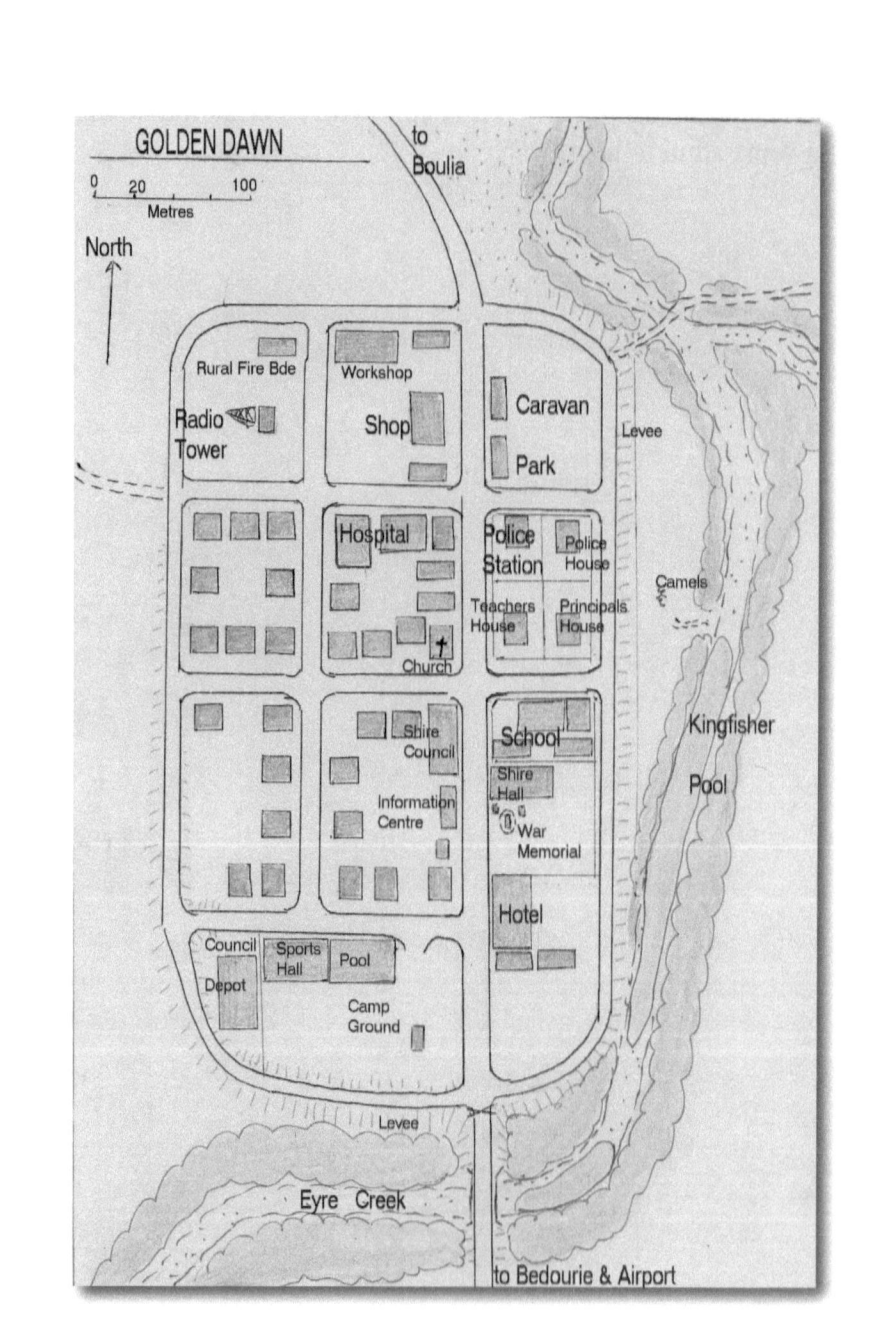

GOLDEN DAWN

to Boulia

0 20 100
Metres

North

Rural Fire Bde

Radio Tower

Workshop

Shop

Caravan Park

Levee

Hospital

Police Station

Police House

Teachers House

Principals House

Camels

Church

Shire Council

Information Centre

School

Shire Hall

War Memorial

Kingfisher Pool

Hotel

Council Depot

Sports Hall

Pool

Camp Ground

Levee

Eyre Creek

to Bedourie & Airport

Chapter 33

LOCAL KNOWLEDGE

Vaughan looked at him and shook his head.

"What are you planning to do?" he asked.

"I have to find the policeman and tell him, preferably without the crooks knowing," Donny replied.

"What if he's not there?" Sharlene asked.

"Then I go to the council offices and get adult help. Uncle James can't take the whole town hostage. Please, Vaughan, look after Sharlene."

Vaughan looked at Sharlene and she gave him a grateful look in reply, and nodded, "Yes please. I'm not used to this much physical effort. You go Donny, and good luck."

"You look after her, Vaughan," Donny said, then blushed at having revealed his concern and admiration.

Without another word he turned and hurried off. It was 1620hrs and he was aware that there were only about two hours of daylight left. He was also very conscious that the crooks might be on the lookout for him and would try setting a trap. For that reason he went down the face of the dune quickly, risking a fall, and then started running. The direction he took angled away from the town and airfield.

That took him almost parallel to the dune to begin with, but he thought the most likely place the crooks would have a watcher was in the trees where the highway went into the trees bordering Eyre Creek. From there Eyre Creek flowed towards him for several hundred metres, then curved and went away to the north. Along its whole length was a dense growth of trees and bushes. Off to the right, Donny saw the end of the sand dune. That was now about two kilometres away and another line of trees came from around it and angled across his front to join Eyre Creek about three kilometres to the north.

The Washaways branching off, he told himself.

Which meant he was now running into a U-shape of creek lines but was way out in the open grassland. Already he was feeling winded and had to slow down. He estimated he had covered about a kilometre and

269

was nearly level with the east-west section of Eyre Creek at the highway bridge.

There was a barbed wire fence running East-West right across the flat and on over the dune to his right. He rolled under and kept going.

That was the boundary of Craiglie. I am on the Town Common now, he thought. Which was very heartening. Now safety looked to be so close! *If the crooks are watching how can I avoid them?* he wondered.

He shook drops of perspiration from his face. It came to him that his main advantage might be local knowledge. But how to use that to win? He had now reached a point where a person hiding at the bridge could no longer see him, so he abruptly changed direction and headed for the radio tower near the hospital.

I will cross the creek at the top end of the Kingfisher Pool and do a bit of scouting, he thought.

He knew the area fairly well from nature projects when doing days at the school. In his mind the easiest option was just to cross the creek and go straight to the police station, which was only a few hundred metres from there.

But he was now puffed and feeling very sore and drained. He estimated he had run two kilometres in fifteen minutes and was still about half a kilometre from the trees along the creek. Pushing himself to keep walking fast, he strode across that open ground, cattle getting up and scattering as he advanced. He was heading directly into the afternoon sun now and was very glad of his hat. His eyes kept scanning the trees for any sign of danger.

I don't want to walk straight into a trap, he told himself.

But he saw no-one and, apart from the cattle and a couple of birds, no sign of any other movement. Panting with anxiety but more than lack of fitness, he reached the trees and immediately went into a crouch behind a tree trunk. For a minute or two he looked carefully in all direction and used his ears. Nothing stirred and nothing happened. A lizard scuttled on the dead leaves, and he jumped and then grinned at his reaction.

He could just see glimpses of the creek and the buildings of the town through the trees, so he moved cautiously forward to another tree. From there he got a view down into the creek bed.

"Ah! Kingfisher Pool!" he muttered.

Right in front of him was the top end of a large pool of water that extended out of sight to his left. It had a green scum around its muddy edges, and he was glad he didn't have to drink it.

I can cross here, he told himself.

Almost directly opposite him an overgrown vehicle track went up the other bank. Through the gap in the trees, he could see part of the schoolteacher's house. The police house and station were just out of sight to the right.

But before he ventured out into the clearing of the creek bed he did a careful study of the trees and bushes along the other bank. Seeing nothing and very conscious of the march of time he stood up and quickly made his way to a cattle pad that led down the steep bank to the bottom.

Now he was out in the open and his heart was hammering faster with anxiety. Then he silently cursed himself. His fast movement had disturbed some water birds on the pool to his left. A white bird, an egret or stork or something, and some ducks, went hurrying into the air with a whirring of wings.

Down in the bottom of the creek bed, Donny felt very exposed but he could see no other option (Honourable option, that was!) but hurrying forward to get under cover again. So he went up the vehicle track into the trees. The track had a good cover of leaf litter and grass and obviously hadn't been used for a long time. At the crest, Donny paused and peeked out through the gap in the trees and then at the trees close to him. He found he was gasping with anxiety as though he had run another kilometre!

Quickly he made his way to the right, in amongst the line of trees and bushes growing along the top of the bank. Again, he crouched behind a tree, ready to bolt if any alarm was raised. But it all stayed silent, so he crept forward to a tree right on the edge of the open ground in front of him. He had known that was there, but he was also aware that the only way to avoid it was to go to his left for many hundreds of metres to the area where the highway crossed the creek. There the trees grew right close to the road.

That area of open ground was only about 50 metres across, but on the other side was what Donny had known was there: a massive grassy mound that encircled the entire town. The mound or embankment, a levee actually, was about ten metres high and now, this close to it, hid all of buildings. Only the top of the radio mast showed above it. The levee was covered with grass and small bushes and Donny knew it had a bitumen road along the crest. A barbed wire fence extended right along the base of the levee.

When he had jokingly mentioned that Golden Dawn only had two streets, he had not considered the road on top of the levee, which actually gave it four: East, West. North, South. It had three cross streets, five counting the levee. Now he paused and made a conscious effort to reconstruct the exact layout of the town in his mind. The first problem was this open ground. Not only was it 50 metres wide but it extended the entire length of the town. To the south (his left) it ended several hundred metres away at the trees where the creek curved to go west at the highway. To his right it went on for hundreds of metres to where another sand dune began just past the end of the levee. And sitting in the middle of the open area almost directly in front of him were two camels!

Bloody camels! he thought irritably.

He swore as both were looking at him and one now stood up. Donny swore again. He knew they were tame camels used for the annual camel races at Boulia, but he did not like them. He also knew they were African dromedaries, descended from the camels imported in the 19th Century for transport in the desert. But tame or not they were potentially blocking his path. There was no danger they would attack him or bite him, but he was worried they might give away his presence to any observer. Worse, the camels were in the direct line to the police station! There was nothing for it but to move to his right.

I can't keep waiting here, he told himself. *If the crooks did see me cross from that last dune, they will come looking for me soon.*

So Donny moved back into the trees a bit and made his way 50 metres northwards. As he did, he was annoyed to note that the camels kept turning their heads to watch him. There was nothing for it but to take his courage in both hands and cross that open ground.

Mum and Dad are depending on me, he thought.

Then an image of Sharlene formed in his mind. That stiffened his determination. He saw no point in trying to crawl as the grass was so short. But equally he remembered hearing (or reading?) that running was more likely to attract attention.

That meant walking; and as he strode forward out into the open, he found his mouth dry and his heart hammering. He was resolved to just make a sprint for the police station if he had to. To further annoy him, the other camel now stood up. Both kept turning to face him as he walked across the open. Reaching the barbed wire fence along the base of the mound, Donny just rolled under it through the weeds, an action he instantly regretted as he picked up a few bindis as he did.

There was a tiny little rill washed out in the side of the levee bank, and he went up that using hands and feet. The slope was so steep that he needed to, and of course there were more prickles. He swore but kept climbing. As he got near the top, he slowed both to check and to get his breath ready for that sprint.

It was as well he did because just as he peeked over the top he noted movement out of the corner of his right eye. It was a white 4WD, a Prado. It had just driven out onto the north end of the levee bank. His first reaction was to snatch his hat off and lie down in the rill so that several small bushes hid him from any casual search. He had just had time to note that he was directly across the road from the Principal's House and that the police house and station were another 50 metres to his right.

To his horror, Donny heard the vehicle approaching, its tyres crunching on the loose stones on the rarely used bitumen of the levee. His heart hammered even harder, and he tensed, ready to run. He got a glimpse through his tiny bush of the vehicle coming to a stop only about ten metres away. He was still unsure who might be in it, but when its engine was switched off he flattened himself even more. This was very hard to do, partly because the rill was such a tiny washout but mostly because of the burrs and prickles. They were so painful it took real self-control not to cry out.

Have I been seen? he fretted.

A door opened and then closed, and boots crunched on the bitumen and sand. To his horror, he saw Thug appear on top of the levee. Donny was horrified and got ready to spring up. It seemed that his heart was hammering so loudly that Thug must hear it! But the man stopped and leaned back against the vehicle, staring out at the trees along the creek.

He hasn't seen me! Donny realised.

A tremor of shaking went through him and he stayed low. But the man only needed to move forward a couple of steps and look down and he must be seen!

Then, to add to Donny's anxiety, the sound of another vehicle came towards him from directly in front.

That is along the middle cross street, between the school and the teacher's house, he thought.

It drove almost to the grassy edge of the levee and then stopped. Donny tensed, ready to run or fight. He could not see it, did not dare lift his head. Its motor stopped and a door opened and then more boots were crunching only metres from him.

Uncle James spoke from just above him, "So where did Ringer say this little bastard was?" he said.

Donny tensed, trying not to even breathe. But his mind was racing. The odd wording puzzled him until he realised that Thug had not seen him, and nor had Uncle James! They had only arrived there in response to some message from Ringer.

Thug moved a couple of paces back and across to be nearer to Uncle James, then replied, "He saw the little bugger running across the open country on the other side of these trees. So he must be somewhere in front of us there."

That was both a revelation and a relief to Donny. The next few comments clarified it for him. Uncle James asked, "So how do we know he hasn't already made it into town, even to the cop shop? Where were you?"

"Doin' what ya told me," Thug answered angrily. "I was parkin' that caravan in the van park just along there and I could see all this area from there. I came here as soon as Ringer phoned."

Uncle James grunted and then said, "Plenty of cover over there. We won't waste time trying to search it. We will just block him from town. Ah! Here comes Ringer."

Donny now heard a third vehicle approaching, this time along the levee from his left. That made sense too.

Ringer must have been watching from those trees beside the highway, he surmised. He slowly rolled his head that way, ignoring the many stabbing little pains from the prickles and burs. He got a glimpse of the green Land Rover. *Ringer all right! I was seen,* he decided.

A feeling of deep despair at having failed mingled with anger at the men and the entire situation. He tensed while desperation filled him.

The Land Rover was parked, and Ringer joined the other two. Uncle James said, "What exactly did you see Ringer?"

"I seen that little rat runnin' towards these trees here," Ringer replied.

"What about the other two? Did you see them?"

"No boss. He was on his own."

"So where are the other two?" Uncle James asked.

Thug spoke in reply. "They might-a split up to come in from different directions."

Ringer snorted. "Nah! Not them. That other kid isn't fit enough, and they got that girl with 'em. She couldn't cover that sort of distance."

"I agree," Uncle James replied. "And even if they did, this is the real danger point. We gotta stop that little Donny getting to the cops for the next couple of hours."

"When is yer brother arrivin' wiv the money?" Ringer queried.

"He sent a text a few minutes ago. He has just taken off and has the money. He should be here sometime between 7 and 8, depending on weather and so on," Uncle James answered.

"It'll be dark by then!" Thug cried. "How we gunna watch all this in the dark?"

There was some unhappy agreement from Ringer before Uncle James said, "Same as we are going to do now. Benny, you stay here and watch all this. Ringer, you start doing slow laps around this levee bank."

"Around what bank?" Ringer asked.

"This levee they built to keep floods out of town," Uncle James answered.

"And where will you be boss?" Ringer queried in an almost insolent tone.

"I will park opposite the pub and watch along the main street."

"As long as yer ain't in the pub!" Ringer added.

"Don't get cheeky! I'm paying you, and don't forget it," Uncle James replied angrily.

Thug said, "I'll be a bit conspicuous if I park here for hours boss. The copper might come over and ask me what I'm doin'."

"Is he there?"

"Yeah, I seen him washin' his cop car earlier," Thug replied.

Donny wanted to cheer. Constable O'Grady was there! Now all he had to do was get to him!

Chapter 34

GOLDEN DAWN

But how?

The three men were standing there blocking the route and he suspected they would treat him pretty roughly if they caught him. And it hurt just lying there.

I wish they'd bugger off! he thought irritably.

The only good thing was that the slope was now in shadow as the sun had gone lower. But instead they stayed to talk and then argue.

Thug made a snorting noise, and said, "Look at them bloody camels! They're ugly bloody things."

"So are you," Ringer replied.

"So will you be when I rearrange your face!" Thug threatened. "I hate the way they are just standing there staring at us."

"Never mind the bloody camels!" Uncle James cried. "Benny, you go and park in this closest corner of the van park where you can see right along here. Have the headlights facing this way so you can turn them on if needed."

"Will that be enough when it gets dark?" Thug asked.

"Yes! Look up you mug! There is a streetlight at every one of these street corners. They will light up right along here and past the back of the pub," Uncle James snapped.

Thug grumbled, then said, "So when do we get our money? I want to be well away before the sun comes up."

"As soon as I bring David back from the airfield we will divvy the money up and you can have your share," Uncle James answered.

"Whereabouts?" Ringer asked.

"I've booked a room at the back of the pub. Room Four," Uncle James replied. "I will call you."

"We'll be there as soon as you get back from the airstrip," Thug said.

"You wait till I call you! We have to make sure the cops haven't been warned," Uncle James snapped.

It was obvious to Donny that the other two did not trust him.

There was a bit of grumbling and Thug muttered, "What about a proper meal? Can we go to the pub?"

"Yes, but no getting drunk. Ringer, you go at 6 as soon as the dining room opens and then relieve Benny. I will patrol the town as well until the plane lands and will have my meal after you blokes," Uncle James said. Then he muttered something and said, "Okay, let's move off. We are a bit conspicuous here. Ringer, you go straight to the pub. It's already 5:20, and don't get drunk!"

"Yes boss."

There was the sound of boots, doors, and motors, and the vehicles moved off. Donny sighed with relief and then eased himself back a bit. He found he was trembling from reaction and that he had dozens of bindies and burs stuck in his front, especially his forearms and hands. Muttering swear words, he began plucking at them while thinking about what he had just heard.

What was really worrying him now was how quickly time was slipping away. Young as he was, he understood that the police would not be able to react immediately, not in such an isolated location. He knew there was only one policeman stationed in Golden Dawn and the nearest help was hundreds of kilometres away, hours of driving time. But first he had to get to the police, and he could not see how he could do that in daylight, other than just a frantic sprint and the hope that the policeman was there.

That could be very messy, he thought. *Constable O'Grady might not be able to get all the crooks and that could put Mum and Dad at risk, and Vaughan's parents too.*

Which seemed to leave him no option but to lie there until it got dark. He considered going back to the trees along the creek, but the more he thought about other options he still thought that the side of town where he was offered the shortest and best route to get help.

At least I'm out of the sun, he told himself.

Then reaction set in and he began shivering almost uncontrollably. He found he was aching all over and had a real thirst. Plus, he was sick from the heat and the sun and then his stomach churned and, despite all his efforts not to, he farted.

Oh, bloody hell! Just as well I didn't do that when the crooks were here, he thought.

That led to a bout of anxiety and then tears, but not many as he was too dry. To add to his concerns, he was aware that the camels were still staring at him. All he could do was hope that the crooks did not notice. Minor irritations like flies and ants he just brushed at or endured. It was all tiring and uncomfortable and required him to be very patient. The only real tension for a while was hearing vehicles drive by every twenty or thirty minutes. One, he was sure, was the Land Rover, and the other he presumed was Uncle James. He knew that the locals did not normally drive around the levee.

And those bloody camels! They had sat down, still looking in his direction. But every time a vehicle came by they stood up and watched it, then stared at him before slowly sitting down again.

With a mixture of shock and relief, Donny noted that the sunlight had almost gone off the tops of the trees along the creek.

Soon be dark. I wonder what the time is? I must ask Dad for a watch for my next birthday, he thought.

Overhead he noted the sky darkening and then the first stars began twinkling. The air cooled perceptibly, bringing more relief. But it was still very wearing and testing just to lie there. There was also fear too when a vehicle that sounded like the Land Rover drove slowly by and then stopped further along the levee.

Is that Ringer taking over from Thug so he can go and have some dinner? he speculated.

The thought of dinner got him salivating and his stomach churning again. This time, with the proximity of an enemy to provide fearful incentive he managed to suppress most of his next emission. He kept it silent, but it was deadly! All he could do was endure his own smell.

Half an hour later, just as it was getting dark, another vehicle drove past from the direction of the hotel. It stopped near the Land Rover and then drove on towards the van park that took up the north-east quadrant of the little town. At this time of the year, at the very end of Tourist Season, the van park was nearly empty. The Land Rover started up and went back past the rear of the hotel and around into the main street.

Now! thought Donny. *Move now!*

But a single quick peek over the top changed his mind. He was almost under a streetlight, and the road and the wide, grass footpath beyond were too well lit. After slipping back down he studied the layout of the streetlights and decided that further to his left, closer to the back of the hotel, offered the best chance. He knew, from something his father had said, that the levee was all the same height so there was no dip or drain to slither through.

Having made that decision, he moved carefully down to the bottom of the mound and started walking slowly south, towards his chosen crossing point. In his mind he mapped a route that should give him as much cover as possible. It was now that his intimate local knowledge of parts of the town was of real value. It was fully dark by then and he guessed it was probably about 7:30pm. *I need to move fast or Uncle Dave will fly in and the crooks will grab the money and run,* he told himself.

Spurred by that urgent need, he walked on, continually stopping to listen and to look around, noting with a shock that the camels were standing nearby and still staring at him.

"Bloody things! Bugger off!" he hissed.

They ignored him and he didn't dare make a real noise. It was so quiet too, apart from mosquitos and crickets, an occasional dog bark in the distance, there was no noise. There wasn't even a breeze to rustle the leaves.

Then headlights swept around the curve near the back of the hotel, lighting up the trees along the creek and making everything down where he was very visible. Donny lay flat, heart hammering, and ready to run if he had been detected. Then a spotlight beam sprang out from the vehicle and swept along the flat ground and nearer edge of the trees and his anxiety shot right up.

The vehicle kept moving towards where Donny had taken cover flat against the mound. He saw that the beam could be directed right down the slope but that most of it was illuminating the trees. As the beam swept closer, he took several deep breaths and clenched his fists with worry. But when the vehicle was directly above him the beam lit up the camels. These sprang to their feet and went lolloping away until the beam came off them. Then the vehicle was past him and continued along toward the north end of town. Once past the van park, the spotlight was switched off and the vehicle went away. Donny lay there for a couple of minutes, breathing fast and shivering with reaction and illness. Then he got to his feet and pushed himself to move, suppressing the pain from prickles, chafe and sore muscles.

Dry mouthed with fear, he crept on until he judged he was halfway between the streetlight he had left and the one at the corner of the levee just past the back of the hotel. Hoping he would not be silhouetted by that streetlight, he crawled up to the crest of the levee and peeked over. Yes, there was the back of the hotel, with four or five vehicles including a big truck parked on the open ground over to his left where the road curved around back to the main street, which was an extension of the highway.

If Ringer is parked in front of the pub and Thug is all the way back at the van park, I should have a good chance of not being seen, he thought.

Taking a big breath, he crawled over the crest and out to the edge of the bitumen. But should he stand and walk across or stay low and crawl? There seemed to be a good argument for both, but now he decided to crawl. It hurt his elbows and knees, but he set to work inching across flat on his stomach.

I hope Ringer or Uncle James don't come driving around now! he thought.

A minute later he was off the bitumen and onto a gravel driveway that angled slightly down into a car park at the rear of the hotel, the famous Drover's Arms. There was a 4WD utility parked there and the place was a blaze of lights. Quickly he crawled into the shadows of the truck and on across a shallow drain and the grass sidewalk. That put the back fences of the school and houses beyond it between him and Thug, who was now at least 300 metres away.

Now Donny's local knowledge really came into play. He understood that his best option now was to crawl along inside the back fences but curiosity about his enemy's locations caused him to detour.

O'Grady will want to know exactly where they are, he thought.

To the right of the hotel was a small park containing a children's playground, some ornamental gardens and the town's war memorial. The whole area was in darkness but along the main street on the opposite side were more streetlights, one at each corner and one almost directly in front of him across the street. There were also lights at the front of the single-story buildings there: the Information Centre for tourists and the Shire Council offices. But the lights also cast good shadows, so Donny got to his hands and knees and moved at a fast crawl over behind a picnic table under a shelter shed where he had a good view towards the front of the hotel.

Directly in front across the street was the Information Centre and, to its left, an area of open garden. The Land Rover was parked there on the other side of the street. Donny could just detect the blur of a face seated in it: Ringer, he presumed. Beyond the Land Rover was a museum area with the first house built way back in the 1880s, a low structure of white-washed mud with log posts supporting a corrugated iron roof. To his left was the hotel. It was also a single-story building built in the early days of settlement of mud walls and log posts supporting an awning over the front. There were people and lights there and three vehicles parked along the street. But no sign of Uncle David.

Apart from the voices and laughter from the hotel, the town was quiet save for an occasional dog bark and the flap of some night bird's wings. Having decided he had learned all he could, Donny turned and crawled away, returning to the back of the playground. From there he turned left and made his way into deep shadow behind the Shire Hall, a new brick building.

Confident he could not be seen, he stood up, sighing with relief and plucking at the numerous burs and prickles that were now embedded in his skin and clothing.

Now to get to the police house, he told himself, well aware that the police station was closed at night.

He was just about to walk across to climb the school fence when he heard a vehicle engine start up behind him. Turning, he went back to the corner of the Shire Hall and peeked around. Through the clutter of signs, picnic shelter sheds, and such like he was just able to see the area he was interested in.

I was right. It was the Land Rover engine, he thought. But was it Ringer and was he just doing another of his drives around?

The Land Rover's headlights came on and it pulled out and drove along the main street, passing out of sight in front of the Shire Hall. Donny turned and ran across to the far side and watched. He saw the Land Rover pass across the intersection at the other side of the school. It vanished from view, so he decided it was safe to continue towards the police house.

Ten steps had him at the fence. It was a low wire mesh fence, the netting secured top and bottom to a steel pipe. Donny had jumped it a dozen times (and been in trouble for that often!). Placing both hands on it, he vaulted over and moved forward pass the toilet block and sports shed and halted in their shadow.

Through a gap between the buildings a few metres ahead (The school had only a small yard and no sports field), he glimpsed the Land Rover turning right at the north end of town beyond the shop and service station on the left and the van park on the right. Now he was sure it was just Ringer doing another lap to try and stop him getting into town.

"Too late, buster!" Donny murmured. "I'm in!"

Knowing the school layout as he did, Donny hurried across between the two classrooms: Years 1, 2 & 3 on the right (Where he sometimes had lessons), and Years 4, 5 & 6 on the left. Peeking cautiously both ways from the corner of the building, he checked that the shelter shed to his front and the admin building on his right were clear.

Then he waited as the flicker of a bright light told him that the Land Rover was now driving back along the levee road towards the other side of the school (It fronted on to the cross street).

Better wait! Better to be sure than sorry, he told himself, echoing one of his dad's favourite sayings.

Then there it was. The Land Rover came into view to his right front, went out of sight behind the principal's house across the side street, and then passed under the streetlight at the end of the street where it went out of sight behind him, back towards the hotel.

Okay, now! Donny told himself, his objective partly in sight.

He flitted across the big, covered area where the kids sat to have meals and play during breaks, halting behind a bush in the garden that lined the front fence. Just to his right was the front gate to the school. Across the side street was another big town block. In it were four main buildings and a few sheds. Closest to him and fronting Main Street was a teacher's house. To his right front was the principal's house. Beyond were the police station and police house.

The teacher's house was in darkness. Donny did not care. He knew it was school holidays, so they had probably gone their homes for that. There were lights in the principal's house and the police house, his objective. He was worried about the policeman's dog as Thug was parked just across the next street.

Then he saw a person in the kitchen window of the principal's house and changed his plan.

Chapter 35

PLEASE MISS!

Through the lighted window of the kitchen at the back of the house, Donny saw the school principal, Mrs Pearce. She looked to be washing up.

Miss will be better! he instantly decided.

Part of his plan was to inform the police without the crooks knowing so that they had a better chance of rescuing the hostages unharmed. Yet the policeman's dog was an obstacle to that plan.

If it starts barking at me it will attract Thug's attention. But Miss Pearce will believe me and will be able to contact him without raising Thug's suspicions.

There she was, and time was important. Donny quickly checked in all directions, cursing the flickering bright lights of the school's electronic sign at the corner to his left. There was no-one around the church that was diagonally across the intersection, no movement to left of right.

"Go!" he told himself.

Standing up, Donny limped towards the school gate and quickly opened it. Luckily, it did not squeak. Then he halted and clung to gate post as a fierce cramp locked up his left calf muscles. It was so sudden and unexpected that he let out a little cry of pain. Then he whimpered and punched at it. For precious seconds he stood there in agony, until the cramp just as quickly left him.

For another couple of seconds he hesitated to move, fearing a return of the agony. Very gingerly he set off across the side street. Once more he cursed the electronic sign. The last time he had been at the school it was being used to post a daily joke or riddle, but the same one had been displayed for three days. Donny had to smile as it flitted across his mind (What did the big plant say to the little plant? You are growing, bud!).

Donny crossed the concrete footpath, stepped down over the kerb and hurried across the bitumen road. His boots crunched on the loose bits of sand and, to his horror, the policeman's dog started barking.

Bloody thing! It's two houses away! he thought. To be so close!

He heard a male voice call out and the dog went thankfully silent. By then Donny was on the grass verge on the other side of the street and a moment later had reached the front gate to the principal's house. All the houses were set in their own wide lawns and gardens and had standard government fences like the school. Donny could have jumped the fence but did not want to land in the flower bed on the other side, so he went to the gate and very carefully opened it. Stepping through he pulled it almost shut and made his way to the steps. All three houses were typical Queensland Government designs of the mid-20th Century, built up on high blocks with an underneath used for parking cars and for the laundry and so on, while the living areas were all upstairs. The steps were on the outside and led up to a small wooden landing at the front door.

The steps turned into a bit of a final challenge for Donny. He was dismayed at how much his muscles protested, so he went slow, fearing another cramp. Stair by stair he went up, using his left arm to assist on the railing. Then he was on the landing and the moment had arrived. He was a little breathless by then, both from exertion and from apprehension. He saw what looked like a doorbell, but he did not want to risk setting off electronic chimes in the still of the night. So he knocked, very tentatively. Too soft obviously so he knocked a little harder and waited.

To his relief, he heard footsteps approaching the door but then, to his horror, a light came on next to him!

The door opened and a solidly built man in his forties stood there, the principal's husband. Donny knew he was a mechanic and diesel fitter and owned the workshop on the edge of town at the back of the service station. He looked puzzled, rather than annoyed.

"Yes?" he said.

Donny was speechless for a second and then stammered before blurting out, "Please, Mr Pearce, can I see Mrs Pearce?"

"What? Whatever for? At this time of night?" Mr Pearce said. Then his eyes took in Donny's appearance. "Are you in trouble young fella?"

"Yes sir. Please sir," Donny said.

Then, to his immense relief, he heard Mrs Pearce approach and heard her say, "Who is it, Bill?"

"Some kid," Mr Pearce said and then she arrived at the door and looked out. For amount she looked puzzled and then recognition showed on her face.

"Why, it's young Donny MacAndrew! Donny, what's the matter?"

"Please Miss!" Donny said, trying not to burst into tears with relief.

But before he could speak, Mrs Pearce obviously took in his grubby and exhausted appearance and said, "Donny, are you alright? Has something happened?"

"Yes Miss. Please Miss, turn off the light so that the men don't see me," he croaked, fighting back sobs and trembling.

"Turn out the light!" Mr Pearce said in astonishment at the same time as Mrs Pearce asked, "Men? What men?"

"Crooks, Miss. They have taken my parents and... and... have taken them hostage. I got away and I want the police."

That produced astonished expressions on both, and it was more Donny's fearful look around than his words that prompted Mrs Pearce to reach across and snap off the light.

"You'd better come in and tell us the story," she said.

Donny was ushered into a large room that combined both living and dining as its functions. There was a dining table and chairs and beyond that comfortable lounges and smaller tables. He was directed to the lounges. It took him an effort as he was now trembling almost uncontrollably with relief. But he was also still socially conscious, so when he reached a lounge chair he hesitated and indicated the mud and prickles and grime.

"Miss, I'm a bit grubby. I've been sweating in these clothes for five days. I don't want to dirty your lounge." He was also very conscious that he must smell.

Mrs Pearce stepped across and tugged a towel from a washing basket on an ironing board and quickly spread it on a chair.

"It's fine. Sit down before you fall down."

Donny slumped down and found he was shaking so much he was ashamed. To add to his shame, he began to cry. Mr Pearce looked him up and down and said, "Yeah, you look like you've been in the wars."

"Can... can I... have a glass of water p... please," Donny sobbed.

He was now very ashamed of crying. With an effort of will power he stiffened his muscles and shuddered the sobs to a stop. By the time he was calm enough to speak, Mr Pearce had returned with the water and both adults seated themselves while Donny first sipped and then gulped. The water was lovely, clean, town water and tasted like nectar to Donny. To his added shame, he was shaking so much he spilt some of it.

Mr Pearce came and took the glass. "Another?' he said.

Donny nodded and tried to calm himself, breathing deeply. At the same time, he was marshalling his words to try to explain. When Mr Pearce returned from the kitchen, Mrs Pearce said, "Now Donny, what is this about men and needing the police?"

"Please Miss. My Uncle James and two crooks, no three, came to our place and took my dad and... and his other brother and my grandad and our mothers hostage," Donny explained.

"This is at Clonargh Sation?"

"Yes Miss."

"Go on."

Donny could see that both adults were now looking very concerned but were obviously very curious. As much in sequence as he could, he related the outline of what had then happened.

"So we need to get the police, Miss, and I want to rescue my mum and dad," he said, the tears starting again.

Both adults were astonished. Mrs Pearce shook her head in wonder. "So you and this Vaughan have been out there in the desert for four or five days trying to escape?"

"Yes Miss," Donny replied. "And Sharlene."

"Who is Sharlene?"

"Sharlene Sanderson from Glen Morris Station Miss."

"Oh, I remember Sharlene! Lovely girl, very pretty, with red hair and a lovely personality. Well, well!"

Donny calmed himself and finished the glass of water. "Miss, please get the policeman. But he must not come in uniform and must look casual as there is a man watching the house."

"What man? Where from?" Mr Pearce asked, looking very concerned.

"He's in a white Prado that the crooks took when they made the old tourists hostage as well. It is parked in the corner of the van park in front of the police house," Donny explained.

"Is he!" Mr Pearce cried. He got up and padded quietly off to the front rooms. A couple of minutes later he came back and said, "I can't see the vehicle from here. Is he dangerous? Is he armed?"

"Yes, he's got a shotgun," Donny told him.

Mrs Pearce stood. "I'll phone Colin and he can come over, pretending it is for a social call," she said. "You just sit there, Donny, and relax."

She went and got her phone and went into another room to use it. Mr Pearce stood up as well and said, "Have you had any tea, young fella?"

At that, Donny almost burst into tears and shook his head. The thought of food got him instantly salivating. He explained that he had not eaten a proper meal for four or five days. He was having trouble keeping track of just how many days and nights he and Vaughan had been out in the desert. But now he was sitting in civilised comfort in a normal, modern lounge room with the TV and sound equipment and bookshelves and all the furnishings! He shuddered but then remembered the crooks.

"Please make sure your curtains are drawn so those men don't see me," he asked.

Having watched them, he was afraid he was putting the Pearces at risk. Mr Pearce gave him an odd look but complied and then went to the kitchen. Donny tried to relax while Mr Pearce got him something to eat.

Mrs Pearce came back and said, "Colin, I mean Constable O'Grady, and his wife are both coming over. They have agreed to do a bit of playacting for the benefit of the man in the van park. Do you know Constable O'Grady, Donny?"

Donny did and he blushed. He had been spoken to severely several times by the policeman over the last year or so for a couple of little adventures.

"Yes Miss," he admitted, and then farted.

It caught him by surprise, and he was quite unable to suppress it. And it really smelt awful! Donny blushed scarlet. "Aw Miss, I'm sorry," he cried. "It's the creek water we've been drinking. It has upset our stomachs."

"It's alright Donny," Mrs Pearce said. But Mr Pearce was not so forgiving. He had just walked back in carrying a plate and cup. "Gawd almighty young fella! That would stun an ox! Pshaw!"

Donny blushed again and then stiffened with anxiety when he heard a female laugh at the back steps. Mrs Pearce went to the back door and turned on the light. A very attractive young woman appeared at the top of the steps. She was smiling and carrying a plate with a sponge cake on it. "Brought some supper," she said loudly. She came into the room and cast a curious eye over Donny.

Constable O'Grady, clad in casual slacks and civilian shirt, followed her in. "Hello you two. Thought you needed cheering up," he said loudly.

He waited until the door was closed and the outside light switched off then spoke to Mrs Pearce. "Sorry, didn't want to leave Sally alone in the house after what you told me."

He then stood and studied Donny, who was torn between relief and embarrassment.

"Well, young Donny, you certainly look like you've been through the mill. What have you been up to this time?" he asked.

"Sir, I... er...sir," Donny stammered. Then he took a deep breath and said, "Can I have some of that cake please?"

The sight of the cake had caused him to really feel his hunger. He noted that Mr Pearce had put down the plate and cup on a side table. He noted a sandwich and that the cup had Milo or Hot Chocolate in it. He picked up the cup and mumbled 'Excuse me,' and then drank half of it in one quaff. The adults all sat down, and Donny noted with mixed awe and concern that Constable O'Grady had pulled his automatic pistol from under the back of his shirt before he sat. Seeing the weapon, all black and shiny and potentially deadly, really sobered him. Then he gathered his thoughts and told his story.

While he talked, the cake was cut and he munched at a slice, noting that Mr Pearce was eating the ham sandwich he had brought him. The adults sat in silent amazement as the tale was told, except for a few questions by Constable O'Grady.

"These men, are they the ones I have been seeing out on the embankment here during the afternoon?" he asked.

"Yes sir," Donny agreed. He named them and their vehicles.

Constable O'Grady looked very thoughtful. "I wondered who they were and what they were up to. I even considered going over to ask them."

"Just as well you didn't, Colin," Mr Pearce commented.

Constable O'Grady nodded. "I think you are right. I reckon they would have just taken me prisoner too. Okay, let's assume they do not know that Donny has reached me. I need to call my HQ and get a few things organised. Then I am going to change into uniform and, depending what my boss says, I might go and have a word with Mr Benny the Thug in the Prado. Can I ask you to back me up, George?"

Mr Pearce nodded, and Mrs Pearce looked very anxious but also nodded. Constable O'Grady then looked at Donny. "Okay, Donny, we will take it from here. Now, I know you want the crooks caught so we can rescue your parents, but I have to tell you that my first priority is the safety of the other two children. So I will organise that. Now, you look like you need a bath and some doctoring, young lad. So you attend to that, and some food too I reckon, judging by the way you have demolished that cake, while I get things organised. Would you please look after him while I do that, Margaret?"

"Of course," Mrs Pearce said. But then she cocked her head to one side and listened.

Donny heard it too, an aircraft! "That will be Uncle David with the ransom money!" he cried. "Oh quick, you must go to the airfield and rescue him. You might even catch Uncle James there at the same time."

He had to almost shout as the approaching aircraft, a twin-engine turbo prop from the sound of it, swept low overhead on its landing approach.

Donny sprang up. "Quick! We must get going!"

Chapter 36

TWO DOWN!

As the sound of the aircraft faded, Donny became very agitated. "Quickly please! We must arrest the crooks and save my parents."

Constable O'Grady nodded. "Okay, we must move fast. I am going home to change. I need to be in uniform for this. Sally, come with me please to help. Mr and Mrs Pearce, please put Donny in your car and when I phone you, drive to the back road, turn left and stop under the next streetlight with your headlights pointing at the corner of the van park. I am asking you to be a decoy while I walk across and speak to the man in the Prado. Quick now!"

Constable O'Grady and his wife quickly made their way out the back door and down the steps. Donny was already on his feet but realised he urgently need a toilet and that took up several minutes, during which time he thought he heard vehicles moving over at the hotel. That got him even more agitated until he felt he wanted to scream to release the tension. He was then guided down the front steps and in under the house by Mr Pearce. The Pearces had their family car there, a Toyota Land Cruiser. Donny was buckled into the back seat and the adults climbed in the front, Mrs Pearce driving.

Then they sat. Minutes ticked by and Donny fretted and itched to be up and doing. But he knew they had to wait until Constable O'Grady was ready. Donny understood that the policeman was going to do a very brave thing (In fact, the sort of brave things country cops do every week, he reckoned). It did not help his composure that he was also assailed by small cramps and stomach rumblings.

Suddenly, Mr Pearce's mobile phone rang. "Now Bill!" was all Constable O'Grady said.

Mrs Pearce heard and at once started the motor and a second later engaged reverse and backed out from under the house and along the driveway through the open gate. Once across the drain and on the grass verge, she switched on the headlights and swung the car towards the van park. A few seconds later, the car was up the gentle slope to the levee road and out on the bitumen. It accelerated and then, just as quickly, slowed to stop under the streetlight. There was a crunch of gravel as the wheels locked and Donny saw that their headlights, on high beam, were shining directly at the white Prado that was parked in the nearest corner of the unfenced caravan park.

Out to the left, Donny glimpsed movement and he saw that it was Constable O'Grady. He was silhouetted to people in the car by the streetlight at the intersection of the main street and the side street but only for a few seconds. Then Donny saw that he had gone the other side of the stolen caravan, his movement hidden from anyone in the Prado by it.

A few seconds later, Constable O'Grady appeared from around the back of the caravan. He walked straight across to the driver's door on the Prado. His left hand was empty and he had a torch in his right. On his belt was a pistol or taser (Donny could not see which). With his right hand he reached forward and opened the door and swung it wide and a second later he reached in and pulled. Out onto the gravel fell a started Benny the Thug. As Benny fell, Mr Pearce, who had undone his seatbelt, opened his door, got out and started running forwards to help. In the bright light of the headlight beams, Benny the Thug looked startled and then frightened. He gaped and then nodded at what Constable O'Grady said and rolled onto his front. By the time Mr Pearce reached the pair, Constable O'Grady was kneeling and starting to apply handcuffs.

"Oh, very well done!" Donny applauded.

Mrs Pearce also gasped her approval and then switched the headlights back to low beam. Benny the Thug was hauled to his feet by Constable O'Grady and Mr Pearce and the man stood there shaking his head and looking bewildered. He was saying things, but Donny could not hear what over the noise of the vehicle engine.

The constable's wife came running across the street to join the group and they all hustled Benny the Thug across the road and into the police station, which Donny now saw had its lights on and front door open. They vanished inside and there was a pause. Mrs Pearce put the Land Cruiser into gear and drove left to park in front of the police station.

As she did, Mr Pearce, Constable O'Grady and his wife came out of the front door and walked over to the Land Cruiser. Mrs Pearce wound down the passenger window.

"That was well done. How did it go?" she asked.

Constable O'Grady leaned down to talk in the window. "Your decoy effort really worked. Benny had been asleep and was still waking up when I opened his door and told him he was under arrest. He was so groggy from exhaustion he gave no resistance." He shifted to look in the back and continued. "But he did grumble and say that obviously that little bugger Donny had made it to town."

They all applauded at that, and Donny felt a real glow of pride and achievement. "I thought he'd struggle," he replied.

Constable O'Grady shook his head. "He grumbled that he and another bloke had been searching for you and the other boy for four nights, with almost no sleep. He did say that he told his boss, your uncle, that they should start running as soon as it got dark, but it looks like greed was a stronger motive. Anway, he's in a cell and we can now go and look for your friends."

Mrs Pearce spoke first. "What do you want us to do, Colin?"

"Take Donny to the hospital and get the nurse and ambulance ready to come as soon as we find the other kids," Constable O'Grady said.

Donny was appalled, "Oh sir! I don't want to go to hospital! I'm good for a few more hours yet. Anyway, you need me with you."

"Oh yeah, why?"

"Because Vaughan and Sharlene will probably only come out of hiding if they hear my voice, and you need me to identify who to arrest," Donny answered, determined to be there at the rescue.

Constable O'Grady looked thoughtful. Then he nodded. "Okay. Get out and hop in the police car. Sandra, you go into the station and lock the door. Then call Senior Sergeant Urquhart and keep him up to speed on the situation. Let's move!"

Donny nearly cheered aloud. For a few moments he fumbled with the seatbelt buckle and then quickly opened the door and clambered out. By then Constable O'Grady and his wife were striding towards the police Land Cruiser parked in the driveway of the police house and Mr Pearce was climbing back into the Land Cruiser. By the time Donny was seated in the front of the police Land Cruiser, the Pearces had driven off towards the hospital (which Donny knew was just a medical clinic with one registered nurse and no doctor) at the far end of the next block along the side street.

Now Donny was wildly excited. The tiredness fell away and he felt ready to go. Constable O'Grady spoke briefly to his wife, kissed her with some emotion, and then checked that Donny had his seatbelt done up.

"You stay in the vehicle and out of harm's way, young fella," he instructed. He climbed into the driver's seat and buckled up. A few seconds later the engine was going and they began to move.

Constable O'Grady drove the police Land Cruiser left and then left again onto the main street. As it turned the corner, Donny peered ahead, cursing that flickering electronic sign on the next corner at the school as it made it hard to see further along the street. But what was obvious was that there were no other vehicles moving.

I thought I heard one a minute ago, he told himself. But there were no headlights visible in the main block.

They drove south past the teacher's house and across the next intersection. As they did, Donny again cursed the brightness of the electronic sign, but could not help reading the thing. 'The frog on the bank asked the frog in the pond how deep the water was. The frog in the water replied, "Knee deep!"'

What the...? Donny puzzled, and the then got it and, despite the drama of the occasion, chuckled.

Amused and annoyed at the same time he shifted his attention back to the main street. There were three vehicles, all 4WD, SUV or Utility types, and all white, parked along the front of the hotel. The veranda of the hotel was a blaze of lights and there were four people sitting drinking and talking at tables. Two of them were indigenous council workers in yellow Hi-vis shirts. The other two looked like tourists.

"No sign of Uncle James or Uncle David," he muttered.

Then his attention was drawn to a scene half a block ahead. Just beyond the last streetlight on the edge of town, the headlights of the police Land Cruiser reflected off the taillights of a vehicle. Then what he was actually looking at registered in Donny's mind. It was the Land Rover, facing away from them and with its headlights on. In the beams of those headlights two people were standing with their hands high above their heads: Vaughan and Sharlene.

"Oh no! That's them! Ringer has caught them!" Donny cried.

Constable O'Grady had been studying the scene and now reached across and activated the red and blue lights on top and the police siren.

The noise was so loud it caught Donny by surprise. He jumped, even as his gaze took in the silhouetted figured of Ringer. Ringer had just got out of the Land Rover and had his back to them, and he was holding the shotgun!

Constable O'Grady's voice boomed out through the loudspeaker system. "This is the police! Put the gun down and lie down!"

Ringer was caught completely by surprise. By then the beams of the police Land Cruiser's headlights were illuminating him. Donny saw his head jerk around and his eyes widen as his mouth fell open.

"Put the gun down! Lie on the road!" Constable O'Grady ordered again.

Donny tensed ready to duck or help if Ringer resisted. But then he saw Ringer shake his head and swear and then lean forward and place the shotgun on the bitumen. With obvious reluctance he lay down. Vaughan and Sharlene stayed standing but were now clutching each other in a mixture of emotions.

The police Land Cruiser drove forward and pulled to a stop a few paces from where Ringer lay. Constable O'Grady killed the siren but kept the red and blue lights flashing.

"You go and get your friends, Donny, and take them to near the Information Centre. Not the pub, the Information Centre."

"Yes sir!" Donny replied.

Hastily he unbuckled his seatbelt and got out. By the time he did, Constable O'Grady had already moved forward and picked up the shotgun. This was placed safely aside and, as Donny ran past him, he heard him say to Ringer, "Arms behind your back!"

Donny ran forward past the prone Ringer. As he did, Ringer lifted his head to look and then swore again. "Oh bloody hell! You, you little toad! I might have known it!"

Donny almost whooped with joy over the downfall of his enemies. *Two down, one to go!* he told himself (He did not think the pair at Glen Morris would be any trouble to the police).

But to jangle his emotions a bit more, there were Vaughan and Sharlene, and she was looking very matey with Vaughan. They blinked into the bright light with anxiety until they recognised him. Sharlene spoke first.

"Donny! You made it! Oh, thank heavens!"

"You were supposed to stay hiding until I came to get you," Donny said.

"You said wait till 8 o'clock," Vaughan replied. He had obviously been given a real fright and was upset as a result.

Donny wasn't quite sure so didn't argue. "The policeman said come with me to the Information Centre," he said.

He reached out towards Sharlene, who had let go of Vaughan. But she did not take his hand. Instead, she just started walking. Vaughan followed, both staring wide-eyed at where Constable O'Grady was placing handcuffs on a very angry Ringer.

As the trio went past him, Ringer looked up and glared. "Little bastard! You've wrecked everything. I'll get you one day!" he snarled.

Donny felt a simultaneous surge of fear at the threat and jubilation at seeing Ringer under arrest. "You've got to be good enough!" he retorted.

Then he ignored him and walked on, both Sharlene and Vaughan limping along with him. They passed under the streetlight and Donny kept glancing back. He saw Constable O'Grady lift Ringer to his feet and then move him to the back of the police vehicle. After placing Ringer in there, the policeman then took out his mobile phone and began talking.

Donny led the other two onto the concrete footpath on the left. The Information Centre was a hundred paces ahead. The same distance away on the other side of Main Street, was the pub. There was now a crowd of half a dozen people standing at the front, staring along the street. Seeing that group sparked a sharp little stab of concern in Donny.

Is Uncle Dave there? he wondered.

Then four more people came out of the front door of the pub, the famous Drover's Arms. By then Donny and his friends were only fifty paces away and walking under the streetlight in the middle of the block. One person Donny recognised as the publican. Another was dressed in a pilot's uniform: dark long trousers, white shirt with black shoulder boards with little gold bars on them. It was the last two who grabbed his attention: Uncle James and Uncle David. Uncle James was looking very worried and carried a black briefcase.

Donny saw Uncle James look along the street towards the flashing police lights and vehicles. Then, with a sort of inevitability, he looked across the street and their eyes met. There was a flash of recognition in Uncle James's face, but it was Donny who reacted first.

Pointing, he yelled out, "There he is! Grab him! Uncle Dave, grab him! The police have his gang all under arrest."

There were stunned looks on the faces of the other onlookers, many of whom turned to stare at Uncle James. Comprehension dawned on both uncles at the same moment and Uncle David grabbed at Uncle James.

"Help me!" he shouted.

Uncle James screamed like a wild boar and wrenched himself free, staggering out onto the road. Uncle David came after him, grabbing at the briefcase. That really set Uncle James going. He began to shout obscenities and to hit at Uncle David. Uncle David called to the people beside him, the pilot and the publican.

"Help me! He's a crook and he's got our money! Grab him!"

Uncle James's face became contorted with fury and he stepped back, tugging at the briefcase with his left hand while reaching behind him with his right. To Donny's horror, that right hand came back into view holding the automatic pistol.

"Let go!" Uncle James screamed.

The sight of the gun caused the others to all back away and Uncle David also released his grip. Uncle James, his chest heaving with huge gulps, stepped back, his eyes wild and the gun in his hand moving in a threatening way at the crowd. That caused a general retreat by the onlookers. For a terrible few seconds Donny wondered if Uncle James was going to shoot Uncle David.

But then Uncle James turned and hurried away along the street to the front white vehicle, a 4WD Utility. As he did, he kept looking wildly around, and then his gaze settled on Donny.

"You, you little mongrel! You've wrecked everything!" he screamed.

He raised the pistol in one swift movement. Donny gaped, then survival instinct kicked in and he jumped sideways. But the gun did not go off. Uncle James looked at it stupidly.

Donny could not help himself. He had endured so much pain and fear already at the instigation of this man that he shouted angrily, "Ah, ya jerk! It isn't cocked! You should have paid more attention in Bruce Willis movies!"

Uncle James's reaction was to drop the briefcase and then to use his left hand to pull back the slide to cock the pistol. His face ugly with rage he raised the gun and aimed it at Donny. But Donny did not wait. Spurred by pure fear he was running and then suddenly changed direction back.

Bang!

Donny nearly wet himself, the unreality of the situation suddenly swamped by the terrifying knowledge that it was real! But his instincts were still working and he had already changed direction away again.

Bang!

Another miss! This time Donny sprinted away along the foot path past the Council Chambers. Acting on an idea, he momentarily appeared to pause and then dropped to the grass behind a small monument to some explorer of the old days.

Bang!

Donny had no idea where that went but he was now hyperventilating and fleeing on pure adrenalin. Rolling frantically to one side, he sprang up and continued running away. As he ran, he glanced back and noted that both Sharlene and Vaughan had taken cover behind some tourist information signs.

That sign won't stop a bullet, he thought. But another glance showed that Uncle James was not even looking for them. *And he's lost interest in me!*

Uncle James had turned, snatched up the briefcase and was backing away, while pointing the gun at the people outside the hotel, most of whom were now backing away or putting their hands up. A moment later, Uncle James slid the gun out of sight. Donny realised that he needed to use that hand to dig out his car keys. He unlocked the vehicle door, opened it, flung in the briefcase and then climbed in himself. The door was slammed, the engine roared, and the vehicle accelerated away with a screech of tyres.

Donny had stopped running and now looked back. He could see that Constable O'Grady had climbed into his vehicle, started it up and was turning it around in a U-turn.

He hasn't seen what happened, Donny thought.

"But he must have heard the shots?" he muttered.

The policeman seemed to be his last hope to catch Uncle James. But that evaporated a few seconds later when Uncle James drove his car around the wrong side of the police Land Cruiser and accelerated off into the night, heading south.

Donny came hurrying back, the reaction now setting in to make him shake. His arrival back in front of the Information Centre coincided with Constable O'Grady pulling up.

"What the hell's going on?" the constable shouted.

"Uncle James shooting at me. He's running away with the loot. Quick, after him!" Donny yelled.

But Constable O'Grady just parked the police Land Cruiser. "No. I'll chase him with a radio and have all the roads out of the area blocked. He can't possibly drive to any other town like Windorah or Bedourie before the police there are ready for him."

"But he's got a helicopter at the airport. He'll get away!" Donny almost screamed.

It seemed so unfair, and he was shaking, much to his shame.

Chapter 37

OUTSIDE THE DROVER'S DOG

"Cheer up Donny. We got two of them. Only one to go," Constable O'Grady replied.

He switched off the engine and climbed out as an ambulance came hurrying from the direction of the hospital, the Pearce's car following. Both came to a stop, but Donny was so worked up, now with anxiety over what Uncle James might do to his father and mother, that he could not let it rest.

"Oh, after him! He's getting away and he might hurt my mum and dad," he cried.

"Calm down, Donny! Let me sort things out here first," Constable O'Grady said.

"But... but what if he steals the plane Uncle David came in?" Donny almost shouted.

The pilot had come over and was listening. He shook his head. "That's my plane and it's locked, and I have the keys. It's not going anywhere. Besides, it needs fuel and the refueller wasn't there when we landed," he said.

"That's right," agreed another man, one of the council workers who were standing nearby. "That's my job. The Shire Council run the airport, and I act as the refueller when needed. I was off on a job along the road towards Boulia, and I didn't refuel that helicopter either. So he won't get far."

That was some comfort to Donny, but he was still very agitated. The group was now joined by Vaughan and Sharlene, Mr & Mrs Pearce, and three people from the ambulance. Uncle David at once rushed over and embraced Vaughan, who did quite a bit of sobbing, which Donny forgave him in the circumstances.

Uncle David rumpled Vaughan's hair and hugged him tight. "Vaughan, my boy! Where have you been? What happened when you and young Donny drove off in the Land Rover?"

Vaughan eased himself out of his father's arms. "Aw, Dad. It's a long story. Not now. We just ran away and hid. Donny was the one. He knew how to survive in the desert."

That praise really softened Donny. "Oh, fair go! It was you who knew how to navigate," he said.

Vaughan looked him in the eye and said, "Then it was a team effort, once I started to pull my weight," he replied.

That sent Donny's opinion of Vaughan right up. *He's come a long way in a week,* he thought. He decided never to mention how Vaughan had nearly broken down several times during the ordeal. *It really was a team effort,* he conceded.

Then his feelings were tested when Vaughan reached out and took Sharlene's hand and drew her forward.

"Dad, this is Sharlene Sanderson. Her parents manage Glen Morris station."

Seeing them holding hands was a sharp blow to Donny's hopes and pride, and he was glad he had not made any declaration about his feelings for Sharlene.

Bugger! He's a fast operator, Donny thought. He had to admit he had no chance, being a few years younger. But he was still jealous!

One of the people from the ambulance was a nurse and she now stepped forward and interrupted. "Let's check you over. I hear you have been on the run in the desert for a week, so I want you to come to the hospital for a check-up."

That statement drew a murmur of appreciation and surprise from the assembled crowd. But Donny wasn't interested.

"No way!" he cried. "I want to rescue my Mum and Dad."

Mrs Pearce now stepped forward. "You be sensible, Donny. You obviously need a bit of doctoring, and a bath and a feed too. So calm down and do what Nurse Jenks asks."

Donny wavered. "Yes, Miss, but..."

"No buts, Donny. And don't you go expecting Constable O'Grady here to go haring off into the night, on his own, chasing a madman with a gun into the desert in the dark. That's not fair. He's done a mighty job already and I'm sure he has things to organise."

Constable O'Grady nodded. "Too right! The first thing I need is to organise a roadblock to stop him escaping back northwards if he can't fly the helicopter."

The other council worker stepped forward. "That's a job for Cyril and me, Constable. We will lock the flood gate just there and organise a roster to man it all night so you can get things moving and get some sleep."

"Thanks Geoff. Can you organise the keys?" Constable O'Grady asked.

"Too right boss!" Geoff replied with a grin. "It'll be a pleasure to phone the Shire Clerk and get him doing something. Cyril, you drive the council vehicle down to the flood gate and park it across the road and then start rounding up the others in our crew."

Donny understood that. Just where the bitumen road along the top of the flood levee crossed the highway there was a substantial steel gate which was closed to stop travellers from using the road when flooding was happening. He thought that a good idea. He was so interested in watching the policeman organise things that he resisted several tugs at his sleeve.

"Yes Miss, in a minute," he said.

At any moment he expected to hear the helicopter start up, but more minutes went by without that happening. To Donny's surprise, Sharlene was next to speak.

"We had better warn the people at Craiglie in case he goes there looking for fuel or a vehicle."

"You are right," Constable O'Grady agreed.

At that, the publican said, "I'll do that. My sister is their housekeeper and cook so she'll believe me when I tell her its serious."

With that he turned and moved away to use his phone. Knowing that other people were being kept safe made Donny feel better.

Uncle David turned to him. "Okay, Donny, where do you think James will go? Where is my wife and your mum and dad?"

That put Donny on a spot. He did not think Uncle James would go to any of the places he had in mind.

If I was him and had the loot I would just be trying to get right away, he thought. But he said, "My mum, all our mums," he amended indicating Vaughan and Sharlene, "and Grandad are being held hostage at Glen Conner homestead."

"And probably the old couple who gave us a lift in their caravan," Sharlene added.

301

"Who is guarding them?" Uncle David asked.

"That nasty Reggie guy and his old hag of a missus," Sharlene replied.

"Ma Baker, we called her," Vaughan put in.

That drew a gust of laughter from the assembled group, most of whom actually knew the hag. Constable O'Grady tried to hide a grin, and said, "Do you think they will give any trouble?"

Vaughan answered before Donny could. "They've both got guns, but I reckon they will just give up."

Donny nodded and opened his mouth to speak but Sharlene beat him to it. "They are just horrible lowlifes, but they are cowards. And I don't reckon Uncle James has told them the whole story."

"He might go to Clonargh," Vaughan suggested.

Donny shook his head. "Only for fuel. I don't think there is anyone there."

"So where do you reckon your dad is being held?" Uncle David asked.

"I only have a rough idea," Donny admitted.

Constable O'Grady now spoke. "Okay, let's discuss all this in an hour or so. I need to make phone calls to organise roadblocks at Bedourie and Windorah, and get a special squad of armed police to do the rescues. I will be in trouble if I don't follow procedure and try to do it on my own."

That comment drew a murmur of appreciation and much head nodding from the people. Donny also nodded. He already thought Constable O'Grady was a real hero.

I won't give him any more trouble in the future, he told himself.

Constable O'Grady went on. "I have to question these two prisoners, and I would like you there Mrs Pearce, as Justice of the Peace, and the Shire Chairman if we can find him." Mrs Pearce agreed so Constable O'Grady continued. "Mr MacAndrew, you come to the police station too. I need to understand your part in this," he said to Uncle David, who looked very crestfallen but nodded.

Constable O'Grady turned to the council workers. "You blokes go and set up the roadblock, and no heroics. If a vehicle won't stop just get out of the way and stay safe. Now, Mr Pearce, would you go and open up the service station so we can refuel vehicles, and you kids go with Nurse Jenks to the hospital and get looked after."

"Don't you go without me!" Donny cried. "You need me to show where to go."

"And me!" Vaughan added. "I can help guide."

"Okay, Constable O'Grady agreed. "Now get going!"

The gathering broke up in a buzz of preparations and talking. Donny, Vaughan, and Sharlene were ushed into the back of the ambulance with Nurse Jenks and a paramedic and were driven the two blocks to the hospital. But even that short drive was enough for some of Donny's muscles to stiffen up and he groaned and walked stiffly when they got out and were led into the building. Nurse Jenks seated them in a front waiting room and she and the male paramedic took some basic details.

When she got to Sharlene, Nurse Jenks looked at her sunburnt and grimy state and shook her head. "Oh, you poor little girl, lost in the desert for days," she said.

Sharlene was indignant. "Fair go, Miss! I'm nearly fifteen, and I not some silly little city kid. I am station kid and live out there, and I'm in the army cadets at my school. We were never lost. These boys knew exactly where they were and where they were going."

"Oh sorry!" Nurse Jenks replied. "Anyway, you can tell us the story after you have had a bath and a feed. Now, come with me into the female ward and Mr Carpenter here will take the boys to the male ward. Shower first, then food."

Donny and Vaughan were led along a corridor and into the male ward, a long, modern corridor with a polished vinyl floor and rooms either side and a nurse station in the middle. They were led into a room with two beds in it and the door closed.

The paramedic pointed to chairs and said, "Boots off first, then clothes and into the shower. There's a towel and soap. I'll go and get you some pyjamas."

Now Donny had a problem. He did not want to admit it but finally had to. "Before you go, would you please help me get these boots off?" he asked.

The paramedic paused at the door and came and helped ease off Donny's right boot. Then, what Donny was afraid of, happened. The paramedic wrinkled his nose up and asked, "When did you last change your socks?"

Donny was now very aware of the horrible smell from his socks and feet and blushed with shame. "Four or five days ago," he answered. "We've been on the run ever since."

The paramedic put on rubber gloves and peeled the sock off. Trying not to breathe, he carried it with two fingers and tossed it into the bin.

"We aren't going to try to save this pair," he said. He then held Donny's foot and studied it. "Hmm! You are on the edge of getting trench feet young fella," he commented.

Donny looked and saw that his foot was a mixture of grime and pasty, wrinkled, white flesh. And it did smell. The other boot and sock were taken off and then the paramedic helped Vaughan.

Then he stood up. "Now one of you into the shower while I get you something to wear. Those clothes can go in the bin too."

Vaughan pointed to the shower. "You go first, Donny. You look more of a wreck than me and you've earned it."

Donny did not dispute that, but he found it hard to stand up and he literally hobbled into the shower cubicle. Taking off those grimy, sweat-stained and bur encrusted clothes was also an effort, but also a huge relief. He was then astonished and appalled to find that his whole body seemed to be covered with bruises, welts and scratches and there were still lots of prickles and small thorns embedded in his wrists, hands and knees.

But that shower was bliss! He could have stayed there all night, except that Vaughan began calling out and Donny reluctantly turned the shower off and stepped out to dry himself.

The paramedic knocked and came in. "Here are some pyjamas. Just put the pants on till we've checked you over," he instructed.

Donny did so, feeling a bit ashamed of what he thought was his scrawny physique. He then made his slow and painful way out to the chairs in the room. While Vaughan showered, the paramedic went out to tell Nurse Jenks and she came in and took his pulse, temperature, and blood pressure before studying the scratches and bruises.

"My word, you have been in the wars," she commented.

She then began washing the scratches, chafe and grazes with lovely warm water. The dabbing of antiseptic was not nearly as nice. Donny winced and tried to pretend it didn't sting. While she was doing this, the paramedic went to check on the meal preparation, it being well after the normal hospital mealtimes.

To his horror, Donny realised he was going to fart. Appalled, he struggled to control it and even thought of asking the lovely lady nurse to leave. But too late! Out it came, an enormous and loud explosion which mortified him.

"I'm sorry, Miss! It's the water we've been drinking. We had to drink from cattle troughs and water holes in creeks, he explained."

"It's alright. We will get something to settle your stomach," she said, but Donny could see she was embarrassed and that shamed him even more.

Then the paramedic came back in and immediately wrinkled his nose. "Bloody hell! It smells like we've got a dead pig under the bed!" he commented.

Donny flamed with embarrassment. Nurse Jenks looked up. "There's no need to embarrass the boy, Jack. He can't help it," she snapped.

"Sorry," the paramedic replied, but then he grinned at Donny. "You'll be alright, young fella. If even half of what I have been told you did you are a champion. But you should bottle that and sell it as natural gas."

At which Donny blushed some more. Nurse Jenks and the paramedic then got to work plucking out thorns and prickles. Then Vaughan came out of the shower and was also checked over and doctored. The food then arrived, and Donny realised he was truly hungry. It was only a meat stew with vegetable and gravy, but it smelt and tasted wonderful.

Then he and Vaughan were hurried into bed. Those clean linen sheets felt just wonderful! But anxiety gnawed at Donny.

"You will make sure we are woken in time to go with the police won't you, Miss?"

"Yes, don't worry. We have to go to as well and we'd like some sleep before then. So lie down and go to sleep."

"Promise Miss?"

"Yes Donny, promise."

Donny was asleep almost before his head hit the pillow.

Safe! he thought as he slipped into a deep sleep..

Chapter 38

I THINK I KNOW

"Wake up Donny, wake up!"

Donny jerked awake as reality flooded his mind. He saw that it was Mr Pearce.

"What time is it?" he asked, sitting up.

Mr Pearce glanced at his watch. "Just after four. We want to be on the road by five. So get up and here's some clothes for you," he said.

"Whose are they?" Donny asked as he glanced at the khaki shorts and blue shirt he was being offered.

"They were my boy Alan's," Mr Pearce replied.

"Will he mind?" Donny asked.

Mr Pearce gave a short laugh. "Bless you no! He's twenty-four now and a diesel fitter at the Phosphate Mine up near Cloncurry." He handed the clothing over and turned to Vaughan, who was also now sitting up. "And these used to be Lawrence's; and no, he has outgrown them too. He's twenty-six and an engineer building motorways on the Sunshine Coast. Now dress, toilet, and be out the front in ten minutes."

The boys did. Despite having only about six hours of sleep, Donny felt rested and only a few sore muscles and chafe bothered him. He and Vaughan were soon outside ready. It was cold out there but not chilly. There was even a thin layer of cloud obscuring the stars.

Mrs Pearce was there helping Nurse Jenks load blankets and water bottles into the ambulance. Both said a cheerful hello and Nurse Jenks came over.

"Are you boys feeling alright? You don't have to come if you don't want to," she said.

"I do!" Donny said quite fiercely. "I want to see my mum and dad."

"Alright then," Nurse Jenks added. Then she said hello to Sharlene, who had also appeared. Sharlene was asked the same question but also said she wanted to be with the rescue party.

Donny was now fidgeting with impatience to be on the move. "Has anything happened during the night, Miss?" he asked Mrs Pearce.

"Not really. A big truck arrived at our roadblock, but it was just hauling freight and had come from Birdsville. The driver had not seen anyone. And the people at Craiglie reported a vehicle which might have been driven by your Uncle James going east at about 9pm."

"Didn't he go by helicopter?" Vaughan asked.

Mrs Pearce shook her head. "No. It is still at the airfield. Now get in the back you lot."

They did, Donny on the left, Sharlene in the middle, and Vaughan on the right. Nurse Jenks and the paramedics climbed into the ambulance, and they drove around to the police station. Constable O'Grady spoke briefly to them, mostly with a warning to stay out of trouble and not to take any risks. He was driving the police Land Cruiser and had another policeman with him. That officer had driven south from Boulia during the night. A third policeman was standing out front of the station. Constable O'Grady's wife was busy loading their car with supplies.

"Food and drink. These men are really only boys and need looking after," she commented to Mrs Pearce.

Then, just before 5am, they were on their way. They drove south through the town to the roadblock, exchanged cheery greetings and 'good lucks' with the men there, and then continued on. Donny was now gripped by a mixture of excitement and apprehension. Worry about what might have happened to his parents, especially his father, clouded his thoughts so that he wasn't even too jealous of Vaughan sitting next to Sharlene and seeing him adjusting a rug to keep her warm.

The vehicles drove south for nearly 10 kilometres to the junction of the Min Min Highway. The place was deserted and Donny found it slightly spooky in the headlights. From there they turned left and went east along the Min Min Highway. A few minutes later they passed the lights of the Craiglie homestead but did not stop. For the next few kilometres they went over the succession of sand dunes, and Donny experienced several vivid memories of struggling over them on foot. He began trying to add up the distance he and Vaughan had walked since they escaped.

As they passed The Washaways, Vaughan pointed out to the Pearces where they had run off to get to town after the caravan had been stopped.

"Just here it was Miss, Uncle James landed his chopper... I mean his helicopter, here on the road. Donny jumped out of the caravan and knocked him down the bank, just here, then took his gun off him."

Donny relived that scene with some satisfaction but then his eyelids somehow just closed and he went to sleep, missing the Government Bore and only waking when the vehicles drew to a halt in the middle of a blaze of lights. Blinking stupidly, it took him a few moments to recognise where they were.

The roadworker's camp, he told himself. He saw they were parked in the quadrangle among the buildings.

Everyone else climbed out so Donny joined them. He learned that the roadworkers had been warned by satellite phone and had been manning a roadblock at the junction since midnight. The roadworkers crowded round, full of questions.

Constable O'Grady pointed to the three friends. "These kids came here yesterday morning looking for food and water. They had to hide for hours from two of the crooks who spun you a line about them being thieves."

A big, burly man in workman's Hi-vis shirt looked the three friends over and then said, "Well, they are! They definitely took some food from our kitchen."

Donny was indignant. "Not just us! That crook, Benny the Thug, did too, before your cook turned up and locked the place."

The big man then grinned. "Good fer you, young fella! From what I hear, you are welcome to come into our kitchen any time you like."

Constable O'Grady interrupted to complete giving instructions for the roadblock there and the safety of the work camp. Then he allowed a few minutes for a toilet break and a drink before ushering them all back into their vehicles. The workers helped and then sent them off with a cheer.

"Drop in next time you are passing, kids, and tell us the whole story," called the big man.

"We will!"

And then it was back onto the highway and on east to the turn-off to Glen Conner. It was after 6am by then and it was still dark. Donny could see that the moon was just peeking above the skyline and the sight made him smile.

I'll never be lost again! he thought.

Constable O'Grady got them out of the vehicles at the gate and told them to gather around. "We are waiting here until we get the all-clear," he said. "An aircraft with a team of armed officers is flying from Brisbane and is due to land on the Glen Conner homestead airstrip at dawn."

Donny nodded. He had seen the airstrip once. It was simply a dirt landing strip to the south of the swamp where he and Vaughan had hidden. He knew that every homestead in the shire had an airstrip in case the Flying Doctor had to be called.

Sharlene said, "What if they need a doctor?"

"They have a police surgeon on board," Constable O'Grady replied.

"Has there been any sign of Uncle James?" Donny asked.

Constable O'Grady shook his head. "No. They had a roadblock in position at Bedourie by 9:30 last night and he hasn't been seen there, and the one at Windorah was in position by about 10, and he couldn't have driven that distance quicker than that. So he's still somewhere in the district," he explained.

That was worrying news to Donny, who began to speculate where Uncle James might have gone and where he might be hiding.

And what might he do if he is desperate? he pondered.

All there was to do was sit and wait. They were all glad of the rugs as it grew colder until the first grey glimmer of sunrise showed. Then they walked up and down talking and trying to keep warm.

Donny found the waiting particularly trying, his mind roving over unpleasant possibilities. It wasn't until nearly 7am, when the sun was lifting above the horizon, that they got the call on the satellite phone that the hostages had been rescued and it was safe to come to the homestead.

"Is everyone safe?" Sharlene asked.

"Yes, nobody was harmed. The two people who were guarding them have been arrested but have a very strange tale to tell, claiming they were misled," Constable O'Grady replied.

"I'll bet they have!" Sharlene replied.

Donny put his hand up. "Sir, Constable O'Grady, is my dad safe?"

Constable O'Grady shook his head. "He is not there. We don't know where he is. Now get into the vehicles and let's go."

Hearing that sent Donny's anxieties soaring. He was very pleased that his mother and grandad were safe, but what had happened to his dad? He climbed back into the vehicle and barely noticed the next hour of driving. He was aware that Vaughan and Sharlene were discussing their night ride and walk along that road, but to Donny it was just 50 kilometres of irritating dust and corrugations.

It was such a relief to see his mother and to run to her arms that Donny did not care who saw him cry. She was also almost beside herself with relief and joy.

"Where have you been?" she asked, tears mingling with annoyance. "Those men told us you had run off into the desert and were probably dead."

"Not me," Donny boasted, glad his grandad was listening. "We just hid from them and came to find you to rescue you."

"How could you possibly hope to do that? How could you possibly think you could get away from grown men with guns and Land Rovers?" his mother asked, her relief giving way to a whole flood of emotions.

These were interrupted by the arrival of Donny's grandfather, who limped out with the aid of a broom handle.

"Hello Grandad," Donny cried, rushing to hug the old man.

Then the questioning began again, and nearby Vaughan and Sharlene were both experiencing similar questioning.

Donny shrugged, then grinned. "They weren't all that good. Vaughan and I, well, we just hid from them and followed them. I mean, Vaughan knew how to navigate using the sun and stars from being an army cadet and... and," he noted Vaughan's anxious glance. "Well, we just worked as a team and we got better and fitter and it worked."

"But in all that desert!"

"Mum! We live here! It was no big deal," Donny said, determined not to embarrass Vaughan by mentioning their weaker moments.

"But the distances I have heard you walked," his mother said.

Donny had already done a rough calculation of how far they'd trekked over the past five days. "About a hundred and twenty kilometres I reckon," he said. "But we had lots of stops along the way."

There was a lot of headshaking at the improbability of the tale, then his mother turned to him and asked, "Do you know where your father is?"

Donny shook his head. "No, but I think I know where he might be."

"Where?" his mother cried, attracting the attention of the others.

This included a grim-looking police inspector dressed in black, with body armour and webbing and festooned with weapons and gadgets.

"Yes boy, where?" the inspector asked.

"I think he is at the Number 1 Yards," Donny replied.

Chapter 39

NUMBER 1 YARDS

"Number 1 Yards? Do you mean cattle yards?" the inspector asked. "Yes sir, for sorting and loading cattle onto road trains," Donny replied.

"Where are they?" the inspector asked.

"About twenty k's north of the Clonargh homestead," Donny answered.

His grandfather stepped forward. "They are on a side road about ten kilometres south of the highway off our main station road. The yards are three kilometres from that junction and back onto Burke Creek. That's why they were built there, as there is a big permanent waterhole. Yabby Billabong we call it."

"Can you draw me a map?" the inspector asked.

Donny spoke up. "I can do that, Grandad. I'm good at maps," he said.

The inspector took out a notebook and pencil and handed them over. Donny thought for a moment and then started sketching. "This is Burke Creek and the Yabby Hole," he explained as he moved the pencil tip. "Now this is the road in, and this is north." He put an arrow with N at the top. "Mr Cavallaro said you should always put a north pointer," he explained to the inspector.

The inspector kept a straight face and nodded. Donny went on. "The scale won't be right but here are the yards backing onto the creek, cattle mustering yards, you know."

The inspector, who had served twenty years in Western Queensland again kept a straight face and nodded. "Yes, go on."

"This is a big dusty open area where the road trains come in and turn around after loading the cattle. And there's a side track to the waterhole with a poly pipe and pump for water. There are water troughs in all the yards, and also a small shed with a kitchen in it for the stockmen and truck drivers."

Donny's grandad agreed. "I had it built years ago. I got sick of seeing people standing around in the dust and flies trying to have a feed. And I

312

had a proper dunny built at the back of the hayshed too. There are two big water tanks here near the shed don't forget," he prompted.

"Oh, the hay shed," Donny cried. "It is big, here at the far end of the yards. I drew this bit wrong. The track to the waterhole goes further out and around it. And the water tanks are here." He set to work making changes. "There are a couple of big trees here too, Ghost gums. They are the only ones in the whole area except along the creek."

"Is there an airfield nearby?" the inspector asked.

Donny's grandad answered that one. "Yes, just here to the north about half a mile, I mean a kilometre or so. I had it put in when we started the bull sales so that buyers could just fly in."

Donny looked at the sketch and shook his head. "That's a bit messy. If you don't mind, I'll use another page and draw you a better one," he said.

The inspector nodded so Donny got to work again and soon had quite a neat sketch map of the area.

"The scale isn't right," he explained. "That's about a hundred metres."

"That will be fine. Thank you, young fella, that is really good work," the inspector said. "Now, if you folks will just wait in the shade, I will brief my men and get things moving. Stay out of the house and outbuildings please so we can do forensic stuff."

Constable O'Grady's wife now intervened. "We will park the vehicles under those trees over there and swing out the awnings to have breakfast. Come on."

This was done. Both her vehicle and the Pearces had side awnings that swung out and these provided enough shade. There were only four folding chairs though, so a rug was spread under one awning and the chairs were given to Donny's grandad and the two grey nomads whose car and caravan had been stolen. Food was placed on a folding table and water bottles, cups and thermos flasks of coffee. Donny was impressed with her thoughtfulness and thorough planning.

He also took the opportunity to thank Mr & Mrs Ross. "We didn't mean to cause you all this trouble and upset," he said.

The old couple took it in good part. "As long as nothing has been broken or lost," Mrs Ross said.

Mr Ross grinned. "Sounds like you and your mate have done a mighty job. Grandad, you should be very proud of these boys."

Donny's Grandad nodded and smiled. "I am. They are real MacAndrews, chips off the old pioneering block!"

Donny glowed inside at the praise and knew that life would never be quite the same again. He sat on the rug next to Vaughan and accepted a sandwich with boiled egg filling. It tasted wonderful to him, and he happily sat there munching until his nose detected a really foul smell.

Who farted? He wondered, casting a suspicious glance at Vaughan.

Vaughan grinned and said, "Donny!"

The implication caught Donny by surprise, and he cried indignantly. "It wasn't me!"

He saw his mother frown and blush. But then he did fart, a noisy, lengthy eruption that he had been trying to suppress for some time.

Vaughan began waving his hand in front of his face. "Donny!" he cried.

Donny burned with shame and saw that his mother was embarrassed by it but too good mannered to speak. Not so Grandad. He grinned and said, "Bloody hell, Donny! That would smoke out a skunk!"

"It's the water we had to drink!" Donny cried.

All of a sudden he wanted to cry. But Sharlene was there and the last thing he wanted to do was have her see him cry! With an effort of will power, he lowered his head and took another bite from the sandwich.

Sally, the policeman's wife, came to his aid. "Here is some Coca Cola, Donny. Drink some of that. Sugar kills germs and there is enough sugar in Coke to fix your upset tummy."

"Thank you, Miss," Donny mumbled, still blushing with shame.

Gratefully he took a sip. It was bit too cold for his palate, but he had a big gulp before handing the bottle back, not wanting to appear a glutton. Then he burped as the gas in the Coke came back up. That got him blushing again and both Vaughan and Sharlene giggled.

Slowly the conversation started again and during that time Constable O'Grady used his Land Cruiser to ferry the armed police team and police surgeon to the station airstrip. A few minutes later, the police aircraft took off. As it dwindled into the distance, Constable O'Grady returned. He parked and walked over to accept a sandwich from his wife.

"As soon as we have eaten, we will all move to the road junction near these Number 1 Yards. As soon as the area is secured and safe, we can go there."

After that statement, all Donny wanted to do was get into a vehicle and rush there to look for his dad. But he had to wait until all had been given some food and drink. Then they began loading. As they did, two more police vehicles arrived with four more police. Constable O'Grady got up and went to brief them. They parked and two of them went to the homestead and came back with Reggie and Ma Baker. As these were being put into the back of one of the vehicles, Donny saw Sharlene poke her tongue at Reggie.

"Horrible pervert!" she muttered.

Then they were seated in the cars. The three mothers went in the policeman's private car with Grandad. Donny and his friends resumed their seats in the Pearce's car. The old couple stayed, to be given a lift back to Golden Dawn by one of the other police vehicles. The ambulance followed the three vehicles.

There had been a debate between the adults over the best way to go, but Donny's mother settled it by saying, "We must go by our place. There must be dogs there that haven't had water for a couple of days, and the chooks."

"Your stock will need some attention too," Sharlene's mother added. "I'll get onto Frank and he and Michael can come over and help for a day or two."

So it was agreed. For the next hour they drove along the poorly graded, rutted and potholed track that connected the two homesteads. Along the way Vaughan pointed out where he and Donny had crossed Camel Creek and the side road they had crossed in the dark. Donny barely glanced at them. His thoughts were focused on worrying about his dad's whereabouts and welfare.

It was after 10 o'clock when they reached Clonargh homestead. Another hour was spent looking after animals and poultry. Donny really just wanted to keep going but understood the necessity. So he took the opportunity to show how he had snuck in to get food and how Sharlene had helped. She positively glowed at the praise from him and the adults over how she had acted so calmly, even though she admitted to being very scared.

Donny took the opportunity to take some food and some sugar lumps out to Min Min. The pony had come trotting up as soon as the vehicles had arrived and the other saddle horses had followed. Water was no problem to them as they had access to the creek, but they were given some oats and hay.

Then it was on northwards along the main station road. It was another half hour of dusty, bumpy, dirt road before they arrived at the road junction where a large sign pointed west and read: NUMBER 1 TRUCKING YARDS.

Constable O'Grady stopped them and came walking back. "The inspector has radioed and said we can come in," he said.

"Have they found Dad?" Donny asked.

Constable O'Grady shook his head. "No. Sorry."

Now the tears welled up and Donny got all choked up and unable to speak.

I was sure he would be here! he thought.

As they drove in along the access road, he went over in his mind all the little clues he thought he had picked up from the crooks. The last few hundred metres were the worst, and Donny could barely see through his tears. On the left were the steel fences of the cattle yards and their associated loading ramps, and the big parking area on the right, dusty as he had described, little whorls of dust being picked up from it by the breeze that had sprung up. At the far end to the yards was the big hay shed and around the corner were the water tanks, shelter shed, kitchen, and toilet. The vehicles drove to there and stopped in the shade of the three Ghost Gums.

The inspector met them, looking baffled and apologetic. "I'm sorry! We've searched the whole place and there is nobody here."

That really upset Donny and his mother, and even his grandad looked downcast and teary.

"You've looked everywhere?" his mother asked, her lip trembling with emotion.

The inspector gestured around. "There's not much to search. But we will keep looking."

"The river?" Donny suggested, pointing to the line of trees a hundred metres away.

The inspector looked that way. "No. I'll send a couple of men now."

"Can we help?" Donny asked. He was starting to feel desperate.

The inspector shook his head. "No. It is much too dangerous with an armed man on the run. We don't know his mental state."

The inspector gave orders, and three armed police spread out and moved widely spaced towards the trees along the creek. There were a few minutes of tension before they vanished out of sight. 'Nothing,' was the report.

That really deflated Donny, and he looked around in frustration. In the distance he noted the aircraft parked out in the heat shimmer and nearer the flat plain of short grass with a few fences. Then another idea came to him.

"If he came here where is his car?"

Nobody knew. Even a casual glance showed that the whole area had tracks everywhere: vehicle tracks, animal tracks, and boot prints. Donny gloomily studied the dusty ground, trying to work out how old most of the tracks were.

Then another problem arose. His stomach gurgled and he looked around anxiously. Remembering his previous embarrassments and humiliations, he decided to slip away so nobody would notice. Next to the shelter shed was the big hay shed. It had a corrugated iron wall facing him and on the north side, where the worst of the weather came from when it rained. The side nearest the cattle yards and the far end were both open. More pressure in his lower body decided Donny to move quickly. He walked across to the corner of the hay shed and then slipped around it and out of sight. There was a vehicle track there between the shed and the steel rails of the yards.

Donny glanced back. *I'll go a little bit further,* he thought, remembering how loud his last emission was.

So he strode along between shed and yards. On his left was a wall of rectangular hay bales that went up almost to the high roof. Deciding he had gone far enough, Donny stopped to ease his body. As he did, he glanced idly around and down. There, clear in the dust, was a boot print facing towards the nearest hay bales.

That's odd? Donny thought. Curious he glanced up, and then gasped.

Staring down at him from between two hay bales right near the top was Uncle James! Their eyes met and Donny immediately yelled, "Here he is! Here he is!"

"You little mongrel!" Uncle James snarled.

He crawled out of his hiding place, his face suffused with rage. And in his right hand he had the pistol!

Donny did not wait. Remembering how Uncle James had shot at him in Golden Dawn, he bolted, sprinting on along the side of the stacks of hay bales. As he ran, Donny screamed, yelling for help rather than out of fear, although there was plenty of that.

Behind him he heard Uncle James also yelling, snarling in rage. "Little bastard! You've wrecked everything! Cop this!"

Donny understood that and swerved, just in time.

Bang! Dust flew up right near him and Donny nearly voided his bowels as he knew it was a bullet strike. He had seen plenty of animals hit by bullets and clearly understood the terrible damage they could do, and then he tripped!

Down he went, sprawling in the dust and prickles. Just as well, as another shot cracked past close beside his head.

Now actuated by the adrenaline of sheer survival, Donny scrambled to his feet, glancing back as he did. To his horror, he saw Uncle James jump down, only about 25 metres from him. The pistol came up to aim straight at him!

Donny's options were limited, blocked on his left by the wall of hay bales and on his right by the steel rails he could only duck and weave as he ran away.

Bang!

"Aaargh!" Donny yelled.

It had felt like a red-hot poker had been whacked across his right buttock. But he kept running, glancing back as he did, and what he saw made him skid to a stop in the dust.

Vaughan had come around the corner of the shed behind Uncle James and now dashed forward and launched himself in a desperate tackle. He and Uncle James went down, Vaughan reaching desperately for the arm holding the pistol. And he had it! Donny saw that Vaughan was now gripping Uncle James's right forearm and clinging on grimly.

Bang!

That shot went into the hay somewhere, but Donny had started running back. It was obvious that Vaughan was not strong enough to hold Uncle James. Worse still, Sharlene has appeared and was running to Vaughan's aid.

Sharlene! Oh no! She might get shot!

That fear spurred Donny to run even faster. He arrived gasping next to the struggling pair and dithered, trying to decide if he should try to wrestle the gun free. The notion of breaking Uncle James's little finger again crossed his mind but then a better idea came to him. There, right near his right hand, was an old branding iron leaning on a post of the shed. Without hesitation Donny grabbed it and lashed out at Uncle James's hand.

Whack! Crack! Bang!

Donny saw the pistol go flying away to land in the dust near Sharlene's feet. Uncle James screamed in pain and then started swearing, hitting at Vaughan and trying to break free. Donny lifted the branding iron to strike again but hesitated lest he hit Vaughan instead. The pair were rolling in the dust, Uncle James yelling threats and swear words.

"Sharlene! Sharlene, grab the gun! Grab the gun!" Donny yelled.

To his relief, she did, picking it up by the body and holding it to one side. Then there was a big, burly police sergeant in black. He pushed past Sharlene and stopped to pull out a yellow object, a taser. As Uncle James broke free and raised his left fist to punch Vaughan, the sergeant fired the taser. Donny watched in amazement as Uncle James shuddered and twitched.

Just like on TV! Donny thought.

Then he dropped the branding iron and raced in as Uncle James fell flat. In desperation he grabbed one of Uncle James's legs. The police sergeant was joined by another and then the inspector. For a minute or so there was a furious struggle in the dust before Uncle James was subdued and lying on his face with his hands handcuffed behind him.

Still swearing, he was dragged to his feet, just as the three mothers and his grandad came hurrying around the corner. Uncle James glowered at Donny as he scrambled painfully to his feet.

"You little mongrel! You've broken my hand!" he shouted.

"Serves you right!" Donny retorted.

Uncle James glared back. "You little troublemaker!" he spat.

"Where's my father?" Donny demanded to know.

Uncle James curled his lip and gave a short laugh. "Do you think I would ever tell you? Like hell I will!"

"Then tell me where my son is, son," called Grandad.

Uncle James looked shocked and he visibly wilted. Then the shook his head and stiffened up.

"No! You find him. He's your favourite!" he shouted back.

"You were all my favourites," Grandad cried, but it was obvious to Donny that the comment had really wounded him.

Donny's mother tried next. "Where is my husband?" she pleaded.

Uncle James just gave her a cold stare and walked on between his guards. Donny watched them go with a sinking heart.

Where is my father? he thought.

Despair began to swamp his battered emotions.

Chapter 40

WHERE?

Donny walked over to his mother and embraced her. Tears flowed as she hugged him.

The inspector waited, then asked, "What happened then?"

Donny described the incident, but was careful not to mention why he had walked around to the side of the shed on his own! As he talked, he noted that Vaughan was still seated, leaning back against a post, with Sharlene dabbing at his cut lip with her handkerchief. Vaughan's mother joined them, giving Sharlene puzzled looks while she did. Sharlene's mother just watched, pursing her lips and shaking her head.

Vaughan looked up and met Donny's eyes. "Thanks, Donny. I couldn't hold him. He was too strong for me."

"And for me," Donny agreed. "Thanks for saving me," he added.

He walked over and put out his hand. Vaughan reached up and they shook hands. For Donny it was a good feeling, or would have been if he had not been so worried about what had become of his father.

"You are going to have a good black eye, I reckon," he said to Vaughan.

Vaughan grinned. "Better than being shot in the bum!" he answered.

That remined Donny that he really hurt and now he tried to twist around to see the damage. He had turned his back to his mother, and she now cried out with concern.

"Oh Donny, what's all that blood? What happened?"

Donny wasn't sure but tried to make light of the wound, even though he was now trembling with reaction. His mother hurried over with his grandad and they both bent to look, much to his embarrassment.

Then his grandad snorted. "Huh! Nothing much! Just grazed his bum," he said.

Vaughan laughed and Donny burned, then also laughed. His mother was not amused and hurried away to get a First Aid kit. The inspector shook his head and smiled with evident relief.

"So where was your Uncle James when you saw him?" he asked.

Donny pointed up. "Up there in a little gap between those two hay bales," he answered.

At that moment, the three police who had run to the river returned, puffing from the exertion. The inspector turned to them, and said, "Well?"

"Found his vehicle sir, hidden under the trees," replied a Senior Constable.

"Who searched up on the hay bales?" the inspector asked, one eyebrow raised and a sardonic expression on his face.

A constable put his hand up and looked abashed. The inspector pointed up. "Well, you and Bullock get up there again and search properly this time," he snapped.

The two policemen at once ran around to the front of the shed where Donny knew the bales were always left stacked in steps so people could climb up. The third policeman was directed to secure the pistol, and he immediately pulled on gloves. He then picked up the pistol, making sure it was pointed away from everyone and ejected the magazine. Then he cocked the weapon to eject the round in the chamber and all three items were placed in a large evidence bag he took from one of the big side pockets on his trousers. It was carried away. The sergeant began taking photographs and also picked up the branding iron, much to Donny's.

Now in almost a state of numbness, Donny was led by his mother and grandad back to the shelter shed. Here he was further embarrassed by his mother getting him to turn around while she pulled his shorts half down. Nurse Jenks and the paramedics followed but he allowed her to do it, just providing First Aid stores when needed. The male paramedics both snickered and made silly jokes which caused Donny to blush until Nurse Jenks told them to 'act their age'. His mother washed his bum, then added antiseptic before putting on a Band Aid.

His grandad watched this with a mixture of pride and concern. Then, as Donny pulled his pants back up, Grandad grinned and said, "You won't be able to show that scar to the girls for a few years yet lad."

Donny's mother looked shocked, who turned on Grandad and snapped, "That will be quite enough talk like that, thank you!"

Grandad chuckled and Donny saw his eyes twinkle. That caused him a stiff face as he tried not to grin in reply. But then he had to sit down as he started to shake so badly he had trouble controlling his limbs. He was offered a drink of hot Milo by Constable O'Grady's wife and that helped.

Vaughan and Sharlene and the other mothers came back and joined them and then the inspector. Constable O'Grady came back from where Uncle James had been placed in the back of one of the police vehicles under guard.

"He won't talk. Just demands his lawyer," he said.

That upset and annoyed Donny even more. He had a big drink of cold water and then gratefully accepted a corned beef and pickle sandwich. They began to discuss what had happened and where Donny's father might be. Donny's real fear was that his jealous brother might have killed him, but he did not voice that so as not to upset his mother even more.

Then there were calls from the front of the hay shed and soon the two policemen appeared, carrying the black briefcase.

"Found the ransom money," one called.

The briefcase was placed on the table and the inspector, now also wearing rubber gloves, tried to open it. But the briefcase was locked.

"Go and see if that fellow has any keys on him," he instructed.

Constable O'Grady went to do this and returned a few minutes later with three keys. The inspector picked one and tried it. It worked and the locks sprang open. The briefcase was opened and the inspector spread several large evidence bags on the table. He then began placing items on the table while the sergeant took notes and put them in more evidence bags.

To Donny, the ransom looked substantial. There were bundles of bank notes, some jewellery and half a dozen small gold bars that made a real clunk when dropped on the table.

As that was being done, Donny noted the other two keys lying on the table. To him they did not look like car keys or house keys. One had a small key tag on it and Donny picked it up and read it. 'Container' it read. Then something that had been niggling at the back of his mind got him standing up.

"What's wrong, Donny? Sit down! You are shivering," his mother said.

"I need to go away to do something," Donny replied, not wanting to raise false hopes.

I need to check, he told himself.

Very gingerly he walked off around the side of the hay shed again. Each step hurt and he realised that he was even more battered and bruised from the fight. Worse, the wound in his buttock had gone stiff and hurt when he moved. But he persevered, anxiety gnawing at him.

He walked all the way to the front of the hay shed and looked back at it. He had been there a dozen times at least over the last few years and it was a familiar location, but something did not look right.

"Now what is it? What's wrong?" he asked himself.

The shed was very full, the hay bales stacked almost to the roof. That was not unusual as they always stocked up in the winter ready to feed during the three hot dry months of the summer before the rains started in December or January.

Then it came to him. *Where is the storage container?*

For years there had been a steel 40-foot shipping container at the side of the hay shed against the sheet steel wall. It was used to store tools and chemicals and keep them locked up from casual pilfering. Donny scanned the huge stack and began to get excited. He could not see the shipping container and did not remember hearing his parents discussing disposing of it.

Now so excited his heart was hammering, Donny hurried back around to the shelter shed. Everyone there was looking very gloomy, and Donny hesitated to start false hopes. But he knew he had to.

"Mum, did you and Dad get rid of the shipping container?" he asked.

His mother looked puzzled. "No, not that I know," she replied.

"What container?" the inspector queried.

"There used to be a 40-foot shipping container at the front over against the corrugated iron," Donny explained. "So where is it now?"

"Show me what you mean," the inspector instructed.

Donny led them to the front of the hay shed and pointed at the huge stack of hay bales, saying, "The container used to be there, against that wall. The door was near this end so we could put stuff in it easily."

As he said this, his gaze roamed across the stacks of hay bales. Over to the left they were a bit untidy, the ones at the front starting low and building up in steps so that a person could easily climb up. But on the right the stack was a high and very neat wall of bales.

"It's been hidden!" he cried.

With his heart hammering with hope, Donny ran over and scrambled up the pile until he was level with the top of the neat section. The bales were a metre long and way too heavy for Donny for pick up (Although he knew grown men could, the trick being in the technique rather than in pure strength). So he pushed at the bale and sent it thudding down.

As it landed in front of the astonished faces, the inspector nodded and called, "Sergeant Black, get you men to remove these bales, quick now."

Three police were detailed to drag the bales aside down at ground level and the other two followed the sergeant up to help Donny pushing them down. The top three front row bales were gone in a few seconds and then a policeman lifted a bale from the next row in and swung it over the side.

Down behind where that bale had been, Donny glimpsed grey steel. "It's here! Here it is!" he cried.

They redoubled their efforts and everyone who could began lifting or dragging the bales away as they tumbled down. Within a minute, what Donny had said was obvious to all of them as the top and end doors of a steel shipping container became visible. Hope soared and Donny grabbed frantically at the bales until told to move aside by one of the policemen.

"Let us do this, young fella. We can do it faster if you move aside. You might get hurt otherwise."

Donny did not want to stop but saw the sense in what the man said. He moved away and then climbed down and ran back to the shelter shed and snatched the key labelled 'Container' from the table. Clutching it, he ran back, then stood gasping and sweating while the bales were dragged away. His mother was helping, and even Grandad was doing his bit. Within another few minutes the front of the container was clear. There was a padlock holding the locking bars and the inspector told one of the police to get the key.

"Here it is!" Donny cried, holding it up.

The inspector took it and inserted it into the padlock. As he twisted the key, Donny remembered hearing the horrible stories on the TV news of illegal immigrants dying of suffocation in containers.

Oh! I hope Dad is alright, he thought, his heart again hammering with anxiety.

The locking bars were moved, and two policemen swung the doors wide. They were well greased and moved easily. As they opened, daylight flooded in and Donny gasped and let out a sob.

His father was there! He was crouched in the far corner, covering his eyes against the bright light. But he was alive!

"He's alive!" Donny yelled, along with most of the others.

Despite a waft of foul air, he went to run in, as did his mother, but the inspector stopped him.

"Wait," he said. "He's chained up."

"The third key," Donny cried.

He went to run back to the shelter shed but a policeman stopped him. "I'll go mate," he said, setting off at the run.

A minute later he was back, and Donny's father was free. The sergeant took pictures, then Donny and his mother were allowed in to hug him. Donny's dad stank of unwashed clothes and faeces, and he had a week's growth of stubble on his cheeks, but Donny did not care. He hugged both his mum and his dad and wept with joy.

"How did you find me?" his dad croaked.

His mother pulled Donny around. "Donny worked it out. He did it!"

His dad reached out and rumpled Donny's hair and then hugged him. "Thank you, little mate." Then his voice broke and he let out a few sobs. In a voice that trembled, he said, "I thought I was going to die in there!"

That set Donny shaking. The ghastly thought came to him that Uncle James had been prepared to let his brother die rather than tell where he was! It was a very sobering and sad notion. Donny just cried. He could not help it, and only later did he remember that nobody thought there was anything wrong with that.

Grandad was there and he reached out and gripped his son's hand. Donny's father gave a weak smile, and said, "Hello Dad. Good to see you."

"Good to see you too, son," Grandad replied. He then reached across and drew Donny to him. "Here is the man you really need to thank. Young Donny has been a hero all week. He has saved the day. He is a real credit to you."

Donny glowed at that and was even more touched when his father hugged him again. Being called a 'man' and a 'hero' by men he thought really were set his tears flowing again, but also gave him great pride.

Nurse Jenks and the paramedics then took over. The ambulance had been driven to the end of the hay shed and Donny's dad was eased up onto the wheeled stretcher. Nurse Jenks began examining him while the inspector hovered to ask questions and the sergeant took more photos.

After that it was just administration really. Donny's dad was weak and suffering badly from dehydration and lack of food, having been fed only once in the six days. But he could sit up and was taken to the aircraft and flown to Golden Dawn and put in hospital. The police were left to do their procedural stuff and everyone else was transported back to Clonargh homestead.

"We have to look after the pets and the chooks and the stock!" Donny's mother pointed out.

Once there, the three friends were bathed, doctored, dressed, and fed and then put to bed. They were questioned by the police and asked to write full statements. Life began to settle back on an even keel.

When Donny's dad and Uncle David came back there were more tears, of joy this time. And more praise for all three when the full story was told. Donny was very pleased.

Dad thinks I'm okay, he told himself.

Then the school holidays were over. Sharlene had left a few days earlier and Donny knew he would always admire her. But his crush had faded to realistic proportions. So he wasn't too jealous when he learned that Vaughan had persuaded his parents to send him the Northern Goldfields College in Charters Towers, rather than back to his posh school near Sydney.

"The sneaky bugger!" he muttered.

But he was pleased when, a few weeks later, he learned that Vaughan had settled in at the college and rejoined the army cadets.

"He says he plans to go on the corporal's course in December," his mother said.

"Good!" Donny replied. "It was his army cadet training that made it all possible. And mum, when I am old enough and have to go to boarding school, can I go to the Northern Goldfields College?"

And I might join the army cadets too, he reckoned.

Author's Note

To really get the feel of this amazing country, my wife and I recommend driving from Windorah to Bedourie, overnighting at the Monkira Rest Area. While there take the time to sit out in the dark to study the amazing display of stars and, maybe, you might be lucky enough to see the Min Min lights. Bedourie and Boulia are both worth a few days visit, and for the real flavour drive the Lake Machattie track. But be safe and tell those most helpful people at the Bedourie Visitor Centre where you are going and be prepared with water and food. This is 'Remote Area' driving and we want you to arrive safe and well, and to read more books.

Enjoy more C.R. Cummings stories

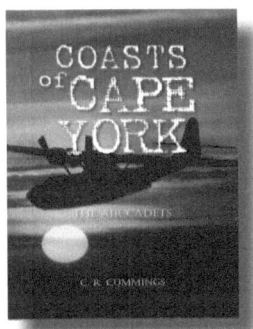
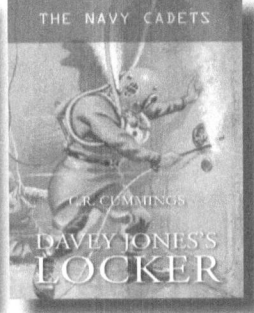